THE ATTIC CHILD

Lola Jaye

THE ATTIC CHILD

A Novel

WILLIAM MORROW
An Imprint of HarperCollins*Publishers*

This is a work of fiction. Names, characters, places, and incidents are products of the author's imagination or are used fictitiously and are not to be construed as real. Any resemblance to actual events, locales, organizations, or persons, living or dead, is entirely coincidental.

HarperCollins books may be purchased for educational, business, or sales promotional use. For information, please email the Special Markets Department at SPsales@harpercollins.com.

Published in the UK in 2022 by Macmillan.

FIRST US EDITION

Library of Congress Cataloging-in-Publication Data has been applied for.

ISBN 978-0-06-326037-5

22 23 24 25 26 LSC 10 9 8 7 6 5 4 3 2 1

For Ndugu M'Hali, Omoba Aina,
Dejazmatch Alemayehu Tewodros, Mbye Otabenga
and all the other children . . . taken.

Until the lions have their own historians, the history of the hunt will always glorify the hunter.

African proverb, quoted by Chinua Achebe in
"The Art of Fiction," *The Paris Review*, no. 139

Prologue

I open my eyes to death.
But I'm still here. Why hasn't she claimed me?
Apparently it's my birthday tomorrow; not yet thirteen.
Yet nobody knows I exist.
Each of the days melt into one long stretch.
Weeks fly by.
Endless.
I'm no longer afraid of the dark.
The blackness, warm.

*

Breathe.
Footsteps.
Is anyone out there?
I hope not.
Happy to stay here.
Forever.
If that's what it takes.

PART ONE

Chapter One

Dikembe
1903

We sat under the tall limba tree that day, with no idea these were the last days of paradise.

The branches and leaves cowered over us, a welcome protection from the blazing afternoon heat. Behind, an uneven, sandy path through a row of trees which flourished majestically under a hazy sky. This was me, almost every day, cloaked in the familiarity and comfort of my favorite spot with my favorite brother, Kabili. Close enough to hear Mama calling for help with a chore, yet far away enough for the illusion of solitude, free to privately discuss pressing issues of the day, such as what it would be like to catch the multicolored thick-toed gecko currently moving toward the top of a tree.

"I almost caught one yesterday!" said Kabili, my elder by three years. I believed the beginning of his story to be true because I'd never doubted anything from his mouth, even if Kabili was well-known in the family for telling half-truths. Just like when he insisted he'd been involved in the killing of the ram Mama served up last Sunday; an unfounded boast because everyone knew Kabili was the first to vomit at the sight of dripping blood.

Being the youngest in my family, a host of questions

permanently rested on the tip of my tongue—*how do you outrun a gecko?* the least important of them all.

"Kabili . . ."

"Yes, brother?"

"Where do you go . . . when you go with them?"

The sound of my name punctured the moment.

"Dikembe!"

Even when raised, my mama's voice rang sweet inside my ears. Being the youngest of five and likely to be her last, I believed that of all her sons, I was the special one. I only felt this because she constantly made me feel this way with her words. Whispers mixed with an aroma of freshly made stew as we stood over a cooking fire: *"A good child, that is you."*

Mama often complained that not having a daughter meant being unable to pass on how to prepare the tastiest of dishes for the home, yet I was a willing student, soaking up all she was willing to teach about cassava, or the importance of banana leaves, while also being able to spend precious moments with her, as if I still remained attached to her breast. My older siblings, which sometimes included Kabili, would accompany our father on journeys outside the village and be gone sometimes for weeks at a time. Mama said they were working with my father in the timber trade. My father was a skilled craftsman and sculptor who had been taught by his own father, a skill I one day hoped to master. My favorite carving of his was a footstool melded around the shape of a man with an elongated head, which he had sold at market. However, I hadn't seen anything he had made lately as my father no longer carved at home. Mama explained that my father and brothers now simply worked away, yet I'd also never seen any items they had made. On the few occasions I got to sit with him, it was with an audience of others. He did sometimes speak lovingly of the trees of his childhood. I once asked if he could take me back to where those trees stood, and his expression hardened.

Luckily, in a few short years, I would also be joining my brothers and father at work, and I would be able to see for myself what they did. For now, though, my happiness came when nearest to my mama, hearing her talk, laugh, or just entwined in her arms on a floor mat, lying in comfortable silence—as if waiting for something to interrupt the delicious contentment.

At the age of nine, my journey into manhood seemed to trudge along slowly.

Kabili was now twelve and regularly accompanied my father and brothers out of the house to work. They would return spent and would retire straight after Mama (with some help from me) had served an evening meal. Kabili would complain that work was not what he had imagined it to be and that he wished he too could stay home.

I couldn't understand why he would say this. When I asked as much, he glanced at me with what I could only describe as anger, as if I had said something wrong.

Of course, I still enjoyed my time with Mama, but an envy often nestled deep inside me which refused to leave. I was no longer content to be an outsider looking on as my kin embarked on a mission to feed and clothe the family.

Men worked the land and toiled, while women kept the home.

I was not yet a man, but this did not stop me from counting the days until I would be allowed to join my father and brothers.

Home was a wooden hut under a palm-frond roof that housed everything we would ever need: mats for sleeping, a space to store our clothing. We lived away from the main village, an area I was forbidden to venture into. I was only allowed as far as "our tree" and when I once asked why, my mama just said she would beat me if I disobeyed her. She said this with tears in her eyes and this, along with the fact she had never beaten me in my entire life, confused me. So I basked in the joy of sitting by my mama's knee listening to stories of the past, until I succumbed to the afternoon sun, falling asleep with my head in her lap as the sound of her sweet humming danced into my ears.

I never went past the tree.

Until, one day, I made a decision.

"Are you saying you don't want to stay with your mama anymore?"

Mama didn't appear angry and I was relieved by this. I had simply grown tired of hearing the triumph laced in Kabili's voice as he reeled off tales of exploits with our father and older brothers; as they chopped wood and carved the pieces into shapes and styles to sell on; of the dangers they faced from cheetahs who hid in trees. I was ready to take up the mantle of manhood that each of my brothers already held on to. I was ready to contribute to the upkeep of my family—even though I was actually unsure of what this truly meant, only what I imagined it to be.

When I believed that momentous morning to have arrived, I approached my father.

"Not yet, my son."

My father did not approve of outbursts of emotion, so I swallowed mine down as best I could, yet couldn't help but be brave enough to ask, "Why?" None of us ever questioned our father and up until that moment, I had never had reason to. Most of my time had been spent with Mama anyway, and talking to my father wasn't something I knew how to do easily. But I felt this injustice deeply and needed to know the answer to my question.

"I said, not yet." His words were firm and spoken with a finality that saddened me. He quickly pulled away and drew my mama into a private communication. I couldn't hear their words, but she held her face to her hands as my father rested his palms on the back of his head. Their bodies spoke of defeat, but I could not imagine what for, as I had only asked to accompany my father and brothers to work. I was ready. Surely this was a good thing?

The following morning, I watched as my father and brothers prepared for work. They very seldom ate before they left, but Mama sent them off with provisions which they would eat as soon as they got to their work destination. I followed closely behind them, managing to remain hidden, thanks to the welcoming presence of a line of trees which covered my tiny frame as I sprinted from bark to bark, my chest puffed out and mimicking how my father and brothers moved, face upturned and shoulders erect, just like one of those trees. With Mama I had felt safe and warm, but with my father and my four brothers, Kabili, Yogo, Djamba and Pako, I felt a surge of energy I was not familiar with. I hoped to observe them long enough for me to learn everything I could about how they spent their days and see perhaps why I had not been allowed to accompany them. My aim was to be back home before Mama even noticed I had gone. The trees were sparse so there was always a danger of losing sight of my family as I trailed behind and attempted to remain out of sight. I was certainly relieved when they reached the edge of the stream and stopped. Two men dressed identically in blue jackets and red fezzes on their heads greeted my father. They reminded me of the birds I had seen a few times, with coats the brightest of blue, yellow beaks and red-topped heads. This amused me until I noticed what looked like weapons of some sort tucked under their arms.

I slapped away a fly and may have made a sound of annoyance, and it was Kabili who looked back and toward me. Kabili, who sometimes knew what I would say before I said it.

It was always going to be him.

Our eyes locked.

The man in uniform now had his hand on my father's shoulder, and it seemed to me that my father began to shrink before him. My tall and brave father, now in an instant shorter in stature, as this man raised his voice to him in a language I did not understand.

None of what I was witnessing made any sense to me. My father ran a timber business and had taught my brothers everything they knew about wood. So why was he taking an order from another man, while my brothers looked on as if this were an everyday occurrence?

My mind attempted to explain what I was witnessing, just as the second man spoke hurried words to my brother Pako, before raising his hand and bringing it down upon the right side of my brother's face with a force I never knew was possible.

I gasped and then covered my mouth.

I waited for my father to spring into action, but the silence felt piercing and prolonged because he did nothing. Even as Pako helped himself to his feet, my father simply watched as if he could not see what I saw.

My expectation grew into a state of confusion.

Once the uniformed men had moved away, Kabili walked quietly toward my hiding place.

"Dikembe, I knew it was you!"

"But what of Pako and—"

"You better go home or else I will tell our father! Go, Dikembe. Go!" he hissed.

I felt his hand on my back as he shoved me in the direction I had come from. Kabili had never treated me in this way before. We were the closest of brothers. I knew him the best and he knew me. However, in that moment, I did not recognize him.

"You must go back to your mother," said my father, finally noticing my presence as he walked toward us. My body was inches away from collapsing into the tantrums of a toddler. I wanted to go with them. I also wanted to ask who those men were and why they had struck my brother, and why my father had done nothing.

Instead, he did something that day I had never witnessed him do with any of us boys before: he knelt down to my height and placed each of his hands in mine. The small world around us seemed to cease. His touch was unfamiliar yet welcome, his hands drier and coarser than my mama's; instead of her sweet aroma, the scent of sweat.

"Listen, my son, this is no place for you. Not now, and if I can help it, not ever. You go back to your mother now before they see you. We will not tell her about this."

"But—"

"Go now, before they see you!"

"Who are they?"

"Oh, Dikembe," he sighed.

I looked into his eyes and once again saw something I had never seen before in those rare moments when I had got this close to him.

Now, in his eyes, was fear.

I blinked rapidly, blocking the emotion threatening to embarrass me in front of my father, let alone my brothers, who in that moment I had forgotten about.

"Dikembe, you will do as I say. You will go home."

Something in his voice lacked the firmness I was used to and I felt sad, so desperately sad. "I will go home." I turned and ran as fast as I could from the unfamiliarity of that moment back to the safety of the cooking fire.

And my mama.

It was nightfall before they returned. Impatience lodged in my throat because for once I wanted Kabili to explain every detail of what had happened. But as soon as we boys had eaten, Mama and my father became embroiled in a deep conversation with no place for childish chatter.

"They are talking about the white men again," whispered Kabili as he shrugged his tired shoulders. Ever since he had begun accompanying my father and brothers, Kabili often appeared sleepy and ready for slumber while I still had enough energy to run around the yard manymore times.

I had a thousand questions. "Who were those men, this morning?"

"I must sleep, Dikembe."

My brother, usually so full of stories, gave no answer.

"Why did they do that to our brother?" I said.

"This work is not easy," he mumbled as he lay on the floor, head resting in his palm.

That night as my father and brothers slumbered, I felt a restlessness which did not allow for sleep. A hollowness resided in my chest, a space that could only be filled by my mama.

She was outside, scrubbing the pot she'd used earlier to cook the cassava leaves.

"What is it, my Dikembe?" She tilted her head to the side.

"I am unable to sleep, Mama."

She smiled, placing the pot to one side.

"Come," she said.

We sat close together on the floor, and with her damp hand she smoothed my head, humming the same tune as always and yet one I had never asked the name of. I simply enjoyed the way it danced unapologetically into my ears, sounding delicious and familiar. Her smell—like the sweetest of fruit—allowing me to slowly succumb, surrender to the nighttime. I wanted to ask her about what I had seen, but if I did that, she'd know I had defied her.

"My Dikembe," she said.

"Yes, Mama."

"My last born. *Mwana muya.*"

"Yes, Mama," I said.

The way she exhaled and patted my shoulder with a graceful hand told me what was to come—and a fizzle of excitement rose within me.

I looked up at her face as she began my bedtime story.

"There were once two kings who ruled our land. The red king is named Nkongolo Mwamba, and he is a cruel king and very unforgiving. He does not know how to control what he does and he is a brute."

"He is not nice, Mama."

"He is not. But the good king is named Mbidi Kiluwe, remember?"

"Yes, Mama."

"He has beautiful dark skin and it shines, even in the night. They call him the Black king, and he is the one who brought a great civilization to our lands. His voice is very soft, and he knows how to behave. He is good, just like you."

"Yes, Mama."

"This is why I call you a good child."

I nodded my head.

"He knows how to control himself."

"He sounds much nicer than the red king, Mama," I said, stifling a yawn.

She placed the back of her delicate hand onto my cheek and smiled. "You must always be like Mbidi. You must always be the Black king."

I opened my eyes the next morning before dawn, which should have been the first indication something was amiss and unbalanced. Usually, my brothers and I would remain sleeping until the cockerel crowed, each of them stepping over me in a race to wash first. There was seldom enough water left for me in the container and I hoped this time, I wouldn't have to fetch more or go to the stream and wash with our neighbors.

My father had left alone, ahead of my brothers, as he sometimes did, with Mama saying he had an important meeting with the village elders and "decisions needed to be made about the future." He had set out early, promising to be back before sunset.

Ina Balenga was our closest neighbor. She lived nearer to the village and had a gap in her teeth. She often brought yams or the ripest mangoes for my family, which I suspected was just another excuse to sit and talk endlessly with Mama. Mama referred to her as a good friend and my father called her a gossip. To me, she was just a lady who brought us delicious things to eat, and one of only a few people other than my family that I saw often.

Today, though, she came empty-handed, her lips quivering over her gapped teeth as her eyes searched toward the floor. "Where is your mama?" she said. I tried to find her gaze, but she refused to meet mine.

"She is out back."

"I will wait in the house," she said.

She sat on the floor, on the mat Mama had placed there earlier. I offered her some water which she declined. I wanted to ask her why she wasn't smiling, why I could no longer see the gap in her teeth.

Like the events of the previous day and waking up before the sound of the cockerel, this was unfamiliar and slightly unsettling.

When Mama returned, Ina Balenga failed to greet her the usual way. This was a greeting bereft of "womanly laughter" as my father called it; instead, they remained inside, talking quietly while I waited outside the hut as Ina Balenga had instructed.

They remained inside for the longest of times, even after my brothers had returned home. I flinched at the raised sounds coming from our house, which sounded not unlike an injured animal. Forever obedient, Kabili and I stayed put, but our three older brothers, Yogo, Djamba and Pako, rushed inside.

Minutes later, when my brothers emerged from the house, their faces were fresh with tears. This I did not understand because men were not supposed to cry, my father always said so. He had not *actually* told me that, but had said as much to Pako, who then relayed it to me passionately as I tearfully folded myself into Mama's arms after falling over outside.

I moved closer to the sound of the wounded animal, which now sounded closer to its demise, pain, fear and sorrow etched into one long agonizing howl.

I peered inside and Ina Balenga was comforting my mother, her hand smoothing the braids on my mama's head as she sat in front of her. My mama's hands were curled into fists, beating her own chest. Ina Balenga spoke hurriedly as Mama continued this physical onslaught, screaming her pain—and I wanted to run to her, console her just as she'd done for me on so many occasions. I was her last born, *a good child, her special child*, and it was my job to do so!

Ina Balenga stood and turned to me, halting my approach. Her face was awash with tears.

"What is it, Ina Balenga?" I asked.

"Your father . . . it is your father. The Belgians. The Force Publique."

I could no longer hear Ina Balenga's voice. I did not know what some of her words meant anyway; my mind remained locked on the image of my mother so distraught she was beating herself.

"I do not understand, what do you mean?" I said, watching my mama carefully as she fell silent, her mouth parted, her eyes open but without focus, her whole demeanor like a goat about to be slaughtered when it no longer has the strength to fight.

My legs became weak and unsteady as I began to perceive the seriousness of what had happened, even before Ina Balenga said quietly, "They killed him, Dikembe. Your father is dead."

Chapter Two

Dikembe
1903

At first I believed I had done something wrong.

Mama did not speak and no longer beckoned me into her arms for comfort. She no longer even acknowledged me—or anyone. Instead, when I attempted to meet her eyes, she would simply look away, her focus on anything but us, her children. Ina Balenga and her daughter brought us food and made sure we still tended to the yard. The daughter would help Mama dress while Ina Balenga plaited her hair. Mama could only utter her discomfort at how tight it felt, while I was simply happy to hear her voice even if her words never mentioned my father or any of us.

It did not feel so strange at first to have not seen my father for many days. He and my brothers often went away for long periods to work. The longest he'd been away before was when he'd tended to his own sick father in another village. I had never met my grandfather or anyone in our wider family, and I remember begging to accompany him. It had been my grandfather who had made the bone necklace my father always wore, after all. So, I did not understand why I was not permitted to meet him. That time he had returned with a limp and blood on the side of his leg. He said he'd fallen over in the bush and no one dared question it. Yet now, I would give anything for him to come home, along with those afflictions. But this time would be different. He had now traveled to a place far away from any of us and apparently would never be returning, and this finality felt like a permanent blow to my stomach, yet still not as painful as seeing my mama cry every single day since it had happened.

A different kind of life began to exist in an unfamiliar haze. I was no longer able to spend any time with just my mama, without others around us. Although the visitors were not plentiful, there were enough for glimpses of her to remain hidden by another person, the sound of her voice smothered by the wailing of another.

My brothers had not been around since the day after our father had been taken from us, having traveled out to work, their tears not even dry. So I was reduced to listening to snippets of information from the people in my home, although most were in whispers.

"They tried to overthrow them."

"He was a brave man."

"A stupid man—why could he not just leave it be? Did he believe it would be different for him when others before him had failed? It's never going to change and now he has paid with his life!"

I soon began to miss my mama even as much as my father.

The familiarity of the area in which I had lived my entire life now appeared disrespectful somehow. The crooked sandy path which led to the tree I was never allowed to walk past; the happy birdsong; the unrepentant existence of mahogany, iroko and limba trees. My father had taught us all there was to know about these trees and yet it felt that they had turned against him by simply staying the same, never bending to the grief that had infected us all.

When my brothers finally returned home after a month away, I immediately cornered Kabili, pleased to finally have somebody I could express my confusion to.

"I have missed you, Kabili," I said, as my brother began to

remove the dirtied clothing he had been wearing. He had not said much since his arrival; indeed, he had not even looked at me.

"Kabili, have I done something wrong?" I asked when he didn't speak.

"Maybe if you weren't such a baby, you would be coming with us, then you would see."

"See what?"

This was not the Kabili who'd left the day after they had taken my father. This was an older, angrier version who felt so very far from me, even though he stood close enough for me to feel the fury in his breath.

"You have no idea what they sacrificed for you!" His gaze shifted from the tip of my head to my feet. "The good child, the special child!" His voice was laced with a venom I had never heard from him before.

I sat under our tree alone and drew a nonsensical shape in the sand with a twig. I no longer recognized my own life and those who occupied it.

At least the sound of humming was familiar, and I assumed my mama had finally come outside to embrace me; then I realized the sounds were coming from my own mouth.

1904

My father had been gone for some months now. My brother Pako, who liked to keep a check on everything and everyone, perhaps wanted to step into his place. I could easily tell he was trying to fill the space left by our father, yet failing in my eyes because there'd never be anyone like him. I felt both resentful and relieved that Pako was at least attempting to take up the mantle.

I saw Mama standing in the yard one day, her face in her hands, repeating my father's name over and over again. My brothers just stood and watched helplessly as I, without any thought, ran to her.

Her words turned to hums, and even if it was just instinct kicking in, she embraced me anyway, kissing the top of my forehead. It was the comfort I had longed for and, as I closed my eyes, soaking up this goodness, I realized that maybe she had needed this too.

Sometimes, the afternoon sun would render me helpless as I slowly succumbed to sleep. One such day I was awakened by my mama's heightened voice, which soon turned into screams. I followed them to the front of the hut, in time to see my brother Djamba limping toward her with the aid of my brother Pako.

"What have they done? What have they done?" she screamed. I rubbed at my eyes, recalling with a chill in my chest the last time I had heard her scream like this.

I walked closer to the scene, my brother's right arm wrapped in what used to be white cloth, now stained with the stark redness of his blood.

"What have they done?" my mother kept shouting. My brother simply shook his head, his mouth pursed shut. Why was he not speaking?

"What have they done to my son? Where are the rest of my children?"

It was as if Pako's ears were clogged with leaves, ignoring Mama as he helped Djamba onto the ground and bent over him to further inspect his wounded arm. I moved closer to them. My eldest brother looked up and we briefly made eye contact. It was only now that I noticed how much he resembled our father. The mark on the bridge of his nose was not the only similarity, but his presence, which you could feel as soon as he stood before you; a silent strength you could either admire . . . or fear.

"Go back inside, Dikembe. Now!" he commanded. I wanted to tell him he had no right to ignore our mama, and that he was not my father and I didn't need to listen to him.

Djamba squinted his eyes and made a sound.

"Go!" said Pako.

I quickly did as I was told and headed inside our home, accompanied by my mama's questions: "Why? Why?"

Djamba appeared to be in a trance, even when he struggled to eat using his left hand, which was not something I had ever seen anyone do before. Mama kept the wound clean and wrapped, but I was surprised when Djamba prepared to return to work with the others after just two days.

"Why are you going to work now, my brother, should you not be resting?"

"I will be back tonight," he said without looking at me, as if to do so would reveal an anger toward me which had no reason to exist. Surely my older brothers loved me as I loved them? Although we had never really spent much time together as they were always at work, there was this underlying and silent kinship which would always keep us close—we were bonded together by blood.

"You are wounded. How can you work?"

"What do you know about work, little brother?" The way he said the word "brother" sounded like it was something laced with dirt from the ground.

That night, I asked Mama if Djamba hated me.

She could only stare toward me blankly, which I guess in my mind confirmed he did.

That night, my brother Djamba returned home alone. The two of us fell asleep without words and hours later, I shot up quickly as if awakening from a trance. The light of the moon shone upon the space usually occupied with three others, as well as illuminating Djamba's face. My gaze shifted to his bare arm where the cloth had fallen away during the night. My stomach flipped, my mouth agape at what I saw. Convincing myself I was in a dream, I struggled to fall back to sleep.

*

The rest of my brothers returned a week later and my heart lifted upon seeing Kabili. My fears that he remained angry with me were unfounded, as he reeled off stories of a wild beast who had stared at him as he chopped wood.

"I believed he would eat me!"

"What did you do?" I asked.

"I fought it to the ground of course, brother! What else?"

Despite the tallness of his tales, I was happy to hear Kabili spin them. It was like it had been before. Almost.

That evening, Kabili and I stood outside our hut, listening to the raised voices of Pako and Mama.

"He tried to stop them and now it is our duty to continue what our father started!" said Pako in a tone that sounded more determined than usual. I did not understand much of what he spoke of, only Mama pleading with him, begging him to put an end to such thoughts.

"You must not do this!" she screamed.

"Why? You know what they have done to the rest of our lands. The only reason they have left us alone till now is there is less to reap here! Instead, they are using our bodies to carry items much too heavy and without enough food or water. When will Dikembe be next? Or you? Do you know what they do to the women? They not only work them to death like the men, but they force them to lie with them. They beat them, they—"

"Stop your words! Your father made sure Dikembe and I were safe here. He spoke to one of the chiefs who assured him that we would never be forced into any of it—"

"Ah, yes, the same chief who signed away our land thinking they were friendship pacts! Those idiots?"

"Pako, where is your respect?"

"Lolo, please," he said, sounding so much younger than his years. "There are children smaller than Dikembe working for these people. They work the trees in the forests and they carry goods for the men and . . . and . . . they are very . . ." His voice broke, but only slightly. "What they did to Djamba is nothing!"

My questions, while plentiful, couldn't get past Pako's tone. If our father were alive, my brother would never have spoken to Mama in this way.

"No! You do not do this! You do not!" she screamed.

"Our father said we should never bend to the enemy. Never!" Pako's raised tone had returned. "He was ready to fight and so am I!"

"Do you want them to do to you what they did to your father? For me to actually see your lifeless body with marks around your neck where they hanged you like an animal? Holes in your body where they shot you? The elders did not allow me to see your father's body. They all said I would not be able to live after such a sight. But yours I would see, because I would insist on it. I would make sure of it! Is this what you want for me to endure? Have I not suffered enough?"

I almost toppled where I stood, unable to process the words that had fallen from my mama's lips. The words were almost as awful as the sound of weeping, which I realized was coming from Pako.

I ran away from the sounds and straight into Kabili's path.

"What is it, Dikembe?"

"Let us go. Let us just go."

He followed behind me just as I knew he would. My heart raced along with hurried steps, my bare feet unconcerned with the tiny stones lodged between my toes.

I did not stop until I got to our tree, a place I had not been with my brother for some time. Questions rested on my lips, not unlike how they used to. This time, instead of inquiring about a simple gecko, I wanted to ask more about my father's death. Had Kabili seen his body? How had he been killed? As most of what I had heard were just parts of stolen conversations, Mama's description was the most vivid yet. But, as I opened my mouth to speak and nothing came out, it was clear that something deep inside me had made the decision for me.

"Would you like me to tell you the story of the time I climbed up a giraffe?" said Kabili, to which I nodded my head.

1905

The first time I saw a white man, I was taken aback at how pale he looked.

I had decided to follow my brothers again one early morning. I had planned to be back home before Mama even realized I was gone.

When he spoke in my native tongue, my fascination quickly waned. Were these men just like us, yet paler and perhaps more prone to the harshness of the sun? I'd heard my father tell Mama more than once just how much he hated their presence in the neighboring villages, and that they should go back to their own country. At the time I had not understood.

They were dressed in a lighter uniform to that of the Black men who had struck my brother the last time I had ventured far enough away from our hut. The red hat I would never forget, the hardened expressions with dark foreheads dripping with sweat. What they carried were rifles and I only knew this now because Kabili had told me.

The white men began shouting orders at my brothers and a group of other men who had joined them. Pako, the most hotheaded of all of us and so much like our father, Mama would say, simply did as he was told. His shoulders hunched, inches seemingly taken off his height.

Again, and just like with my father before, I waited patiently for a retaliation which simply did not come.

According to Pako, our father had been gone for long enough that my mama's tears should have eased, but I suspected they were about more than my father's death.

I was no longer allowed out of her sight, and as my brothers still worked away for days, or even weeks at a time, it was mostly just Mama and me with hardly any visitors, just Ina Balenga on occasion.

More than ever, I was keen to say and do such things as I assumed would please my father, to fight the feeling that nestled deep inside me—one that told me I was beginning to forget what he even looked like.

When I had said as much to Mama, she simply said, "Every time I look at you, Dikembe, I see him."

One day, Mama appeared, dressed in a patterned cloth my father used to compliment her on. I was sitting alone under the mid-morning sun before it became too hot to tolerate.

"I am hungry," I said, standing and circling my arms around her waist. I could feel the disapproval of each of my brothers, even though they had not been home in days.

"What do you have to be hungry for, did you not just eat?" She placed my palm into hers and it felt like the power of life. I looked up at her and squeezed her hand, just in case she was about to let go. "Come, my Dikembe. We must speak."

I began to sort the questions in my head, deciding which to ask first as we sat under my favorite tree, cross-legged.

Whenever she smiled, which was a rarity these days, my heart would lift, that one act filling me with warmth more satisfying than the sun, and with it an optimism that could not be quantified. Little did I know that within minutes it would be marred with a request that I, at first, could not understand, and when I did, would make me want to run away from my tree and the sanctuary of my mama as fast as was humanly possible.

Ignoring my tears, Mama told me to remain calm and to listen as she explained once again.

"We have been struggling ever since your father was taken from us."

"Yes, Mama, but why does it have to be me?" The force of my tears affected my voice as if I were a toddler rather than a boy of ten. I didn't care, though. Nor did I care what she or my brothers thought, and as such allowed my tears to defiantly flow down my cheeks. "No, Mama! I don't want to!"

I had never shown such disrespect to her or any elder, but I was falling deeper into an abyss and there was no one waiting at the bottom with open arms, no one to hold me and tell me I didn't have to do this. The only person who could save me was the very person pushing me down the hole!

She shifted closer to me. "You are always saying you want to work, like your brothers. Now is your chance."

My head buzzed with confusion. What I'd seen of my brothers' work so far terrified me, but I was willing to partake in it because it was my birthright as a member of this family. Yet what Mama spoke about was something I knew my father would not have liked. Something I had never, ever considered would be asked of me.

"You are the one who can help our family, Dikembe. You want to help us, no?"

I nodded my head weakly.

"It would not be for long, don't worry. Remember, you are like Mbidi Kiluwe, the Black king, and you must do what is right."

"Yes, Mama," I said, in between streams of tears.

"You must do as they tell you, even if it seems like something you do not understand or are not clear about. When that happens, just think about what the Black king would do."

"But why—" I began, as her delicate finger pressed against my lips.

"Please, Dikembe." My mama also began to cry, which only increased my distress.

"Listen, my child," she said, wiping her eyes with her hands. "Your father would want this. He always protected this family and he would want you to do this."

Her words confused me. My father had always spoken ill of the white man; I was the youngest and not the eldest, so why had Pako not been tasked with this? Perhaps the real reason was that Pako was her favorite and not I.

My mama's own explanation was simpler as she slowly placed my father's bone necklace over my head.

My breath caught in my throat quickly. The last time I had seen this necklace was around my father's neck. Had he been wearing it the day they shot and then hanged him?

"You will wear this," she said, smiling through her tears.

I ran my fingers over the beading and then smoothed them over the clawlike spikes which hung down my chest. I could not speak.

"You are the last born and your father wanted a different life for you. He would want you to have his necklace too. You children and this necklace are all I have left of your father and now it . . . it belongs to you," she said, rearranging each of the claws to decorate my neck.

My mama's clumsy attempt to appease me with the necklace only made me react more at the unfairness of what was being asked and for actually wearing it, an honor I had not earned. Instead, I was about to betray my father in the worst way.

"Do you understand now, Dikembe?"

I nodded my head, tears blurring my vision.

Her voice no longer resembled sweetness but was laced with a desperation I hadn't noticed before. "Look at me, Dikembe." She gently tilted my chin upward. "Listen."

The whites of her eyes reddened. I blinked rapidly, her face in and out of focus because of my own tears. "Yes, Mama."

"You are the only one who can do this."

"Yes, Mama."

"No one but you, Dikembe. *Mwana Muya*."

My good child.

Chapter Three

Dikembe
1905

Each of my brothers lined up outside our hut in order of age: first Pako, Yogo, Djamba and then Kabili. Apparently, it was only through the kindness of the white man that they were allowed to be here for this goodbye. A gratitude I was unable to voice because I for one did not want to be there or for this to be happening at all. But at the age of almost eleven I had been tasked with looking after our family the way my father would have, by working and ensuring they would not go hungry.

"Goodbye, Dikembe," Kabili said as I stared up at him. "I will miss you," he added in a whisper. He'd grown inches away from me, and now we were to be separated by an endless sea, two different countries and another language. I was headed to a land I had heard my father speak of many times, but always with disdain. If I just told myself I'd see him again soon, this would prevent any tears from falling. It would allow me to leave this moment as a man worthy of the necklace I wore around my neck.

"I will see you very soon, brother," I said, my voice tinged with hope. I had no idea when this reunion would occur, though; Mama had said a month or slightly longer. I just knew that one day soon, I would see my brother, Mama and the rest of my family again.

All I needed to do was this one small thing. Wasn't that what

Mama had called it? Yet it didn't feel small considering my brothers were able to stay here and with my mama.

The long sleeves of my robe felt itchy under the warm sun, but Mama had insisted I dress in my best clothes for the occasion.

"I am happy you will be with an Englishman," said Kabili.

"Why?"

"Because he will not be like the white men here."

This I did not understand.

Ina Balenga had come to wave me off and it was her I saw gently grip Kabili's shoulder as I moved away, both with tears in their eyes. If I was due to return in a month or slightly longer, surely there was no need for tears?

It was my mama who accompanied me on that long walk through the village, past the now-permitted tree and into a clearing I had never seen before. It felt unfamiliar, as I had only ever known my mother within the proximity of our hut. What was also strange to me was that we were not alone. With us was a white man, with hair that looked slippery to the touch, and that did not match the thick grassy texture that lived above his lip. He was dressed in long boots almost up to his knees, and the three of us walked that dusty journey past scatterings of beloved trees my father would know the names of, mostly in silence, save for the large birds squawking overhead and the sound of his weight hitting the ground as he walked.

The man started to converse with my mama in our native tongue, his pronunciations not as clumsy as I would have assumed. I should have listened, but I was more intent on keeping up with them as they hurried along the sandy track. We stopped a few times for water; in the first village I spotted a commotion—a boy not much older than Kabili on his knees, holding on to a block of wood as another white man dressed in white stood over him, carrying what looked like a black snake but was actually a whip made from what I would learn later was hippopotamus hide. The same man addressed the crowd with warnings as two women dressed in robes, their dark foreheads glistening with sweat, looked on, fear in their expressions and in the way they stood, alert yet hopeless. The man in white turned to us and smiled. My mama looked away, as did the white man walking with us, yet I couldn't keep my eyes from that scene.

"Dikembe!" called my mother, just as I turned back to her and a multitude of sounds mingled with that of the birds which flew above us.

We arrived at a village, where the white man walked away and Mama took my hand. "Come, Dikembe," she said.

I followed her to a hut where I lay inside the crook of her arms, falling asleep instantly, convincing myself that this was where my journey would end and that Mama of course would be staying with me.

"Wake up, Dikembe!" she said, as I rubbed at my eyes some hours later. Within minutes we were on that journey again, and between that village and our first water stop three men slowly passed by us, their necks and wrists bound in iron chains, as a white man, again dressed in white, walked behind them carrying a rifle. Beside him was a man who reminded me of my brother Yogo, though he was dressed in that uniform again with the red hat. I could not read the expressions of the three bound men, but one of them looked toward me and we locked eyes. He reminded me of my father—what I could recall of him—and I immediately felt helpless.

"Dikembe, keep moving," beckoned Mama, as my gaze followed the back of the last man, his skin covered in welts, open and glistening under the rays of the sun. I watched until the men disappeared.

It was hours before we made our final stop, which landed us at a view that looked out over a very large expanse of water. I had never traveled this far away from my village before and perhaps if

I had, what rested upon that water would not have come as such a great shock to me.

It looked so high it could have touched the clouds, this vessel, this ship like nothing I had ever seen before in my life. Mightier than the rhino Kabili claimed to have spotted and more magnificent than the tallest of trees!

I had not really believed it when Mama had said we would be seeing one, yet there it was, large and overpowering, a metal beast!

In the past I'd heard them described from the mouths of others and never thought to be privileged enough to rest my eyes upon one. I knew of the little curved riverboats that some of the villagers used to catch fish, but they were surely like swarming flies next to this vessel that balanced itself perfectly on top of the water.

"What do you think?" asked the white man, whose name I had forgotten in the midst of my excitement. He stared at me with a sort of anticipation.

"Say thank you to Mr. Richard," said Mama, gently squeezing my shoulder.

"Don't be frightened," said Mr. Richard.

I looked up at my mama and there were tears lodged in the corners of her eyes. Tears of happiness, I suspected.

"This is the right decision," he said to Mama, as I moved closer to what Mr. Richard explained was called a steamer.

There were a number of men already on board, and this made me hold back at first and proceed with caution, one small step at a time. They were all white, and I couldn't be sure what they would do to me if I went any further. Perhaps they'd be nice like Mr. Richard and not like the others. Yet, for a chance to be closer to the ship, I would have to risk my fate and hope I did not end up like my father or the men I'd seen in chains.

Now closer to the ship than to Mama, I glanced over at her and Mr. Richard, who was placing a piece of cloth into her hand, which she used to wipe her eyes.

My gaze alternated between Mama and that ship, and when she ran toward me, I turned away from the beauty of it and allowed her to scoop me up. With a strength I did not know she had, she held me off the floor, right up there in her arms.

"I love you," she said. This always sounded sweeter in our native tongue: *Nkusanswa*. I responded in kind, unsure of why her tears were so plentiful or why she tilted her head as if she'd just asked a question. I would be seeing her again very soon. A month, she had said. Or slightly longer. I was not leaving like my father. I would come home! Sure enough, the impatience I felt to return my gaze to the ship was greater than my need to stay in my mama's arms. So I extracted myself from her embrace and followed Mr. Richard onto a plank of wood I was sure would falter, and I would fall to my demise. Yet it was sturdy enough to take his weight and mine as the small cluster of men aboard stood watching, smiling. I nodded my head in greeting, the smoke from their cigarettes resting in my throat.

I so wished Kabili was here to see all of this.

Inside, the ship appeared much smaller than the outside.

"Look, Mama!" I screamed through one of the many windows. She looked toward me; I waved at her to come aboard but she slowly shook her head.

I ran off the ship and back to her, breathless. "I am not going for long," I said. Indeed, by the time I returned, I might be as tall as Kabili and everything would be as I had left it!

She bent and kissed my forehead. The vessel looked like it was already moving, and my stomach lurched with disappointment at the possibility I wouldn't get to stand on it once more.

"Come along now!" called out Mr. Richard. I looked at my mama again, but the sounds of the ship demanded my attention. She kissed me once more, this time on each of my cheeks and back to my forehead. It was as if she did not want to stop. Our hands released from one another as I quickly turned and jumped back onto the ship. Soon it was actually moving and on the water, the entire ship pulling away from where Mama stood. No one I knew had ever ridden on such a thing, and this felt like a wonderful dream I wished would never end. I waved at Mama but she had already turned away.

Looking back, if I had known—if I had just known—I would have tempered my excitement with questions, so many questions. Or I would have stayed on the shore and I'd never, ever have left my mama's arms. I would have begged her forgiveness for whatever I had done to deserve to be sent away, and I would have insisted on staying in my village, with my brothers, with her. Or I would have gone back even further—to the time I had woken before the sound of the cockerel. I would have found my father that morning, held tightly on to him, and simply begged him to stay with us and forgo that meeting with the elders, not to leave that morning.

To stay.

To simply stay.

Chapter Four

Dikembe
1905

I could no longer count how many days we had been on that ship, only that, according to Mr. Richard, we were edging toward a new year. The majority of the first leg I'd spent hunched over vomiting, or sleeping off illness and nursing an ache in my chest for my mama and brothers. It felt like a similar loss to what I had felt for my father, yet different too. Because along with it came the fear of living each day on a giant vessel that somehow managed to balance on an endless body of water, and with no one for company but white men who spoke in very loud voices and in a language I did not understand.

Luckily, Mr. Richard spoke my language while the others made hand gestures to communicate with me, which thankfully wasn't that often. He insisted I learn a little English but I found this very difficult at first, each syllable sitting uncomfortably on my tongue. When some of the men laughed at my attempts, it would only shut down any further efforts.

"There is not much else to do on such a voyage home, so I will teach you all you need to know. I cannot have you picking up words from our boys here . . . the language of the average seaman is . . . what can I say . . . rather colorful. You shall also learn to write!"

Mr. Richard was always talking, even when I just wanted to

close my eyes and dream of my mama. He expected me to match his excitement at learning English, sitting on a ship strangely called the *Lady*, which was once an object of my joyful curiosity but now felt overfamiliar, along with the contempt that came with it. It did not help that it smelled unsanitary and had long ago lost its shine. As had this adventure.

We ate a lot of beef with salt, which I did not like. I often wondered why there wasn't much fish, considering we lived on the sea! I enjoyed the fried flour dumplings, as well as something called marmalade. Mr. Richard scoffed when I discovered the joy of eating them together. However, my appetite was lacking most days as my stomach could not get used to the motion of the ship. Every time I failed to keep my meal inside, a burst of laughter from one of the sailors would follow as I bent over the side, heaving uncontrollably.

One such day, one of the kindlier men proffered a handkerchief and I simply looked at it.

"It's clean, lad," he said. That much I understood. I took it and wiped at my mouth, no longer embarrassed by my sickness as its frequency had brushed aside any modesty.

Slowly, as my seasickness abated, a smidgen of appetite returned, with Mr. Richard insisting I eat as many dumplings as I wanted while he sat beside me, reciting more English words for me to learn. This ritual appeared to be the only shining light in that endless sea we remained on for what felt like an eternity, with not much else to do but eat and sleep.

I watched others prepare the food and clean the vessel and they were chores I longed to join in with as soon as my strength returned, but Mr. Richard insisted I was never to engage in such "low-class activities."

His response confused me.

We changed transportation more than once, each time to something even more magnificent in size and splendor. But the novelty of this was no longer able to excite me, as my body weakened with grief and something new. As I lay stricken in the bed of our cabin one day, Mr. Richard wiped at my brow with a damp cloth, and said I now had something called the "flu." I managed to ask a question which had rested on my lips for weeks now: "Why am I here?" The room spun, and every ounce of my strength felt like it had been extracted from my body. I'm convinced Mr. Richard could only put my question down to delirium, for it was a question I simply lacked the courage for when in good health.

"You are accompanying me to England, dear boy, where you will live with me in my home. Your mother has explained this to you."

"As your servant?"

"Who told you this?"

"My mama."

"No, dear boy, that will never be your fate. How amusing of you to think so!"

This explanation at the time felt incomplete and insignificant to me because, plainly and simply, *I just wanted my mama.* But it was something to digest, as the cabin began to sway and a feeling of nausea invaded my stomach once more.

1906

We finally reached our destination, weeks or even months later; I could no longer tell! England and this long-awaited arrival had turned into an anticlimactic moment that I would not have even noticed, if not for the startling change in scenery. I had already experienced the stark difference in temperature the further we traveled on the ship, so the eye-watering breeze as we disembarked was not a shock—though the harbor, awash with white ladies, men and children, was. I had never seen a white woman before and they were adorned with long flowing robes and hats, while the men dressed in layers of clothing that would have caused them to sweat profusely back in my village. My own thin layers of clothing felt overly scant as I pulled the oversized jacket Mr. Richard had given me closer around my shoulders.

"When we get to the house, there will be plenty of clothes to keep you warm. Ones that fit!" said Mr. Richard with a smile.

My first ever trip in a motor vehicle should have been a cause for celebration, yet all I craved was a bed to rest my body after such a seemingly endless journey.

Mr. Richard was explaining the mechanics of the machine to me, his voice triumphant. "The Darracq Flying Fifteen automobile isn't owned by many on this earth and is fresh from France!"

I couldn't be bothered to work out how he could have transported such a contraption to England . . . yet hadn't he just done the same with me? My eyes flickered as the machine maneuvered us on the road. A moment that should have matched the excitement of seeing the steamer for the first time was simply a prelude to much-needed rest; a desperate fight between wanting to drink in my new surroundings yet also wanting to just close my eyes and sleep. However, I remained engaged at the sight of such tall and stoic buildings, the strangely smooth path of the roads without a single pothole. It was only when I spotted another automobile on the opposite side of the road that it truly dawned on me that I was actually sitting in one!

When we pulled up at a building that shone brilliantly with artificial light, I felt a semblance of fresh energy.

I carefully stepped out of the motor vehicle and immediately looked up to the moon in the night sky—at least that was familiar to me. But as I turned my gaze to the steps, I noticed the outline of two creatures either side of the door.

I opened my mouth to speak, yet no sound could emerge.

"Don't worry, they are not real. Besides, I thought you'd be used to the real thing!"

I did not understand this comment; indeed, nothing made

much sense. I was in a cold land where no one who looked anything like me existed, with two creatures made of stone staring down at me with menace, daring me to come closer, which I did, albeit very cautiously.

As I slowly climbed the steps which elevated me high up above the automobile, I soon recognized the creatures as lions, but with faces that appeared human to me; a ridiculous concoction, not that I would ever echo my distaste. Mr. Richard clearly thought the stone creatures to be the epitome of taste.

"Welcome to your new home. I think you're going to have a wonderful time!" he said grandly.

Each step sapped a little more of my strength than I had to give, and when I reached the top, the mouths of the creatures looked ready to consume me. I laughed at such silly thoughts. They were not real, after all.

Yet with hindsight I can now see that walking past those two beasts and into that house was the beginning of an ending that would change everything about my life forever.

Starting with my name.

Chapter Five

Lowra
1993

As he breezed past me, the smell of alcohol and stale cigarettes followed behind him.

"My office, please, Laura."

I hated when my boss called me that. He knew how to pronounce my name and was just doing this to provoke a reaction. He wouldn't be getting one.

"I'm just finishing up, Mr. Rice," I said, peeling off the thin disposable gloves. I'd just finished a shift at the university cafe and was ready to get out of here, even if it was to simply sit at home, watch TV or read a magazine. I dropped the gloves into the bin as I went after him.

"Never mind all that." His voice was a command with not enough power to affect me as it did the other staff. Nevertheless, being summoned by Mr. Rice couldn't be good.

I followed him outside and into his "office"—a cramped yellow van parked in the university car park.

"Is there a problem then?" I said, sliding onto the seat beside him. The van reeked of ash and coffee, the stains on the floor and dashboard telling the same story.

"Laura . . ." The pause was for dramatic effect, no doubt.

"It's Lowra," I corrected.

"I've been told you haven't been pulling your weight."

I stared at him probingly: this was me pretending to care.

"It has been brought to my attention that on more than one occasion, you have been asked to waitress at graduation ceremonies and you have refused."

"I'm a catering assistant."

"Sometimes they get short-staffed. It happens. Everyone has to muck in."

"I was hired as a catering assistant, Mr. Rice. I don't have any waitressing experience or a silver service qualification, so—"

"So, it's a university cafe, not a fancy restaurant."

Mr. Rice was one of those middle-aged men who'd probably never been good-looking even in their youth, plowing all that pain into becoming the most successful one in the family and then choosing to look down at everyone else every chance they got. Little did he know I'd been up against worse than him.

"I do the job I am paid to do, Mr. Rice."

I looked straight ahead through the window, now speckled with raindrops, and from the corner of my eye I caught the side of his mouth twitching. Idiot.

"Fact is, we can't afford to have complaints about our staff. This university's a big contract."

I nodded my head to show I was listening.

"I get the feeling you're not taking this seriously because you're agency staff," he said.

My "don't give a crap" attitude about things often riled him, just as it did others, especially those who tried to pull me into some type of unwanted friendship. Most gave up trying, preferring instead to go along with the idea I was just a rude little cow, a loner, or both. Not that I cared. There wasn't much in this world I actually did care about.

As long as I could muster up enough strength to step out of bed in the morning and turn on the shower, that was a win.

"I do my job, Mr. Rice. I don't know what else you need me to do," I said, shifting to look out of the side window. I twirled the bottom of my hair with fingers still smelling faintly of bleach. I'd only just had it cut. The hairdresser had tried to make a connection with me: "Good job the bob hardly goes out of fashion—you've had the same style for years. You must really like it . . ."

Of course, her statement only led to surface talk and the odd lie. That I had been obsessed with the singer Betty Boo a couple of years ago and the hairstyle stuck. I wasn't going to tell her the truth: that I had to have that style because it was the one *she* liked. The one she wore in my photograph and probably the same one she died in. I wasn't going to say that.

My eyes focused on a little girl skipping past the greengrocers with a woman—probably her mother—trailing behind in a pair of pointy heels which had to be uncomfortable, or at the very least impractical for the task of running after a child. She caught up with the little girl, clasping her hand tightly, while almost yanking her arm out of the socket. It took everything in me not to jump out of the car and confront that woman.

"Lowra?"

Not even his voice could drown out the image now forming in my head: of a woman, her brown hair in a bobbed haircut, bending down to kiss my hand, half the size of hers. "Lowra," she'd said—my name with an added Spanish flourish to the pronunciation.

"Lowra, are you listening?" he said, bringing me back to the present.

I took a sharp intake of breath. "Of course."

"Do better, or else I'll have to take you off that site. All the others are full, so . . ."

"You'll sack me if I get another complaint, is that it?"

"I would have to let you go, yes."

He'd have to let me go from what? A job that didn't even pay sick leave and hardly put enough food on the table?

"It won't happen again," I said, with a lack of emotion I knew he'd find frustrating.

That same day at home, I did what I usually did after working the early shift—I sat in front of the television, not really concentrating on anything. Yet this was better than sitting there in silence, alone with my thoughts. That was never a good thing. Thoughts led to more thoughts and then to more, until—

The sound of the phone startled me. No one ever rang except cold callers trying to sell double-glazing or timeshares, and I hardly gave my number out. There was no one I needed or wanted to keep in touch with *that* much. Plus, there was a safety in keeping myself to myself. Marnie from work dared to ask for my number once, and I pretended not to hear her. Recently, she'd overstepped her place in my life by turning up at my home without an invite. I had no idea how she'd even found me, considering I had just said, "I live on the Boston Estate, fifth floor." At the sound of the intercom, I'd basically cowered in the corner of my lounge, hoping she couldn't hear me breathe, even though it sounded louder than it usually did, my hands covering each of my ears, eyes squeezed shut. Some might find me weird for doing this, but my flat on a council housing estate in Croydon was more than just a building, or even a home—it was where I felt safe from everything and everyone. Letting just anyone through the front door wasn't something I could do without any preparation and thought.

I stared at it, the telephone on a stand in the lounge, waiting for it to stop ringing, that intrusion into my private space. It did. Finally.

Some might think having spent almost three years in a noisy children's home with eight girls in one room had a lot to do with why I valued my space so much.

But that wasn't it.

I'd left the children's home twelve years ago at the age of eighteen, with keys to a new rented flat, a grant, and no idea of what to do next. I was meant to start living life as an adult apparently, and in a world I knew nothing about.

My social worker may have been helpful, but really everything was now my responsibility. The bills, a flat, my life, everything; and these required skills I'd never been taught.

The money I received from the government every two weeks was useful, but I'd always run out midmonth because I spent most of it on takeaways, having never learned to cook anything more than beans on toast. I also began to get used to red letters falling through the letterbox. Silly, really, because I'd always have enough money to pay them but just hadn't got into the habit of doing so on time. It's not as if I ever went anywhere, and I hardly bought myself things most teenaged girls did, like makeup and fancy clothes. Then again, I wasn't like anybody else. At the age of eighteen, I was content enough to sit in my flat most days and just think. Overthink, some would say. Thoughts of my dad and my mother as I sat staring at the one photograph that existed of the three of us together, as a family. Thinking about what could have been if only she'd lived. If only they'd both lived.

When I was nineteen, I took an afternoon computer course at the local college and a Spanish one in the evening—perhaps it was all too much, too soon, because I only lasted a month before I quit both.

My life suited me and never really changed—until I reached the age of twenty-five. That's when I started to feel not a part of it. Like someone looking in on another person's existence, I started to feel like I wasn't in my own body, disassociated from everything and everyone around me. People tried to get close to me, whether it be at my job or in the library, when all I wanted to do was be distracted by the books. I even started going out with a boy, who said I was pretty after watching me carefully weigh four oranges in the greengrocers.

It never felt like I was actually participating in any sort of real life.

I'd watch people on television having more of a real experience than I ever could. I wanted to feel something, anything. So when my boyfriend touched me with his fingertips and I felt the sensation against my skin, I craved more, yet at the same time I was terrified, allowing him to go further because I just wanted to feel. But then it was as if he forgot I was there and just continued with what he was doing, his breath hoarse, his excitement escalating as he asked me over and over again if I "liked this." I couldn't answer as once again I simply ended up looking down at this person being touched, kissed, probed, and feeling no connection to her whatsoever.

It wasn't long after this that I started to feel like the comfortable world I had cultivated for myself wasn't mine anymore. The boyfriend wanted to come round too often, spend time with me, even rearrange my flat. He spoke about the future, our future, while all I could ever feel was a sense of panic until he left me alone and I could be in my room, safely by myself. But here's the thing: it—my home, my life—no longer felt safe. It felt contaminated, and I didn't know who I had become, if that makes sense.

It made sense at the time and then it didn't, and when it didn't, that's when all I could see was nothing.

I stood up and rolled my neck to ease the tension the ringing phone had caused. I looked for things to do around the flat. I puffed up a pillow and ran my finger along the TV cabinet. Of course there was no dust, as I kept my small flat fantastically clean and presentable even though I was usually the only one who crossed the threshold. On the rare occasions a repairman walked through my home, it felt like an intrusion. Their angry boots stomping all over the floor, each step as if they were crunching the bones of my torso, and feeling faint when one asked to use the toilet, making sure to disinfect the whole area twice over before I could even think of using it again.

I took the phone off the receiver.

*

At work the next day, Marnie caught up with me just as I was about to finish my shift at the university.

"Fancy a drink?" she said.

"Bit early for me."

"Lunch?"

"I have some leftovers waiting for me at home. I'll grab that before my evening shift." The agency had recently offered me work in a local gym cafe.

Marnie linked her arm in mine and I stiffened, quickly maneuvering myself away from her strong grip.

"Come on," she said. "We can make an afternoon of it. I have a couple of hours until I go get the kids."

"Maybe a quick bite . . ." I agreed, while trying to ignore the deep feeling of unease resting in my chest. Marnie was nice enough but she asked too many questions. We'd worked together for two years and I knew everything about her: two kids, a husband who snored, and a dog who weed itself whenever a firework went off—and yet it was all information I had little interest in. It was only after I'd overheard one of the other girls saying something about me being "weird" that I said yes to one of Marnie's frequent invitations to lunch. Not because I particularly cared what others thought of me, but because it was Marnie who'd stood up for me, told the girl to "fuck off" and that "Lowra's a lovely girl if you bothered to get to know her!"

Ironic really, because Marnie didn't know me at all. I was polite to her, as I was to all my colleagues, and perhaps she had mistaken my silence for being a good listener. But she had defended me and I wasn't used to that, so I felt she was at least worthy of an hour of my time now and again—however uncomfortable and unnatural it felt. As long as she never made unwelcome visits to my flat again . . .

Marnie scanned the laminated menu as a large man in a white apron stood over us.

"I'll have a tea, and the ham and cheese panini, please," she said happily.

"I'll have the same . . . but with tomato. Thanks."

"I like tomatoes too. Just not in a toasted sandwich because it makes it go all soggy."

She seemed to be pleased at extracting yet another bit of useless information about me, however pointless.

The sandwich tasted surprisingly good. The excuse of a full mouth prevented any responses to the barrage of questions coming from Marnie, and for that I was grateful. She said something about being glad we were "friends" but I just smiled and chewed.

There were numerous ways my life could have turned out. The one that seemed most like a fairy tale yet tied in with what really could have been was the one where Marnie would not have existed in my life. That life would have been full of chums made at a fee-paying school, I suppose, and by now I would have been living in a house just down the road from where I grew up, in a seaside town miles from here, with regular trips to my parents' nearby as well as to Valencia, my mother's favorite city and where a lot of my childhood holidays were spent. I may even have had a husband and a handful of children by now. Perhaps a dog too; a white fluffy one that also peed over the carpet when a firework went off. In that life I'd smile almost every day, and people would comment on just how much I looked like my mother.

Of course, in reality, if I looked closely enough at the photograph I carried in my purse, it was my dad I looked more like. Thin, long nose, slim lips and an oblong-shaped face, while my mother's resembled a love heart—at least that's how I saw it. A large, beautiful love heart! While her olive skin was clearly a shade darker than mine, along with my Spanish name I'd inherited enough of my mother's genes to look, as Marnie once described it, as if I'd "just come off holiday!"

Marnie was talking once again about holidays now, happy enough with my nods of encouragement. "I've always wanted to go to Italy, visit the Colosseum and all that. I wanted my other half to take me there on our honeymoon, but we went to Bognor instead. He's such a cheapskate!"

My stomach tensed because I knew what was coming next.

"How about you? Been anywhere nice?"

I answered her question by reeling off a fake trip to Devon I was yet to take. My "regret" at never having been abroad. Omitting to mention the frequent trips to Spain I remembered from my childhood. The accompanying murmurs and nods of her head told me I was giving her what she needed, though, which was a description of a life that basically didn't exist. If I told her the truth about the first half of my childhood, it would have read differently: passport at the age of five, regular trips with my parents, and long hot summers in Valencia. The sunshine, sea and fancy foods served to a child who at that age couldn't really appreciate them. Splashing about in a pool bathed in a neon light; running on an open field under a scorching sun; my beautiful mother leaning toward me in a swimming costume and oversized straw hat and wiping sticky melted ice cream from my chin; my dad calling me a "messy pup." And the laughter. So much laughter.

"Tell me more about this holiday you're going on this summer, Marnie. America, isn't it? Disney with your husband and the kids?" I asked cunningly.

"Don't get me started on all that. The kids want America but Rod says we're going to that new one in France."

Beyond the guise of wanting to talk about me, Marnie really just loved talking about herself. She was no different from anyone else who attempted to get to know me. Most people were simply in a rush to talk about themselves, using interest in my life as a ruse. And as the relationship progressed, their "love" for you simply became about how you made them feel and nothing much more than that. The boy who said he was my boyfriend had taught me that.

Yet everyone seemed to crave these relationships—except me, of course. I had absolutely no interest in anyone or anything.

My interest was simply to survive.

Chapter Six

Lowra
1993

The early hours of the morning, my favorite time of day.

The world still asleep, unbothered with what lay ahead. The sounds of wildlife as they ruled their own little world without the onslaught of humans. Enjoying my own stillness, where I could almost forget my past and what I had seen, and the actions of others.

A moment in time when it was possible, just possible, to exist without assumptions or judgments—to just *be*. I sounded a bit like one of the books Dr. Raj had recommended and I'd scoffed at, but for a few moments in the early hours of a bright morning, it all made sense.

This morning, though, the quiet and stillness was broken by the angry sound of the telephone ringing. Again.

"Look here, I don't want any of what you're selling so—"

"Is this Miss Lowra Normandy Cavendish?"

I swallowed. This man, this voice, had just said my entire name, including the middle name I never used or even liked—because it sounded too posh.

It belonged to another person, another life.

"It's just Lowra Cavendish."

"Splendid."

I took a deep breath, hoping by the time I exhaled, none of this would actually be real.

"Who is this?"

"My name is Mr. Philip Danvers and I have been entrusted by the estate of Nina Cavendish—"

I dropped the handset at the sound of that name. I could no longer hear the voice, just a blinding noise in my head. I could not have the intrusion of this in my home, my sanctuary. I did not want to hear any of this!

"Miss Cavendish? Miss Cavendish, are you there?"

I stared down at the phone and the disembodied voice of the man.

He was just a man on the other end of a phone. He couldn't hurt me.

Just as she couldn't hurt me anymore.

I bent down and placed the tip of my finger on the cream-colored, smooth surface of the phone. It was starting to look like a snake, but it was just a phone.

"Miss Cavendish, are you there?"

The noise in my head began to ease. It was just a phone. Nothing bad could happen to me through a telephone. I lifted the handset back to my ear but he must have hung up, thinking it had cut off.

I took another deep breath.

When it rang again, I swallowed. "Hello, yes, I'm still here."

"Miss Cavendish, we have been trying to get hold of you, hence the early call."

"I'm here now."

"I have some very bad news."

I swallowed.

"It's regarding Mrs. Nina Cavendish . . ." There was a lengthy pause.

I tried to think of something to say in response. Something normal. Something dramatic. Anything. "Is she . . . ?"

"Yes, I'm afraid she's deceased. She has died . . ."

"I know what 'deceased' means."

"Yes, of course. I am so very sorry to have to tell you this over the phone, but we have been trying to find you for some time . . ."

I slid to the floor, my hand clutching the phone still pressed against my ear.

"I am so very sorry."

"Please stop saying that." My voice was a whisper.

"Sorr—"

The call lasted all of five minutes. After my initial confusion, each of his words sounded clear, concise and final. I replaced the phone onto its cradle and slowly stood up again, standing with my back stamped against the green wallpaper, which had taken me two days to apply. The walls used to be gray, but a presenter on one of those makeover shows had called the color "oppressive" so I changed it. A rare attempt by me to change something about my life; to add a spark of "funky fun," I suppose. It hadn't worked because I realized soon enough that brightly colored walls were not going to stop my thoughts or the memories.

I closed my eyes, the solicitor's words echoing in my mind, which started aimlessly listing the polite words people use when someone dies: deceased. Gone. No longer with us.

The voice on the telephone had asked if I remembered the address and if not, did I need to write it down.

I told him I did not.

I knew exactly how to get there.

The gray, aging buildings of London slowly gave way to flashes of color as the train sped up, then slowed down to reveal fields and pot-bellied animals grazing the land, then sped up again to mesh everything together, causing it to look like a continuous sloppy canvas. The further away from the city I got, the less I could recall of Mr. Rice's furious voice on the phone earlier: "You can't take days off work without notice!"

He had only piped down once I reminded him that, in the absence of a permanent contract and since I worked through an agency, I could. The only reason he hadn't fired me on the spot was my assurance that I'd arranged for "my good friend Marnie" to take over most of my shifts.

The train slowed down again, stopping by a house where I was able to focus in on the garden—a red plastic slide along with a miniature brown dog, happily chasing its short tail: signs of life and a family. I hated to stare but couldn't help it. My eyes fixed on the scene even as the train gently began to move away.

As the train edged closer to the end of the line, its final destination, my heart began to race and my forehead felt clammy.

I wrapped my scarf tighter around my neck as I flashed the station guard my return ticket and placed it back into the side pocket of my bag. Outside the station I was instantly bathed in a flood of sunlight. The atmosphere was so very different from London, yet familiar as I walked the almost empty road that headed toward the seafront. The seagulls above me yelled violently and I wanted to shout back at them: *I don't want to be here either!*

The local sweetshop I vaguely remembered had now been replaced with a post office that also sold seaside tat, including large inflatable sea life. Next to it was a small cafe called the Flamingo Club which used to be a diner. Now, a miserable-looking man sipping tea by the window turned and glared at me. Who came up with these names?

I turned into a road of smart Victorian houses that would gradually lead to the last one at the end of the street—number 109—and I took a sharp intake of sea air.

I was getting closer.

Dr. Raj insisted I be mindful of sights, a sound, a familiar smell that could trigger feelings from the past. Perhaps this would account for the tightness in my tummy and my shoulders leaping up to almost reach my ears.

A man and a little girl carrying a cute puppy walked slowly by. The man's head nodded in my direction but his eyes were narrowed as if questioning who I could be, because clearly one look at me was enough to know I didn't belong here. Or perhaps these days everyone knew everyone around here, happily entrenched in each other's business, yet when I had desperately needed them to be in mine, they had remained silent.

Number 109 was finally in front of me. The large steps, once massive to a child, were now clearly in need of one of those makeovers shows I liked to watch. The two weird-looking lions either side of the door were just tacky, that brass door knocker outdated and pointless.

The front door was ajar, allowing voices to drift out, and for a terrifying second I thought it must be her.

She is no longer with us.

This was going to be OK, I muttered to myself, as my heartbeat felt like it had quadrupled in speed.

I stood at the bottom of the steps, my vision purposely tunneled, not intending to absorb anything around me. Not the sunshine hovering over me, or the perfect row of detached houses lining the street. Nor the bed of neon-pink flowers sprouting from a large pot at the side of the door—a new addition that just didn't fit with what I knew of this house or the secrets which existed behind those walls.

"Hello, can I help you?" said a woman dressed in ripped jeans, the skin of her knee visible. She stood at the top of the stairs in between the "creatures." "You've been standing there quite a while."

"I'm Lowra Cavendish."

"You're the new owner, right?"

"Y-yes . . . I suppose so."

"I've been hired by Danvers and Harding, the solicitors."

I knotted my eyebrows, as if any little bit of information felt like too much.

"They often use us for house clearances. Sorry for your loss," she said, and with that one comment, I could feel my body jerk backward through time and I was slowly being transported *there* again.

My hair in pigtails, sitting on the bottom step, watching each car pull up and expecting him to show up, perhaps with a giant Minnie Mouse and wet kisses all over my cheeks. Instead, each vehicle that arrived was simply ferrying more people to the front door; some with dishes of food, some with flowers, never once with the only person I actually wanted to see.

"Sorry for your loss," they said over and over again, until I was sick of the words, hated every single syllable.

"They told us you were coming," said the girl in the ripped jeans, cheerily.

I took my time up each of the steps as she carried on talking, forcing myself to engage in small talk. "What are you going to do with everything?"

"The expensive stuff will be sold off or given to charity," she said. "She left strict instructions for which charity would get what."

I reached the top of the stairs.

"Cats' home?" I said absently.

"No, the bulk of it's going to kids' charities. Nice of her, wasn't it? I bet she was a lovely lady. Are you her daughter?"

I swallowed. "No."

The woman stood aside as I placed one foot over the threshold and then the other. As my feet hit the black-and-white tiles of the hallway, the rush of emotion I feared didn't come . . . only a numbness, which was good. This was exactly what I needed to get through what was next. Whatever that was.

"Such a beautiful grand house. The best on the street, I'd say. Back in the old days it must have been quite a sight. If you don't mind me asking, how were you related to Mrs. Cavendish?"

I opened my mouth to speak and then shut it. She carried on anyway.

"Not wanting to speak ill of the dead, but I think she must have let the house go a bit."

"Where is Mr. Danvers?"

"He had to dash off to some meeting, said he'd be back very soon."

"Right."

"He also left instructions—if you wanted to take anything, now's the time. Only the valuable stuff is listed by name in the will for sale. Maybe there's something sentimental you want to take?"

I nodded my head.

"Lovely house, this is. Three floors—stunning. But I guess you know that already?"

I looked up toward the grand staircase.

"She had a lot of nice stuff."

I wanted to tell this woman, this stranger, that this house had belonged to my mother and father and not *her*. But that information, and so much more, remained entwined in a ball I had no intention of unraveling.

"Where do you want to start?" she said.

I breathed in. "The attic."

"Really?"

I closed my eyes briefly. "Yes, the attic," I repeated, my eyes locked on the staircase. She'd never know just how much energy it had taken to utter those words.

I turned my gaze away, settling on a box by the door in front of the downstairs cloakroom.

"What's in there?" I said, walking over to it; to stall for time, I think, having suddenly lost my nerve.

I bent down and peered into the box, and immediately I knew that inside was my father's old black Brother Deluxe typewriter, now covered in a film of dust. I wasn't tempted to take it out of the box, because the memories were already emerging.

Six-year-old me, just a little while after my mother had died, sitting on his knee as he tapped away. Me pinching his nose as he called me his "messy pup."

"Stop that, Lowra!" he'd say with a smile.

"Stop it, Daddy!" I'd say with a loud giggle.

"STOP IT! JUST STOP IT!" she would yell, in the loudest voice I had ever heard in my life. It was four years later, when I was ten. Dad would be at work and she and I would be at the desk doing lessons, and suddenly her mouth would lean in so close to mine I could feel her breath. "You think it's OK to laugh about me, don't you? I heard you both, the other night."

"We weren't laughing at you."

"You're always plotting, whispering things about me."

"That's not true!"

The desk where just moments ago we'd been working out algebra was now a weapon, as she wrapped her hand around my hair and smacked my head against it.

That first time I couldn't believe what had happened. Or that it had happened at all. I placed my hand to my head as it slowly began to throb.

"Look what you did!" she said with a slight whine to her voice. She fingered the butterfly brooch on her left lapel, purple and sparkling. "Why do you do this, Lowra? Why do you insist on making me angry?"

I didn't speak during the remainder of that lesson, just in case she did something else like pinch me, which she sometimes did when I got a sum wrong.

At the end of the lesson, she stood up, her eyes searching the room. Her voice had changed. "We don't want your father worrying that we don't get on, do we?"

I shook my head slowly, which only made the pain in my head feel worse. I wasn't even sure what I was agreeing to, I just wanted her to leave me alone.

"Go and clean yourself up. You're going to bruise. Tell your dad you fell."

She left the room. I wouldn't see her for the rest of the day, or at least until Dad came home from work. Then she would be all over me, with compliments and kisses. Her hand on my shoulder, gushing about what a good little girl I was and how she loved her new, ready-made family.

What she said often confused me. One minute she was Miss Range, my home tutor who helped me with my math and poetry; the next, she and Daddy announced they were together and she'd suddenly changed toward me.

That night, the bruise freshly revealed itself on my forehead and I was all set to tell my dad everything.

But that was the night they announced their engagement.

I was now ready for the attic.

"Go ahead. We haven't touched up there yet, so I'm not sure what to expect," she said. "We've taken care of everything on the bequest list, so I suppose the rest belongs to you."

"Can you leave the attic alone for now? Do what you need to with the rest of the house, but the attic stays put," I said with some authority—an emotion that did not match what I felt inside.

"Oh, right then . . . saves us a job, but—"

"I will speak to Mr. Danvers." I didn't want to miss anymore stuff of my dad's—or my mother's.

"You OK?" she said.

I breathed heavily through my nose. "I'm not sure," I began, yet my feet followed another set of orders as they headed in the direction of the attic. "Will you be close by?" I said.

"Of course."

It was just an attic. A place she stored stuff she no longer wanted, discarded items with no place in the main house. A dark and damp place, which sometimes felt suffocating and airless.

It was just a room.

"Are you sure you'll be all right? You look like you might pass out!"

"I'm fine."

"Just stomp your feet if you need me."

"No, I would prefer it if you were waiting at the bottom of the second set of steps."

"Scared there'll be spiders up there?" she said with a smile.

I nodded my head, not about to confide in her my real reason for feeling this way.

"We do these types of jobs all the time and it's never easy. Here, take this." She handed me a tissue. "It's clean."

I placed my hand to my cheek. There was no wetness.

"For the dust, love. You never know."

"Oh . . . thanks. Will you be . . . ?"

"I'll be right here."

Each step felt like a succession of mini explosions of memories going off in my head. I reached the top of the second set of stairs and as soon as I opened the door, dust particles tickled my throat and I began to cough.

"You OK there?" she called out.

"Just don't leave!"

"I'm right here."

"You promise?" I said, sounding like a child. I hated how weak I sounded, yet I needed her reassurance in that moment.

"I promise," she said.

The darkness was blinding. The light switch on the left outside the door, just where it had always been, would help shine a light not only on the vast attic space, but on a past I had buried deep inside me. My instinct was to turn back and run as fast as I could, until I got to the station and back to London, to my small and humdrum but adequate life, never to return here.

Instead, I stood in the doorway unable to move, unable to turn on the light, feeling powerless once again as a myriad of emotions threatened to knock down the walls I had worked so carefully to build around me.

I knew that once I opened the door to this attic, I would never be able to close it again.

Chapter Seven

Celestine
1906

I had now spent either a handful of days or even a week in a strange country, mostly in a deep and dreamless slumber. I at times woke up with a start, my forehead dripping with beads of sweat, feeling unwell but not like it had been on the ship. Or perhaps I wasn't unwell at all, just afraid to step out of the safety of a bed so vast in size and comfort, I was simply content to float on a stack of soft pillows, as my toes and elbows molded happily into the warmth of the cotton sheets.

I could recall Mr. Richard entering the room from time to time clutching something warm in a cup, tea or sometimes soup. He would at times speak and I'd mumble a response, just to let him know I understood. I always understood, of course, but sometimes it felt easier to pretend I couldn't hear him. The cocoon of this bed felt like a sanctuary, far away from what lay beyond the bedroom door and the rest of this house I was expected to venture out and into at some point. The warmth and comfort, so reminiscent of my mama's embrace.

"Are you sure you don't want to have a quick walk up and down the stairs?" he'd say with encouragement. Or, "Dear boy, you can't stay in bed forever! Ranklin awaits!" with a loud guffaw.

Sometimes there were two voices.

"Is he sick, doctor?"

"No, the poor boy is simply exhausted. Who knows what he could have brought with him from that wretched country, though. Isn't sleeping sickness rife over there?"

I kept my eyes closed, extracting the voice of familiarity from the two. The deep baritone sound of Mr. Richard was somewhat comforting—familiar in the unfamiliar.

I'd open my eyes from time to time, but mainly enjoyed the blackness that closing them would bring and then the flowing images that followed. Like sitting cross-legged under the tree with Kabili; standing at the cooking pot with my mama; my father's mouth slightly curved into what looked like a smile, one of pride as he looked toward me. Sometimes that image of my father would change, his strong lips shrinking into his face along with the deep, round holes on his neck growing until they devoured his entire being.

I squeezed my eyes shut until water rimmed the edges and the images ceased. I had not cried for him in so long, yet my tears were less of grief and more of the betrayal.

I was now in a European country, in a house owned by a white man, enjoying its comforts.

What would my father think of me now?

A name was called and my first response was to ignore it.

After all, it wasn't the name given to me by my parents, but one I'd first heard on the steamer and quickly put down to delirium. Now I had recovered and could ignore it no longer.

"Celestine, are you awake?" He peered from the side of the door with a large smile.

"Yes, Mr. Richard." I pulled the cover to my chin as he moved closer to the bed.

"Splendid. Then we are making progress."

I nodded my head slowly as he sat on the edge of the bed.

"Mr. Richard . . ." I began.

He placed his cold palm onto my forehead. "Your temperature does feel normal," he muttered.

"My name, sir. It is Dikembe." I felt my own heartbeat stop, hoping I had not offended him.

"Dear boy, of all the things you are on the verge of experiencing now you have arrived on these shores, of all the resources I have put in place, the English you are now starting to grasp more easily, is it not only fair I have one wish granted of my own?"

A wave of confusion confronted me. Was it during my delirium that I had asked for any of these things? Perhaps so.

"My request is that you be called Celestine."

I ran through the names of each of my brothers and how my own name fitted in at the very end of that line of children. Dikembe. *A good and special child.*

Confusion mixed with sadness threatened me from within. My father calling me by my given name and Mama telling me to "do everything Mr. Richard asks of you, my son."

"Yes, Mr. Richard," I said, failing to add that this would be a temporary measure, considering I'd soon be back home. Indeed, for now, I would simply be obeying my mother and not this white man.

This was what I told myself.

Another day passed, and when I was sure no one was in the room, I climbed out of the bed, my haven, my cocoon, and stood at the curved window, not yet ready to view beyond it. A lot of the furniture inside that room was made of wood, and this reminded me of my father. I ran a finger over the dark mahogany wardrobe standing beside the bed, which I now realized could be one and a half times my height in width. Crouching down to inspect what it was I had been sleeping on for these past days, I discovered a metal frame and headboard. A potential weapon if I was able to disconnect it.

But why would I need a weapon?

My arms quickly developed a rash of goose bumps and I could feel the pulsating of my heartbeat under my clothes. Where was I? I wanted my mama, I wanted Kabili. I wanted to be back in my village again with Ina Balenga and my brothers. I wanted to be in my mama's arms as she hummed me a song I had never bothered to ask the name of. I wanted to be anywhere but here!

The door flung open. "Ah, Celestine!"

I exhaled softly, the space between my eyebrows softening.

My tongue touched the roof of my mouth as I silently spoke my name.

Dikembe.

My name is Dikembe.

"You look a lot better now. Ready for the world! As it should be. Soon we'll get you into some good clothes."

I hoped such garments would not be like his attire, which didn't seem to be much different from what he had worn on the ship: an army uniform consisting of beige trousers tucked into long riding boots, making him appear as if he were about to wrestle a rhinoceros.

"Mr. Richard," I began.

He moved closer, pulling a pipe from his pocket. "Dear boy, you have been resting for four days now, and that's wonderful because your body has needed it after such a tumultuous journey to England. But here you are, dear boy, here you are!" He placed the pipe firmly between his lips, and I truly hoped this would tone down his words and allow them to sound less alarming to my ears. When he pulled the pipe from his mouth, stretching his thick moustache into a smile, my hopes were dashed.

"It is splendid you are here with us, Celestine, and we are lucky to have you."

We? I wanted to ask. Instead: "When shall I start work?" Mama had said I'd be a huge help to him and, in turn, our family. I assumed my work would be similar to what my father and brothers did. Working the land, returning home covered in beads of sweat, ready for food and slumber yet satisfied with what they had achieved. Yet when I mentioned this to Mr. Richard, he simply began to laugh.

"Oh, dear boy, you're so full of jest! I can see having you around here is going to provide this household with much-needed joy!" He proffered his hand. The first time he'd done this, we were on the ship and I—weak with sickness—was only able to urinate with his assistance. Here and in this vast brightness of the house, though, I couldn't help my pangs of discomfort every time he had assisted me to the toilet, too weak to hide any hint of my genitals.

"Come on!" he encouraged. A fresh wave of embarrassment appeared as I took his hand.

"Do you need to use the—"

"No, Mr. Richard. I am now able to do so alone."

"Come on then, let me show you your new home." His skin was smooth to the touch, while my father's had felt like the edge of wood before it is smoothed over. "Hopefully you will like what you see!"

My room and adjoining bathroom had only given small clues as to what the rest of the house looked like, and the reality was more than I had ever seen in my entire eleven years of life. Wallpaper decorated with flowers; a huge feat, I feared, considering I had only ever seen plant life protruding from the ground. My bare feet sinking into the thick carpets and rugs on the ground (some reminding me of what was above Mr. Richard's lips—but I would never dare tell him so).

Mr. Richard's home had three floors and appeared to go on forever. So many rooms—a living room, a parlor and a dining room—in which to eat.

My speech was stunted as I took it all in. Every last decoration appeared carefully chosen; from the painting of a bright white house I was soon to realize was the one I stood in, to the porcelain figurine of a man on a horse gracing the top of the dining room cabinet—Meissen, Mr. Richard said—which housed hand-painted china and gold-plated crockery.

"Artifacts you may find more familiar are in the study—which we shall save for another day," he said.

A quick introduction to the staff followed: a young woman and an older lady who instantly warmed me with her smile. Mrs. Cuthbert was round and kindly looking, in a black dress decorated with a crisp white cotton apron and a matching mob cap on her head. She stood with an air of impatience which I believed had something to do with the aroma of food wafting in from the kitchen.

"Nice to meet you, Master Celestine."

This confused me. Surely, as a boy, I could not be her master?

"I'm sure we'll get acquainted soon enough," she said, her accent sounding looser than Mr. Richard's. The younger woman was called Enid. Her uniform appeared too big for her and as Mr. Richard kindly introduced me, her eyes remained fixed on him, as if I were not even in the room.

"You are probably not used to this," he said, as we moved away from Enid and Mrs. Cuthbert.

I shook my head, feeling somewhat overwhelmed by it all, moving from one room to the next, my eyes resting on items I had never come across in my entire life.

"You will have plenty of time to acquaint yourself with everything. We don't have many staff anymore as it all seemed such a waste. But from time to time we have people come in and help us out—especially if we are entertaining."

My mind rushed again to my impending workload. Any staff was better than none if I was to assist in cleaning this entire house.

"Time for lunch, I believe!" Each time he spoke, it sounded like an announcement.

"Yes, Mr. Richard."

"Celestine, now we are home, in our own domain as it were, could you refer to me as Sir Richard?"

My eyebrows knotted in confusion.

"It's just what everyone calls me here, and something I have earned due to the work I have done and intend to do more of."

"Of course, Sir . . . Richard."

"I will tell you more about that work another time. Contrary to what you may think, it isn't just about exploration and meeting new people. It is so much more."

"Yes, Sir Richard."

"For now, we eat!"

"What would you like for me to do?" Judging by the aromas radiating throughout the house, no food needed to be cooked. Although I was unsure of how I would get my hands on a batch of cassava leaves.

"Dear boy, nothing!" he said, his face awash with a smile. He beckoned me to follow him back into the dining room, transformed since the last visit. Now, the large wooden table had been unashamedly dressed in a cotton cloth; on top of it, a large roasted chicken trimmed and surrounded by a plethora of colorful vegetables.

"Mrs. Cuthbert usually prepares a light lunch for me, but as this is your first real day here, it should be special, don't you think?"

"Yes . . . Sir Richard."

The aroma of vegetables and meat jostled for attention, causing my mouth to water. All I wanted to do was dive into that chicken and pluck all of its flesh, while desperately packing as many of the colorful vegetables into my mouth as I could—even though I did not know what most of them happened to be. Instead, I silently stood by.

"Tuck in!" said Sir Richard, sitting at the head of the table as I tentatively sat on one of the chairs, which had a cushioned seat.

"Celestine, eat!"

I nodded my head with uncertainty. I was being served by a woman, a white one no less, and Sir Richard was addressing me as if I were his equal. This was not what Mama had told me to expect, her words now a confusing jumble of sentences.

"But what does he want with me?"

"To work, of course . . . What else would he want?"

"Is the food not to your liking, Master Celestine?" said Mrs. Cuthbert, her smile somewhat counterfeit.

I stared toward the chicken leg which had somehow landed on my plate. "It is very lovely," I said, waiting for Sir Richard to realize a mistake had been made. As the youngest in the family, I knew that such parts of the chicken were generally reserved for the elders. Yet Sir Richard appeared content enough spearing his own breast of chicken with his knife and chewing slowly. So, I followed suit.

Each morsel of food in my mouth tasted like a burst of the sun. I was comparing it to the food on the ships, of course, my mama's cooking being far superior to anything I would ever taste.

"I don't want you getting used to this, now, Celestine!" He laughed, as did Mrs. Cuthbert, who stood nearby. I felt a rush of concern for her strength, having to stand by as we ate. She was not a young woman, perhaps the same age as Ina Balenga.

"Mrs. Cuthbert is one of my oldest staff members."

"Enough of the 'old,' if you please, sir!" she said with a smile that appeared to be a little more genuine.

"Or should I say, longest serving? I would be lost without her."

"That you would, sir," she said.

I smiled, pretending to understand everything they said because their sentences sounded rushed. It was now clear just how much Sir Richard had been slowing down his words whenever he spoke English to me, which was now all of the time.

Once we had finished our meal, my immediate future began to take shape.

"Celestine, I want you to think of this house as your home." He brought a glass to his mouth and sipped. "You will have free rein of this house, and that means you are free to go anywhere you like. However, my study is out of bounds unless I am in it."

"Where will I be staying, sir?"

He looked up at Mrs. Cuthbert as if she had asked the question.

"In the room you have been in since we arrived, of course. What a question!"

"That big room, sir?"

"Why, yes. It's all for you."

I crinkled my forehead in confusion. "What will be my duties?"

"You are to be my companion," he said.

When Mrs. Cuthbert cleared her throat, it sounded deliberate. Perhaps she was keen to sit down.

"A companion?"

"Yes, dear boy. In your language that means—"

"Yes, I understand the meaning, Sir Richard . . ." What I did not understand was how I could be such a thing to Sir Richard. What of our ages? Surely neither of us had earned such a title?

"Don't look so confused. Many of my acquaintances have a companion from another land and, well, you being so much younger means I can regularly draw strength from the nectar of youth, doesn't it, Mrs. Cuthbert!"

"Yes, sir," she said, this time not even bothering to hide her concerned expression.

"Celestine, you will live and be taught in a way that is refined . . . dignified. You will have a life you could never have dreamed of, a splendid existence where all of your needs will be met."

I still found it difficult to understand what this meant, and not simply because of my weak grasp of the English language. So I stood and bent to clear away the crockery from the table.

"No, Celestine," said Sir Richard, urging me to sit back down. "We have Enid who will do that for you. Silly boy!"

I sat back down, the food inside my stomach swirling uncomfortably.

"Come inside," he said, opening the door to the study, his left arm announcing my entry rather grandly.

I couldn't help the fresh wave of fascination that flew over me as I entered Sir Richard's most private domain in the house for the first time. By the door was a cabinet displaying a number of objects not really in line with the decor of the rest of the big house. The first one to catch my eye was a bird sitting on a plinth.

"That, dear boy, is a fish eagle from the Shona people in southern Africa. Legend has it they stood on the walls of a city built in the twelfth century."

I only heard his words intermittently, as I found myself drifting in and out from the past to the present. In and out of England, across the waters to the continent that was Africa and back again to England. The uncertainty of where I actually stood in this moment felt unsettling.

"It is a privilege to have traveled to so many lands. To have experienced their people. My memories will one day fade, so it is important to have a reminder. A proof of one's travels, so to speak. I do this through writing, and also collecting."

I asked about each of the artifacts, with genuine interest. Although unable to recognize most of them, I felt a warmth inside my chest, as if somehow I belonged to them and they to me.

I moved on to a curved object shaped like a jug and decorated with triangular patterns in black, white and red. It stood out, held its own audience.

"It is very colorful," I said.

"It is called *imigongo*."

I ran the word over my lips.

"That, dear boy, is made from cow dung."

"Do you mean—?"

"Yes! It's mixed with ash, which kills the nasty part of it all, including the smell, I may add. It is then left to harden. Fascinating to watch the women who do this."

"You have seen women make these?"

"But of course, dear boy. I have spent many years traveling the great continent of Africa and seen many beautiful and wondrous things."

The geometric patterns were almost hypnotic, which added to the strangeness of being in the presence of such greatness: items, objects, carvings, art; painted and created by people like my father, my brothers, my mama.

People like me.

"If I could have brought more back with me, I would have."

I searched the remainder of the cabinet, this special object in a room of grays and beige. An oasis in a room that promised so much, but with the capacity to leave me with an emptiness I could not articulate. I had walked into this study to ask a simple question—of the exact date I would be going home—and had now amassed several.

"I assume you are looking for something from your part of the world."

"Yes, sir." I ran my fingers under the lapel of my shirt, feeling the outline of my father's necklace.

"Well, it is right here, dear boy." His arms flayed about again and I tried to follow their direction with my gaze.

"Where, sir?" I said with alarm, thinking he meant the necklace.

"Well, you, dear boy. You are my prized possession from the Congo! The most valuable, and one I will make sure is looked after and taken care of to the best of my abilities. That, I promise you."

Chapter Eight

Celestine
1906

I had been in England for three weeks, and the experience had not even come close to my expectations. Indeed, it had exceeded them.

Each day, Mrs. Cuthbert would enter my room and ask if there was anything in particular that I desired for lunch. My answer was always the same: anything. I would eat whatever she provided, because although it did not resemble anything I had grown up with, it was flavorsome enough. Mrs. Cuthbert also allowed me to watch her prepare and cook said food, although never permitting me to assist, and this brought me happiness. The way she hummed to herself while preparing the food brought on a feeling of warmth and comfort. As for Enid, I never saw much of her as she worked nights, according to Mrs. Cuthbert. She'd made this remark with a smirk that I did not understand. Nor did I understand why Sir Richard would need anyone to work when we were asleep.

Perhaps it was boredom that lured me into regularly shining the tops of Sir Richard's shoes where they had scuffed. I had done them first without being asked, and he'd reluctantly approved of my work so much he insisted only I could shine them from now on. I enjoyed this as there was a usefulness in it. More so than spending my days following Sir Richard around the big house, or sitting beside him while he wrote correspondences with a fountain pen he constantly dipped into a silver inkwell.

"I know it is not the done thing to use an inkwell these days, but the words feel much more important this way. As though they mean more. Words are powerful, dear boy." He now only spoke to me in English and would quickly translate if I failed to understand a word or phrase. I wanted to impress Sir Richard and make sure he never assumed he had made a mistake in choosing me to come to England, so I did what he asked, like studying the books he gave me, which felt much harder than when he'd begun teaching me English on the ship. I enjoyed the writing of English much more.

Whenever he insisted on an impromptu test (which always seemed to be after breakfast or dinner), I made sure to show I was as good a student as I was a companion.

I stood behind him and peered over his shoulder; a letter he'd been writing for a few days now was addressed overseas. To Africa. I knew this because he'd said so in between sips from his glass. I'd come to realize that when Sir Richard sipped from a glass, he was more forthcoming with subjects he would usually deem beyond my need to know.

"The work going on in that part of the world is vast, but we must not lose sight of those in need. I am trying to get that across as much as I can in this letter."

"Yes, Sir Richard, like my family," I added, grateful to find a way of discussing them. Being halfway into my allotted time in England, it was perhaps prudent to at least be dropping hints, as my plans to ambush him with a direct question never seemed to transpire.

Sir Richard took another sip before placing the glass to one side. "There is absolutely no need to reinvent the wheel, and as many have begun work in earnest, I will do all I can to assist. I have a fund-raiser planned for next week to help with the much-needed money for my next trip in the coming month."

I swallowed. "Will I be going with you?"

"Of course. You will be the guest of honor, dear boy."

At that very moment, my heart could have burst with pleasure. I was going home, possibly in three weeks as per my calculations. My life, while very comfortable here, still meant nothing next to the reality of being with my family again. I couldn't wait to feel my home soil under my feet once more, and more important, to feel my mama's arms around me; to sit with Kabili under the tree; to bask in the sun of the land that was all I had ever known.

I was going home!

"When shall I begin packing?"

"No need for that, dear boy. Just make sure you look smart. We shall go to my tailor and get you fitted for an excellent suit!"

I felt a lift in every part of me. A joy louder than could be heard. "I am excited, sir!"

"So am I! It is my firm belief that people are much more capable of parting with money once there is something to look at."

My eyes made a circular motion as I tried to think of what he meant.

"Money, dear boy, is something I hate having to ask for, but I will do so as a means to a greater good!"

I nodded my head as the reality of seeing my mama again began to sink into every part of me. Oh, how I had missed her!

"Once they see that real human beings are in need, well, the parting will be done with less sorrow! Now, you look perplexed. What is it?"

"What has money to do with me going with you onto the big ship?"

"The big ship?"

"I am to go with you onto the ship, Sir Richard."

"What gave you that idea?"

"You said . . ."

"Oh, dear boy!" He placed his large hand to his mouth and began the first of his overly loud and very irritating guffaws. This time, instead of joining in with the false joviality as usual, I remained stoic. The joy switched off, momentarily.

"I can see you have questions," he said.

"Am I accompanying you? Home to Africa?" I said.

He beckoned for me to sit on a cushioned chair. I did as I was told, staring at the floor, fearful yet still hopeful of what he would say next. My eyes caught the glint of my shiny black shoes and the bottom of my carefully pressed trousers, and when I looked up, Sir Richard was staring toward me.

"Oh, dear boy, has there been a misunderstanding?"

I did not answer, as to do so could pierce any hope I had. But in the silence that followed, he simply smiled and brought the glass of whisky to his lips once more.

As several days passed, I chose not to bring up the subject of going home because of the potential disappointment and words I had no interest in hearing. I concentrated on the upcoming fund-raiser instead, matching Sir Richard's excitement as he discussed the menu with Mrs. Cuthbert and decorations for the table. Apparently, along with Enid, more staff would be brought in to assist on the night.

I was warned by Sir Richard that our trip to London was going to be a long one. Yet I doubted it could be anymore exhausting than the last big trip I had made.

I carefully stepped out of the motor vehicle, which I was finally able to appreciate. The color was red like fire and inside were green leather seats. I admired the steering wheel from the back of the vehicle as the driver—or as Sir Richard referred to him, the chauffeur—Gordon drove us slowly along the street, specks of rain falling against the glass. Minutes later we were at the station, in front of a contraption which resembled a bloated snake with a head that blew out bellows of angry smoke. I had been taught to stay away from reptiles and this was the most exaggerated and angriest I had ever seen.

"Oh, dear boy, I thought we had discussed this—it is simply a train to take us into London the quickest way. The experience is a sheer joy to behold!"

I nodded my head rapidly, slowly becoming used to wanting one thing yet readily agreeing to the opposite.

"We have first-class seats—you will enjoy it, that I promise." He turned to me, crouching down to my height. "Do you not trust me, Celestine?"

I wanted to shake my head. "Yes, sir, I do." An avalanche of guilt followed. Had this man not fed and clothed me for weeks? Had he not taken hours of his time to sit with me and teach me how to write English as well as correctly pronounce phrases I had found difficult, and without ridicule? Had he not given me everything I could desire?

"I would never allow harm to cross your path. You must know that," he said.

I nodded my head in agreement, and as I stepped into the reptile-like container, I was tempted to squeeze my eyes shut until the journey was over. My body remained rigid instead, and not until I had been in my seat for ten or so minutes did I experience any semblance of calm, upon the realization that this was simply a lesser version of the ship I had once lived on. Only this time, surely I was safer being on dry land, which meant in theory I could leave at any given time?

In theory.

Looking out of the large train windows, I made sure to curb any heightened emotion as I was reminded of the last time I'd encountered a large vessel. I had never heard of this London before, yet now whenever Sir Richard spoke of it, his animation, his excitement became infectious.

As the train moved further away from the station, past the

green fields and, according to Sir Richard's commentary, closer to London, my anticipation grew.

When we left the train, another motor vehicle was waiting to drive us into the frenzy of London Town and its busy roads and endless people. To my left and to my right: activity, chatter and laughter; the relative tranquillity of the place called Ranklin and the big house firmly left behind. I was used to handfuls of people passing by as we rode in the motor vehicle, many acknowledging Sir Richard with a wave or a nod. Yet here in London, he was just . . . anonymous.

The buildings appeared tall and smart, with everyone around us looking rushed. My head turned toward the seemingly endless rows of shops, motor vehicles, carriages and large trams powered by rows of horses, as well as the waste that went with them, swarms of flies congregating around fresh excrement. Sir Richard had sold London to me as something great and spectacular, yet I couldn't see anything I would deem special so far. Even my perception of Sir Richard momentarily changed, as he now appeared to be just one of many white people gathered in a large area, even that booming voice inaudible among the throng of people.

The Sapphire Hotel, on the other hand, appeared imposing and nothing short of palatial. Inside it was lofty and spacious, with vast pillars in red and gold and a large front desk paneled with walnut wood, bordered with velvet embellishments. Music wafted in from another room. The ballroom, apparently; the word was displayed prominently in gold lettering on the huge double doorway. Sir Richard said I could go up to my room with the bellboy while he waited in the bar for a friend who was staying at the nearby Cecil Hotel.

The bellboy must have been twice my age and it felt ill-fitting to refer to him as a "boy." I thanked him profusely after he left the suitcase Sir Richard had gifted me on the bed. The room was grander than my room at the big house, the cotton towels softer than Mrs. Cuthbert's terry cloth versions; the bath in the adjoining room deeper and with taller legs than the one I submerged myself in every chance I got.

I laid my head on the pillow and fell into a deep sleep, only to awaken when I heard the sound of the door from the adjoining room where Sir Richard was staying. I could hear echoes of his booming voice alongside another . . . that of a woman, I think.

The following morning, we sat at a table adorned with the crispest of tablecloths, a large transparent ceiling above us and a piano playing as a backdrop. Breakfast included hot muffins, omelettes, fruit and veal chops.

"Are you enjoying the trip thus far?" asked Sir Richard.

"It is very good, Sir Richard," I said. "One day I would like to have one of those." I pointed to the glass ceiling. "You can see the sky through it." I did not want to add that I hoped it was the same sky my family could see. That looking up to it could in some way mean we were close.

"I'm sure you too will own an atrium one day," he said.

We headed to Sir Richard's favorite tailor, Henry Poole & Co., where I sat comfortably on a chair by the window, looking out onto Savile Row and the dignified gentlemen in their three-piece suits with slim trousers and smart hats. There were fewer people than outside the hotel and this gave me a better sense of calm.

Hats and shirts and freshly pressed trousers lined every corner of the shop, all of which did not excite or concern me in the slightest. I was simply counting down the hours to when we would return to the big house. London with its crowds and ornate buildings had left me feeling slightly overwhelmed.

"Celestine, come and say hello."

I stood to attention as a gray-haired man ran his gaze from the tip of my head to the soles of my shoes and back up again. "Yes, we can measure him up for a suit. For a fund-raiser, you say?"

"That's right. Although I suspect Celestine will be attending a number of special evenings at the house. Especially as he is about to become a man of society."

The man looked on with narrowed eyes. "I can already see him in one of our finest lounge suits . . ."

I wasn't sure why any of this was necessary. I already dressed in bespoke clothing provided by a tailor in Ranklin, so this felt rather excessive. But who was I to question Sir Richard?

"Let's see what you have, then."

The promise of suits I was to wear to other functions was not proof that I would be staying here past the allotted time. It simply suggested that as a companion, I had to look a certain way when presented in society—even if I did only have a limited amount of time left in England.

We departed the shop that day with the promise of an outfit that would include a white silk shirt with a wide-spread collar and a waistcoat made from gold swirl material. It was certainly the most exquisite thing I could ever have imagined wearing.

Later that day, we visited a place called Madame Tussaud's waxworks, where I almost passed out with the thought of these life-sized beings coming to life. But after Sir Richard's quick and still implausible explanation, I was only partly assured I was not in danger!

"Perhaps one day you will be immortalized here," he said.

"Yes, Sir Richard." I was used to answering him this way now. *Yes, Sir Richard.* The standard answer to anything I didn't have a response for, or to hide disappointment.

Also, a response that hid a plethora of emotions.

Chapter Nine

Lowra
1974

He was missing. Dad was missing.

Not dead, but missing. Which meant he could still be alive somewhere in a foreign country, trying to make his way back to me.

The last time I'd seen him, he looked so happy, and it was in that moment I made up my mind never to tell him about what she was doing to me.

Also, as she put it, who was he going to believe?

Instead, I dressed up as a flower girl in a pink and white dress with daisies in my hair; danced at the reception; squeezed my arms around Dad's waist and kissed him goodbye as he told me to be good for my grandma.

Then they left for their honeymoon and I never saw him again.

I waited and waited for him to stride through that large door, past the lions and with a neatly wrapped present under his arm.

But he never did.

My grandma never said a word; actually, no one did in that house. All they did was cry.

Only when I took a look at the newspaper she threw at me one day did I stop with the questions: HORROR CRUISE: SUCCESSFUL LOCAL BUSINESSMAN PRESUMED DEAD.

The Attic Child

1993

A few false starts here and there, but there I was, standing inside that attic. The woman downstairs had promised me she wouldn't leave.

"You're still there, right?"

"Still here," she said.

At that moment, she was everything, even though I couldn't remember if she'd even told me her name and I would probably never see her again. Nevertheless, at that moment she was the difference between falling and standing, crying and holding myself together.

I stepped one plimsoled foot over the threshold. Then the other.

I can do this.

Another step forward and another one.

"It's just an attic," the woman had said. Yet it was more than that to me. It was more than just a room, a space, and was powerful enough to make me turn back, run down those stairs and get away from Ranklin as fast as humanly possible. But I had to at least stay long enough to see if *they* still existed; if they had survived the last fifteen years as I had. Or if they'd withered away, taken to a place they could never be found. A place I had also been to once.

Another step.

The air was different; musky, old. Suffocating? No, not that.

Breathe.

Since I had been here last, there were new additions. Boxes piled high, probably with things like Christmas decorations and old paraphernalia presumably belonging to *her*. The watercolor of a pink and purple butterfly, balanced against a box, sent a slight current down my arms. Luckily, I saw my dad's old brown leather briefcase tucked in a corner and immediately picked it up, the dust coating my fingers. It was a surprise to see it, even more so when

I realized it contained a wad of papers including my parents' marriage certificate and my mother's passport. My heart instantly warmed, yet my stomach churned. These papers represented bits of a life that promised so much and yet had delivered nothing.

I placed the briefcase outside the door. This wasn't the place to go through my parents' things. The space felt soiled, wrong. I would do it later and far away from this house.

Ignoring the dust this time, I fell to my knees and pulled another box away from the wall, and immediately began to trace my fingers along the curve and shapes of what was carved into the wall. I pulled my fingers away quickly. It was still there. Of course it was. I hadn't imagined it all those years ago. *The message on the wall.* And just like then, the floorboard below it was loose, and I exhaled, thinking I knew what was to come, removing the board quite easily and then another one, not caring whether a mouse ran out at me because I needed to do this.

I reached into the hollow rectangular space.

"You OK up there?" the woman called.

My hand shot back up. "Yes, thanks!" I replied with irritation. What was I doing here, on my knees in a dusty attic? I needed to get up and cross the threshold back to another world and another time, because inside this attic was the complete opposite to that. I had to leave before the memories flooded back because I couldn't afford for that to happen. Not after all this time. I had to find what I was looking for fast, or leave.

I placed my hand back inside the space . . . and there it was.

Just as it always had been.

I exhaled.

"Would you like a cup of tea, love?" this stranger said as I reached the bottom of the stairs.

"I think I'm just going to go."

"What about Mr. Danvers, aren't you going to wait for him?"

"I'll call him. I have his number."

"Is that it?" She stared toward the collection in my grasp. A very old canvas bag filled with items I had not looked at for many years, and my dad's briefcase.

"Would you like a proper bag for the rest of the stuff? That one looks like it's on its last legs. Unless you want to put it all in the briefcase," she said.

"I don't want to mix the stuff up," I said. I don't suppose this made any sense to her.

I hadn't wanted to follow her into the kitchen, but I did, again not allowing myself to absorb anything that came into view.

"You look like you need a glass of water or something."

"No. No, that's all right." My words came in spurts as my breath began to take over. I needed to leave . . . now.

"What happens next?" I said, almost through the front door of the house.

"We will continue cataloguing and clearing out the listed items for sale, and the rest—well, that's up to you."

"Remember not to touch the attic," I said. I hadn't planned to, but it now felt more urgent than ever, though I wasn't sure why.

"I don't think there's much up there of financial value, love, so don't worry, we'll just leave it alone, as you wish."

I shut the huge door to that house and stood between those two silent creatures, the briefcase and bag both safely tucked under my arm. I'd taken them from one world—that of the attic—straight into mine, and I had no idea what this would mean for me. The items were so very precious, embedded with stories of the past . . . and its secrets.

Chapter Ten

Celestine
1906

The boy in front of the free-standing oak mirror wasn't me.

This figure breathed when I breathed, moved when I moved, yet I still couldn't place him. This had nothing to do with the suit from Henry Poole & Co. which had arrived the day before, or the gold waistcoat wrapped around my middle. It had more to do with the English words Sir Richard had gone over with me in preparation for the evening, because for the first time, I spoke with confidence and a pronunciation not far off his own: proof I was slowly becoming what Sir Richard had described as an *English gentleman*.

Sir Richard would say this was excellent progress, that in almost five weeks I had already started to read key phrases. Yet to me it felt like an erasure of Dikembe and everything that had accompanied him so far.

It also felt like the fiercest of betrayals of my father.

"Celestine! Come down and look at what they've done with the rooms!" called Sir Richard.

I blinked rapidly, and yet there I still stood, in all that finery with freshly cut hair. The image had not disappeared, or been replaced by the boy who had stepped onto that steamer dressed in a robe and barefoot. Here stood this counterfeit English gentleman.

"Celestine?"

"Yes, Sir Richard. I am coming."

Downstairs, the big house also demanded a new gaze. It had acquired extra uniformed staff for the evening, including a man dressed in a jacket that fell way past his buttocks at the back and shortened at the front—a butler, I was told. He announced each of the six guests as they arrived and accompanied them to the drawing room. I wasn't sure of what to say as I stood on the staircase watching it all unfold. This newness. This new life I occupied.

I made it off the staircase with much coaxing from Sir Richard, and in earnest began to form the words I had been taught.

"How do you do?" I said.

Of those who replied, I could only smile in response, forgetting the greetings I had been taught and the formalities to go with them. The men wore suits not unlike the ones displayed in Henry Poole & Co., the women in long-flowing gowns which dragged graciously on the floor behind them. Some of them looked on with curiosity and others with warmth—I thought. I found it difficult to decipher the expressions of the British, as they always appeared to have their noses elevated and their upper bodies rigid.

The aroma of freshly cooked food caused a rumble in my belly as I accompanied the last of the guests into the dining room, just after the butler announced that dinner was served. Each of the guests sat in front of a name card at the elaborately decorated table set with flower-filled vases, tall candlesticks and shining centerpieces. British names rolled comfortably off my tongue: Daphne, Roger, Muriel, Archibald, Rupert and Gertrude. I had been told that the big house had been host to many such gatherings in the past, its current predicament a mere fraction of what it once was.

My name card was thankfully beside Sir Richard's, who sat at the head of the table. CELESTINE, it read. Dinner was to be served *à la russe*—Sir Richard had earlier explained that this had been introduced by a Russian ambassador into British society. This, as well as a lot of what he explained, only served to confuse me. Especially as Sir Richard regularly pressed on me the importance of England being everything that was right about a country, and yet at the same time lent itself to so many outside influences. Indeed, wasn't Sir Richard by definition an explorer? If England was so great, then surely there would not be a need to explore . . .

I looked on guiltily as the staff presented us all with a succession of courses, beginning with Mrs. Cuthbert's delicious pearl barley soup. The silver cutlery and crockery, brought out for this special occasion, looked impressive in such a setting. The mustard pot, a shining silver circle, resembled a crown just like one I had seen in a painting in the corridor of the Sapphire Hotel.

The guests chatted among one another, three women and three men. Their mouths moved to the sway of their laughter, their plummy voices commenting on the delectable food Mrs. Cuthbert and her assistants had so expertly prepared.

While my English was now sufficient for me to follow conversations, I was still shy in company and this allowed me to at times forget any command of English I may have learned. In desperation I turned to a smiling Sir Richard, my translator, my ally, for assistance. But his shoulders had already turned away from me and toward his guests seated on the other side.

I moved the spoon slowly to my lips again, my eyes scanning the room which had taken on a boisterous life of its own, yet with no place for me. I indeed felt more like an impostor.

It was Mr. Roger who addressed me first. The moment he'd walked through the door behind his wife, I had sensed a kindness in him which set him apart from everyone else in this room. He was Sir Richard's oldest friend and his lawyer. That much I remembered.

I smiled warmly as he clumsily spoke a few words of my

language, asking how I was finding England, and I appreciated this greatly even if we then had to return to speaking English.

The other guests were not so graceful. Sets of eyes began to rest upon me as I placed the spoon to my mouth again, this time a hushed silence making each slurp sound exaggerated in my ears. I looked up at the chandelier. Anything to block out the stares. Or perhaps no one was actually staring and this was all part of my imagination.

"Is everyone enjoying Mrs. Cuthbert's soup?" said Sir Richard in his booming voice, which I was actually grateful to hear at that moment. "Please rest assured that with the next course, she has a jolly treat for you all. Mrs. Cuthbert is an expert in culinary delights, as you can already gather!"

I was grateful for Mrs. Cuthbert's brief appearance, even if it was only to chastise one of her temporary staff members. I longed to be inside the kitchen with her, watching her peel, prepare and bake. Anywhere but here.

By the third course, I had lost my appetite and still hadn't said much. Although Sir Richard had been boasting just how fluent I now was in English, his expectation did not match my confidence.

"Daphne here is asking how you're enjoying your time in England," said Sir Richard. I had heard her the first time, but became mute at the sight of those long and sparkling shapes which dripped from her ears like the chandelier above us. Her lips were painted red in a way that afforded the illusion of a fuller mouth. A fruitless endeavor, I thought.

"My stay here is very good," I replied.

I did not understand her laughter, sure I'd used the correct order of words.

"Isn't he just delightful," she said with a contradicting frown.

A barrage of questions then came at me from the others.

"England must be much better than your homeland?"

"Is this your first time using a knife and fork?"

"What does it feel like to wear clothes?"

Sir Richard shook his head at times and yet laughed at others, while my body could only stiffen at the possibility I was becoming the subject of ridicule.

Mrs. Cuthbert's lemon tart silenced the room again, and I felt a rush of relief with almost everyone now only concerned with the deliciousness on their plates. All except Daphne, who seemed to be looking at me with a curiosity that made me want to loosen my collar.

"Remarkable," she kept on saying, with her eyes narrowed.

Sir Richard beamed with happiness at "a successful evening so far," and I took the opportunity to quietly lean in and ask, in English, why he'd needed this fund-raiser in the first place, considering he was already such a wealthy man. At times I would surprise Sir Richard with my high level of English. Thanks to the phrases regularly spoken in Mrs. Cuthbert's kitchen, it was clearly better than he thought and with added colloquialisms thrown in. I wasn't even sure why it felt important to mislead him like this. A way of holding on to something, I suppose. To have this secret for myself; to have *something left* for myself.

His voice was not the whisper I had hoped for. "It isn't simply about providing material means, but also about educating people here on what is truly going on in other countries." He smiled toward his guests, signaling he was no longer talking only to me.

"There is just so much more to do . . . and, well, this will require funds," he said, shaking his head and soaking in the audience's attention.

"Of course! These countries are in dire need and it is good people like yourself who answer the call!" said Archibald, the man seated next to Mr. Roger's wife.

"Hear, hear!" said Sir Richard, raising his glass.

I remembered my father saying it was the white man who had

plundered the area around our village. My father had never included me in much discussion, but I had heard snippets here and there, and of course Kabili and I had dissected what we could as we sat under our tree. Of what I knew, those people had been from Belgium, so it was right to assume Sir Richard had a good heart because he was a British man and clearly just wanted to help.

Daphne placed her hand to her chest, a crumb from Mrs. Cuthbert's tart lingering on her bottom lip. "How awful it must have been."

"Celestine is one of the lucky ones. Being an explorer is more than discovering other lands, their people and their animals. It is not enough to just walk away then and not do anything to help," said Sir Richard.

I spoke in very careful English. "What if they are not in need of help? What if people go there to help themselves?"

The room was silent except for an exaggerated sigh from Daphne. Even at the age of eleven, I still felt the clangs of my father's impassioned words and beliefs, and repeating them felt exhilarating—as if I were honoring him in some way, even if I didn't understand the full meaning behind what I was saying.

"Ask these questions later, Celestine. We have guests."

As the evening wore on and glasses were refilled, the previously labored words and "properly" spoken sentences, at least from the men, began to fall over each other, and my brain was unable to decipher the meanings and sounds or link them with what I had learned.

When the men retired to a different room, they appeared even more animated over their glasses of port. Each word, sentence and point of view moved back and forth like a ball.

"You can't fight facts or science."

"The African is a harmless, docile race."

"I'm not sure about that, Archibald, I've been exploring the region for years . . ."

"Just keep yourself to yourself, I say. What if liberal explorers like yourself start to breed with them, what happens then? An impure race, that's what. Then what do we do?"

"For the record, Rupert, I have never lain with an African before and do not intend to. I do not go there for that, and find it somewhat insulting that you would think such a thing of me."

"Sorry, old chap. Fill us in then, why do you go? It's hardly a paradise, is it?"

"It's actually one of the most beautiful continents I have ever visited."

"All those . . . *natives* . . . Sounds rather frightful to me!"

"My aim in that wonderful country is simply to help them."

When Sir Richard insisted we rejoin the ladies, the conversation expanded.

"As you know, last year I had the pleasure of traveling to America," said Rupert.

"I can't take to the Americans," said Daphne.

"Are they not simply our cousins, and with the ability to make things bigger? Take the St Louis World's Fair, for instance," continued Rupert.

"Did you go?" asked Sir Richard, suddenly interested.

"Indeed, and it was a most remarkable spectacle, especially the selection of pygmies on display. I'm still surprised you didn't attend, Richard old boy!"

"It's not something I had planned to."

"Anyway, one of the pygmies was called Ota Benga. He and his . . . *natives* . . . gave a real insight into their behavior. Very interesting indeed. There are rumors of an exhibit next year at the Bronx Zoo where all the pygmies get to be lined up with the animals."

"I'm not sure I like the sound of that," said Sir Richard.

"I would certainly attend. I just wonder if anyone will be able to tell the difference!" said Daphne.

"I'm not sure that would be a suitable endeavor, Daphne—and this of course will not be Celestine's fate."

I dreaded being invited into the conversation again.

"Celestine here is from a rich and beautiful land with rivers and beasts and breath-taking greenery. A young boy from a hardworking family too, isn't that right, Celestine?"

"Yes, sir."

"What does his father do?" asked Daphne.

I opened my mouth to speak.

"A carpenter," said Sir Richard.

"So not even an African chief or a king? I would hold him in much more regard if he were more than just the child of a common workingman!"

"Oh, Daphne!"

"I'm just saying, he is no better than a costermonger in the East End of London, is he?"

"Just somewhat darker in hue!" said Rupert.

"Celestine is a dear boy who keeps me company and will one day hopefully accompany me on an expedition, if he so wishes. He will want for nothing, even when I am no more of this world."

"You need to find another wife. A woman would make a far more suitable companion, old chap!" said Archibald.

"I've been saying much the same. Can't be good for one's health, all this trekking," added Daphne.

"Forget what Daphne here says. It's a bloody good thing you're doing and because it's you, Richard, I am willing to donate some of my ancestors' hard-earned money to your cause!"

"Thank you, Archie old boy. Indeed, to open civilization up to the only part of our globe which has not been penetrated, to pierce the darkness which hangs over entire peoples, is a crusade that is worthy . . ."

"Good speech! Where did you hear that?" said Rupert.

"Just something I listened to many years ago and from someone

I once admired. It's stayed with me ever since and influenced my first ever expedition. The speech that has led me to the here and now, and to the presence of our dear boy, Celestine!"

I shuddered at the thought of a mere speech being responsible for me being taken away from my mama. It made no sense. Indeed, being in the presence of a room full of white people, being served by white people and speaking a language that up until just two months ago I had never heard before, made even less sense.

And yet it was I, Dikembe, who had stood before the mirror that morning and not recognized myself; it was I, Dikembe, who was sitting in the grand room full of people, all eyes on me, yet feeling as if I were actually invisible.

Chapter Eleven

Lowra
1993

I couldn't sleep that night and sat up in bed, my eyes wide and bloodshot.

I padded into the living room, heading straight to the canvas bag. Kneeling on the floor, I stared at the weird-looking necklace made from what resembled some type of wood or bone, three pieces of weathered paper, a pen, and a large and rather ugly porcelain doll.

Except for a little dust here and there, they were still amazingly intact—identical to how they were fifteen years ago when I'd last seen them. Although even then, they had looked *old*.

I sat back against the sofa and pulled the doll onto my lap. The yellowing dress and scraggy hair did nothing for the pure creepiness of its face, those glassy and expressionless eyes staring back at me. I still wasn't that sure why I'd "rescued" these items from that house. Random items with no obvious connection to each other.

Yet, there was no way I could have left them behind either.

Once I'd stepped back over the threshold of that attic, they'd once again become part of my world.

I turned to the pieces of paper. One was light brown with age and only some of the writing was still legible.

Lola Jaye

1974

I had forgotten what the sun looked like, so I closed my eyes and went searching . . . Not for the sun, no, just someone to chat to, to tell me a joke. Another voice. Maybe that way I'd know I existed, that I was real. That this was real.

I no longer hoped for this to be over, though—I just wanted someone to stay with me until it was.

On my clearer-headed days, the blocked-out window felt a bit mocking and I'd sometimes imagine a superhuman strength allowing me to bust it open.

I hated looking at it. Yet just underneath it, on the wall, were shapes—letters, I think—and I told myself this was a message. A message for me, carved into the wall!

My knees were scuffed almost to the point of flesh, as I frantically ran my finger over the shapes or letters or gobbledygook, over and over again. Perhaps nothing was there after all, and like the imaginary people I sometimes made up to keep me company, this too did not exist. I often felt out of it, the room floating from side to side like a ship. Like the one my dad was on before . . .

A pen peeked out of the floorboard. Old-fashioned, like the ones my dad favored. Maybe it was his? I pulled at the floorboard, watching it shift with a further tug, but not too much because my strength wasn't what it used to be. I finally pulled out the pen, rubbing it free of dust across my sleeve, and noticed it was black with a gold tip. Snazzy.

I placed it to one side, immediately noticing something else poking out of the floorboard. More stuff! A treasure trove! Perhaps not that, but I did manage to pull out a weird-looking beaded thing and a really ugly doll. I'd never been one for dolls, but in that moment it was the best thing I'd ever seen in my entire life, and even more important than the piece of paper that fell to the floor.

Sometimes, I held her tightly to my chest as I closed my eyes and tried to go to sleep. Other times, I'd talk to her and pretend we were sitting inside a diner eating ice cream together—like the one I used to go to with Dad.

The doll didn't answer when I spoke to her, but at least she was company.

I took a look at the piece of paper, squinting my eyes in the faint light. The words looked odd and like nothing I'd ever seen before. I slowly ran my finger over each word.

Al??e
?????? away
Mayhe?
??????
Ka?ili
Ma??
D?kem?e
M?ana M?ya
N?ngula

Chapter Twelve

Celestine
1906

A month, or slightly longer, my mama had said. So if half of a month is two weeks, that would make six weeks at most.

So why had I been in England for seven weeks?

In my mind, the smallest of fires had already begun to form during the sixth week and by the seventh had turned into a raging inferno.

Fuelled by the flames, I headed toward Sir Richard's study with such emotion I forgot to knock on the door.

"Come in, why don't you?" His voice sounded animated. The glass in his hand was empty.

"Sir, I would like to speak with you."

He placed the glass to one side. "I will forgive your intrusion because I am in the best of moods. I am headed to Africa!" he said, and anything I had been thinking of before that moment disappeared.

"To Africa?" I said, sitting on one of the cushioned chairs.

"Indeed, dear boy, I'm to be reunited with that excellent continent once more."

A shiver of excitement ran through my body. "When do we leave, sir? What date?"

"Oh, dear boy, you're not coming with me."

"Sir?" I said, believing I had misheard him.

"Africa is but a huge continent!"

"Of course, but—"

"I will be venturing into west Africa, and to the wonderful Kingdom of Benin. I have been before, some years ago when it was . . . let's just say, somewhat in transition. But it is a land so magical in its beauty that I am unable to stay away, despite the consequences. I will not be traveling to any part of the Congo."

"But you could leave me there and I will find my way home." I moved closer to him, just so he could see how serious I was.

"And how do you intend to do this?" His eyebrows rose.

"Well, sir, I can go on a big ship again."

"Oh, dear boy, these are ludicrous thoughts you are having. But I do understand what it is to miss home. I myself would be away at boarding school for months at a time . . ."

"Sir, I must come with you."

"Your mother and I had an agreement."

I threatened to fold at the mere mention of her, my sweet mama.

"This agreement being that you would receive a full education that would lead you to become an upstanding gentleman worthy of this country."

My heart rate had increased, as if I were running with speed. "Am I not your companion, sir? Would a companion not accompany you on such a trip?"

"Celestine, have I not afforded you a good life here?"

"You have, sir."

"Then I am fulfilling the wishes of your mother, and my agreement with her has not been completed as of yet. Therefore it would not be gentlemanly to send you back home."

I exhaled. No, this was not making any sense to me. All I could decipher was that Sir Richard was traveling to Africa and I should be going with him.

"How about this . . ." he said, as hope began to live inside me again. "When I arrive, I will immediately try to get word to your family. To your mother. Now, how does that sound to your ears?"

Tears rested in my eyes as she was mentioned once again. Words lodged in my throat.

How I longed to hear her voice speaking softly to herself that I was her good child, a special boy that would go on to do special things. I smiled at such a memory.

I nodded my head slowly as if my body's strength was gradually being drawn away.

"Then it is agreed! Hopefully, I will find a fellow traveler and they will get word to your mother, and she will say something to you in return, to reassure you of what I have already said—that you are here to receive an education and become a fine upstanding English gentleman."

The fire still remained, yet had dimmed as it mixed in with a helplessness that felt debilitating. I clenched my fists tightly, as if this could control the tears desperate to fall.

"Oh, dear boy. It is not my intention to see you sad." He moved his chair close to me as ours knees connected slightly.

I began to speak again, as if to erase the last few moments. "Please, sir, may I please come to Africa with you, please!"

He placed his hand on my knee and my instinct was to flinch. However, physically I felt trapped and forced to remain in that position.

His hand pressed harder onto my knee. "Oh, Celestine, why are you not understanding me?"

Only when he leaned to his side to retrieve the whisky bottle, releasing me from his grip, did I move my chair backward. I watched as he filled the glass almost to the rim, which also told me there was no further conversation to be had.

I ran to Mrs. Cuthbert.

"My words don't carry any weight here, unless it's about

cooking! This has to be between you and Sir Richard," she said, mixing the gooey contents of the bowl, which would soon become a cake. "What I don't understand is, why would you want to go back there?"

"It is my country, Mrs. Cuthbert. What a question."

"What I mean is . . ." She stopped the mixing, staring at me with an expression I could not decipher. "I just thought it would be the last place you'd want to go. Sir Richard said . . ." She resumed with the mixing, turning her gaze back to the bowl.

"What did he say?"

"He said your people were destitute and had no choice but to give you to him. You were found running around all alone, naked, he said."

A level of shock began to form inside me. "Why would he say that, when it is untrue?"

"I must have heard him wrong," she said.

The days leading up to the departure felt like a slow and painful countdown to what was inevitable. I never left Sir Richard's side, as if my mere presence would remind him that I needed to accompany him on his latest expedition. Every couple of days I would allude to the fact that my presence on his trip would only be beneficial to him, with comments such as, "What if you get lonely on that ship, sir?"

"Dear boy, I have been doing these trips by myself for longer than you have been alive."

Even after consuming a quarter of a bottle of whisky in one sitting, his resolve remained.

"Dear boy, how does this sound? I will send a message to your family letting them know you want to return home, and then who knows, perhaps after a year you may do just that. Yes, that's what I'll do!" he said, before collapsing into a fit of guffaws.

"A year?" I said, but he was no longer listening.

When the day of his departure came, all too quickly, any

stubborn resolve slithered away as I eyed the trunks piled up in the hallway, ready to be shipped, along with Sir Richard, out of this house and away from any chance of me accompanying him.

My voice sounded deliberately calm as I made one last attempt to make him see reason. He was scheduled to leave later that day and I could have my belongings packed up in that time. Indeed, I wouldn't need to take much, happy to leave in the clothes I had arrived in.

"Do not make this more uncomfortable than it needs to be," he said.

"Sir, I miss my family."

It was the first time I had verbalized this to him. My reluctance in the past was more to do with not appearing ungrateful and also not to anger him so much he'd throw me out onto the street, which was always a possibility, even though he had never made such a threat.

My feelings often confused me: full of gratitude, yet bubbling with frustration that this man was all that stood between me and my mama. That his decisions and the direction of his mind would determine whether I saw them sooner rather than later.

I suddenly felt bound in chains that were invisible. The desperation to be released was strong and all-consuming.

"Sir Richard, I will do anything. Please, just let me go back with you."

"How many times do I have to tell you, Celestine, I'm not going to the Congo?"

"I DON'T CARE!" I said this so loudly and with such rage it was as if the whole world was silenced.

My fingers clenched within my palms as I allowed my tears to fall.

"I just want to go home. That is all I want. P-please, sir, I just want to go back to my mama." My shoulders heaved with emotion, and in that moment I was not an English gentleman in waiting but an eleven-year-old boy who just wanted to wrap his arms around his mama and to sit with his brother under a tree.

"Oh, Celestine."

"I do appreciate everything you have done for me, Sir Richard. The food you have given me, the . . . the beautiful garments and the . . . the chance to be an English gentleman. But, sir, I would rather give it all up just to be back with my mama and my brothers in my village. I beg of you, please take me back with you!"

I didn't realize my eyes had been closed, and when I opened them, with wetness around the edges, he appeared to be staring at me with horror. His forehead was creased, his mouth open.

The silence between us seemed to go on forever. I had said so much and yet not said any of what I really wanted to communicate.

"This is a most undignified display, Celestine."

I wiped my eyes, using the back of my hands.

"We will speak no more on this matter. My decision is final and I will soon be on my way. During my absence, Mr. Lattery will tutor you and Mrs. Cuthbert will stay here with you and tend to your day-to-day needs."

"Mr. Lattery?"

"Yes, I have engaged the services of an excellent tutor to guide you further in your English language pronunciations, as well as having you proficient in the three Rs."

I gazed toward the floor, angry at my tearful display and even angrier at my lack of headway.

"As my father used to say, these tears and female theatrics are not helpful, not now, or in life, Celestine. I can only hope that when I return home, it will be more of a young man I see than the child before me."

He turned away, and I was left with not only disappointment but confusion, which increased that burning anger that refused to die.

I ran to my room. The one with a big, comfortable bed and a wardrobe full of smart clothes. I dived onto that bed and despite his words, surrendered to my tears and the sounds that came with them. I looked around that room in my blurry, tearful gaze, wishing I could burn the entire lot to the ground. Then go back home. To the place of my birth. The place I had been happiest, even in the midst of grief and being apart from my brothers most of the time. It was my home, the country in which my mama still resided, and I needed to be back there.

I needed her.

Though all I could see was darkness as my face remained buried in the pillow, my clenched fists punching the sides forcefully and with abandon, muffling the screams I needed to expel into the ether.

Perhaps if I screamed loud enough, my mama would hear me.

Chapter Thirteen

Lowra
1988

They called it a breakdown. I called it acceptance.

He was never coming back.

It had only taken me fourteen years to get to this stunning conclusion. Yet this quickly turned into some sort of release and maybe a relief at not having to fight anymore, to be free of the expectation and constant disappointments. To just feel my weight against the kitchen cabinet as I brought my head backward and forward, the numbness setting in. My voice with a life of its own until someone called the police, and my so-called boyfriend held me up by the arm, almost dislocating it, asking what was wrong. Even though I'd stopped answering his calls days ago, here he was, uttering my name over and over again and with so many questions.

I don't really remember much else about that night, only the huge oblong moving shape with lights screaming out of it outside the tower block—yet with no sound. That seemed so weird to me: an ambulance with no sound.

1993

Now, five years later and ignoring the sound of my telephone, I switched channels on the TV. Snooker was one of the few programmes I tolerated. The quiet concentration of players like Steve Davis I found relaxing, bringing me the level of calm I sometimes found hard to achieve, especially when the thoughts returned.

I picked up the phone after the third set of rings.

"Miss Cavendish, it's Mr. Danvers. We must discuss the house. *Your* house!"

I looked over at the doll, now sitting on my mantelpiece. "Just sell it, OK, and pay off any debts. Leave anything left over in my account." I wanted nothing to do with that money. I didn't care that it was rightfully mine, because everything to do with that house was poison. Everything except the items I had rescued from the floorboards in the attic. They were lights which had kept me going through my darkest moments there, and like me, they too had been trapped. "I thought we'd been through everything, Mr. Danvers."

"But there's so much history in that house."

My tummy constricted. "I'm sure there is, but I am not really interested in history."

"If it once belonged to your father and perhaps his family before him, does that not mean anything to you?"

I allowed my mind to wander again and then straight into blackness. "Or my dad just bought it after my parents got married. It doesn't matter who it belonged to, please just sell it."

"Well!"

The judgment in his voice didn't concern me. At all.

"In any case, Miss Cavendish, it might not be that easy to just sell it."

This house was fast becoming a headache. I had no interest in it and I resented the fact it had entered my life once again. I resented every piece of 109 Ranklin Road.

"A very well-known person once resided there and English Heritage may be interested in marking it as a listed building."

"I don't see how. I mean, it's my family home . . . and, well, my dad wasn't famous . . . as far as I know." I was only six when my mother died, but my scant memories of her did always involve trips on planes, swimming pools, and what some would regard as a "fancy life." Other memories of my mother involved her looking like a princess dressed in floaty dresses as she glided from one room to another, possibly in ballerina shoes. But it wasn't as if I should rely on the memory of a six-year-old.

"You see, from the Victorian era through to Edwardian times, that house was very famous in Ranklin and beyond. I thought you would have known that, having lived there."

"I didn't. I was a child."

He cleared his throat. "It will take some time to draw up the paperwork and get the house sold, especially with its historical significance, but I will be in touch."

"Thank you, Mr. Danvers," I said quickly, because I wanted and needed this call to be over.

"Miss Cavendish, I don't think you have any idea of the huge local and national significance of that building, and that is unfortunate. Did you know—"

I hung up. Mr. Danvers and his opinions were irrelevant to me. I may not have known the "national significance' of that house, but I knew all too well the secret side of it no one else knew. No one except me and Nina.

And she was no longer with us.

I placed my hand to my chest. My heart rate was rapid again. I closed my eyes then inhaled and exhaled in sets of four. Dr. Raj had taught me this, a technique I hadn't needed for a long time . . . until now.

At work, it was difficult to concentrate on much. Marnie, of course, didn't notice, too busy talking about something I couldn't really bring myself to care about. I asked an Asian lady, who worked in the office upstairs, if she recognized some or all of the words in my notebook that I'd copied from the piece of paper.

"So because I'm Sri Lankan, you think I will automatically know what this means?"

"Sorry, I didn't mean to offend you."

I walked away in disgust—at myself. In my haste to find out what was written on a piece of paper, I'd forgotten any common sense or manners. Why was I so bothered about a bunch of words written on an ancient piece of paper, anyway? I was only bothering because of what Mr. Danvers had said. Perhaps this and the other items had something to do with why the house was famous and could potentially stop me from getting rid of it quickly.

The memories kept trying to burrow through to my thoughts.

Dr. Raj had told me about displacement activities, so I bought a ticket for the matinee showing of *Falling Down*, yet watching it just reminded me of how easy it would be for me to be tipped over the edge again.

1988

Apparently, I spent a whole month in a psychiatric hospital.

Of that time, I do remember just how patient Dr. Raj was with me and how I felt so unsure about leaving the safety of my room. So many of the others were in a rush to get out when all I wanted to do was stay put, as the thought of leaving the hospital would send me into a blind panic.

But I did leave, and because I was deemed "vulnerable' I was given a new council flat on the day I left the hospital. It wasn't as nice as the privately rented one I'd had in my old life, when I'd worked as a reasonably paid office manager in a private law firm, but it was mine and paid for until I could find a job.

The employment agency with the dusty tables asked no questions about my whereabouts for the past month, and within twelve days had found me a job.

I was settled, I suppose.

I had an income, basic but regular, coming in. There was food in the cupboard, including ten jars of Marmite and other items I stockpiled. This gave me some sense of safety, according to Dr. Raj, who said this had something to do with control. I'd laughed in his face but wanted to tell him that the drugs he signed off on had put paid to any real control I had.

The job kept me busy without being a major distraction. I needed the routine, apparently. The psychiatric nurse Deidre often used to say so. That's when she wasn't lecturing me about her childhood in Zimbabwe and how lucky British kids had it. This was clearly a dig at me and her take on why I had ended up in a psychiatric hospital. I'd always wanted to tell her she knew nothing about my life as a kid, and perhaps she ought to go into another profession.

Luckily, I wasn't the same girl who'd entered that hospital. I had changed. For the better, I hoped, so I was able to approach this new life, this new chance, with a better outlook.

This wasn't the first time I'd emerged from nothing to nothing, anyway. The future never scared me as much as the past did.

It was months later when my onetime boyfriend, the one who'd found me that day, got in touch and took me to dinner.

"This thing that happened to you . . . it's huge, Lowra."

I bit so far into the burger there were only three good bites left. "Not really. Not in the grand scheme of things."

For as long as we'd "known" each other, I'd never revealed anything about my past and he had never asked. Yet now he'd seen me at my lowest, he wanted to know it all and had suddenly become an expert in mental health, yet with a qualification in computers. All this talk about "loving myself," unsolicited advice and expressions of concern, and none of it meant a thing to me. The burger was delicious, though.

In fairness to him, he could have just exited my life without providing a reason because I was used to that. Yet we both knew he was only sitting there watching me eat a burger to appease his guilt. He was a "nice guy," and always wanting to be the good guy wasn't a bad trait to have, especially when we exist in a world where some people do not care how their actions affect others, happy to just destroy everything in their path like a finger on a trail of dominoes. Yet I didn't need my onetime boyfriend, or whoever he now was, to be the good guy. I just needed him to understand. But of course, he didn't. How could he? No one ever could, which was why it always just felt safer to keep myself to myself, so I never needed to explain.

1993

I woke with a start. My bedroom was blanketed in semidarkness. Another nightmare. In this one, words were etched onto a large white wall in an empty room. A loud voice I recognized as my own spelled out each letter: M . . . D? Now awake, I could not remember the other letters. Perhaps I *had* worked them out in the attic all those years ago and they were now stuck in the deepest depths of my mind, waiting to be discovered. Or perhaps they weren't letters after all.

The glare of the streetlamp illuminated the glassy-eyed stare of the doll sitting on a side chair and staring straight at me.

I could have left it on the mantelpiece but I wanted the doll near me when I slept. Just like before.

Having it close by used to give me comfort, especially after I'd convinced myself it had once belonged to my mother. That she'd left it in that attic just for me to find one day. A story which now, with the full clarity of a thirty-year-old woman, made no sense; because if she had, she'd have to have known what would happen next.

And for her to have known that would mean my mother had hated me.

Chapter Fourteen

Celestine
1906

I had been living in Britain for almost six months now and Sir Richard had been away for most of those.

At the beginning it was easy to count the days until his return when I would receive word from my mama, but as Mrs. Cuthbert reminded me, time was more likely to speed up if I just "got on with things' and that I did.

I had grown somewhat in height, the changing seasons something I still needed to get used to, and after a shaky start had really begun to enjoy my tutoring sessions with Mr. Lattery. He was a stern yet quiet man, who took great delight in teaching me English as well as the three Rs, while failing to show much interest in anything else. He never appeared to smile and that was fine, because from the start he let me know we were here to work.

And work was what I did. The lessons ignited an excitement in me that told me learning was all I wanted to do. The more he taught, the hungrier for knowledge I became.

Math was my favorite subject: working out problems and conundrums and watching Mr. Lattery's face soften when I answered a question correctly. I also enjoyed using a dictionary, something Mr. Lattery said every boy should own.

"I shall see you tomorrow," he said, just as class came to an end at 3:00 p.m. sharp. Mr. Lattery was on time for everything and expected the same in return. I admired his discipline and commitment, as it reminded me of my father.

I spent the rest of my time in the kitchen with Mrs. Cuthbert as she prepared my meals, and this quickly became something I looked forward to.

That first night after Sir Richard had gone, I had emerged from my tear-soaked bed and asked why she was bothering to cook elaborate meals, as I was happy to eat whatever she did.

"I'm under strict instructions," she'd said.

I found this to be rather wasteful, but didn't mention it again as one of the things my mama had taught me was never to be ungrateful. I would gratefully receive whatever Sir Richard insisted on giving, however inauthentic that may have felt. And it did feel so. Especially when all I could really think about was him traveling across the seas and to the land where I was born, while I was here and wanted to be *there*. Those thoughts consumed me daily, and it was only the presence of Mr. Lattery and Mrs. Cuthbert that gave me some relief.

Watching Mrs. Cuthbert in the kitchen sometimes felt like I was watching my mama. The utensils my mama had were modest in comparison and her space was much smaller, but the similarities, however minute, I noticed and latched on to. Like Mama, Mrs. Cuthbert prepared meals with precision and dedication, soon allowing me more than the job of peeling potatoes.

She spoke much more freely now. She had a grown-up daughter with three children, and Mrs. Cuthbert was called Maida, and I was welcome to call her that. Of course, I never would.

She'd been working for Sir Richard and his father before him for almost forty years.

Every so often, after vigorously kneading dough or mixing in a bowl, she'd wipe her brow with great drama and say strange things like, "All this mixing will have me arm off, if I'm not careful."

I liked Mrs. Cuthbert, and although I accepted that children were not equal to adults, she spoke to me in a way someone like Daphne never would.

One afternoon as we waited for a pie to bake, I stood beside her as she leaned over the worktop, complaining about her back. I pulled up a chair for her to be seated.

"Thank you, love," she said. "Never did this much work when Lady Eloise was around because there were so many of us then."

"Lady Eloise?"

"The place always had fresh flowers too. Of course, there was more money then."

I stopped. "Who is this Lady Eloise?" I repeated.

"Sir Richard's wife."

"Sir Richard is married?"

"Yes, he was, and in those days the house had a real woman's touch to it. Although she was hardly that. Not much more than a girl really. But it wasn't my place to talk."

"I did not know any of this."

"Why would you, love? You're but a child. Anyway, he's got rid of anything to do with them."

"Them?" Sometimes I mistrusted my interpretation of certain English words, but she had certainly said *them*.

"She died in childbirth."

I leaned over the counter, weighted by this barrage of new information about Sir Richard. I'd never seen him as anything more than an explorer of countries, with a booming voice and a love of what rested in a bottle.

"Can you tell me more, Mrs. Cuthbert?"

"Here, peel these." She stood up and moved a bowl of potatoes across the countertop, a job I took on with gusto and precision even though it would only be me, Mrs. Cuthbert and perhaps the bread boy, Bill, who would be eating them.

She stopped and looked toward me. "It was a little girl she birthed. I remember seeing her, Lady Eloise, holding on to the little mite who was wrapped up in a blanket. They even named it, which I thought was mighty strange. You don't do things like that, do you?"

"I would not . . . know, Mrs. Cuthbert." Words were not coming freely to me as I struggled to digest this new piece of information.

"Sir Richard doesn't ever talk about it, so don't go asking him when he gets back."

I shook my head vehemently. "I would never do such a thing."

"You're a good boy."

I continued with my task, my mind absorbing all these new facts about my benefactor.

"It's been a good while now, and Sir Richard is a most eligible bachelor and could have his pick, but he chooses to run around in Africa all the time. I have no idea why. He needs to settle down and have some children." She stopped the mixing. "Maybe that's why he brought you over. Maybe he wants you to be his son."

"I already have a fa—" And then I remembered.

"I didn't mean anything by that, love. Just making conversation," she said. However much I liked her, this comment moved me further away from her.

"Celeste," she said.

"Celestine is the name Sir Richard gave me, Mrs. Cuthbert, you know this."

"I mean . . . it's been a few years now, but I remember it clear as day."

A splash of water caught the countertop as I plopped a potato into the bowl.

"No, I mean that was what they named the baby—it was Celeste."

Chapter Fifteen

Celestine
1906

I was still reeling from the news about Sir Richard, but in his absence I had no place to speak of it further. Mrs. Cuthbert believing she had "said too much" meant she quickly shied away from any further mention. Besides, upon his return it would be news of Mama that I craved to converse with him about, and not his past. Yet the name chosen for a baby that had not been able to live . . . this I couldn't freely remove from my mind. Or the question of whether he wanted me to become his son as a replacement.

The similarities were already apparent. I felt as if I had not been allowed to live too—yet in a different way.

Mrs. Cuthbert was right, of course, and we all needed to just get on with day-to-day life, at least until Sir Richard's return.

Mrs. Cuthbert said it was best I seek someone my own age to talk to, but that meant the bread boy Bill, who came around every other day even though much less food was being consumed in the house. He often departed with leftovers, which I didn't mind, as it would have been wasted otherwise.

"Hello, all!" he said, bounding into the kitchen. He appeared to walk lopsided and not in a straight line. As usual his face was speckled with dirt, his knee-high trousers frayed at the ends, his speech fast and brash. My own garments, thanks to Mrs. Cuthbert's upkeep, were always spotless and smart.

Bill seemed accommodating when I asked him to stay behind and . . . converse.

"So what's it like without the old man?" he said.

"It has been very good," I replied.

"It must be. Look at yer! All spruced up and nowhere to go. No one can believe the likes of you get to stay here like this. I mean, you see the odd one the further south you go, but around here, you're not what we're used to."

I felt a relief when Mrs. Cuthbert appeared.

"Leave him alone, Bill. I only let you inside because Sir Richard's away. Carry on like that and you'll be out again."

"What? You know it's true. Now the old git's out the way, I should bring the lads round to see for themselves."

"I said, stop it! If you want to get fed around here, you'll do well to keep that shut." She pointed to his mouth.

I swallowed. What Bill had said sounded threatening. His words were a reminder of what Daphne and Sir Richard's other friends had said at the dinner party, poking at me with words: that I was different from them in ways that were to do with more than just the color of my skin.

Even after he'd gone, his words lingered. And as I headed up to the first floor and to my bedroom that evening, my thoughts once again turned to Sir Richard. There'd been no word of when he would be back. His friend Roger had visited with a telegram a month earlier, assuring us he was safe, but nothing since.

It was hard to concentrate on my math the next morning and Mr. Lattery was less than impressed with my lack of concentration.

Halfway through the lesson, he'd clearly had enough.

"Am I keeping you?" he asked.

I knew enough about the British people to know they seemed to clutch on to sarcasm quite a bit.

"No, Mr. Lattery."

"Your concentration seems to be anywhere but in this room today."

"I have been thinking of many things."

"You may want to think about what you are squandering here."

I exhaled slowly and hunched my back.

"You've been given a brilliant opportunity, one that many of the local street urchins out there would die for. At first I could not understand why Sir Richard had embarked on this, but it was not my place to question it. He is paying for a service which I will deliver. However, I have seen your determination to learn and greatly admire it, so I am somewhat bemused as to why you are behaving like this today."

"I'm terribly sorry," I said, straightening my shoulders and speaking in the best English I could muster.

"It is not me you should apologize to. But perhaps to yourself. Shall we get on?"

I greatly respected Mr. Lattery, just as I had my father.

"I will do my very best not to let you down," I said.

When I was not studying or peeling potatoes, I amused myself with games like quoits even if I had to play by myself, but today I requested that Bill stay behind and join me.

"No, ta. Not really my thing. Surprised to see you playing anything. You always got yer nose in a book."

"I prefer study to playing."

"That's silly!"

"It is?" I said, quite enjoying this sarcasm thing.

"You live right by the sea—don't you even want to see it?"

I wasn't about to admit to Bill that every time I even thought of the sea I became clouded with memories of home that forced tears into the corners of my eyes, followed by a longing for something that felt so out of reach. It was the sea that had brought me here, after all, and my relationship to it was that of an enemy.

"We won't be long," promised Bill, as Mrs. Cuthbert stood with her arms folded.

"You'd better have him back here in an hour, you hear me?"

"Yes, Mrs. Cuthbert," he responded in a mocking tone.

I hadn't actually agreed to go, but like my life so far, I did what others expected of me and reluctantly followed him outside.

By foot and not by motor vehicle, the street appeared more textured and intense in its appearance, and I was gripped by a wave of apprehension as we edged closer to the sand.

"Come on!" beckoned Bill.

The sun felt warm on my back, the breeze from the sea instantly cooling as I looked out onto the horizon. I suddenly felt I was the only one present, with this endless ocean right there in front of me, an expanse that had brought me here and could also lead me back. Any tension I had been carrying, guilt at sometimes forgetting to wear my father's necklace over the past six months, or days gone by when I had not thought of Kabili or the others, swiftly rose out of me and was replaced by fields of hope. All this time I had avoided the sea, and yet it was the one thing that could have actually made me happy.

Just as it did now.

I turned to thank Bill for bringing me here, but he was gone, and as I turned to the other side, my rising panic abated when I saw him walking toward me, joined by three bigger boys.

They were dressed not unlike him, with their torn waistcoats, ill-fitting blazers and caps—all of which needed a good amount of washing—and just like his, their shoes were worn and threadbare. Nevertheless, they were within my age group, so perhaps spending time with them wouldn't be so bad.

"There he is! I told yer!" said Bill. The other three were

pointing and chuckling—with one holding his stomach—as they moved closer to where I stood. My happiness turned to uncertainty. Their laughter aside, none of this felt friendly as they advanced upon me, and for a quick moment I pondered if I should jump into the sea. A ridiculous thought, because Bill was not about to harm me!

The four of them surrounded me, thumbs resting in their pockets.

One of them prodded my arm with his finger. "Blimey, it's real."

They all began to laugh, except Bill.

"Of course he is. That's what I told yer," said Bill.

"Speak then!" said one.

I opened my mouth to do so, then thought, *Why should I?*

"I said, speak!" I felt specks of spittle on my face as the boy stepped in closer, yet still I did not oblige. I would not oblige. Ever.

"Leave him alone," said Bill. "He's all right."

"What is it, though?" said another boy. "Ain't he like one of those apes in that book we saw?"

I wanted to say that I doubted he had ever opened a book in his life.

Another boy began to laugh rather animatedly, as if this was the funniest thing he had ever heard, and I simply wanted to say that he was more ape than I, with his lack of manners and unkempt demeanor.

"Can it speak English, then?"

"I said, he's all right," said Bill.

"Do you think it bleeds?"

This comment made me take note. It had come from the boy directly in front of me, the one who hadn't said much, his squinted eyes telling me more than I wanted to know.

"Why don't we find out?" I wasn't sure who said this, my mind fixated on the shining slick of a blade which shone from the fingers of the silent boy.

"Come on, boys, let's not get silly," said Bill. I didn't like the fear that sounded in his own voice, as if overpowered by a situation he had started.

I was unsure of what I should do. My mind was spinning.

"Let's see!"

"Do it!"

"Give him a poke!"

"Maybe it's black too!"

"Come on, boys, stop it!"

"Go on!"

"Do it!"

The blade flew up into the sky, slowly at first, and then smacked onto the pebbly ground. I could see the back of Bill's jacket, the feet of one of the boys shuffling for superiority, just as I lunged toward the ground, grabbing the blade. I was running before I could breathe my next breath, my pace slowing down only once my feet no longer connected with the pebbles on the beach.

My heart raced.

With no idea of where the big house was in relation to where I was, blind panic navigated my way. Those I passed stopped to look at me as if I were a stranger to the area, the ladies clutching whatever possession happened to be in their hands, the gentlemen grabbing hold of their ladies, like possessions.

The blade was safely folded away inside my pocket, my mind fixated on recalling the route we had taken. I'd never realized just how close in proximity to the sea the big house stood, until now.

When I made it back to the big house, I pounded the door for Mrs. Cuthbert to let me in.

"What's all the racket?" she said, standing before me. I said not a word as I threw myself into her arms, collapsing into the fabric of her apron.

"What is it, love?"

I held on to her tightly, as if she were my mama.

Just moments later, as Mrs. Cuthbert insisted on disappearing to the kitchen and preparing me some tea "for the shock," Bill stood at the front door, which I had left ajar. My body tensed as I stood before him in the hallway.

"Glad you're all right. Sorry about that."

"Where are you going?"

"I wanted to check on yer. Saw the door was open . . ."

"You will use the back door as always," I said.

"I said I was just checking if you're all right."

"This does not mean you can abuse the fact that Sir Richard is away by entering through the front door. You will enter by the back door when you deliver goods. Other than that there is no reason for your presence in this house. Do you understand?"

"All right then," he said. But I was far from finished with him yet.

"I will also inform Sir Richard of what you did today, and he will be sure to secure the services of another baker and bread boy."

His expression was of surprise and confusion. "But I didn't do nothing."

"You mean, 'I didn't do *anything*.' And actually you did, by doing *nothing*."

"Yeah, but it was me that stopped them—"

I slammed the door and blocked out his voice.

His remorse was of no importance to me because I did not care. The humiliation of that fund-raiser, although months ago, had just been reignited via Bill and his friends; it clearly still burned within me. Placing those feelings back onto Bill felt like a good way to try and rid myself of them, while also feeling satisfying. At least in that moment.

Yet when I returned to my bedroom, the anger resurfaced with a twist.

I was tired of hearing about the "wonderful opportunity" Sir Richard had foisted upon me—because I hadn't asked for any of it. What did the likes of Bill or even Mr. Lattery know about who

I was or what I wanted? Every time they looked at me, it was always about *him*, Sir Richard Babbington and how "giving" he was. No one ever saw who I was or what my life had been before here. Before England.

It was as if they believed my life to have started the day I stepped off a ship and landed in England! It was only Mrs. Cuthbert who ever appeared mildly interested in my life before, especially when I corrected her on Sir Richard's dubious account of things, and yet her power in this new world of mine was limited, nonexistent even.

I gazed at the pocketknife resting between my fingers. The high carbon steel blades snapped strongly when I opened and closed them, each inscribed with a triple S symbol and appearing to be of excellent quality. No doubt it had been stolen by one of Bill's ruffians, and now it would belong to me. I would for once take something that was not my own, just as everyone else seemed so adept at doing.

Three months later, I finally heard Sir Richard's booming voice. I had been "playing" with the pocketknife in bed, something I sometimes did when I wasn't studying, no longer interested in playing any games. I slid it back into my pocket, believing I was imagining Sir Richard's voice, while a feeling of elation threatened to topple me over as I ran downstairs to his study. The door was ajar and he was sitting on his chair smoking the mahogany pipe he favored, smiling once he spotted me at the doorway.

"Come closer, dear boy!" His skin had turned a slightly darker shade, and his moustache as well as his body frame appeared thinner.

Questions tumbled out of my mouth.

"One word at a time!" he said.

My words were accompanied by spurts of impatient breath. A desperation to know of my village, my family and when I would be returning home. I had waited too long for his return and now it was here, I had so many words, questions that really only required one answer.

"Dear boy, allow me to reacquaint myself with my home and Mrs. Cuthbert's delicious cooking. Then and only then will we proceed with this conversation."

I had waited this long. What was another mere hour?

An hour turned to three, which included Sir Richard retiring to his bedroom. He finally called me into his study and told me to sit down. I sat on one of the cushioned chairs, my palms resting in between my thighs, my heart beating loudly.

"You have questions," he said.

"Yes, sir, you sent word to my family. My mama."

His eyebrows squinted and I wondered if he had forgotten to do what he had said. "Oh yes, that."

"When may I return home, then?"

His forehead softened.

"Of course I am grateful for all you have done for me thus far, but it is my intention to return home. My mama needs me. I believe she must be missing me, sir."

He gazed toward his lap. "I see."

"Sir?"

"When I was a little boy, my father felt it best to expose me to the harshest of truths, whether they be damning or simply what would propel me on to better things. More often than not, I would refuse to understand his true intention."

I did not understand what he was saying; my only interest was what Mama had said and when I would finally be going home.

"I was duped, dear boy!" He bowed his head slowly. "At the beginning of all of this, it was for the people—to help, to assist—when all along . . ." He shook his head and I simply wanted to place my hands onto his shoulders, squeeze and then shake his entire body. Why was he tormenting me like this?

"It would appear the true intention of one man can indeed have devastating consequences for many."

I shifted in my seat.

"Celestine." He said the name more softly than he'd ever done. "What was found in your village . . ."

I swallowed.

"There was simply nothing there."

I did not understand.

"Burned to the ground, the entire village, and by those who claim to have wanted the greater good!"

"What?"

"What I am trying to tell you, dearest boy, is that your village is no more."

My mind had not deciphered what this could mean. Perhaps purposely so, because to do so would mean an unthinkable reality.

"But how would you know this?"

"What do you mean, dear boy?"

"You said you were to send word . . . that you were going to Benin. So you could not have seen this with your own eyes."

He looked away and then back to me again. "No, but I am reliably informed by my contacts in the region that there is nothing left."

"My mama . . . ? My brothers?" I said.

"Dear boy, you must listen to me."

"I do not understand!"

"There was no trace of any of them."

"What do you mean, no trace?"

"Celestine, your English has much improved since my voyage . . . when I say no trace, I mean—"

"I know what it means!" My voice had risen to a volume I did not recognize. I turned to him with a quieter tone. "Mr. Richard—"

"Sir Richard," he corrected.

"Sir Richard, I do not understand." I said this with my eyes squeezed shut, because to open them would let out a pain I wasn't sure I was ready for—also, to do so would mean I believed him.

"I am terribly, terribly sorry," he said. Yet I could only see blackness. This man had lied before. He had told Mrs. Cuthbert that I had no family. How could I believe this story?

I looked into his eyes, to see if the lies danced within them. They appeared sorrowful, while all I could feel was rage.

"I am sorry for not realizing this earlier, for not seeing enough. For being taken in by that impassioned speech by Leopold. One that left out details of the cruelty and the depravity."

I had no idea what he was now talking about, the babbling and false sentiment of no interest to me. Where was the letter? Where were my family? What he had said my mind refused to acknowledge. I needed to hold on to something that was real, believable. I needed to hold on to the fact that I would be going home!

Sir Richard brought a glass to his lips, his eyes closed, and simply said, "I'm sorry for your loss."

Chapter Sixteen

Celestine
1906

If you asked my brothers which of their memories they were most fond of, I hoped they'd recall times spent accompanying our father to work, cutting down trees and then standing by as he expertly worked and carved the wood into something beautiful enough to sell.

This was something I had never seen him do, instead relying on tales from my brothers and even his own mouth. His love for trees was evident in every sentence he spoke to me.

If anyone asked of my fondest memories, they were of my mama and Kabili.

Her tender hands rocking away my distress as I fought sleep, my anxieties instantly soothed by the humming of an unnamed song; the secret knowledge between us that spoke of me being *a good child*; stories she told, especially of the two kings Nkongolo and Mbidi; and of course, sitting under the tree with my Kabili.

These were the fondest memories of my childhood, and after what Sir Richard had disclosed, they were now all I had left.

Days later, I still could not accept that my family had experienced the fate he described.

Where was the evidence? Indeed, the entire village burning to the ground could have had a multitude of outcomes—one being that my family had escaped.

Sir Richard had lied before, so there was no reason to believe he wasn't doing so now.

As usual, he was much more forthcoming while sipping from his glass, so I constantly topped it up with his favorite drink as I asked the questions.

"Did they see them?"

"Who?"

"My family!"

I topped up his glass once more.

"Dear boy, I have been lied to and deceived by someone I respected."

He had been muttering much the same for almost an hour now, over and over again. I wanted to tell him I understood the pain of being deceived. I also wanted to grab him by the shoulders and shake him until the words I longed to hear—the truth—came tumbling out.

"Did your friend see anyone from the village, like Ina Balenga?"

He narrowed his reddened eyes. By now, he'd consumed at least half a bottle of his favorite whisky, his skin almost matching the color of his bloodshot eyes.

I persisted. "Baba Mbuyi? He would sometimes visit—but only rarely. Or . . . or one of my brothers. Kabili?"

He was no longer listening, though, his eyes closing once he brought the glass to his lips.

"This can make it all better, if only for a moment," he said. "If not for your tender years, dear boy, you too could experience the utopia and forget your questions. If only for a moment."

More sips followed and Sir Richard was soon asleep in his chair.

"I'm off home now, love," said Mrs. Cuthbert. "Best leave him to sleep it off. Don't worry yourself. Last time he was this bad was when his wife died, so he must have seen a lot on this trip. But let's face it, he's always been a drinker. See you tomorrow."

She turned toward the door and then spun around. "You want some advice?"

I nodded my head weakly.

"Let it go."

"Pardon me?"

"Ever since he got back, you've been asking him all sorts and all he's done is drink himself to oblivion. I know it's hard, but sometimes we have to accept things."

"Even when they are untrue?"

Her smile was straight. "You see what happens when you don't let things go," she said, pointing to Sir Richard's crumpled state. "All I can say is, you have no choice but to pull up your boots and get on with it."

"Boots?"

"It's just a saying. What I mean to say is, you have two choices: to stay and torture yourself, or to stay and make something good come out of this horrible situation. See you tomorrow, love."

Her words were sharp, short, yet hit me to the core. I respected Mrs. Cuthbert a lot more than Sir Richard, yet as before, her words felt like daggers. I was not ready to stop asking about my mama, my family, my village. I needed to know the truth, didn't I?

That night I sat on my bed, surrounded by all the trappings my trip to England had afforded me, yet overwhelmed with a sense of helplessness. I lived in this house full of wealth yet did not have the personal means to change my own destiny. I was at the mercy of a situation I both enjoyed and despised, all at the same time.

I was a lifetime away from my country, with the only person linking me to it a drunkard who insisted over and over again that everything I had ever held dear was gone. Even in his drunken state the words stubbornly refused to change, which meant they had the capacity to be true.

With a tear drifting toward my cheek, I decided that evening to place any feeling of hope I had inside an imaginary box. A box I would open again one day—if I wished. But, in order to survive this part of my journey and get to a position where I could begin a search for my family, I had to allow myself to absorb what Sir Richard was offering me, knowing that in time, when age was my companion, I would be able to do so much more. At the age of eleven, I had to admit that I was limited, even though I had more opportunities than the likes of Bill. I just needed more time. I already dressed well and spoke like an English gentleman—and these were the tools I would one day use to take me back home.

Most days the box in my head felt easier to contain, to keep closed. But one day as we rode in the motor vehicle, I peered to my side, the wind making my eyes water, and I spotted a lady in a long flowing dress and a picture hat on her head in the same colors as one of my mama's favorite cloths, maroon with specks of white. My heart immediately felt heavy, my eyes refusing the onslaught of tears which threatened to expose my feelings.

There would be no more tears.

My thoughts and feelings had to remain inside the box. So as Gordon stared intently toward the road ahead, I closed my eyes on the pretense of shielding myself from the wind.

The next time the box slightly opened was the result of a vision, a memory that just decided to appear as I lay in my bed. That morning and without provocation, a tug, a longing in my heart had shifted to the entirety of my being, and in that precise moment of intense pain, I knew with all the certainty in the world that I would give everything up—the tailor-made clothes, the succulently cooked chicken and the big house, everything—for just one last day with my mama. It wouldn't have to be a lifetime—just one day, an hour, a minute, a second.

At first I embrace her, and then she strokes my head and kisses the tip of my nose. She asks how I've been and wants to hear everything of my life in this Great Britain so far. I loop my arm in hers, my smile almost as big as my face, as we walk back to my village, but not before Kabili runs over to us, asking me to recount my story of what life has been like without them. My adventures and my excitable tales, which I exaggerate to fit the moment, he takes in with smiles. Then the remainder of my brothers join in, each and every one of them—Djamba, Yogo and Pako—all vying for my attention and anything I can tell them about this new country. But when night falls and it's just me and my mama lying on the floor on a woven mat, her arm resting around me, my head snug under her arm, we hardly speak. My nose rests on the cloth of her dress, taking in her scent of fresh fruit one more time before she is lost forever. I am sensing the nearness of our time being cut short. A part of me quickly grows in resentment as she pulls herself up from the mat and starts to walk away. Her back is toward me as my arm rises, hungry for just one more touch.

With my arms open, I realized where I was: in England, in my bedroom. This had to stop. It was not becoming. I was trapped in a place of being too old to cry for my mama yet needing her more than I ever had before.

Then a rush of more emotion, this time confusing: anger toward my mama because she'd sent me away with this man.

Yet what was clear was that I had to accept I was never going to see her again.

So this I decided to do.

I closed the box.

PART TWO

Chapter Seventeen

Lowra
1993

I may have been walking along a pavement in Ranklin again, but this time I was determined to stay away from that house.

I could do without the memories and the intrusions in my head.

You see, ever since leaving hospital five years ago, I'd been stable, yet still aware of the possibility that I could one day land right back in there if anything in my life went off kilter, and that's why I preferred things to be just so. Yet *her* dying had unbalanced bits of my life which had also shifted things in my head.

And I was worried.

So it felt logical to me that if I just found out who that doll belonged to, I'd also find some sort of peace again. I would eventually sell the house, give the money to charity, and get on with my life back in London. That's all I wanted. That's all I needed.

I stood in front of the tacky Flamingo Club cafe, which, when it was a diner, was a favorite of mine and Dad's, especially after my mother died. Once he'd arranged for a trip there with *her*, that had ended in total chaos when a blob of my chocolate ice cream landed on her white lace dress. Dad and I giggled as she flapped about madly, as if it was one big disaster. Which for me it was, because after that there were no more trips to the diner, or to the sweetshop with its large jars of bonbons and aniseeds, and a lady with hair like Grandma's weighing out sweets and scooping them into a white paper bag.

Nothing was the same after she stopped being my tutor and became my dad's fiancée.

The woman at Ranklin Library eyed me above her glasses with a gold chain attached, her little silver-colored badge which read HAPPY TO HELP slightly annoying, to be honest.

"You'd like to find out who lived at your old house?"

"They were well-known, apparently."

"Why don't you just ask your family then?"

"Because they're all gone," I said without expression.

"Sorry for your loss," she said.

Sorry for your loss.

There it was again.

"Is it number 109 Ranklin Road?"

I held my breath. "How did you know?"

"This is a small seaside town and it's the only famous house for miles!"

I looked toward my shoes. The white plimsoles were badly scuffed and I would soon need new ones.

"I can tell you all you need to know about that house."

"That would be great," I said, looking up with a false smile.

I could not match her happiness and just wanted to get this over and done with.

She set up the microfiche machine, but not without giving me the whole rundown of that house's famous former inhabitant.

"The Babbingtons lived at that address from the early nineteenth century."

That sounded a bit far back, but who knew how long that doll had actually been there.

"Sir Richard Babbington was one of this country's greatest explorers. Imagine that? And he lived in little old Ranklin!"

"In that house?"

"Yes, 109 Ranklin Road. Isn't that just wonderful!" she squealed.

"So, did this Sir Richard have a family?"

"As far as I know, he had no offspring."

"You're sure of that?"

"Oh, wait . . . I do remember reading an article about him, mentioning that his wife, Eloise, gave birth to a daughter who died shortly afterward. His wife too. They say that's why he went on all those expeditions."

"Because he was grieving?"

"I suspect so," she said, nodding her head.

"What about his family who lived there before he took it over? Was there a little girl?"

"As far as I know, he was an only child."

"And you're sure of that?"

"As sure as my name is Jean!"

I smiled politely, because I couldn't bring myself to chuckle.

"Look, if you want to be certain, the best way of finding that out now is probably to look at old cuttings from the *Ranklin Gazette*. The Babbingtons would have shown up to charity events and the like as they were so very well-known around here. We have them on microfiche. Do you have the time to take a look?"

This already felt like hard work, but I would press on at least for today.

I sat at the machine with Jean standing over me and it felt really awkward to have someone so close, to be inside my personal space like this. Feeling the warmth radiating from her body, the smell of her musky perfume—I hated it.

"Could you stand back a bit, please. Sorry," I said, feeling like an idiot.

"Oops, sorry. Messing up that lovely hair of yours, aren't I? Just so excited to see what we're going to come up with!" She pulled up a chair.

Jean was a good instructor as I operated the small screen in front of us. But I could never get as excited as she did when the first picture popped up.

"So this article is about the Babbingtons donating money to charities in 1899. He was very philanthropic and spent a lot of time abroad helping poor countries."

It felt like we were straying away from anything to do with the doll. Perhaps the doll had belonged to his daughter.

"Is there a notice . . . you know, for when he died?" I said.

"Oh, you mean an obituary? Of course. There were numerous notices. Even one in a national newspaper!"

Minutes later I was staring at it.

> We regret to announce that Sir Richard Babbington has died. The famous African explorer fell to a mystery illness, perhaps one which had lain dormant in his body as a result of numerous expeditions to the darkest depths of the African continent.
>
> His demise removes yet another of the gallant and brave explorers of our time who enabled the rediscovery of the African continent and one of the oldest civilizations in existence. Sir Richard Babbington, along with Livingstone and Stanley, will forever be connected with making the continent known to us all, and making possible that "scramble for Africa" which has so profoundly affected the powers of this great country of ours and the rest of Europe in the African continent.
>
> He was born . . .

"If we go back even further . . . here. This is him after he'd just returned from Brussels in 1876."

> Richard Babbington spoke with great affection of the International African Association formed to oversee

> the ending of the slave trade, and open up the people to civilization as well as new roads for its citizens' travel, schools for its children, and hospitals for a healthier nation.
>
> Babbington said he would persist and follow in the footsteps of King Leopold II as a fervent humanitarian, and has received funding from the King to embark on his first trip to the continent.

"So after that date he started going on all these expeditions?"

"Yes, and mostly to the African continent."

Which was probably where the beaded necklace was from, and not in fact Asia.

"You know a lot about this man, Jean. Looks like we don't even need the micro machine thingy."

She smiled, clearly taking this as a compliment.

"Well, of course I do. He's Ranklin's most famous son and everyone here is very proud of him!"

All I saw was a thickly moustached man in a hat and very long and inappropriate boots staring smugly toward the camera, but each to their own.

"So the guy who lived in that house before we did went on trips abroad and gave to charity."

Her face reddened. "Sir Richard Babbington was more than that. He was a man who risked his life traveling abroad and helping others, and was recognized for all he'd done. He was even made a Knight Grand Cross of the Order of the Bath in 1899. I can look up the write-up for that."

"No, thanks." This all suddenly felt a bit pointless. What did this smug, self-serving man have to do with me, anyway? Nothing. I was wasting my time.

She clicked her fingers. "Give me five minutes."

I pulled a roll of gum from my pocket and by the time the

sweetness had started to fade, she was back, carrying a stack of books in the crook of her arms.

"You might want to stay and look at these," she said, placing them on a table. "These are Sir Richard's books."

"An author too?" I said with a disinterest she would not have heard.

"He published two—*The Trek to Africa* and *The Princely Joy*—and there's even an unpublished manuscript floating about! No one here's happy about that. We feel it should have been returned to Ranklin where it belongs. How it ended up in that exhibit in the stately home in Rinchester I will never know."

I opened up the first book, *The Trek to Africa*, effectively obscuring the cover—a grainy black-and-white picture of a uniformed Sir Richard Babbington with his arms folded. Hardly a book I'd usually read, and flicking though the pages it was clear why. The old-fashioned language was a bit tedious as well as a little patronizing.

They looked upon me like a golden nugget on top of a bed of weeds. Wonderment at this pale-faced stranger they could see beyond, recognizing the potential for friendship and love.

"If you're local, I can sign you up and you can take them out," she said.

"No, no, that's OK," I said, feeling slightly sick at the thought of ever living in this area again. "I'm from London. Maybe I'll just buy them."

"There's a lovely vintage bookshop up the high street. They'll have all of his books."

"Thank you."

"Oh, and I also noticed this," said the librarian, handing me a shiny A5 flyer. "There's a big art exhibition on Africa coming up and apparently our Sir Richard is featured. You might get some clues there . . . It's in London. Didn't you say you were from London?"

"I did," I sighed. The Richard Babbington fan club was something I had no interest in joining, and what did she mean by "clues'? Jean was clearly more excited about all of this than I could ever be.

"There might be some more info there about him, you know, if you were interested in finding out more about that lovely house. Just a thought."

"I suppose so."

"Just want to help," she shrugged.

I looked down at the flyer in my hands—TRAVELS OF THE NINETEENTH CENTURY: A PHOTOGRAPHIC JOURNEY FROM AFRICA TO EMPIRE—before folding it up and placing it inside my pocket.

That evening on the train heading out of Ranklin, it was as if my entire body exhaled. That tacky, small seaside town still held something over me, and perhaps if I found out who that doll belonged to, it wouldn't anymore. Some hope. The plan sounded sensible in my head, but in reality . . .

I unfurled the flyer. A museum was one of those places I'd never usually visit, so this would be a first.

The marbled floor of the gallery looked impressive as I walked the length of a long corridor that smelled of lemon cleaner and led to an information desk.

"We have the Africa department on floor two. That's where the exhibition is being held," the receptionist said.

I followed her directions, stopping now and then to gaze at some of the artifacts: beautifully formed busts of women under the title THE MAGNIFICENT KINGDOM OF IFE; perfectly shaped sculptures lining the inside of a large glass cabinet, dominated by a huge masquerade costume in a multitude of colors; a carefully carved wooden footstool in the shape of a woman. Each item fascinating me and opening up a need to know more. So I read the accompanying texts, conscious of getting sidetracked. I was here to take a quick look at an exhibition on Richard Babbington and perhaps to find a clue to the original owner of that doll—nothing more, nothing less.

Considering how grand the gallery appeared so far, I wasn't prepared for the tiny room afforded to the exhibition. The bright side was, I could be out of there within a few minutes.

Two people with their backs to me, holding hands, studied a photo of a young man in a princely costume. He had to be royal because of his turban, decorated with jewels. The quality of these photographs was so much better than I expected for prints almost a hundred years old. According to the flyer they'd been produced on glass plate negatives, which was probably cutting-edge technology at that time. One print of a beautiful young woman which could have been taken last week held my gaze, because her eyes were smiling toward the camera, but just slightly. An anomaly; apparently, no one smiled in Victorian pictures.

I moved over to the next photograph, entitled THE SOUTH AFRICAN CHOIR'S TOUR. According to the blurb, they'd toured Britain in 1891 and sung for Queen Victoria! I wasn't sure what I'd expected from this exhibition but this wasn't it. I felt drawn to read each and every story, however brief the write-up, telling myself I would follow through with looking them up in the library, but knowing I wouldn't.

I was yet to see anything connecting Richard Babbington to these photographs.

Until I did.

A young Black child, no more than eleven or twelve, looked straight down at the camera. I say "down" because his eyelids appeared to be gazing in that direction, as if dragged by an invisible force. The result was an expression which spoke of this being the last place he wanted to be. Unlike subjects in the previous photographs, he was dressed in a western-style three-piece suit and was standing by a chair, his right arm resting on top of it, one leg crossed in front of the other and his shoes beautifully shined.

I looked into those eyes again and I saw defiance.

I moved over to the next photograph.

This one looked a little yellowed with time, but the same child sat on a different chair, this time his arm resting on a circular table and his legs slightly apart. His expression was full of sadness. I swallowed, feeling deep inside a pang of recognition despite the decades that separated us. In the third picture, the child's torso was wrapped in a striped cloth, his bottom half dressed in trousers and boots, and he leaned against a rock. The fan in his right hand was yet another weird prop which looked like it had been thrust into his hand. His eyes once again drew me closer, telling me not to leave. This beautiful little boy looked as if he was not even a willing participant in the scene, that he had somehow taken himself away from it all: that studio, the flash of the photographer, the moment . . .

It wasn't until the next photograph that I recognized Richard Babbington with his long boots and ridiculous dome hat, carrying a gun. He wasn't alone. Behind him, the same child was dressed in a wrap, his belly button exposed, carrying what looked like a spear. The sadness in his expression was easy for anyone to read. I turned away quickly as Jean's tales of admiration echoed in my memory, feeling an unease as sudden questions I did not know the answer to floated in the air. Why was this young Black boy posing with an old white man in pictures which had clearly been taken in a studio?

I turned back to the second picture, moving closer and perhaps seeing what no one else in this museum could: an expression that told me he'd suffered. A lot. And it was those eyes which refused to leave me as I began to walk slowly away from the photograph and on to the next one, not of him. Yet just as quickly, I turned back to him, drawn to this little boy as if something, someone, was pulling me back like an invisible force, silently pleading with me not to leave. Telling me to stick around and listen—to what I do not know, but I had to stay. I had to stay.

A well of emotion rested in my throat. My eyes actually began to brim with—what, tears? What was happening to me? Was this the start of another breakdown? No, I was OK. I was in control. These were just photographs, old ones at that, and they meant nothing to me.

I gazed down at the block of information displayed in a glass enclosure. It was all about Richard Babbington, with little about the child by his side—only that his name had been Celestine. No surname, no age, only that in 1907, when the photograph was taken, he had been a "companion" to this Sir Richard Babbington.

I returned to the last photograph, not quite believing how I had missed it.

The necklace.

Even in black and white, it was clearly the same beaded claw necklace draped around Celestine's neck. The necklace I had first discovered as a lonely eleven-year-old under the floorboards of a cold and dusty attic.

I needed to sit down, but no seats were available.

This was real and not a hallucination.

In that picture, around the neck of a child named Celestine, was the necklace.

It was at that precise moment that something in me shifted.

This was no longer about who once owned a creepy doll; I now had to satisfy this need to find out more about that necklace and the little boy wearing it in the photograph.

Celestine had lived in my parents' house all those years ago as a "companion" to this Richard Babbington. What did that even mean? Where were his family? How did he end up in Ranklin?

How did his necklace end up under the floorboard of the attic?

That day I told myself I was going to find out more about Celestine. I wasn't sure how, I just knew it was something I had to do—as if my life, in some small way, depended on it.

Chapter Eighteen

Lowra
1993

I returned to the museum the next day because, according to the helpful woman at the information desk, Montgomery Alburn, an expert on African history, would be giving a talk. Marnie had been reluctant to cover my shift at short notice, but after I confided a story about a sick friend, she agreed.

This time I had a Polaroid of the necklace, because now I knew how old it was, I wasn't about to carry such a precious item in a canvas bag, on the bus. And it was precious. The necklace had meant something to that little boy, and the least I could do was look after it for him.

I heard his voice before joining the small crowd gathered inside the room I had been in only yesterday.

"So, where do we start when it comes to the wondrous artifacts of Africa? A continent with over fifty countries, vast beauty and wealth. From the unmistakable pyramids of Egypt to the exquisite statues of Benin."

Mr. Montgomery Alburn was not what I'd expected. He wore red-framed glasses and had a full head of curly hair with light brown, flawless skin and a small dimple in the middle of his chin. Half the people in that room were enchanted with every word he spoke, with each movement of his hands and wrists, his words bringing this subject alive. The man was clearly passionate about everything he spoke of, and in turn forced his audience to feel the same.

Afterward, I stood in line as a number of hangers-on took his attention. I waited until the last person had left and a woman leaned to whisper into Mr. Alburn's ear.

"I wondered if I could have a word, please?" I said, not wanting to come across as one of his museum groupies—if they existed.

"Of course." His voice sounded relaxed and less rigid than during the talk. "Is it going to be a long one?"

"It could be?"

"In that case," he said, "why don't we move onto the terrace? You'll have to excuse me while I eat. I'm starving, and my assistant has just popped downstairs to get me a sandwich. If you don't mind me eating it in front of you?"

"No, that's fine."

I introduced myself as we moved out onto the small balcony and I sat on the chair opposite him, feeling a rush of awkwardness. "So, you have an assistant?"

"In reality she's an art history student who I pay with knowledge. It doesn't cover her rent but luckily her father does that."

I smiled, just to be polite.

Thankfully, his "assistant" returned with a sandwich and a carton of juice.

"Cheese and pickle and a Capri Sun. My weakness," he said.

I nodded my head with a false smile. I had absolutely no idea how to start this conversation.

"There's something quintessentially British about the cheese and pickle sandwich. So mediocre but delicious at the same time," he said.

"Mr. Alburn . . . ?"

"Just call me Monty. You're probably thinking, he doesn't look like a Monty or a Montgomery for that matter."

"I wasn't thinking anything about your name or your sandwich. I'd just like your help with something." I knew I sounded rude, but that probably had more to do with feeling anxious than a lack of manners.

"You're very direct. I'm all ears," he said.

I pulled out the photograph, but hesitated. This story needed context.

"I was clearing out an old attic and I found this," I offered by way of explanation as I handed it to him. "I didn't bring the necklace itself, but . . ."

Chewing slowly, he gazed at the picture in his clean hand. His eyes widened then narrowed and then widened again.

"You recognize it, don't you?"

"I'm not sure . . ."

"Celestine . . . the little boy in the pictures. He's wearing this exact necklace."

"What pictures?"

"One of the subjects in the African exhibition."

"They're not my photos and the exhibition has nothing to do with me. I'm just doing a talk here. But wait . . . you're telling me a boy in a photograph in this exhibition is wearing the same necklace you've found?"

"That's right."

He placed the sandwich back into the box. "You found this in an attic, you say?"

I thought about telling him it was from Babbington's house—the one I'd lived in for fifteen years of my life—but I suddenly didn't feel like being affiliated with Richard Babbington. "I suppose I'd like to find out more about Celestine . . . this little boy."

He abandoned his lunch and we moved back inside to look over the picture of Celestine. We both stopped at the photograph of the little boy dressed in a wrap, the necklace displayed proudly around his neck, standing behind the long-booted Richard Babbington.

"I'm sorry to say, I have no idea who this boy is or where he's from."

"As you can see, there's nothing much known about him," I said, fighting a sudden sense of frustration.

"From what I know of him, Babbington toured a lot of the continent and the child could have been from anywhere."

"That's what I thought . . ."

"How do we know it's the same necklace? It could simply be a copy."

"Because I found it in the attic of the house where Richard Babbington used to live." Blurting that out wasn't so bad. I just hoped it didn't come with a host of other questions.

It came with one.

"What were you doing in Babbington's old house?"

"Can you help?" I said, evading the question, of course.

"The necklace will point us in the right direction once we find out what tribe or even country it belongs to. It won't be easy to find out more about the boy. Can I take this photograph? It isn't that clear but it's something. I'll put some feelers out in the historian and museum community, which sounds grander than it actually is!"

I wrote my phone number on a piece of paper and felt the need to apologize as the weight of self-blame came tumbling onto me. "I should have brought the original, it was stupid of me."

"No. It's best you didn't. If this is the necklace in the Babbington photograph, and I'm pretty sure it is, then it's a very rare find. Leave it with me."

Chapter Nineteen

Lowra
1993

"This is . . . this is bloody exquisite . . . just wow," he said, outlining each of the six "claws" of the necklace with gloved fingers. Monty occupied a small office a few streets away from the museum, which smelled of freshly brewed coffee and could do with a tidy-up.

"So, what is it? Where does it come from?" I said.

He ran a finger over the beading. "I showed the Polaroid to a couple of colleagues and they agree with me. I'm fairly certain it's a buffalo bone necklace, which is typically from the Luba people. We can't be sure but it's the closest lead I have at the moment."

I wasn't even going to pretend I knew what he was talking about.

"It's absolutely more beautiful in person. Sublime," he said, pushing his glasses further up his nose."These are typical to certain regions of what was formerly known as the Congo."

I couldn't help feeling a little impressed at how much he knew.

"Did you find anything else in this treasure trove?" he said.

"Just an old porcelain doll and something written on a piece of paper. I don't know if they're from the same time—and I didn't think to bring them."

I could see the disappointment and I avoided berating myself. But I had presumed he was only interested in the necklace.

"What was written on the papers?"

"Paper. Just one." It was important to correct him, even though I knew there were actually three pieces of paper. "As for what was written—well, I couldn't make it out. I'm not even sure what language it's in, to be honest."

"What's written could give us a connection to the necklace and Celestine. I can take a look, or if it's really difficult, I can fax it to my handwriting expert at the Smithsonian who could help."

"You have a handwriting expert?" I wrinkled my eyebrows at the oddness of this conversation.

"Someone I went to university with, yes. It's his passion. Yes, I know, weird."

I smiled and it was genuine.

"So you found them in an attic in Babbington's old house. In Ranklin, I presume?"

"Yes, he used to live in that house and . . . and so did I."

His eyes studied me above his glasses. "I see." His eyebrows lifted, his mouth pursed. "Do you know much about Babbington?"

"Not much. Only from the bit of info I got at Ranklin Library and what I read at your exhibition."

"As I said, that wasn't my exhibition. I just get asked to do talks on Africa when a museum does its annual 'something about Africa' exhibition."

It was as if we were both trying to distance ourselves from this man.

"Is he related to you?"

"Not that I'm aware of," I said.

"Good, because I've never liked the man or people like him." He stood up and pointed to the small, untidy bookshelf behind him. "I have stacks of books about people like him, and a lot more stored at my parents' house."

He sat back down. "I suppose in those days Babbington was seen as an upstanding citizen, and at that time he would have been. But judging by the pictures of Celestine, I think we can safely add 'child trafficker' to the list. What a guy."

"So you think he was taken against his will?"

"It's probably child trafficking in the modern sense, but if it walks like a duck . . ."

"What?"

"Never mind. Just a saying. Anyway, this type of thing was quite common in those days."

"I can't believe people did that." But of course I did. People were capable of anything.

"Have you heard of Sarah Forbes Bonetta Davies?"

I shook my head.

"She was a Nigerian girl given by a British captain as a gift to the *noble* Queen Victoria. They were all at it then and even further back, in Tudor times."

"To think, this happened . . . this actually happened, here . . ." I said, sounding and even feeling a little out of my depth.

"Where do you want to go from here, Lowra?"

"What do you mean?"

"A child was taken from somewhere in central Africa. Brought to England by Babbington to stay in a seaside town called Ranklin in the 1900s. That much we know for sure. You find a necklace that belonged to him. There's writing and an old doll. So where do you want to go from here?"

His questioning felt probing, and my mind was still on the bit about child trafficking and so-called companions.

"My guess is, that paper you found may hold the key to more than we could imagine. Celestine may even be the author."

"No way! That's . . ."

"Plausible."

I gazed toward the bookshelf behind him, full of large and probably dusty books on history I'd never been interested in. I started to see him again. Celestine.

"Didn't you say you felt as if Celestine's eyes were speaking to you?"

I was surprised I'd told him that much.

"Y-yes."

"Maybe he's speaking to you on that piece of paper."

I wasn't sure if Monty was just humoring me, telling me what he thought I needed to hear, because he was intrigued about this little boy but for different reasons and wanted to know more. Yet I'm not sure it mattered. He was my best shot at finding out more about Celestine, so I suppose in some ways, sticking with him meant I had a greater chance of doing just that.

"I have a good feeling about this," he continued.

"You do?"

"I can't wait to see what we find out at the house."

My breath caught in my throat, followed by a bunch of made-up reasons as to why I wouldn't be accompanying him back to that house. Something about having to catch up with work and that I'd be happy to give him the keys.

"I can't wait to see what *I* find out, then!" he said excitedly, his voice full of expectation and sparkle that felt a little infectious. I also felt a small rise of envy because whatever Monty was about to discover could also be part of *my* story. Wasn't I the one who'd hidden this "evidence" for fifteen years? Didn't I also need to see where this story led?

I needed to see this through with Monty, but in a way that wouldn't compromise my mental state. I had to, because for the first time in my life, I had a purpose.

I needed to know who Celestine was, what was on that piece of paper and how it all linked to the doll—or if it even did. Celestine was real, a human, a little boy who also once lived in the house where I grew up.

Perhaps seeking him would also mean being able to discover who I, Lowra Cavendish, truly was. That perhaps I was more than that eleven-year-old kid whose world had been torn apart; more than the fifteen-year-old runaway sitting at a bus stop with nowhere to turn; more than that twenty-five-year-old with the weight of her entire life experience crushing her shoulders, lying on the kitchen floor and unable to get up.

And, simply put, more than the thirty-year-old with a life of unanswered questions.

That house held so many secrets and a dark past I'd refused to face for so many years. Yet now a little boy I'd never met who was born in a different century was forcing me to do just that.

Chapter Twenty

Lowra
1974

Nothing made sense to me anymore. At the age of eleven, everything I knew and loved was gone, and my life could never be the same again.

Yet the house had never been fuller. Sometimes they arrived with dishes of homemade food and left empty-handed; other times they'd leave with the dish tucked under their arm and with the satisfied expression of having done something good. As if a plate of lasagne could ever make up for everything.

It was always after they left that she would start shouting about something. I zoned out mostly, or if I had my radio on, it was easier. Especially if ABBA came on. I loved ABBA.

"Your dad has left us with hardly anything, and I don't even know how I'm expected to clothe and feed you."

She said this every day and I was sick of hearing it. Nothing she said was ever of interest to me anyway—I only wanted to hear one thing from her and that was what had happened on that honeymoon. Why had she returned and not my dad?

Every time I looked at her, I felt a rage heat up inside me. I resented her space in the house, in the room and in this world. She should have gone missing, presumed dead, and not him.

"What happened to my dad?"

She looked at me with her eyebrows raised. "What?"

"Where's my dad? I want my dad!" My voice was louder than I had expected it to be, my fists clenched into a ball.

We both just stood there, squared up to one another. The top of my head was level with her chin.

Her eyes grew.

"What did you do to him?"

"I beg your pardon?"

"I said . . ." I began, as her hand reached the side of my face. I hadn't realized she was holding on to a clump of my hair until her strength began to move me toward the door and up the tall flight of stairs. I took one step at a time, careful for us to move in sync as I truly believed that any wrong move would mean losing my entire scalp.

We arrived at the first floor and outside my bedroom, where she held on tighter.

"Ow, ow, you're hurting me!" I screamed, not quite registering what was happening. Her breath was loud. The both of us were standing outside the room my dad had painted pink—just for me. The room I had long since grown out of, but still loved. The room where my dad had reeled off stories about princesses and dragons.

I assumed she'd leave me to go into my room where I could cry myself to sleep, like I did every night. But instead, with her hands still gripping my hair, she shoved me up the second flight of stairs and my anger grew into confusion.

"Where are we going?" I said. She may not have answered but her breathing was even louder now. For me, fear had yet to register, but when she used her foot to kick open the door of a room, it came.

She let go of my hair and we stood in front of the opened door.

"You think you are so special, don't you? With your stupid made-up name. Well, your dad isn't here anymore, I am. I'm the one keeping a roof over our heads, me!"

This was my dad's house, I wanted to say, but to make her angrier than this was a risk I no longer wished to take.

"Speak to me like that again, Lowra, make any unfounded accusations, and this is where naughty girls get to spend the night. Is this what you want?"

I shook my head, not wanting to give her the courtesy of my words.

She turned on her heel, mumbling something to herself as I stood in front of that door, tears streaming down my face and missing my dad more than ever before.

When I knew she was definitely gone, I switched on the light which was outside the room, watching the space illuminate faintly in front of me. It was an attic and a section of the house I had never ventured into.

Dust circulated around the lightbulb which hung from a sloped ceiling, and there were boxes in every corner, most of which probably contained my dad's stuff, maybe even my mother's. Old photos, perhaps. Memories.

I switched off the light, and quietly made my way back downstairs to my pink room.

1993

A level of excitement rose within me as I opened my eyes to a new morning, along with just a sprinkling of anxiety.

Traveling into Ranklin with Monty made the experience a little different, less tense, yet as soon as I set foot outside the station I felt a chill, even though the sun was beating down on us.

As agreed with Monty, I was to wait in the Flamingo Club cafe as he ventured up to the house alone, with the keys Mr. Danvers had sent me in the post.

I wasn't about to go back to that house anytime soon.

As I waited for my tea, I pulled out my purse. Inside the plastic compartment was the item I cherished most in this world—a picture of my mother and father standing side by side with me held up by both of them in the center, each of my arms around their shoulders. My smile was almost as wide as my face. I must have been either five or six years old, and this could have been the last photo we ever took together. Thanks to the mysterious disappearance of all our photo albums in the months after his death, this photo was the only evidence that I was once part of a real and loving family.

I was halfway through my tea when Monty walked back in, his long legs dressed in straight-cut jeans, the sides of his corduroy jacket flapping. Already so much taller than me, his height looked exaggerated as he stood over me.

"That was quick," I said.

He sighed loudly, placing his face into his palms.

"What is it? Did you find anything?"

"I didn't actually get a chance, because there was a knock at the door."

"From who?"

"I didn't ask his name but he wore a uniform."

"A police officer?"

"Correct."

"Why was he there?"

"A neighbor reported me apparently, and he wanted to know who I was and what my business was there. I showed him my card and told him the owner of the house had given me the keys—hence no break-in—but he wasn't listening to any of it."

"Why would the neighbors call? They know that house is up for sale, so people are going to be in and out!"

My mind wandered to when I had been in that house alone, scared . . . where had these neighbors been then?

"It's obvious why they called the police," he said, pulling me from my memories.

"Why?"

His eyelids closed. “Never mind.”

“Monty, what is it?”

“I just don’t have it in me today. Let’s move on.”

His statement sounded a bit dramatic, and it was easier to just do as he suggested and move on. But I didn’t want to.

“Monty . . .”

“Nice house, though. Impressive.”

“You’re changing the subject.”

“I know. So, anyway.” He cleared his throat. “We need to go back to the house together.”

“We?”

“I’m not going back alone after what just happened.”

He exhaled again, this time with exasperation.

“I don’t want to go back there,” I said.

“Why? I mean, when you said you didn’t want to come with me earlier, I thought it was weird, but now you literally *have* to come and you’re still saying no.”

I cleared my throat, buying some time. “What I mean is, we can’t go back without a plan.”

“What do you have in mind, then?”

“We keep it simple. We can ask around . . . I mean, Richard Babbington is famous so it won’t be hard. Let’s at least gather some facts first so we know what to look for when we do go back to that house.”

He nodded slowly. My quickly thought up explanation was working.

“That’s actually a good idea.”

I exhaled.

“Let’s start with you, Lowra.”

I caught my breath. “Me?”

“You grew up in that house, surely there’s things you know.” He pulled a polka-dot notebook from his jeans pocket, and the colors and shapes reminded me of one of my grandma’s dresses.

"I wouldn't have pictured you with polka dots," I said.

"I'm full of surprises, me. This will help us keep track of what we find out."

I swallowed. "There isn't much I can add to what I told you before. My father and mother lived at the house with me . . . until she died when I was six. Then he got married again, to her . . . to N-Nina"—her name felt like poison on my tongue—"when I was eleven and he . . . he died the same year, on their honeymoon, and then I left home at fifteen."

His eyes told me he knew there were parts of the story I was leaving out, but he didn't press me. He felt it; he knew I wasn't prepared to tell him all of it. That some parts, most parts, were just for me.

"And the items—you came across them one day when you were playing in the attic?"

"That's right. I always used the attic for hide and seek. It's a good spot," I said.

The roads had become slightly busier than when we'd first arrived, but Ranklin would never resemble a busy seaside town many wanted to visit. It was pretty enough with its dark sandy pebbled beach and large Victorian houses, but I truly believed those waves spoke a story of endless pain which then transferred into the atmosphere and kept people away. Or maybe the place itself was fine and it was simply that house. That evil house at 109 Ranklin Road was the real problem.

A gust of sea air hit me as I stepped onto a crack in the pavement. By suggesting a visit to the Ranklin tourist information center, I had basically been delaying the inevitable.

Going into that house.

I think Monty must have realized this but didn't say anything, simply keeping pace beside me as we headed into the town center, seagulls screeching above us.

"There it is," I said, moments later, pointing to a large statue across the road. "The statue the woman at the tourist information center was talking about."

"The woman who kept gushing about how wonderful this town is, and how brave and gallant Babbington was? Yeah, I switched off after that bit."

"It's probably worth a look. Maybe there's something in the inscription. A clue?"

"Go ahead. I'll wait here and converse with the seagulls."

I turned to him. "What's wrong?"

The expression in his face had tensed. His lips pursed together and his eyes narrowed. "I'll find a bench that doesn't have seagull poo on it and I'll wait."

I shook my head slowly and headed across the road. If I was able to set foot in this awful town after everything, surely he could look at a dumb statue.

I stood in front of the tall sculpture, supposedly a likeness of the man in the photograph. His face appeared wider, the moustache almost covering his entire top lip. The ridiculously long boots and hat did look similar to those in the photograph, though. His arm was minus the gun, but he stood in a pose that suggested anyone looking up at him was beneath him—and more than just in their physical location.

I turned back to look at Monty, who appeared preoccupied with the map he'd picked up at the tourist center.

I stared at the plinth again.

Sir Richard Babbington
Great Explorer of Africa 1857–1907

This memorial was erected by the town of Ranklin in recognition of the great services rendered by Sir Richard Babbington to his country and to Africa.

My stomach swished about uncomfortably as I read each word out loud, without realizing that Monty was standing beside me.

"Services to his country and to Africa," he said, without hiding the disdain in his voice.

I slowly shook my head. "I know!"

"It's fucking insulting. Come on, let's go," he said, already heading off in the other direction.

I ran after him like a child trying to keep up with its mother. "Hey, wait up."

"I didn't want to see that stupid thing anyway and now it's just riled me up." He stopped and turned to me. "It was bad enough studying at Oxford and seeing those types of statues everywhere—of men I knew had done the most atrocious things to African people. The likes of Cecil Rhodes staring back at me as I ate a sandwich. Everyone else just rushing past as if it meant nothing. But it did. It meant so much, and I just don't understand why no one gets it."

"Monty . . ."

"Come on, let's keep going. The sooner we get what we came for, the quicker we can get out of this town."

I had wanted to say something, that I understood. Yet somehow the words didn't feel like they would be enough. So I said nothing.

When we arrived at the local bookshop, it looked nothing like the ones which had recently sprung up in London, where you could buy coffee and cakes while soft music hummed in the background. This was a little antiquated, with films of dust taking pride of place on the shelves.

"May I help you?" said the older man behind the counter. Even the till appeared to be vintage, like something from the Victorian era.

"Yes, I hope so. We're looking for anything you have written about Richard Babbington, Ranklin's most famous resident!" said Monty with the widest of smiles.

"Of course—we have many copies of his work too."

"Why wouldn't you? He was a local hero. And has a statue too!"

"Impressive, isn't it?"

"That's one word for it."

"There are quite a few books on him. Not all of them very good, but I can recommend a few."

"Sure, but I was also hoping a man like you would know more than the books."

"I know enough, I suppose."

"The house at the end of Ranklin Road, number 109."

I swallowed upon hearing the address. I could feel myself shrinking away from this conversation.

"Yes, the biggest house, number 109. He was a bit of a drinker by all accounts, and with an eye for the ladies, apparently. But you didn't hear that from me."

Monty's smile was even wider.

"I only moved here within the last ten years, but there are many who've had the pleasure of living in Ranklin their entire lives. I can give you the names of a couple, if you like."

As if suddenly released from some kind of Richard Babbington appreciation trance, the man appraised Monty, his eyes moving up and down. "Who did you say you were?"

"A historian. Here's my card." Monty placed the beige card on the counter.

"Lovely," he said absently, as if trying to reconcile who was in front of him with the name and occupation printed on the card. The energy in the room had changed, from Monty's false joviality to this stillness I didn't understand.

The shopkeeper pointed out the Richard Babbington books that lined the shelf, before moving on to serve a customer who had just appeared.

"You don't have to buy them out of guilt, Lowra. I think we know all we need to about people like Richard Babbington."

"You probably think you know, but it's best to hear it from the horse's mouth. Besides, I was thinking about buying these after Jean at the library showed them to me. They may have some clues about Celestine."

"Sir Richard Babbington published two books in his lifetime: *The Princely Joy* and *The Trek to Africa*," said the shopkeeper, inserting himself back into our conversation.

He placed both books in my hands, updated editions of those in the library. These editions displayed on the covers photographs of a tall and proud Sir Richard Babbington.

"Do you know anything about Celestine . . . the little boy who lived with him?"

"I do not." He shook his head for added conviction. "But you may like to speak to Matilda Ainsworth."

"Who is she?"

"Only one of Ranklin's oldest citizens."

"This town really is weird," whispered Monty.

"She also has links to Sir Richard Babbington. Distant relative, I think. Or at least, every time there's a feature written on him, she always claims to be! Wows everyone at the nursing home where she lives. It's not that far up the road, faces the sea. Winter Pines, it's called."

The words felt like spikes across my skin.

My grandma, who used to sing along with me to my favorite film, The Sound of Music, *now just looked past me whenever I saw her, sometimes staring at the wall, her mouth drooping, white hair like a melting snowball on her head.*

"What's the point?" she'd say. "First my husband and now my son? What's the point in anything anymore?"

My grandpa had died many years before but my dad was only missing. Only presumed dead. That wasn't final. There was no proof he had died.

Only the say-so of one person, who was also the last person to see him alive. Her.

Yet, like everyone else, Grandma had given up on him, and at the same time me and herself.

After my grandma moved into Winter Pines nursing home, I saw her once and then never again.

The shopkeeper placed my purchases into a paper bag.

"She'd have to be rather old to have even met Babbington," said Monty.

"She was a child. I don't know much of the story, but she can tell you more. Some call her a bit of a busybody, but she's probably just a historian like you!"

Had Matilda Ainsworth been around when I needed help? I couldn't help but wonder.

"We can't just walk into the nursing home, can we?" I said.

"It's worth a try," said the shopkeeper. "Will you both be going?" He attempted to look at Monty, who was in the process of heading to the door without so much as a goodbye to the man who had been incredibly helpful.

"If we do go, it will be Monty asking the questions and not me. He's the historian, after all."

"Probably better if you ask the questions, miss. You know what older people are like."

Monty held on to the shop door after it pinged and just stood there. I wasn't sure what was going on.

"Thank you so much for your help," I said as I followed Monty out of the shop.

We continued in the direction of the nursing home, with Monty rushing ahead. "Wait up! It's like you're trying to lose me or something. What's got into you?"

He stopped. "Can you just leave it?"

"Did I say something, Monty?"

"No."

"The shop guy, then? He was a bit odd, but then everyone in this town is. It's a bit creepy how they all seem to love this Richard Babbington."

He rolled his eyes. "Just forget it, you wouldn't understand."

"Understand what?"

He exhaled. The both of us were probably tired.

"Shall we stop for a bit . . . Regroup, I don't know . . . ?" I suggested.

"Perhaps you're right. Let's hold off on this Matilda Ainsworth until we have more information and questions to ask her. I don't want it to be a wasted journey."

"Exactly. Let's just settle down, have something to eat . . . Let's just stop for a moment."

The Flamingo Club cafe was the place to regroup. Surprisingly their paninis were better than the ones in London, and Monty was easily pleased with his cheese and pickle sandwich.

Everything felt calm again as we headed to our next stop—the local church. It was a beautifully tall Victorian building with colorful stained-glass windows. Stacks of pink and red roses bloomed in large terra-cotta pots at the end of the pathway.

The images came at me without warning.

The rows filled with people, some I had met, others never before. The church, full of flowers with no smell. The sound of her fake tears in the middle of the pew.

No casket. No body. A memorial service, not a funeral.

"You OK there?" said Monty.

"Of course," I said, leading the way to Reverend Townsend, who greeted us warmly and introduced us to his wife, the parish secretary.

"Thank you for meeting with us at such short notice," said Monty.

"Not at all," said Reverend Townsend. "I will leave you in the very capable hands of my wife."

Mrs. Townsend led us into the vestry, where we sat at a table with a very modern-looking typewriter and a records book, open and displaying yellowing pages and distinctive cursive writing.

"This is very precious, so please be careful." She spoke in an Irish accent.

Monty pulled out his own special gloves before turning the pages of the book. Rows of names and dates filled each page.

"Every marriage, christening and funeral is inscribed in the parish records. No doubt you should find what you are looking for inside."

It wasn't long until we spotted a familiar name. "The marriage of Richard Babbington and Eloise Ridley. Married in 1887," I said. Looking at their birth dates, he'd been thirty and his wife sixteen years old. Yuck.

"You must have come across a lot of information on Richard Babbington," said Mrs. Townsend.

"Yes, but not the real stuff, just the admiration," said Monty.

"Only half the story, I suppose. The comfortable part," said Mrs. Townsend.

"In my work, it's always been clear to me that history is on the side of the powerful and not the weak."

"Indeed," Mrs. Townsend agreed. "When you told us about the boy, Celestine, I was appalled yet not surprised."

Monty ran his finger over the 1907 log, the year of the photograph in the exhibition, and still nothing stood out.

"What now, then?" I said.

"We continue. There's something here, I just know it."

Reverend Townsend reappeared.

"We know Celestine lived here because there is photographic evidence, but there is nothing official," said Monty.

"May I interject?" said Reverend Townsend.

"Of course, please," said Monty.

"If he was"—he cleared his throat—"bought, there might be a record of purchase or something like that."

"Purchase?" I said.

"I thought of that, Reverend Townsend, but from what we know, he was possibly brought back from one of Babbington's expeditions somewhere in central Africa and more than likely the Congo, now known as Zaire. We know this because of the necklace. There might not be any paperwork of a transaction in existence."

I suddenly felt invisible.

"What he and people like him did was immoral," said Reverend Townsend. His wife nodded.

"It's refreshing to hear you say so. Everyone around here seems to think he's wonderful," said Monty.

"You can take us both off that list," Mrs. Townsend said vehemently.

Two hours later we still hadn't uncovered much.

"Tomorrow's another day. We still have a possible lead with this Matilda Ainsworth at the nursing home, and we've yet to go back to 109 Ranklin Road."

I held my breath.

"We'll have to do that another day," said Monty.

I wasn't sure how manymore times I could make the trip into Ranklin, what with work and what it cost me to take time off . . . or the emotional expense.

Dr. Raj would have told me not to think about the future if it involved fear. To take each day as it came. And that was exactly what I intended to do.

Chapter Twenty-One

Celestine

1907

Perhaps from an outside perspective, people would see me as harboring some type of acceptance of my situation.

At the age of twelve, I had everything any living, breathing human being would desire by way of shelter, clothing, books, and even little trinkets like the golden cuff links and shoes apparently all the way from Paris! Whatever I desired to eat, whether it be a roast chicken or one of Mrs. Cuthbert's pear tarts, was available on demand. These trappings I appreciated, did not take for granted, though they never held my attention for more than a moment.

"Open it then!" he insisted. Another gift. Another oblong box.

"This is for me, Sir Richard?"

"Who else, dear boy?"

I slid open the top of the box; a slim and shiny black pen rested regally inside. I felt a stirring of excitement. This was useful, this I could use.

"Do you like it?"

I placed the box to one side and twirled the pen between my fingers.

"That is a Parker and it's quite the new thing. It contains an eyedropper and, as you can see, a gold nib."

I wasn't sure of the usefulness of a gold nib, but the way it shone against the black was breathtaking. I knew then that I would use this pen with pride.

"It's called a Black Giant. I find that very apt, don't you?" The guffaws which followed I did not understand. My mind was already fixated on what I would do with this beautiful item. I couldn't wait to show it to Mr. Lattery as it was sure to make him smile, even though nothing really did.

"There is an ulterior motive for gifting the pen, Celestine."

I tore my gaze away from it.

"It's symbolic really, because . . . drum roll, please!"

I stared at him blankly. This white man had clearly been sipping his whisky once again.

"You are going to school, Celestine!"

I opened my mouth to speak but allowed it to morph into a hesitant smile instead. "That is wonderful, Sir Richard."

My mind as well as my emotions were conflicted. It had been a wish, a dream of mine, to attend the halls of education and to put all I had learned with Mr. Lattery to good use. Yet any feeing of extreme happiness always felt overshadowed by things from the not too distant past.

"You will be attending my old school, but not as a boarder. You will come home every day, back to the house from Ranklin's finest! How does that sound?"

"It sounds wonderful!" I said.

"That school has made me who I am."

What, a man who many times smells purely of alcohol and old sweat because he has forgotten to bathe after a particularly raucous night?

I kept these thoughts to myself, allowing myself to bask in this good news. This very good news.

By the time my final lesson with Mr. Lattery arrived, the enormity of how my life was about to change yet again finally hit me.

"Over the last year you have exceeded my expectations and

should be able to catch up rather quickly with what is being taught. No doubt Sir Richard will have explained your exceptional circumstances and you will be in a class of younger students, of which you will undoubtedly be the brightest among them. Indeed, even with your own peers, you would still be so."

"So why am I being placed with younger students?" I said.

For the very first time, Mr. Lattery appeared stumped by my questioning.

"Indeed, I do not have a clear answer for that, so I will not attempt it."

"Will I see you again, Mr. Lattery?" I asked as he packed up the last of the books.

"I begin a new post on Monday, but Celestine, you no longer need me. You have everything you require and more. Study hard, make good use of the English dictionary, ensure you are not distracted, and I do not see why you will not succeed academically. Good day to you," he said with a tip of his hat. Indeed, Mr. Lattery had left me with a wealth of knowledge I had devoured gratefully. Yet I was still unsure of how this would translate outside the big house. Education had been an outlet to express myself and think less about home, and more about the here and now. Yet now my tutor was gone, it felt like just another loss, even though this man had only ever parted with his knowledge and not much else.

The morning I was to attend a school in England for the very first time, Enid had left a freshly pressed uniform on the edge of the chair in my room. She assumed I was sleeping, but I had watched. First as she stood and stared at my surroundings, peered at herself in the mirror, and then carefully placed the uniform on the chair. She wasn't to know I no longer experienced a good night's sleep. That every hour my eyes remained wide open, and I would sometimes use the lavatory three or four times in a night. She also wasn't to know I sometimes heard her giggling, along with the deep groans of a familiar voice as I walked by Sir Richard's study late at night.

I held the short trousers up against me, as well as the matching gray blazer and socks. Almost everything in this country needed to be gray, it seemed, just like the sky. The shirt was at least white, with its stiffened rounded collars and a waistcoat to wear under the jacket. The little cap was something which amused me until I realized I'd have to wear it. I admired the exquisiteness of my new shoes, which were made from sealskin and insulated for both hot and cold weather.

It was very seldom that I left the comfort of this home, and when I did, it was generally with Sir Richard by my side and inside the motor vehicle.

"Come on, dear boy! We must not be late for your first day," boomed Sir Richard. He'd had company last night, which I suspected was a lady—perhaps Enid or even Daphne, who had been here for numerous "private dinners" without a companion. Sir Richard seemed happier and less reliant on what hid at the bottom of a whisky bottle after a night with either of them. When intoxicated, though, he appeared more wanting of my company and my attention, which at times felt uncomfortable, especially when he wished to talk about subjects perhaps best discussed with someone of his own age group. I did not know why ladies were so hard to please. I did not know why his father never respected him. I was only twelve years old!

I sat beside him in the motor vehicle, surprised at how accustomed I had become to this contraption. We passed the row of houses on our road, the sea behind us, before venturing into parts of the town I had never been to before. Unknown streets and houses, people walking in different directions, gazing straight ahead; not like London, but more than what I was used to in my day-to-day life.

We drove up a private gravel road which led to the grandest building I had ever seen. Unlike the Sapphire Hotel in London, the Ranklin School for Boys stood alone in vast green grounds and looked even more magnificent in its own right. I counted eighteen large windows just at the front, surrounding a mammoth-sized door which I feared would eat me up if I dared to get close.

"This, my dear boy, is the establishment where I received the best education money could buy. My hope is that it will provide nothing less for you!"

"Sir Richard, I would like to say something first."

"As long as it's quick, we must not be late. Principal Gallagher is a stickler for punctuality."

We stood beside the motor vehicle facing one another, both smartly dressed and prepared. Mr. Lattery's rare words of encouragement echoed in my head. To not be distracted was the key here, if I were to achieve any of what he believed I could academically.

So, standing outside the Ranklin School for Boys, I knew this was what I wanted, and constantly thinking of my family was a distraction with the power to thwart this part of my destiny.

It would be in my best interests to believe what Sir Richard had said: that I had no family left and that he, England and the big house were all I really had. Therefore, it would be necessary to quieten my anger and instead reach deep into myself and force into my mouth the two words this man deserved, for all he was doing for me.

"Thank . . . you." The words appeared with more difficulty than I had hoped.

"Oh, dear boy, this is just a small taste of what is to come for you. Shall we?" he said, leading the way for me to walk in front of him, up those mighty stairs and into the giant mouth of those doors.

The principal's office was filled with an abundance of books I wished to open, devour and eventually cherish. This man was clearly very learned and I hoped to be like that one day. And even wiser than my father, for my source of knowledge was to be from more than the natural world around me.

I surprised even myself with such treacherous thinking.

"Sir Richard tells me you are from the shores of Africa," said the principal, Mr. Gallagher. He used his index finger to push up his glasses.

"Yes, sir."

"Are you well versed on our ways here?"

"Celestine has been here for some time now and exceeded all expectations with the three Rs. He is also very knowledgeable on how things are done in England—even more so than I, if I am honest. He is very well read, and contrary to what you said regarding his placement here, he will do exceptionally in a class of his own age group."

"I do not think this is a good idea, Sir Richard. Studies show that the brain of the African is far inferior to—"

"I beg your pardon!" said Sir Richard as he stood up. I had never witnessed such anger from him.

"Sir Richard . . ."

"You may have forgotten how much I and my family before me have donated to this school."

Mr. Gallagher's face turned a bright crimson as he cleared his throat. "Indeed," he said. There followed a dead silence before Mr. Gallagher smiled. "You will be pleased to know we almost had another boy from your part of the world enroll here, but alas we lost him to Harrow."

"Why would that be of any concern to us?" said Sir Richard.

"I'm just saying . . ."

It occurred to me that Mr. Gallagher was desperately trying to salvage this situation, which, if I am honest, felt a little confusing to me.

"Well, Celestine is his own man and a joy to behold. The school will be fortunate to be in his company." Sir Richard was back to his usual self, and I watched as the two men conversed about me as if I were not in the room.

"The children in his class are currently engaged in physical exercise. We offer a range of sport, including cricket and tennis."

I had only heard of these activities through Sir Richard and reading about them in books.

Outside, we watched as a group of boys dressed in what looked like white undergarments jogged around an open field.

Around fifteen boys turned to look at me. Not Sir Richard or Mr. Gallagher, but me. In turn I looked back, but perhaps not for the same reason. My eyes searched each one of the boys, who appeared identical to one another, the bright sun lightening strands of their straight hair. Pink, thin lips moved up and down as they whispered among one another. As we got closer, I realized they were not in fact identical, yet no less frightening. I had once been used to being among a throng of loud and rowdy men on the steamer, but to be among boys of my own age and in such a formal setting was yet another unfamiliar experience.

"This here will be your new classmate. His name is Celestine."

They were all silent in response but their eyes spoke for them. While I couldn't decipher what their words would have been, I could tell that each and every one of them was full of curiosity.

"Let's not disturb them any further," said Mr. Gallagher, as we headed back to his office. The tour had been an enjoyable one and I hoped to make "many friends," as Sir Richard had put it. Back home, my brothers and mama had been my only friends, having never been allowed to venture into the neighboring homes or villages. My attempt at friendship with the bread boy Bill had ended in disaster.

I turned around to catch at least six of the boys pointing and whispering, and I was unable to think of a reason for this. It was so rude and very ungentlemanly.

"Celestine, don't get left behind now!" called Sir Richard.

I ran to catch up with the men, and the three of us headed back to the office.

Sir Richard signed some papers and a princely sum for my school fees was mentioned. Having never had to handle any money since my arrival, it was clear that what was being paid for my education was costly. Again, I felt confused; everything that had occurred over the course of the last year hadn't made much sense to me and raised more questions than answers. Such as, why had Sir Richard referred to me as an orphan? No one knew for sure where my mother and brothers were. A gentleman was not supposed to lie, was he? Yet such untruths had rolled from Sir Richard's mouth ever since he had stepped off a ship and into my world, it seemed. I tried to ignore the questions circling in my head and instead to focus on the fact I would soon be going to school.

And this I was looking forward to with much excitement!

My eyes took in the rows of boys sitting at wooden desks.

At the front of the room was a high desk containing a bell, and behind that, a chair facing an audience whose eyes at that moment all appeared to be fixed on me.

I followed the instructions set by the teacher, Mr. Prentice, himself dressed in a black robe and hat, to sit at an empty desk on the front row, and in doing so, the boy next to me shifted in his seat. The atmosphere felt somewhat similar to Sir Richard's fund-raiser, yet unlike then, none of the boys had actually said a word.

"It is customary for a new boy to introduce himself," explained Mr. Prentice, and in my haste I stood up and banged my thigh against the edge of the desk. The boy who sat beside me sniggered.

"Start with your name."

I thought for a moment, feeling the weight of expectation from my classmates and Mr. Prentice.

"Speak up, boy!"

"My . . . my name is Dikem . . ."

"What?"

"My name . . . sir, is . . ."

"Speak up!"

"Celestine . . . sir." I swallowed and looked around at the expectant faces of the boys I'd met for the first time that day. I closed my eyes quickly and then opened them again. This was not the moment I had imagined it to be.

"My . . . my name is Celestine."

"Celestine what?"

I looked toward him, as if I didn't understand his English. I did, of course.

"I asked you for your surname."

I could hear and feel the collection of sniggers. When I closed my eyes again, I could see my father. "My name is Celestine . . ."

Mr. Prentice moved closer to me, his eyes narrowed. "According to signed documents which secured your enrollment with us, your name is Celestine Babbington, or am I mistaken?"

"No, sir," I said, my gaze reaching to the floor.

"Look at me when I speak to you!" he roared, and the entire classroom of boys fell silent.

I felt exposed, naked even.

"Your name"—I could feel his breath on my nose—"is Celestine Babbington," he said.

I nodded my head without sincerity.

"*Say it!*"

"I am Celestine Babbington and . . . and I am from Africa."

"Incorrect. Your life is here now and you must reflect this in your opening statement. Begin again."

I swallowed. "My name . . . my name is, is Celestine Babbington and I am from . . . I am from this great land that is Britain."

Mr. Prentice stood back and nodded approvingly. "But of course you are. It doesn't matter where you may have started, this is where you now live, and it is a land that has given you many opportunities, one of which is attending one of the best schools in the country. You may be seated."

The couple of guffaws I heard behind me did not faze me as much as what I had just been complicit in. To deny my entire existence up to my current age. To deny my own father, my family, my country—and to realize just how easy it was becoming to do so.

I felt a stretch of nausea in my stomach.

Thankfully the attention of the entire class fell to the blackboard as Mr. Prentice formed letters and symbols with a piece of white chalk. His sleeves appeared too big, flapping aggressively as he wrote. I could decipher most of the words quite easily thanks to Mr. Lattery's intense teaching methods.

I assumed it was the end of the lesson when Mr. Prentice pointed toward me. "I would like to invite our newest student to clean the board."

I looked behind me, and then back at the board.

"Celestine?" he said. The boy beside me began to quietly chuckle under his breath, as did others.

I stood up slowly and made my way to the front. Having never once touched a board before, my intelligence told me what to do. And as I glided the duster over the board, a cloud of white chalk engulfed my nostrils. A spark of panic hit me as did puffs of thick dust, causing me to cough relentlessly as the class began to come alive with muffled laughter. I placed my hands on my knees and doubled over, my body reacting heavily to each cough. The laughter in the room increased even after Mr. Prentice chastised the boys as he patted me on my back, which just made me cough all the more.

"Go and get him some water!" he ordered finally. By the time one of my classmates returned with a cup, the coughs had subsided, as had my pride.

Apart from Mr. Prentice, no one spoke to me during that first day.

On the second day of school, a boy named Alfred walked over to me. Alfred had the air of someone who did not feel comfortable, always fidgeting.

"I am glad you are here. We can be good friends," he announced. I decided that this declaration of intent, even though I would have liked some consultation first, was better than none at all. He went on to ask if I had enjoyed my time at school so far, and I assured him I had. Alfred behaved as if he needed constant reassuring. Paler than the others and very thin, he lacked the confidence that the other boys seemed surrounded by.

I placed my pencil case in my desk, delighted to discover it also opened up into a space in which to house a host of my belongings. A mere desk to some, it gave me the sense I belonged there, even if everyone's silence was designed to make me feel as if that were a lie.

On my third day, Alfred asked if I'd like to sit with him at lunch. We sat mostly in silence, only bonding when the subject of trains came up. A couple of the boys swanned over to ask questions: about where I was from and what I was doing in England. The way they approached me was different from Bill and his friends. Indeed, they were dressed better, their faces not smeared with dirt, and they spoke with an eloquence I had only heard from the mouths of Sir Richard and his acquaintances. One of the boys, Sam, couldn't get the words out of his mouth quick enough: "I met a colored boy once. The son of a rich African man my father conducted business with." Another boy, Martin, said he had seen one while out fishing with his father.

To a lot of these boys I was an object of curiosity, and at first I enjoyed the attention.

"So where are you from?" one asked.

I felt a waft of heat rise within my body. After betraying my father by embracing my new name and thinking of his experiences as inferior to my current one . . . I had no interest in taking myself back to that part of my life. Because to do so would become a burden . . . of guilt. Also, as Sir Richard and now Mr. Prentice had said, it was better to forget it all. Britain was my home now.

"I am from here, the same as you."

"No, I mean, where are you *really* from?"

"Come on, shall we go?" said Alfred, which I resented.

"Where in Africa?"

My mind was a muddle of words and images: my mama, my brothers, the tree, Sir Richard, Mrs. Cuthbert, Bill . . . Perhaps it was simpler, easier, to just refer to my former life as a string of words and sentences, in the way Sir Richard had spoken on many occasions. A description of the land I grew up in from the mouth of an explorer: the Congo with its vast rainforests and endless rivers. A beauty that could not be replicated anywhere on this earth. Of all the countries from that great continent, none could hold a candle to the majestic Congo. None.

"I once lived in the Congo," I said.

"Where is that?"

I recalled the map I had found stuffed between two books on Sir Richard's bookshelf, entitled COMMERCIAL MAP OF AFRICA, which was quite unlike the one that took pride of place on the classroom wall. It had confused me at first, with words like "rubber," "copper" and "palm oil" written on a number of the countries. I'd assumed these to be the names of countries before making the real connection through a conversation with Mr. Lattery.

"It is next to German East Africa, and on the other side of Kamerun," I explained to this audience of a few.

"Don't forget British East Africa!" said one. "Part of that lot is ours too!"

It was perhaps that comment which struck me the most, and then floated around a group of school boys who all felt and saw things in the same way. All except one.

Even Alfred could never be on the side I occupied. Not even if he tried his very best to be.

None of these boys would ever be my true friends.

Back at the big house I unfurled the map again. At first it had served as a way of trying to find a route back home, but now it just poured salt into wounds I had never known existed. Because looking at this map, or even the one in the classroom, simply reminded me I had no idea of where to begin. What was the Congo? And if Sir Richard had been telling the truth, which part of the Congo had I been living in? Indeed, I had no idea where *I* had begun, and a wave of humiliation came over me at this lack of knowledge. Just as it had at school.

I had reached the end of my first week at the Ranklin School for Boys.

"I was under no illusions that you wouldn't enjoy it there," said Sir Richard grandly. "And you have already made a friend!"

I couldn't tell Sir Richard that for both Alfred and myself, we were friends out of necessity rather than choice.

"Oh, dear boy, I relished every moment of my time there, but of course I was a boarder," he said, pouring two glasses of whisky. "I believe my father thought it would be good for me. Perhaps it would be good for you too, but I do prefer to have you close to me. You prefer that too, don't you, Celestine?"

The expression on his face was full of concentration so it felt polite to just say yes.

"I'm glad you think so too," he said, handing me the second glass. "Go on, take a sip. You've earned it, dear boy."

A small amount of liquid touched my lips and it burned.

"Keep going then!"

I shook my head quickly.

"Never fear, leave that. I had the new bread boy purchase this sweet concoction." He leaned behind his chair and pulled out an oblong bottle with red liquid inside it. "You might be partial to this ghastly drink instead. Cherry ciderette they call it, and Enid has assured me that those with a softer constitution are partial to it."

Relieved that Sir Richard was still in his right mind, I wanted to keep it that way. "Will you try this softer drink with me, sir?"

"Now, why would I want to drink a liquid with the potency of cat's urine?"

"To celebrate my first week, sir."

He grudgingly poured himself a glass and as the red liquid rested in my mouth, I judged it to be the best drink I had ever tasted.

Sir Richard soon tired of the cherry ciderette and moved on to his usual tipple. We managed to discuss everything I could think of to do with the Ranklin School for Boys until I began to notice the inevitable change in his words, his demeanor and then the subject matter.

"Alas, she claimed I could not satisfy her!" he said, his head cocked to the side.

"I see, sir," I said, shifting in my seat. "Do you mean . . . Lady Eloise?" Although it had taken everything to say the name, it produced no change in his expression or tone of voice.

"Whatever I bought her was never enough. Even if I had produced all the jewels in the world or the entire Paul Poiret fashion collection, nothing would have been enough! They are so difficult to decipher."

I stifled a false yawn, believing it better to just agree with him and then excuse myself.

I stood up to leave, but his hand was quick, grabbing my arm. "Please, stay a little longer. To talk." He stared at me with an intensity I didn't understand and I was desperate to pull myself away from him, yet afraid to do so in case he interpreted this as disrespect.

His expression softened. "You won't leave me, will you, Celestine?"

"No, sir," I said, shaking my head slowly.

"I don't think I could bear that," he said, taking another sip of his drink.

"Yes, sir."

"I will make amends, you know."

"Amends, sir?"

"While there is breath in my body, you will want for nothing. Also, when I leave this earth you will be looked after. You will remain in the class you have become accustomed to. That I promise you, dear boy."

"Yes, sir. Thank you."

"You don't understand . . . I had to do something, anything to atone . . ." He waved his hands as if to shoo away the words.

"Atone for what?" I asked. Yet my sudden burst of interest was lost as he closed his eyes and slumped back further into the chair. His snores arrived within seconds.

I left for my room and must have fallen into a quick sleep, unsure of how long it was before I felt a presence in the room.

My eyes sprang open.

"Celestine, it is only me," said Sir Richard in a whisper.

"What is it, sir?"

"I know, I know," he said, his disembodied voice sounding even more slurred. "I need to make sure that you will never leave me. Everyone else has in the past. The life mapped out for me seems to be all but disintegrating around me. I thought I was helping but I was duped, Celestine, duped by that odious king, all of them. They were all out for themselves. Not me, though. You see, I had the kindest of intentions. Only the kindest. You do believe me?" He was beside my bed, along with the smell of stale whisky.

I sat up. "It may be best for you to go to bed, Sir Richard. May we talk about this when we have both had a good night's sleep?"

"I need you to believe me. I have a pure heart. I only want to do good. That's all I have ever, ever wanted to do." His voice was still a whisper and this felt somewhat unnerving to me. "I need you to believe I have the purest of intentions."

"I believe you," I said, not knowing what I was agreeing to but yearning for him to be as far away from my room as possible.

He did not say a word and my mind wandered to the possibility of him strangling me in my bed. The sober Sir Richard would never do such a thing, of course, but this one had been consuming from the whisky bottle for hours now.

Finally, reassuring footsteps led away and the door closed. I exhaled, yet did not sleep for the remainder of the night.

Chapter Twenty-Two

Lowra

1993

Monty had been busy. This I realized as we sat in a nondescript cafe about a mile from my home; I wasn't ready to invite him into my flat just yet.

"Looks like you got a lot done without me," I said, as he placed his brown case on the table and pulled out the polka-dot notebook.

"I put out a call to a few curators and directors of estates, including the one at Rinchester, and, well . . . someone got back to me yesterday. I'll tell you about that first."

"I had wondered how Richard Babbington's items ended up there."

"Oh, you'd be surprised how many things end up on display at estates they have no connection with. People just want to pay to see Victorian and Edwardian artifacts, and it doesn't seem to matter where they view them or how they got there."

"But that's theft, isn't it?"

"Isn't that how all artifacts are acquired? Did you think the statues from Ife you saw at the museum were given with love?"

"So what did you find out from your friend?" I said, wanting to get back to the point.

"I wouldn't say he was a friend. Anyway, they do have some diaries left by Babbington."

"Personal diaries?"

Monty continued. "Yes, and I told him to photocopy and fax what he could from around 1907. Because of the delicate condition of the book, he could only copy a few pages, but what he sent . . . well, it's enough." Monty placed the photocopies onto the table beside his briefcase. Lines were highlighted in fluorescent pen.

The young swarthy being with unkempt clothing is an object of desire I despise in myself.

This is wrong. I know this. Yet my flesh sings whenever one *appears before me. They are unknowing and unwilling and yet I am aware.*

The silence between us was loud. My mind was racing.

To think of such desires for someone of a darker hue and tender years is unthinkable. Besides, that is not what I am here for—and yet I am powerless.

"We don't know it's Celestine he was talking about," I said.

His eyebrows shot up.

"He made lots of trips. It could have been anyone. According to those tedious books I'm reading, he traveled the world. He went to east, west and north Africa—all over the continent—and met loads of people. Maybe he fell for an age-appropriate woman."

"That thought also doesn't thrill me, but I see what you're trying to do here," said Monty.

"What am I trying to do?"

"Not wanting to think the worst of Babbington."

"No, Monty, I think that ship's sailed, don't you? This is about not wanting to think that after suffering so much, that little boy would have been subjected to . . ." I felt bile rise up in my throat and in that moment felt truly annoyed with Monty. Since the incident at that house, he'd changed toward me. He seemed to pick everything I said apart.

"As I said, my contact was only able to photocopy a few pages and most of these are taken out of context. Like this bit: *With jest but also with sincere longing, I asked him to take a sip of my glass containing the strongest of whiskies. His eyes widened when he experienced the first hit of heat, shaking his head as if to rid himself of the taste.*"

"He's clearly getting him drunk," I said.

"Or he's just documenting what Celestine did. Like here." Monty pulled up another page. "*I told the boy not to engage in menial tasks and yet he is insistent on joining the help in the kitchen. This is not becoming of an English gentleman, but no matter how many times I impress this on him, there is a determination to return to the roots from which I plucked him.*"

There was now no doubt that Richard Babbington was referring to Celestine. I could only hope that not all of the entries were about him. But I was no longer sure.

> *Like many of his ilk in countless villages in Africa, his body is already strong and primed for great exertion. His naivety alerts me of his youth, a reality both intoxicating and terrifying.*

"Are you OK?" asked Monty. I looked up from the papers and briefly saw myself in Monty's widened eyes. That look of concern that could switch to pity at any moment. I didn't want Monty to ever look at me with pity. Never that.

"I'm fine . . ." I cleared my throat, trying to banish the atmosphere that had suddenly appeared in the cafe, with this new realization that Richard Babbington may have had certain thoughts toward Celestine and may even have acted on them. Thoughts of another child suffering in that house, but in a different way from me. I suddenly felt a wave of helplessness, something I had not experienced in a long time.

I needed to banish those thoughts from my head. To be as clinical as the next person, having learned at an early age that to be that way was also to survive. Yet this little boy was tearing that away from me, transforming me into this *feeling* human being, which was a dangerous thing to be for someone like me. Because what if by allowing myself to feel *his* pain, it uncovered my own? My own truths, my own secrets?

"Let's keep on track here. If you look at this next chapter, he refers to a 'Dikembe' more than once, and this may have been Celestine's name. They often gave Anglicized names to their so-called companions."

The random diary entries were out of context. The rational and logical part of my brain understood that, but also believed some things could be explained in isolation, like why a grown man would be describing the contours of a young boy's arms, his calves, and with such detail. Monty reminded me that at the time, studies of Black people included investigations of their likeness to animals, so perhaps this was why Richard Babbington felt it necessary to write these descriptions and it wasn't at all sexual.

This was what I told myself to make me feel better. To soften whatever other thoughts I was fighting against. Celestine was now real to me; he was a person, a child. When I thought of him, I had to work to fight against not only my own pain, but also his.

We ordered tea, allowing it to grow cold.

"There's more." Monty placed the papers back in the briefcase, yet the words written on them were imprinted on my brain.

"Jean at the library was very helpful indeed. She's a whizz with that microfiche machine, and we were able to look up all the exciting things that happened in the area thanks to the *Ranklin Gazette*."

"Hang on, you went back to Ranklin?"

"You always gave the impression you hate being there, so . . . you know, I was on a roll and took a trip. Is that OK?"

"Sure. I mean, as long as you didn't go to Winter Pines without me."

"Never! Besides, the shopkeeper said it was best you ask the questions anyway," he said with a wink, designed I suppose to lighten the mood. So far, today had felt extra heavy.

"Jean and I found nothing until . . ." He rolled his eyes slowly and smiled.

"Monty!" I said with impatience.

"We found this." He handed me a black-and-white photocopy of what looked like an old school photograph. Five rows of boys dressed in identical uniforms.

"Top, middle," said Monty.

He wasn't hard to spot as his was the only dark face in the photograph. And there his name was listed: Celestine Babbington.

"Taken in 1907—the same year as the pictures in the museum."

"This is amazing! Why didn't you show me this first?"

"Thought it best to get the harder stuff out of the way," he said. "We also looked for announcements—you know, a reward for a runaway—but nothing came up."

I sipped at my cold tea; it tasted disgusting. "Babbington—does that mean Sir Richard adopted him or . . . ?"

"Why stop at a first name? Makes sense for Babbington to go the whole hog and completely rename him. Happened all the time in slavery."

"But this isn't that, is it?" As soon as I said it, I regretted the words. Oh, how I regretted them.

I could feel Monty's internal eye roll and I wanted to say more, to cover up the stupidity of what I had said.

He continued. "Anyway, Celestine seems to have been quite active in the year 1907 but after that, nothing."

"So he was at school for just a year?"

"Babbington died in 1907 and there's no record of Celestine after that. It's likely Celestine would have been handed over as part of his estate. There are no purchase records so the house may have been passed on to Babbington's heirs. A married couple are listed in the census, along with a daughter, Caroline, born in 1909."

He brought the cup to his mouth and made a face. "The new owners seemed even more private than Sir Richard because there wasn't even a birth announcement for their baby in the *Ranklin Gazette*."

"So what were their names? Babbington's heirs? The people who took over the house after he died?"

"Mayhew."

I placed my cup down on the table. My heart beat rapidly. "Did you say Mayhew?"

"Yes, why?"

"Mayhew was my mother's name."

Chapter Twenty-Three

Celestine
1907

My classmates soon tired of staring at me whenever I walked into the classroom or sat next to Alfred at the dinner table.

I had blended in as best I could, even though the school photograph on the wall suggested otherwise. In a row of bright faces, mine looked as if it had been shaded in with a pencil, as if eliminating me from an image that Alfred, in all his wisdom, said made me "stand out'.

Yet Alfred remained my only friend, even if half the time he engaged in babbling about something I had absolutely no interest in. Even our shared interest in trains no longer made sense as his enthusiasm was one I could never match.

I would simply watch my classmates as they kicked a ball, longing to join in, yet still without the courage or inclination to strike up any type of conversation.

I wasn't at Ranklin to make friends, anyway. I was there to learn. And while I would never get used to Latin and hardly saw the point of it, geography was a subject I could excel at—yet two weeks in, I had started to despise it.

The large map on the wall of the classroom showed shaded sections occupied by the British. The map I had found in Sir Richard's study may have been older, but I suspected no less relevant.

Inside our books were pictures of what Mr. Prentice referred to as natives and savages, people in desperate need to be civilized. This confused me, more so because these people resembled me more than any of my classmates and yet I myself was *most civilized*. I was well mannered, courteous and dressed in the finest of clothing, and was far from a savage! Yet it was hard not to gaze at such angry illustrations of men dressed in loincloths and no shoes, staring at me from the book. It was difficult not to recall the times I myself had run barefoot with my own brother back in the village, with cloth wrapped around our waists.

The large shaded map hung on the wall proudly, watching over each and every lesson, yet it was during geography that it was given a voice louder than I would have liked.

Mr. Prentice pointed to the darkened parts on the map and asked the question once again.

"Who can remember what the shades on the map signify?"

Every hand shot up except mine, which was undoubtably why he picked on me.

"Celestine, would you like to answer?"

I swallowed as my stomach scrunched. "The shaded parts on the map, sir, they are the countries owned by the British."

"Indeed. Our great land is master over all of these continents and countries, and something to be very proud of indeed."

I gazed downward; an involuntary movement.

Then I heard the snigger.

"Would you like to take the rest of this lesson?" said Mr. Prentice, directing his attentions to a larger boy who often sat at the back.

"No, sir," he said.

"Go over to the map, Celestine, and show us our territories."

I pointed to each of the shaded sections.

"Say them," he said.

It wasn't hard to notice the smiles etched on their faces, with the exception of Alfred.

"The countries occupied by us, this great nation, are . . . ?" he began.

"Africa, India, Australia. It's all there, isn't it?" I said.

"Speak up, Celestine," said Mr. Prentice.

I repeated myself.

"We go to these countries and do our best to make their lives better," Mr. Prentice lectured. "We civilize the occupants so they can become good, don't we?"

Hit with a sudden burst of defiance, I decided I wasn't going to nod my head anymore. He would have to cane me first.

He continued. "I myself have witnessed how fruitless this is with the Aborigines of Australia. Fruitless. It's as though they're stuck in their poor, reckless and savage ways, a mentality which can only lead to no good. Wouldn't you agree, Celestine?"

No, I said in my mind as I headed back to my seat, and Mr. Prentice stopped me with more words, some that burned like fire.

"Celestine?"

"Yes, sir."

"Isn't that why you are here?"

"Sir?"

"To become civilized."

His words rendered me speechless. I could only look back toward the map, trying to block out the images surrounding the continents. Drawings of men, their skin shaded, as those without any color shaded in stood over them. Men in garments just like Sir Richard's: boots up to the knees, military uniforms. But Sir Richard was a good man, wasn't he? A drunk and a liar, yes, but a good man? It was a question I grappled with daily. He was a man who'd offered me a good life and an education. A promise he had kept to this day, even if he did still keep me from my homeland.

My mind was a blur of confusion.

One of the men on the map even had a large moustache, just like Sir Richard, his arms folded, staring down at a shaded man dressed in a white cloth, his eyes crestfallen as he looked up at this aggressor.

I'm unsure how long I was standing but it felt like an eternity.

"Go back to your seat, Celestine. We will be reading from *Chambers's Geographical Reader*, where we will delve deeper into what we have begun so far."

I opened up my copy of the book, his words echoing in my head, feeling like a threat.

Of course, there was no one present in my life who would understand what had gone on in the classroom that day. Ironically it was only Sir Richard who would be in a position to explain even part of it. The man responsible for it all. So perhaps it made some semblance of sense that I wanted to speak with him that evening, though that in itself confused me.

My life at times felt like one large ball of perpetual confusion.

So I stood by the door of his study, where he'd usually spend his evenings either writing, drinking or both. I balled my fist to knock and then heard a voice. Soft and delicate, the total antithesis to Sir Richard's usual noise. The female and male laughter mingled, and I quickly turned to leave as I sensed one of them heading toward the door.

I recognized her voice. "Time for me to go home, I think."

She opened the door and then turned to him, one of her hands buttoning up the top of her dress. My instinct was to look away, as I had never seen a woman other than my mother undressed like this before. I almost tripped over my own feet in my haste to get away, as Sir Richard and Enid appeared locked into their own uncomfortable exchange.

"I'm sorry, Enid," he said.

"I'm not good enough for you, that's all. I scrub your pots and pans. I'm good for that."

"It isn't that, I—"

"So, is it my age then? Not young enough anymore!"

"Stop it! Don't say such things!"

She rushed past me and down the stairs as Sir Richard simply closed the door of his study behind him.

My questions for Sir Richard could wait.

Chapter Twenty-Four

Celestine
1907

My mama would sometimes say that out of us boys, Pako was the stubborn one. But I felt a streak of his nature run through me as I sat on one of the kitchen chairs, watching Enid peel a bowl of potatoes. I hadn't seen Mrs. Cuthbert for a few days now.

"She's been complaining about her back. That's what happens when you start getting on. Anyway, you won't see her as much. Have to make do with me."

"Do you know when she will be back?"

"Shouldn't you be learning your ABCs or something?"

"I have completed the required homework for the evening."

"Hark at you. Speaking all proper and that!P "he rinsed each potato under the tap and I would have commented how wasteful of water this was, when each of the potatoes could have been washed inside the bowl, but I had other questions. "Are you and Sir Richard preparing to be man and wife?"

She turned to me without saying a word.

I rested my chin under my palms.

"Now why would you ask me that?" She turned her gaze back to the sink.

"I saw you—"

"Let me stop you right there. I don't know what you saw . . ."

She wiped her hands on her apron, and we sat down at the table where we both rested our elbows.

Another set of questions moved across my mind as I pondered what would happen to me after such a union.

"Don't look all sad, it's never going to happen. Me and Sir Richard getting married is as likely as it snowing in July."

"What do you mean?"

"The likes of him don't marry the likes of me."

"But you are courting?"

I had never heard her laugh so heartily and didn't see the point, especially as I hadn't said anything funny.

"Let me put this another way. Just like I couldn't marry, say, you, the likes of me would not be allowed to marry Sir Richard. Get it?"

This felt even more confusing now.

"Of course you would not be permitted to marry me. I am but twelve years of age."

Her eyes rolled so quickly that for a moment I assumed they had disappeared from her head. "Say you were nineteen like me, I still wouldn't be allowed to marry you. Don't you get it?"

"I do not."

The tips of her long and graceful fingers moved to the side of my hand. Then I began to understand. The geography lesson at school yesterday and this moment quickly began to mesh together.

"Because I am different," I said, gazing at both our hands, now side by side, resting on the table. I not only stood out in my school photograph and the dinner hall, but clearly here in this house. Of course, Sir Richard's friends and the likes of Bill had always done their best to remind me of that truth, but Sir Richard himself and Mrs. Cuthbert had allowed me a way of hiding from it. And Mr. Lattery had tutored me as I suspected he had all his students before me—his frostiness was directed at everyone. But here was

Enid telling me that we were so very different. I would not be allowed to marry her even if I was of age; although we were both human beings this would never be possible.

"You all right?" asked Enid. I was surprised she could still see me as my entire body felt shrunken to the size of a pea, just like in the classroom previously. Only this time and without any warning, I was overcome with a tiny but true sparkle of determination. It suddenly didn't matter what others thought. I was being raised as an English gentleman and that is what I had become! Even my own mama had seen something different in me, which was why she'd sent me to England in the first instance.

This was where I belonged. In the mother country, in the best schools and wearing the finest of clothes. Food being served to me and being driven in a real-life motor vehicle.

This was the life I truly deserved, no matter what anyone else believed or chose to say. Mama had taught me to be Mbidi, the king with beautifully dark skin that shone brightly and who brought a great civilization. This was who I was; this was who I had always been.

This armor of mine had always been there, though it was covered by my own confusion and at times anger. Yet it had now come alive once more, allowing me to walk into school from that moment on with my shoulders erect and my gaze facing forward.

I was the most studious in that school and brighter than the others, and I was no longer afraid to express this. When asked about a future career, I pondered the list as if I believed I could have access to any one of them: banker, hotelier (one like the Sapphire Hotel, perhaps), merchant.

Mr. Gallagher had prompted me to "think very carefully" about my answer, but as far as I believed, all such careers were open to me, as long as I studied and worked hard in school. I heard the sniggers and the comment "he's not even the son of an African king!" Instead, I chose to focus on the number of possibilities that awaited me.

To me, anything *had* to be possible.

Sir Richard appreciated my diligent and hard work. He was enthused that I had "met and exceeded all of his expectations' and said he could not have felt prouder. My latest reward did not involve a gift wrapped in an oblong box.

"We, dear boy, are going on another trip!" he said.

I chose my finest trousers with the dark line down the seam which stood out flamboyantly, together with the matching waistcoat and jacket, and my laced-up Oxford shoes shined to perfection. Enid helped me pack similar items of clothing as requested by Sir Richard. However, when I saw his own attire, my breath was almost taken away with happiness. His long explorer boots that met his knees, along with the dome hat, suggested Sir Richard was about to embark on another mission across the waters.

My mind refused to acknowledge what I knew this meant, unable to allow myself such joy until it was abundantly clear my suspicions were correct.

The start to this trip involved a lot of waiting. And excitement. Waiting for the train, which was delayed, and then the motor vehicle that collected us from the station.

When we pulled up outside the London Stereoscopic and Photographic Company, my dream, however unrealistic, was once again shattered. The possibility had been weak to begin with, but yet . . .

"Isn't this spectacular?" said Sir Richard, as we both stood beside a man in front of a large wooden contraption with a circular lens in the middle. I had already seen a smaller version of such machines during the taking of the school photograph, but I falsely matched his enthusiasm.

"This wondrous beast was made in 1903," enthused Sir Richard.

I nodded my head knowledgeably.

The man, who had now introduced himself as "your photographer for the day," spoke. "Celestine, you look very smart in your suit, so for this one, I just need you to sit on the chair."

I did as I was told and he bent down to place his hand on my shin, moving it slightly.

"And place your elbow on that," he said, pointing to the circular side table his assistant had just brought into view. Everything about this photograph was contrived, unreal and false. My head refused to spin with the utter excitement that appeared to have overtaken Sir Richard.

"Ready?"

When the light finally flashed, both Sir Richard and the photographer seemed to light up with joy.

"Splendid!" said the photographer, while I hoped this would soon be over as I wasn't having half as much fun as Sir Richard. Perhaps this had much to do with what the day had promised earlier, compared to what it had so far delivered.

"Now we want the both of you together in an image, with some props."

The props were a curious assortment of a model leopard and odd-looking trees made from cloth.

"Put that on," said the photographer, handing over what looked like a bedsheet but in a coarser material.

"I don't understand."

"Wear it, like you did back in Africa."

I turned toward Sir Richard. Had I not just stood before this camera in the finest of garments? And now a man I had never met before was requesting that I wear a bedsheet.

"I want a scene where you're serving Sir Richard something, I don't know . . . a cup of tea?"

"That's not something he does, Kenneth."

"Oh, is that so? Well, it won't hurt to have one, and perhaps also one with the gun."

"Now you're talking, old boy."

"I will take the picture with some foliage in the background, and you with a gun and Celestine standing behind you."

"Yes, that's better," said Sir Richard.

"I'm still going to need Celestine to get into the cloth."

I looked toward Sir Richard but he seemed unconcerned, more excited about finally having this photograph taken. So I stepped into the changing room and out of my fine clothes, and placed the bedsheet around my waist. I focused on what was positive about this entire scene: my beloved father's necklace would now be on show. It had remained a great source of pride for me and at times, I even forgot of its existence. This way, it would be immortalized forever.

I felt a surge of self-consciousness as I walked out, my chest on display to these two men.

"An excellent touch!" said the photographer, pointing to my neck. "Celestine, stand slightly behind Sir Richard and look up at him with adoration in your eyes!"

"To his back? Are you sure?" I questioned.

"Yes, I am sure."

I did no such thing. I wasn't sure what my expression looked like but it was far from admiration. My lips pursed, my eyes clouded over. With my stomach almost touching the back of Sir Richard's shotgun, I began to wonder just how each shape and contour would feel in my own hands. Was this the type of gun those white men in my village had used on my father before they hung him from one of the trees he so dearly loved? What would it feel like to take the gun from Sir Richard's grip and perhaps turn it on everyone in this room? Would I feel a relief, perhaps similar to what my father may have felt when he had finally left the realms of this life? Or would I feel much like that man who had struck my brother, triumphant at what he had done?

Or perhaps I should simply turn the gun on myself. Would this not end the constant questioning that interrupted my sleep? The moving pictures of fire and the destruction of my village; images I had no way of verifying yet were told to me as truth? I had clearly underplayed the day's disappointment. I had believed, for a moment at least, that I was going home. This belief had reignited thoughts and feelings I had carefully placed in a box for survival.

"What an exceptional day!" enthused Sir Richard as soon as we returned to the big house. He'd been saying as much during the journey back, too. "I must apologize for the photograph taken with the cup of tea. It was the only way to appease the man, and he'd worked so hard for us . . ." Within seconds, his "favorite" bottle was in his hands. "Now everyone will be able to see us in photographs! I cannot wait to have them framed and placed on these very walls when they are completed."

"That would be lovely," I said flatly, too spent to comprehend just how bizarre it was for Sir Richard to apologize for a photograph and nothing else.

"Did you enjoy yourself, dear boy?"

"Yes," I lied, because despite my hardest of efforts, this was the start of something. Although I no longer believed much of what came out of Sir Richard's mouth, I now possessed a new emotion toward him.

I had now started to truly hate Sir Richard Babbington.

Chapter Twenty-Five

Celestine

1907

Five photographs took pride of place against the wall of the study. Thankfully, anytime I went in to visit Sir Richard, my back was toward them. If I caught a glimpse, an unwelcome feeling of humiliation would appear in the pit of my stomach. I didn't like that feeling, so it was best to never ever look at them and pretend they did not exist.

When I walked into the study to find Sir Richard snoring very loudly in his chair one day, I simply smiled. Just moments earlier he'd been singing along to a tune in his head, and now this familiar, yet repulsive sound had been my signal to go inside.

Searching along the rows of books, it was difficult to decide where to begin.

Sometimes Sir Richard could stay asleep for hours, other times just minutes, before opening one eye as he poured the final remnants of his bottle into a glass.

I ran my fingers over the books on the bottom row and once again pulled out the one entitled *A Dictionary of Languages as Spoken in Various Areas of the Congo Free State*. This had first caught my attention some time ago, but it was only now that I had received such a substantial amount of tutoring from Mr. Lattery that I actually felt confident enough to seek what was inside of its pages.

A grunt from Sir Richard startled me as I pulled open the pages at random. I then turned back to the Contents page and started again. There was a method to this, according to Mr. Lattery.

"What are you doing over there, dear boy?" His voice sounded weaker than usual, yet still held its authority. I snapped shut the dictionary, satisfied I had actually found one of the words I had been looking for.

When Mrs. Cuthbert announced her retirement, this was no surprise to me as most of her daily chores had shifted to Enid anyway. But I'd miss her. She was the closest I had experienced to a mother since my arrival in England, and it was perhaps ironic that she left on a date referred to as Mothering Sunday.

"I know it isn't much, but here," she said, leading me into the kitchen. On the counter was a round cake topped with eleven marzipan balls. "This is what we call a simnel cake and it's for you, love."

I threw myself into her embrace uninvited. "Oh, Mrs. Cuthbert!"

"You take care of yourself, you hear?" she said.

This level of comfort, my arms wrapped around her waist, was like nothing I'd felt in so very long. She smelled of fresh marzipan and fruit, and it felt like being in Mama's arms again.

"I have to go now, love. You take care of yourself," she said once again, and was gone. Just like that. I stopped in the middle of the kitchen, the cake on the table, a leaving gift that would be eaten over a succession of days until there was nothing left of it. Just an empty plate and crumbs. A feeling not unfamiliar to me.

Enid swiftly moved into Mrs. Cuthbert's role, albeit clumsily. She could not cook and I spent a lot of time assisting her in the kitchen without Sir Richard's knowledge. He was mostly out of the house anyway, appearing during the early hours of the morning smelling of whisky, his words stumbling as well as his feet.

I planned to use the time to sneak into the study once more and retrieve *A Dictionary of Languages as Spoken in Various Areas of the Congo Free State* to translate the words I believed sounded like those I had used back in my village. However, it was no longer where I had left it. It was gone. Hidden, or simply removed.

When Empire Day came around, the school promised it would be a "fantastic day' and one we all wouldn't forget in a hurry. Little did I know, I would remember this day for the rest of my life because it would be the day my life changed once again.

The sun was shining and the entire school remained outdoors enjoying the festivities with members of their families, accompanied by fresh tea and cakes and an actual live band. Sir Richard had promised to attend, just before pouring a glass of whisky down his throat.

When the national anthem played, I mouthed the lyrics, reasoning that this was also a celebration of other countries and continents, as I had been reminded constantly.

The air was filled with joviality and it wasn't my intention to spoil the day for anyone, but I began to feel wretched, perhaps because of the loss of the dictionary—an extension of how I'd been feeling many times since that day in London.

Mr. Gallagher began his speech, bunting in the colors of the Union Jack flowing overhead in the slight wind.

". . . that they might think, with others in lands across the sea, what it meant to be sons and daughters of such a glorious empire . . ." The round of applause followed me as I ventured away from the gathering.

A patch of grass behind the cricket field would be my

playground until I was sure the festivities were over. I wanted no part of this day.

An hour later, Alfred came to find me. I had been summoned to Mr. Gallagher's office.

"Where have you been? Your absence was noted, Celestine, and this is a distinct breach of our rules," he said.

"I apologize." Of course, I did not mean this.

"Besides, why would you not want to celebrate such a momentous day? The sun is shining, it is a joyous occasion—wouldn't you agree?"

He took my silence for agreement.

"If you are in breach of the rules once more, I'm afraid you will face punishment."

That breach came all too quickly and on that very day.

All the boys appeared animated—all except myself and Alfred—at the prospect of another afternoon playing cricket, especially with the extra crowds. For me, standing in a windy field simply meant more time taken away from study—the real gateway to becoming my own man in this strange, strange world.

"Just tell them you're not well," Alfred advised. With his overly pale features and slight frame, he perhaps could get away with it.

This excuse had already worked for me once, culminating in an afternoon spent alone in the classroom, devouring as much of the books as possible. However, this time when I informed Mr. Prentice that I would not be taking part in the "extra special" cricket match, it earned me another trip to the principal's office—the second in one day.

Mr. Gallagher took his glasses off and I knew this was not a good sign. "I am told you are too unwell for cricket, and in light of your behavior earlier, I am inclined to believe this to be untrue. Is it untrue, Celestine?"

My eyes stared toward the floor because I did not want him to see into them. How people like Sir Richard got away with lies I was unable to decipher.

"We have put this down to you falsifying your condition."

I looked at him, my eyes clouding over.

"Here at Ranklin we do not like half-truths."

"What will happen now?" I would prefer a detention, of course. Preferably in the library.

"You will not be punished as long as you go outside now and prepare to partake in the activity. I am told you picked it up very well the first time you played."

"I did, sir, because I am capable. I just prefer to be reading, sir. I am more suited to something academic in nature."

He raised both eyebrows. "Frankly, I simply cannot understand why a strapping young man like yourself would not be more interested in sporting activities. Do you know, my grandfather would travel far and wide to your part of the world and be taken aback by the prowess and strength of its menfolk? You cannot lack ability when it comes to such things."

"My part of the world, sir? I have been told to see Britain as my new world. I am confused. Sir."

His face blushed.

"May I be excused now, Mr. Gallagher?"

"Yes, you may go and get dressed."

"What for?" I said, a heat rising within me. I was fed up with people telling me what I should be and how they saw me, at times even contradicting themselves. Was I supposed to be uncivilized animal, English gentleman or strong athlete? Was Britain my home, or Africa?

"To join the others for cricket, of course."

"I won't!" I said.

His eyebrows arched and his face reddened. "I beg your pardon?"

"I believe that what I said is clear."

"What did you just say?!"

Not even my father had ever spoken so loudly before, so I was clearly in the deepest of trouble. It wasn't until he ordered me to follow him to the office and pulled open his drawer that I realized just how much trouble I had brought upon myself.

I pulled out my hand just as I had seen another boy do, and squeezed my eyes with such force it would be of no surprise if they never opened again.

The first stroke was a surprise, the shock in my body preventing a quick onslaught of pain. By the second one, the burning in my hand increased, and by the third, I had to open my eyes just to check he hadn't dismembered me. My hand was throbbing in earnest and I blinked back any treacherous water lurking inside my eyelids.

"Maybe next time you will think twice about disappearing during an occasion that clearly celebrates you and who you are. You should show more respect to this country and for what it has done."

He waited as if anticipating a response or nod of my head. He would get neither.

"And you will participate in all aspects of the curriculum, whether you feel like it or not!"

I stood before him, my hand still stinging with pain. I would never permit him to glimpse my discomfort. All he would perceive was my straight posture and erect shoulders and the determination in my voice. A dignified presence, like the Black king my mama had always said I was.

When I finally got to tell Sir Richard about the incident, I wasn't sure what I had hoped for. But his rush of laughter in that loud, booming voice felt less than welcome.

"The cane is a rite of passage for any young man. I remember getting lashes for simply wearing my cap inside the building when it wasn't allowed. Try not to go wandering off in the future, dear boy. Especially on Empire Day!" By the time he had finished the sentence, Sir Richard had already poured himself a fresh glass of whisky.

I didn't have to listen to a drunken man. I didn't have to listen to anyone.

That night my hatred for Sir Richard was joined by that for Mr. Gallagher, the other pupils, Bill, his friends, everyone. But most of all Sir Richard, because he'd been the one to begin the chain of events that had brought me into their paths.

These feelings continued, magnified. One night I stood by his bedchamber, him snoring loudly after a full day of pure drunkenness, his pillow discarded onto the floor by his bed. I thought about what it would look like if I held it over his face and pressed down, softly at first, and then when he snorted, pressed down firmer until he breathed his last! These thoughts were not new; they often came clouded in darkness, certainty and uncertainty.

Sometimes I'd be left with shame at having these desires; other times the shame would be associated with not having the courage to follow through.

The next morning, when they found him, I'd been at school for just one hour.

An empty bottle had been found by his side along with an uncompleted notebook, and when they'd lifted his lifeless body onto the stretcher I had already left the school grounds, with Gordon not even breaking protocol to speak with me.

People I did not recognize littered the house, most notably a policeman.

"What is happening?" I asked Enid, who was crumpled on the floor, her face red and wet with tears.

"He's gone," she mumbled.

"Who is?" I knew even as I said the words that Sir Richard was no more.

I sat on the floor, my knees pulled up to my chin, watching the activity unfold around me. Mr. Roger, Sir Richard's friend, spoke with a policeman, but I couldn't hear their words as the cries from Enid became louder and more intense. I had no such tears, though. I was used to loss. Maybe I had already mourned this man every time he had stared down at the bottom of his crystal glass.

Or perhaps I had hated him too much to care that he was dead.

I stayed in my room, trying not to absorb the frantic activity of my surroundings. The big house had always been a quiet sanctuary, save for the booming voice of Sir Richard. A voice I would never hear again.

"What are we going to do with you, then?" she said as the door to my room flung open.

"Mrs. Cuthbert!" I jumped up and straight into her arms.

"I just heard, love."

"How did you know?"

"Ranklin is a small place. Terrible tragedy, it is."

The feel of her arms around me was comforting and warm, and everything I needed in that moment.

"I'll stay with Celestine for the night," said Mrs. Cuthbert after Mr. Roger inquired about my well-being. I hoped she would cook her precious flans and allow me to help with the potatoes. I craved some normality because everything felt abnormal, and once more my world was making no sense to me.

I climbed into bed early that night, thinking about Sir Richard's last moments and whether it was I who had killed him. I had wished death upon him more than once and perhaps there was something I could have done to save him.

The whispers were that it was an excess of alcohol that had caused his demise, and yet many a night I had sat and watched him drink from one glass to another.

And now, the only person who held the key to me ever returning home was gone.

Mr. Roger wasn't able to give me many details, which I probably wouldn't have been able to understand anyway. Words like "property" and "wills" were placed into sentences that made nothing appear any clearer. Mrs. Cuthbert had to go back to her family, and before she left had cooked enough to feed me for a month. It was just myself in the house, with Mr. Roger appearing daily to keep a watchful eye over me. He said nothing about my family or my village or the idea that I might be allowed to return home, merely echoing it was best to go by what Sir Richard had said: that my village was no more. Besides, Mr. Roger would not know how to begin the process of returning me to a country he knew nothing about.

"Celestine, I'm a lawyer, not an explorer."

"If I had money, I could embark on the journey home myself."

"That is correct."

"Sir Richard always said he would make sure I was looked after. Whatever provisions he made for my schooling, it would be better to give to me, so that I could make my way back home."

"It is probably sensible to wait until the estate is looked at before making decisions."

When Mr. Roger finally addressed me almost a month later, it was to inform me my world was about to change once more.

"Richard left everything in a mess and was in a lot of debt. It's a relief his relatives are able to take over the house. At least then, it will stay in the family."

"What family?" The only visitors we had ever received were Sir Richard's friends, and I'd lived here for a year and a half.

"No one implied they were close."

"What does this mean then . . . for me?"

"For you, Celestine, I am not sure. I have impressed on them just how much you meant to Richard and asked them to allow you to stay."

"Stay? But I don't want to stay!"

"Where would you go, Celestine?"

"I will take my money and leave . . ."

"I don't think you understand, Celestine. Sir Richard's estate is almost gone, aside from the house. There would not be the funds to do so, even if we knew where to start and how to do that—and we don't."

A sense of desperation began to grip around my neck. "But I can recall how we got here. All I would have to do is imagine this in reverse. Where the ship collected us; I can tell you what I know. Perhaps Sir Richard has notes?"

"There is simply no money left. If the relatives decide to sell the house, then they could use some of the proceeds, but you would have to discuss that with them. My hands are tied."

What did this man know about being tied? I was tied to a house and a country I no longer wanted, had never wanted, and every strength I had I would use to leave it. Yet the way he had shrugged his shoulders left me engulfed in a sea of hopelessness.

"Let's just take this one day at a time, Celestine. I have much paperwork to sort out and this may take a few months."

"And then you will know what will become of me?"

"One day at a time, Celestine."

His words offered no reassurance. In two days Sir Richard's relatives, who I had never even heard of, would be arriving and moving into the big house.

Chapter Twenty-Six

Lowra
1993

Monty and I were on the train headed back to Ranklin.

Discovering that a member of my mother's family was a previous owner of that house and had been for years was a revelation I hadn't bargained for. A couple of days in, I still hadn't digested the news well, particularly this possible connection to Richard Babbington.

Now I was even more convinced that the doll, Celestine, the necklace and that piece of paper were connected to my mother in some way—I just wasn't sure *how*.

"So, we have Caroline Mayhew, born in 1909 to Agatha and Cyril Mayhew, as recorded on her birth certificate." He handed me the copy of the certificate obtained from St. Catherine's House, the address in Ranklin standing out.

Monty continued. "The strange thing is, I can't find anymore records about Caroline."

"What do you think this means?"

"I don't know, but it's really intriguing. To top it off, these are your relatives!"

"We don't know how they relate to my mother. Just that her maiden name was Mayhew, same as Cyril. I don't know anything about my mother's family. The marriage certificate I found in my dad's briefcase only lists the name of his father. There's a line through my mother's entry."

"Marriage certificates never list the mother—it's ludicrous."

"At least if I could see her mother's name, it would tell us something. I've always believed there to be a Spanish connection somewhere."

"Hopefully there's still stuff we can find back at the house. I'm just glad it hasn't sold yet."

"I'm glad you're excited," I said dryly.

"It appears I'm a historian first and a human being second. How are you holding up with all of this?"

"I've had worse days," I said. I shook my head quickly as if to rid myself of any excess emotion. "Don't worry about the house getting sold—they can't do that without my say-so, and the lawyer says the paperwork with the heritage people needs looking at first."

The train stopped at a station and a crowd of people boarded, followed by a train inspector. I began to feel even more wound up when I couldn't find my ticket.

"Never mind," said the inspector, "just make sure you present it at the other end."

"I will, thanks."

With passengers now sitting beside us, either side of the table, I was alone with my thoughts.

It had been three weeks since we'd started this journey and uncovered so much, but I no longer knew where it was leading. Yet something inside me said there were more secrets, things that perhaps should have remained buried—and this scared me.

The announcement over the PA system prepared us for being stuck at the station "until further notice."

The other passengers finally left and it was just Monty and me again, on this longer than usual train journey.

"Might as well stock up. We may be here some time," he said, before placing a five-pound note into the hands of the food cart assistant.

"Thanks," said Monty, scooping the change from the table and placing it into his pocket.

I bit into the bar of chocolate as Monty opened a fizzy drink.

"So how did you get the name Montgomery?"

"That would be down to my white mother, Suzy Montgomery, and my Black father, Dr. Wilfred Alburn, both narcissists who insisted they raise someone who would be the exact reflection of themselves, hence my full name and the PhD . . ."

"You have a PhD?"

"Sure do."

"So you're a doctor?"

"Without the prescriptions, diagnoses, operations or the wages."

"If I had a PhD, I'd be shouting it from the rooftops. I just about scraped by at school and the most 'learned' thing I did was write the odd poem."

"That's amazing. When you're ready to share . . ."

"They're not very good."

"My mother said I'd get far with a name like Montgomery, and depending on how you look at it, perhaps she was right." He placed the empty can on the table, grabbing it as it began to roll away due to the gathering speed of the train, then crushed it with his palm.

"So what about you? Lowra's a bit unusual, isn't it?"

"My dad told me my mother always loved the name Laura, but the Spanish version. She was worried that if she spelled it the traditional way, everyone would just call me Laura."

"So your mother was Spanish?"

"I used to think so . . . or at least maybe on her mother's side . . . but after finding out this connection to the Mayhews, maybe not." I sounded like an idiot. But as a child, it was easy to just spin whatever you could about a past you really knew nothing about. Holidaying in Spain; my mother's Mediterranean looks in the picture; my name: this all meant she *had* to be Spanish.

She was, to a child with nothing but her imagination.

"So she decided to spell your name phonetically?"

"Yes. Then Dad told me they found out the name actually exists. I think it's Latin."

"You think?"

"I know that sounds horrifying to a historian!"

We both laughed at that.

"It does actually. The first thing I did when I was old enough was research my name."

"What did you find out?"

"Lots." He pulled open the bag of crisps as I waited for more of the story.

I was still waiting a further ten minutes into this extended journey.

"So, your surname . . ."

"What about it?"

"What did you find out?"

"Thought we'd moved on from that."

"Nope."

He removed his glasses from his face, placing them down on the table between us.

"My surname is from my great-great-great-great-grandfather. The rapist who owned my great-great-great-great-grandmother."

I opened my mouth to speak. Nothing. Blank.

"Sorry if that makes you uncomfortable, Lowra, but I thought it was clear I didn't want to speak about it."

"Not uncomfortable . . . just sad."

"Sorry to make you sad, then."

"No need to sound sarcastic, I was just—"

"I suppose when I feel misunderstood, I can get defensive."

"You think I misunderstand you?"

He looked toward the window again. This time I wasn't going to allow him to shut down the conversation.

"Monty, I hardly know you."

"As with many people, but that doesn't stop them making up their own mind about me. Just like the ticket inspector letting you off, and the policeman at the house."

Now I was confused.

"When people hear my name, or my voice on the phone, and what I do, they don't expect a six-foot man of mixed race to walk through the door."

"Your specialty is African history!" That sounded better in my head.

He ran a large hand over his head, and his expression when he turned to me spoke of a tiredness I'd never noticed in Monty before. He'd always been just . . . Monty.

"If I'm honest, Lowra, I don't really have the energy right now. This whole Celestine thing . . . it's bringing up a lot." His voice broke and I didn't know what to do with that . . . or all this emotion. "This is part of the reason I don't like having these types of conversations."

"Let's forget it then. Go back . . ."

"I don't have an on/off button when it comes to trauma," he said.

"I know about trauma, Monty." I felt a rise in my voice, now feeling misunderstood myself.

He looked at me as if silently asking a question, and when I offered no explanation he continued. "I wish you could understand. Even though what happened to the people in my family did so some centuries ago and without me present, it doesn't mean that today I don't feel the pain. It doesn't mean that such legacies have missed me."

His voice broke again. "It also doesn't mean that even today in 1993, I'm not experiencing another version of it everywhere I turn. Just look at what happened when the guy with the trolley gave me back my change by putting it on the table instead of in my hand."

I wanted to say I didn't see anything wrong with that. That it happened sometimes and was just the way some people did things. "I hear you, Monty, I do."

"Do you, though, or are you just saying that?"

He didn't wait for my answer. His exhalation was fast. "Until you walk a mile in my shoes . . ."

I wanted to say the same.

Chapter Twenty-Seven

Celestine
1907

"He's a scrawny little thing, isn't he?"

"His hair—it's all . . . tufty."

"Does it talk?"

I opened my mouth but then thought better of it. Let them believe what they wanted of me. It was probably better they assumed I did not understand, because if their plan didn't match up with what was good for me, at least I could execute some form of escape.

But where would I go? I had no idea where Mrs. Cuthbert resided and whether she would appreciate the sight of me at her front door. I knew the name of Mr. Roger's office, but I had only seen him a handful of times and he hardly knew me.

"Roger insists he speaks very good English," said the man, who was dressed in a suit with a fraying thread at the bottom of his left trouser leg. However much Sir Richard would give in to the weaknesses of the bottle, his clothing would always remain impeccable, even if it did at times appear as if he was heading out on another expedition. The last boots I'd shined for him were still lined up in his wardrobe and this saddened me; perhaps the only piece of emotion I could extend to him.

"Say something then," said the woman.

"Hello."

"Sir," the man corrected. He was right, of course. I would never have addressed Sir Richard as anything less than "sir."

The woman, Agatha Mayhew, eyed me suspiciously as I searched for something resembling compassion beneath the large gray and white picture hat she wore to cover hair that was curled at the sides. She was a tall lady, her husband a few inches shorter.

"Roger was supposed to show us around after the will reading, but he's nowhere to be seen, so you will have to," she said.

"Very well."

"What is that?" she said, pointing to my neck, the top of my father's necklace visible beneath my collar.

"It's some sort of tribal necklace," said Cyril Mayhew, before I could answer.

She made a face of distaste before insisting once again that I show them around their new home.

If Agatha and Cyril Mayhew were indeed the only living relatives of Sir Richard, should they not be aware of the layout of his home? This I wanted to say, but instead I wore a fixed smile of insincerity as they followed behind me, mumbling between themselves.

"I'm sure we can get a good price for some of this rubbish."

"Let's not get ahead of ourselves. Some of this could be very valuable so we don't want to be rash."

"We shall begin here," I said, imagining the surprise on their faces at my excellent command of the English language. However, when they barged past me and into Sir Richard's study, only one matter appeared to concern them both.

"Where did he keep his private papers?" said Cyril. With great reluctance I pointed to Sir Richard's bureau, and within a moment both had their hands pawing at documents, reaching inside for all they could find. The violation of his things felt saddening to me, as I recalled the hours he'd spent with his fountain pen writing down thoughts privy only to himself. Those same thoughts were now in the hands of these strangers.

I desperately wanted to bring up the subject of this will they spoke about. Mr. Roger had implied that Sir Richard was practically penniless, but I did not want to believe that once more he had lied to me; that he had not indeed left anything for my upkeep. Money that I could use to be gone from this house.

"Is there something in particular you are looking for?" I said.

"No, you are dismissed for the night," Cyril said.

I shifted up and down on my toes. "Dismissed, sir?"

"That means we won't be needing you for now."

They were clearly under the impression I was a servant. Perhaps Mr. Roger or even Sir Richard hadn't made them aware of my position here.

I left them to their deeds and headed to my room.

I was not aware of how late or early it was but awoke immediately when I heard the creak of my door.

I sat up quickly. My mind was foggy with sleep.

"Celestine," said a female voice, and for a brief moment I believed Mrs. Cuthbert had come to collect me.

"Yes, miss . . . ?"

"You shall call me madam from now on."

I rubbed at my eyes. It had taken a good while to get to sleep and I resented being disturbed at this time.

"You will need to start on breakfast."

"I was not aware I had to prepare breakfast."

"Who usually cooks?"

"Enid."

"Enid isn't here. We had to let her go because we have you."

"I don't understand."

She walked closer to my bed, her silhouette becoming clearer. "What is there for you to understand? Your English appears fine to me."

"Yes, but—"

"You're here to work and that's what you are supposed to do, isn't it?"

"I am not a servant, madam," I said robustly.

"I don't know what Richard was thinking, but we are not going to be wasteful with money. You will just have to earn your keep like everybody else, starting with breakfast. Is that clear?"

Words rested on my tongue. "But madam . . . ?"

"What?"

"This is—"

"We'll be ready for breakfast in an hour."

She closed the door behind her and all I could think about was how bizarre a request this was, as since arriving in England my role had been clarified over and over again.

I was to receive an education and be a companion to Sir Richard, never a servant!

Instead, I had not been back to school since Sir Richard's death, and now I stood inside the kitchen cooking breakfast, which was only good enough because I had learned from watching and helping Mrs. Cuthbert when Sir Richard had been away. Preparing and cooking food was something I enjoyed, yet under these circumstances, any semblance of happiness was slowly being sucked away.

Cyril appeared appreciative of my efforts, judging by how he pierced the slightly charred sausage and placed it into his mouth while humming. Agatha on the other hand ate slowly, eyeing her plate of food with suspicion. "There don't seem to be any eggs."

"It would appear we are running out, madam."

"Then sort out a new order!"

I stared at her with disbelief. "Yes . . . madam."

"And where are you going?" she said.

"To look at what we need, write it down and make sure it is delivered, like you said, madam." I purposely said the word "madam' as if it soiled my lips. Which it did. Everything about her did not sit well with me: her tone, the way she addressed me and the way I sometimes found her looking at me, as if I were an object of curiosity and disdain all at once.

"Clear these away first," she said.

I inhaled deeply.

"What are you waiting for?" she said as her husband scraped the side of his plate, lapping up the last remnants of the breakfast. "And then you will begin the household chores."

I mixed the carbolic soap with hot water and washing soda, the way I had watched Enid do countless times, and got on my hands and knees to scrub the parquet floors. Cleaning the floor wasn't something I had ever done in England before or particularly enjoyed when it had been my turn to do it back home, but at least I did it with ease. The other household chores I suspected would not be hard to learn, but I simply didn't want to do them. Throughout my entire time in England so far, my current predicament was the worst I had been in, and indeed it had to stop. Now.

They were sitting in the drawing room.

"Sir, madam, with the inevitability of the will leaving me an adequate sum on which to live, I must insist upon my immediate release."

"Is that so?" said Agatha.

"Yes, madam."

"And what funds are these?" I was grateful this question came from Cyril. He was a man of fewer words than his wife but was certainly the most sympathetic of the two.

"He promised me that in the event of his death, he would make provisions for me in his last will and testament."

Cyril's snorts and Agatha's guffaws followed, after which they still had yet to answer me.

"Have you completed your tasks?" said Agatha.

"Yes, madam, so may we discuss—"

"Discuss what?" said Cyril.

"The monies left to me. Sir Richard would have made sure I was comfortable, that I am sure of."

"So you want us to give you money?" he said.

"Yes, sir, eventually. When the details of the last will and testament have been outlined. Or if you prefer to do so now . . ." Even from my own lips it sounded implausible, so I began to waver. "Or when you have sold some of his effects. I have heard you discussing this."

"You did, did you?" said Agatha.

I was conscious we were straying away from the issue at hand: my access to funds that would allow me to leave this house, this country, and seek what was left of my village. To find out to what extent it had been destroyed—if at all. Sir Richard had lied about so many things in the past; I simply needed to see things for myself.

At least I knew where to start—the Congo.

She stood up, a gentler smile on her face. "You poor thing."

"I only would like what is mine and then I will go."

"Of course," she said. I wouldn't have described her voice as soothing, but at least it no longer came at me etched with aggression.

"Come with me, my dear," she said. "Let's go and look for these papers you speak of."

"Really?" said Cyril.

"Yes, my darling. He has been promised certain liberties and the least I can do is help him to find the evidence."

A swell of gratitude allowed me to smile. "Thank you, madam."

I followed her up to the top of the second set of stairs, where we stood outside an attic I had never been inside before.

"Sir Richard kept his personal papers in the bureau in his study. Not here," I said.

She ignored me as she opened the door which creaked, a sign of inactivity. My nostrils were immediately attacked by flecks of dust and I resisted the urge to cough. I opened my mouth to speak and then it all happened so very quickly. The full force of her hands on my back, pushing me through the attic door and onto the floor. My knees landing on the floor, the time it took to turn around, only to watch the light disappear as the door closed in front of me.

"Madam?" My voice sounded weak with disbelief, as I slowly stood up and reached for what I believed to be the door handle; I could not see a thing as the room was pitch-black.

Her voice came through the door. "It might be an idea to be reminded of your place here. My husband and I have been nothing but gracious, even allowing you to reside in a bedroom."

"Madam?" I placed my hand on the doorknob and pushed.

"This will give you time to cool off," she said, sounding a whole world away from me.

"I apologize, madam. Please, may I be let out? The door is locked."

I balled my hand into a fist and banged on the wooden door. "I am very sorry to have offended you!" I said, yet my speech had no audience. She'd gone, and I was alone in the dark. Even so, I banged on that door until my palms were stinging and my knuckles sore. I banged and banged anyway, pain riding up my wrists. Some were harder than others, yet each blow on that door represented my pain, my anguish and my grief. For everyone I had lost and for everything I may be about to lose—my freedom.

Yet surely this was paranoia? She couldn't keep me inside for long. They would at least need dinner prepared soon.

I stood in total darkness, refusing to sit on the floor because that would mean defeat. By remaining standing and upright, I was ready for battle to commence when the door finally opened again.

And it would open again.

When my stomach began to speak its hunger, there was nothing I could do to answer it. I had been in that attic for some time now—an hour, maybe two—and yet still no sound from outside that door. No light. No evidence that a world even existed outside the door.

It was only when I slid against what I felt to be the wall that I was able to sooth my stomach by holding on to myself, imagining the consumption of one of Mrs. Cuthbert's lemon tarts.

I drifted in and out of sleep. The floor was cold against my head.

My stomach told me I had possibly missed two meals.

I awoke with a start into a gray darkness. This told me it was morning or afternoon. Total darkness meant the evening had come and turned into night.

How long had I been here?

It was difficult to hold my urination, but to relieve myself in this room would prove to people like Sir Richard's friends and the scientists who wrote the books Mr. Prentice made us read that I was indeed an animal. And I couldn't do that. I couldn't give them the satisfaction.

Perhaps that was why my stomach hurt, and not from hunger. Perhaps I had only been inside here for one day and one night.

I was no stranger to isolation or loneliness, yet this felt different. Downstairs, outside and in between, was a freedom staring me in the face if I had wanted it, along with a beach and a large body of water that could literally have taken me anywhere, even back home.

This attic offered no such luxury.

I pulled the door handle and nothing. I banged softly on the door once again, aware it would be of no use because no one would hear me.

"Please!" I shouted anyway, my voice weakened by hunger. "I am sorry, madam!" I hated the tears that traitorously ran down my cheeks. I slid down the wall once more, this time clutching my knees, the darkness around me all so illuminating. The loneliness, the possibility of what could become of me. Everything playing out in my head over and over again. Irrationality mixed in with the realization that I was locked in an attic. All alone.

Silence.

Darkness.

A scuttling sound. A rat, a mouse, or my imagination?

I began to shiver because of the cold, or perhaps it was fear—there was simply no way of knowing.

I just wanted my mama.

I lay on the floor and opened my eyes to darkness. I hadn't planned to fall asleep, but tears of exhaustion had caused another brief slumber. I had not soiled myself, or maybe I had and it had dried.

A chill attacked my bones, my throat scratchy. I sat up, a faint light through the door telling me it was morning once more.

When the door finally opened, Agatha stood in the doorway, the light behind her illuminating her smiling face. "It's time," she said.

I remained on the floor, staring up at her, expressionless I imagine.

"It's time to begin your chores for today."

So many questions rested on my lips. Such as: why? But I desperately needed to urinate.

I stood up slowly, my legs wobbling for support, just grateful for the ray of light.

"Did you hear what I said?"

"Yes, madam," I said hoarsely.

She stood aside but I wasn't sure if I was permitted to leave. So with every step I waited, slightly anxiously, for her to call out to me again.

I freshened up and changed my clothing. Once inside my

bedroom, I sank my toes into the flooring and ran my fingers over the lining of the bed. If everything here was real, then what had happened last night could simply have been in my imagination.

I set about preparing what I could with what was available as the bread boy had yet to make the delivery. I had been in the attic from one evening until the morning, yet it had felt much longer.

"Thank you," said Cyril, looking up briefly to acknowledge me as I stood over him with a jug of water. Agatha said nothing.

Back inside the kitchen, Bill was waiting with his arms folded, fresh produce on the sideboard.

"Bill?"

"Well, well, well." He appraised me. His cap was as dirty as could be, cocked to the side like his demeanor. "How the mighty have fallen, eh?"

"Thank you for delivering the produce, Bill."

"No thanks to you, getting me the sack. Looks like they went with the cheaper merchants, where I just happen to work."

I was actually pleased to see a familiar face.

"Finally, you're down to the likes of us. No more hiding behind Sir Richard."

I pretended not to understand his laughter, but I understood.

"Just where you belong," he added.

That evening for dinner, I roasted a chicken the way Mrs. Cuthbert had taught me—with an array of herbs, surrounded by baked potatoes and emitting juices that would make a flavorful gravy. Although Mrs. Cuthbert always complained that recipe books were "no good" and the best learning was from "just getting on with it," for now I found them invaluable.

Agatha and Cyril both uttered their agreement that it was probably one of the best roast chickens they had ever eaten, followed by an abundance of smiles. Agatha even spoke to me once or twice minus the venom, and I hoped that she would never lock me inside that attic again. It had been a one-off incident, an out-of-character moment.

"I'm glad we kept you on. Keep cooking like this and I may grow very fond of you!" she said.

After clearing away the dishes and grabbing a few of the vegetables for myself, I began the task of cleaning up the gravy I had spilled on the kitchen floor. Agatha said I may as well clean the whole floor again, so I obliged, my entire body yearning for rest back in my own comfortable bed.

"Because you were not around for a few hours, many of the tasks have been left undone," she said. I wanted to remind her that I had been locked in the attic, where she'd put me, but Agatha had proven she could turn at any moment and I did not want to upset her.

"So you will be up early in the morning to begin."

"Yes, madam."

That night, I finally made my way up to my room. My underarms reeked of stale sweat and my shoulders ached as if they had balanced an entire tree. I couldn't wait to feel the softness of the sheet and the pillow against my skin, sensations I had taken for granted.

I sat on my bed, just as the door opened.

"What are you doing?" said Agatha.

"I am retiring to bed, madam."

"This isn't your room anymore, Celestine. Surely you know where you will be sleeping now?"

I wanted to avoid the inevitability of the answer.

"Come on, follow me," she said. I stayed put on the bed, but her grip on my arm was swift as she pulled me upward.

"Don't make this harder than it needs to be," she said slowly.

She let go of my arm as I followed her out of my room and up the flight of stairs which led to that darkened place. That tomb of dust. That place away from everyone and everywhere.

She stood by the opened door, her eyebrows raised.

"No, please, madam. No." My pathetic words sounded weak against the force of her palm on my back, as it attempted to maneuver my body into that darkened place once again. I resisted, my feet stamping firmly on the floor, almost tripping over as she increased the force of her palms by shoving me harder, causing me to feel unbalanced and yet rooted to the ground. I assumed she had given up when I no longer felt the pressure . . . until I felt the sting of her touch on my neck.

"I see you still have on that ugly thing around your neck."

My father's necklace.

"Get inside or I will rip it off you, right now as we stand."

My entire body relaxed, and with one shove I fell into the attic and onto the ground, but this time I shot up quickly and reached for the door just as it slammed shut. The sound of the key turning in the lock was the loudest I had ever heard in my life.

"Let me out!" I shouted, loud enough to be heard, even while knowing no one below this floor could.

My anger quickly turned to humiliation that I had allowed this to happen to me once again. There were no more thoughts of this being a bad dream or my imagination; this was real. This was happening.

It was happening to me.

I slid down the wall and pulled my knees up to my chest. I refused to weep. I simply gave in to a feeling of hopelessness which held no escape. A darkness to match the room I could possibly spend this night and manymore inside.

So the desperate roar that left my body was unplanned, yet it refused to give me the release it promised. It simply led to a frustration and a holding in of tears that I would not shed anymore.

I roared again.

I snapped my eyes shut—darkness to darkness.

Silence.

No one, absolutely no one, could hear me.

Chapter Twenty-Eight

Lowra
1974

My voice was no more than a whisper, yet it had taken all my strength to say the words.

I repeated her name again and again—quietly, yet wanting anyone and everyone to hear. I opened my eyes to the semi-darkness, my vision blurred. I stood up and toppled backward, balancing on my feet.

My hands were balled into fists and I pounded the door, weakly.

How had I got in here?

The last I recalled was being called in for dinner which in itself was unusual, as I often just made myself a Marmite sandwich or ate a piece of fruit whenever I was hungry. Dad had always joked his fiancée wasn't much of a cook, yet the spaghetti bolognese she had presented me with had been delicious and I'd wolfed it down with a glass of cool water. That was all I could remember until now, waking up on a cold floor with a dry mouth, my head feeling as if it had been pushed into a brick wall.

I kept pounding at the door, this time with a bit more force. But this only resulted in a sharp pain in my wrist which shot up to my elbow.

I was breathing in spurts.

I'd never been frightened of enclosed spaces and used to play hide and seek with Grandma, so, just as I had then, I waited for someone to find me.

One, two, three, four, five.

I waited.

It was a joke. It had to be. Why else would she lock the door and leave me in an attic? She was always saying how much of a brat I was and that my dad had been too soft with me. She was teaching me a lesson, that was it! That's all this was!

I wasn't going to call out anymore. She'd be back soon; she couldn't keep me here forever.

My belly was rumbling.

I closed my eyes.

I woke up with what I could feel was a trail of spit running down my chin, my underwear wet from where I had weed myself during the night.

How long had I been here?

At least my head didn't feel fuzzy anymore.

If she left me in here forever, maybe that wouldn't be so bad. I missed my dad every single day and it hurt, thinking about the way he held my hands and sometimes danced with me and Grandma around the room until I got dizzy; the smell of his aftershave as my head rested on his chest and we lay down on the sofa in front of the television. I missed the tick-tock sound of his watch as his arm circled around my back every time we hugged for the longest time, and for absolutely no reason other than to tell me he loved his pudding pie.

Now he was gone, so what was the point of anything anyway?

When she did open the door, it was her outline I saw first. To begin with I thought this was a dream, or a nightmare.

"How long have I been in here?" I mumbled.

She ignored my question and simply told me to clean myself up and get ready for breakfast. I was so hungry, I was happy to bypass the "cleaning up" even though I smelled like crap.

Instead of spaghetti bolognese, it was chicken stew and orange squash. I had no idea if it was good or not, but it was food. She even gave me seconds.

When she said I had to pack some clothes, I couldn't even gather up enough thank yous to voice my relief at being sent somewhere else. I did allow myself to believe that maybe Grandma was coming to collect me . . .

I threw what I could into the black bin bag she gave me, including the picture of my mum, dad and me, but my head began to feel a little fuzzy again. It became difficult to walk without wobbling and it was confusing when she told me to head up instead of down the stairs. With my sack of clothes dragging behind me, I took my time up each step. When she held out her arm for support, I wanted to tell her to go away, but I couldn't risk falling back down the stairs. Inside the attic, I chucked the bag of clothes onto the floor beside a bucket she said would be a toilet. I think that's what I heard, anyway. I had questions, but my mouth wouldn't move and the words had to stay in my head. The bang of the door closing felt louder than ever and I was already sitting on the floor, wordless and without an ounce of energy left in my body.

I closed my eyes immediately and lay back on the hard surface. My last conscious thought was, *I hope I don't wake up this time*.

Celestine
1907

Each night Agatha would march me up the stairs where mercifully there was still light, and then shove me into the attic where only darkness existed. The door would close and sometimes I'd catch just a bit of light before it disappeared.

The attic was full of containers, discarded items that no one wanted anymore.

Perhaps that's exactly what I was now.

So many times, I'd bang my foot against a wall or object I did not know was there, sometimes by mistake, other times just to feel a sensation. To remind myself I was still here. The scratching sounds coming from the walls were far from irritating as they represented life, company. Indeed, back home I had been used to roaming wildlife.

Back home. A lifetime away.

In the attic my world was small, and sometimes I didn't want it to be small. I would then think about what it was like outside the attic, the house, in London perhaps. But when I did that I'd have to think about going to a port and a big ship and then . . . home. So it served me well not to think about the world outside this house. It was safer.

It was the cold that affected me the most. The attic felt like the coldest part of the house and it was only after I had located a blanket on top of an object I couldn't see that I began to feel any semblance of comfort.

When the room was coated in a gray and dusty light, I recognized one of Sir Richard's wooden chests which had once been in his study. I pondered when it was that they had brought it up here. What did it matter?

What did anything matter?

Beneath the blocked-out window, the stretch of naked wall felt like a blank canvas in the darkness, but instead of a need to display art, I would use it to vent my frustration.

There was so much I wanted and needed to say, and yet my voice came without sound. My purpose in this house was in stark contrast to what it had been when Sir Richard was alive.

Everything had changed, but what did remain stained upon my body was what he had named me: Celestine Babbington. So, it made pure sense to take out my pocketknife, fall to my knees and stab the wall carefully, so as not to damage it. My elbows and shoulders ached with anger as I carved seven letters into the skin of that wall.

D I K E M B E.

The name given to me by my parents.

Dikembe. Dikembe. Dikembe. DIKEMBE!

My body was spent. The floor felt cold but not wet with my tears. That was a part of myself I'd never give away again. I also no longer tracked the passing of time, but could tell by the changing seasons or just a passing word from one of the Mayhews that six months had passed. Now, at thirteen years old, almost a man, I would have to act like one. Wasn't that what my father would say? I tried not to think too much about my father, Mama and my brothers. What good would it do? Yet as soon as I closed my eyes and curled up in a fetal position on top of what could only be floorboards, it was the first thing I did. I was transported to a collection of happy memories which included sitting under the tree, or chasing a gecko that ran up to the roof of the house, or gazing at Mama's sparkling eyes as she hummed to me.

I questioned the validity of my memories, confused between imagination and reality, as it had been almost two whole years since I had trodden the soil of my homeland, and as I had grown from child to adolescent, it felt longer.

Every day felt the same.

Agatha would unlock the door and sometimes speak, sometimes remain silent. Before the sun came up I would begin the tasks of the day, and not be finished until long after it had set. I began to look forward to the end of the day when I'd find myself once more on that attic floor. At least there I no longer needed to hear Agatha's voice. At least there I could rest and imagine I was elsewhere. That I was *home*.

Embracing the silence of the attic was easy for me, and so it was outside it. Silence when Agatha and Cyril addressed me as "boy" and no longer used the name which had been given to me by Sir Richard. Silence when Bill made the food delivery, able to shut out his words which were always going to be taunts gloating at my predicament. Silence. I would speak only when absolutely necessary.

I had not a penny to my name and absolutely nowhere to turn.

Staying silent was my power.

My only power.

Lowra
1974

My eyes flickered open.

She'd left the light on. I was in there. The attic.

I wasn't sure what time it was, but I hadn't been downstairs in what felt like a very long time.

It was difficult to keep track of time in here because every day felt the same, the time passing fast yet slow. I only knew a day had gone because she'd walk in to change the bucket once in a while. I hadn't noticed the sink earlier and didn't have the mental space to decipher why a sink would be inside an attic and not a toilet, though I was grateful for the sound of running water. Any sound, because whenever she appeared, she never said much. Sometimes a mumble; other times a complaint which had nothing to do with me.

It was only when the stench from the bucket became unbearable that I realized she hadn't been in for a while. Another clue to a long stretch would be leaving me more food than usual. An extra apple; half a loaf of bread instead of four slices. She was unpredictable with what she brought and that sometimes felt unsafe to me. Even more so than being inside that attic.

Luckily, along with my clothes I'd packed a book, a pad, a pen, and of course that picture of the three of us: my mum, Dad and me. I used to keep it under my pillow so I could feel close to them. Now, I simply wanted to be with them, for real. The three of us, together forever.

Sometimes I'd while away the time by writing poems or rummaging around some of the boxes. I found a briefcase. My dad's briefcase! This was where he'd kept his "papers" and "certificates," as he called them. My mother's passport was inside, her beautiful face smiling from the page. The stamped pages confirmed all the lovely trips we had made as a family, mostly to Spain. I wished I remembered them all—every little bit. But inside that attic, I had time to conjure possibilities of what they could have been like, and they were all perfect, of course. Sun-filled sandy beaches and kisses—so many kisses from my mum and dad.

I wrote a poem. I sang an ABBA track or a David Bowie song. Dad loves, I mean *loved*, David Bowie.

Dad.

When I closed my eyes and lay back on the attic floor, I could no longer see his face. Not clearly anyway. It was as if he was fading from my memory. Fading from me. Just like my mother had when I was six years old. I no longer knew what his aftershave smelled like; I could no longer remember how it felt to be in his arms. If it wasn't for the picture, I would have forgotten about the flecks of light brown in his hair and how he smiled.

I didn't think about much anymore. I didn't think about the past, and the future didn't really exist for me. It felt comfortable to just sit and wait for nothing.

Sometimes when someone came into the house—not guests, because she never had those, but a plumber or somebody—I could hear the faint sound of the downstairs doors opening and shutting. I never heard voices, though, because they were too far down, I suppose. Most nights, I felt too sleepy to care anyway. The thought of banging on the attic door sometimes crossed my mind, but I lacked any real strength. I always knew when the house was about to have a visitor because she'd make spaghetti bolognese—a dish I now loved. Sometimes she even put spices in it. I liked that, too.

I never wondered if the people who came to the house ever asked after me. It often felt hard to believe that I existed, myself.

If I didn't exist to myself, then how could I exist to them?

She appeared from time to time, took away the food I didn't eat and replaced it with more. She actually left some ice cream once, which I thought was funny because it melted so quickly, making a huge mess. But it was probably the first meal I had eaten in three days, and it tasted delicious though it made my stomach run. That day or night or whatever, I had to use the bucket for over an hour, sweat dripping from my pores, the stench overwhelming in that attic. The pain arrived in waves, raw, yet it still didn't kill me!

She told me it was a Wednesday, and that my grandma was coming to visit and I should come downstairs and see her. I said no. I was happy in my little room.

"Your grandma wants to see you; don't you want that?"

I actually felt stronger today, not sleepy, and this perhaps made me feel more defiant. "No," I said.

Her mouth was moving and words were coming out, but I decided to no longer listen. Her face grew red—I saw this with clarity under that faint lightbulb—yet still I said nothing. When her left hand came at me and connected sharply with my cheek and my chin jerked to the side, I felt something crack in my neck.

"Your father isn't here anymore, Lowra," she said with a speck of snot flying out of her nose. "You will wash, get dressed, you will comb that hair of yours, and you'll come down and wait for your gran and let her know that everything is fine."

"Why should I?"

"She is an old woman. More bad news could tip her over the edge. Is that what you want?"

Tip her over the edge. Is that what she'd done to my dad?

My defiance felt pointless but necessary. Of course I didn't want Grandma to get sick and die. I never wanted that. Also, a small part of me wanted to see her. A small hopeful part of me needed it.

I looked toward the floor. The floor I had spent many nights asleep on, or fuzzily awake and trying to remember what my dad smelled like.

"OK," I said.

"Good. Now be a good little girl and clean yourself up. Dirty moths never turn into butterflies, do they?"

When I walked out of the attic for the first time after being inside for—according to her—three weeks, there was no fanfare in my head or imaginary balloons flying above me, no level of hope in any part of my being. I was just going to see my grandma.

Inside my bedroom, my real bedroom, it felt the way it did after I'd stayed at Grandma's for a week. Different. Like the walls were bigger somehow. I stared at myself in the mirror, noticing just how much I no longer looked like me. My hair used to be so tidy, in a bun or touching my shoulders; now it just looked like a scraggy mess. Luckily the little sink in the attic meant I could wash using the small nub of soap she'd tossed in one day with the food, so at least I didn't smell.

I pulled a clean dress from the cupboard.

"Are you ready?" she called, as if this were a normal day, week, month. As if she hadn't locked me in a room for three weeks.

"Remember, your gran is not well and you wouldn't want her dying too, would you? Like your dad?"

"Yes. I mean, no."

She bent down to my height, and I could feel her breath brush my nose. "He probably jumped because he'd had enough of you."

I swallowed. My eyes closed. An image of Dad standing on the edge of a ship. His last thoughts about me and how much he hated me.

"Now, go on and see your gran," she said quietly.

A single tear plopped down my face and I wiped it with the back of my hand.

Just minutes later, I was in front of my grandma, who looked worse than I did. The lipstick she used to carefully apply had bled; her hair, fully white now, was cut in a style way too short for her.

"Lowra, my darling, how are you?" She smiled. "You look so much like him."

I couldn't look at her, not with the thoughts of my dad standing on the edge of a large ship, facing the choppy waters. His last thought of me . . .

I said a few things to my grandma, but it didn't seem to matter what I said because she didn't appear to be listening anyway. She was content in her own little world. Perhaps I was surrounded by mad and crazy people because no one seemed right. Then again, I couldn't be sure of what was right anymore because it was as if I too had joined the gang of crazies. I was no longer right. How could I be?

"You can see she's well looked after," she said. "I home-school her, as always."

"He did use to say it was better for her to be schooled at home," said Grandma.

"Just like her dad had been doing since Vivienne died. That's how we met, of course." The giggle that followed I wasn't expecting. Nor had I expected her to say my mother's name.

Vivienne.

I hadn't heard that name in so long. My mother had been a very distant memory, only real in that picture of us in our own little bubble of three. Now it had been pierced with her ugly, filthy mouth, and I was not going to allow that. Not now, not ever!

The fire rising within me refused to burn out. I waited until Grandma headed back to the Winter Pines nursing home before turning to her.

"Don't ever say her name again," I said. My voice was louder than it had been in weeks. My ability to even raise it was surprising to me, but welcome. "You have no right to say her name!"

Her eyes grew as wide as mine, glaring as brightly as the green-encrusted butterfly brooch on her left lapel. "What?" she said.

"My mother" Just as I spoke, the back of her ringed hand connected with my lip with such force I was on the floor within seconds. Then she bent down and grabbed a clump of my straggly hair, pulling me up to face her.

"Who do you think you're talking to, you ungrateful little bitch? Do you want me to call social services or the council and they can chuck you in a home?"

I felt a second slap, then another and another. This time the force of them was not hard enough to keep me on the ground and I stood up quicker each time, like a boxer who wouldn't quit. I tasted blood in my mouth as slaps and even punches rained upon me. When she tired of hitting me, and my own strength was zapped, I lay on the floor as she stood over me with just the sound of our deepened breaths.

"Why do you make me do that, you horrid, horrid little girl? How do you expect to grow into a butterfly if you continue to behave like a common moth? Why do you make me do that?"

None of her mumbling ever made much sense but this sounded

even worse. However, as she turned on her heel and left me there on the floor, tasting my own blood, I felt a wave of satisfaction.

I stood up slowly and placed my palm on my cheek, and then I smiled.

The beating would be worth it if she never said my mother's name again.

Chapter Twenty-Nine

Lowra

1993

"I want . . . I need to tell you something," I said as Monty stood in the corridor of my flat.

It still felt nowhere near natural to see another person in my home, but Monty was different—or else he would be once I shared a part of myself only Dr. Raj had seen.

Part of the reason I felt compelled to do this was because of all the things we'd unraveled so far and what was surely to come. The talk on that train had alerted me to so much of what was unsaid between us, the hidden pain we both carried but for very different reasons.

"You know I said there was one piece of paper in the attic floorboards . . . well, there were actually three pieces."

He sat down on the sofa.

I handed him a piece of paper.

I am awake.
Asleep.
I cannot tell.
I just know that I wish to be anywhere but here.

I handed Monty the second piece of paper.

I open my eyes to death.
But I'm still here. Why hasn't she claimed me?
Apparently it's my birthday tomorrow; not yet thirteen.
Yet nobody knows I exist.
Each of the days melts into one long stretch.
Weeks fly by.
Endless.
I'm no longer afraid of the dark.
The blackness, warm.

I let Dr. Montgomery Alburn into the world I'd inhabited from the age of eleven to fifteen. At the mercy of an abuser; locked away in an attic with only a doll, a necklace and a couple of bits of paper for company. I didn't sugarcoat what had happened to me, yet still I avoided the detail of what it truly felt like to be locked away for weeks on end, with only the occasional respite when an education inspector came to visit. I left out the parts about the stench, the cold, the hunger . . . and the hopelessness.

I told him the abridged version of it all, in a clinical and matter-of-fact way that felt safe to me.

The poems said more than I ever would, anyway.

"I don't know what to say . . ." he said.

"I told you my poems weren't very good."

I also told Monty about my extended stay at the hospital, and he listened without any judgment. I think. His long legs spread out in front of him as he sat on my sofa drinking in each of my words.

"I'm so, so sorry you went through this, Lowra."

I almost said, "It wasn't all bad, Monty," yet had to catch my words.

1976

As usual, she walked in that day, afternoon or evening, whatever it was, placing the plate of food on the floor. Today my head didn't feel like it was filled with mush.

I expected her to turn on her heel as usual, but she remained there. I hadn't said a word, so surely she wasn't about to punish me? I laughed at the absurdity of that thought. Wasn't I already being punished by being locked in this attic? Seriously, my perception of punishments had changed over the years.

"He understood me, you know," she said.

"Who?"

"Patrick."

I sat up then and moved my back against the wall. It wasn't often I heard my dad's name.

"He didn't look at me the way she did."

To my utter surprise, she sat on the floor in front of me.

"All those pretty little butterflies, with their gorgeous colors and flapping wings, all bunched together in one space, trapped . . ."

"What?"

"My mother, she ran a butterfly farm. She was there all hours. I think she loved them more than she loved us."

I looked at the brooch on her left lapel. Even in the dull light, I saw that this one was pink and slightly sparkly. She owned quite a few, and most days I imagined stabbing her in the eye with one.

"You had brothers and sisters?" I asked, pretending to care. She ignored me of course, and got on with saying whatever she wanted to.

"When you're young, you try to do things to make them happy, but they never are. It was as if she hated me, but when Patrick looked at me it felt different."

Her words were beginning to sting, and Dad was now the last person I wanted to think about or talk about with her.

"Then he left me," she said.

I wanted to tell her that he didn't leave, that he fell off a ship, or that she pushed him, but although I felt stronger than I had in days, it wasn't enough to accept the consequences. Not today. So I kept my mouth shut, silently calling her a crazy bitch instead.

She shook her head slowly. "Why did you have to look so much like him?"

1993

I now felt a need to brush it all off. I felt naked and perhaps seen . . . and not in a good way. I didn't want Monty or anyone to ever see beneath my surface, because I wasn't sure what they would find. Yet by showing him those poems, telling him a portion of my story, I had already opened the door.

"I don't understand why social services didn't see something was wrong sooner. If you weren't going to school . . ."

"As far as they were concerned, she . . . Nina was my home tutor when she met my dad, so she simply pretended she was carrying on doing that, always keeping the inspectors happy when they visited, which was infrequently."

He opened his mouth to speak. I knew what he was going to say.

"Why didn't I say anything when they visited?"

"I wasn't going to say that. You were a child. Just like Celestine."

I felt a shortness in my breath, a clue I wanted this line of conversation to end. I hadn't planned to show this level of vulnerability to Monty, but now it had happened, now my secrets were out of the bag, looking up at him, it would seem he was OK with them. There was no judgment in his eyes, just compassion.

I'm not really sure I wanted either.

Lola Jaye

1978

It was thanks to a sparkly red platform shoe that I finally managed to leave that house.

The day was only unique in that it was inspection day, and as usual, I could only look blankly toward the woman in front of me as she scribbled inside her lined notebook. This one was called Miss Jennings. She had her hair pulled up into a bun and everything she wore was beige. The one before her wore sky-blue bell-bottom trousers and a tank top, which I simultaneously thought was weird and rather cool. On "good days," I'd get a copy of *Jackie* magazine with my food, where I got to see what people were wearing. That's how I knew what was cool in fashion, while I just wore stuff she thought looked good on me. Like this hideous belted dress with a butterfly belt clip. Like something out of the fifties! When I at first refused to wear it, she said it was the type of dress only "good little girls" wore. I put it on to keep her quiet; sometimes I just didn't have the strength to fight. It was no longer about the slaps, scratches or—and this was a new one—kicks. It was more about the inner fight. Sometimes it felt easier to give in.

I always knew the inspectors were due because she'd start muttering about how peaky I looked, "encouraging" me to down a load of vitamins so I could at least look healthy. I was already suspicious of these "vitamins" because sometimes I'd feel woozy without any warning, but I rationalized that this usually happened after a freshly made meal. Also, she wouldn't risk that happening just before a visit. Then again, I liked that woozy feeling because I didn't have to think about anything.

Another clue the inspectors were due: around a week before, she wouldn't hit me. Clever, that.

"You seem proficient in all of your subjects. You're a voracious reader, I see?" remarked the inspector. I wanted to respond, *Yes, she lets me study for an hour a day in the attic, and there isn't much else to do except write poetry and sing to myself. Would you like to see one of my poems?*

"I like to read," I said instead.

"Well, that will be all then," she said, smoothing down her beige skirt as she stood to leave. "Oh, actually, one more thing."

When she said this, my breath held in my throat. She knew. She had noticed.

There usually wasn't much eye contact during these visits, and when they bothered to look at me, they weren't really looking.

"Mrs. Cavendish, Lowra looks like she's been under the weather . . ."

"Just a cold."

"Is that so?"

I nodded my head slowly.

They were never able to clock what was going on inside. That inside matched the outside; my body weak from the lack of nourishing food, my skin a little paler than it should be because it hardly saw the sun.

I knew the drill. As soon as Miss Jennings was out of the front door, her body past the half-lion, half-human statues, I'd have to head back to the attic. This time, though, I stuck around a bit longer. Sometimes I did that—to get her riled up or just to soak in a change of bright scenery, look out of the window and stare at a stranger walking past. But when she rushed back to the room, her body just inside the doorway, something unusual happened: her sparkly red platform shoe and a bit of upturned carpet connected haphazardly, making her lose her balance, and then there was a loud thud as her entire body slammed onto the floor, face first!

I stood over her, thoughts struggling to wade through the fuzzy shock. Then, clarity.

Run!

She was moving. Unfortunately.

Run!

Did I even have the strength or the spirit, or had I given up? Each day in the last four years had chipped away what was left of me.

Run!

I moved closer to her and she raised her head. A line of blood drained from her mouth where her butterfly brooch had caught it. I stepped over her and felt her cold fingers clasp my ankle. I have no idea where the strength came from, but I used it to shake my leg so vigorously that the heel of my shoe connected over and over again with some part of her face or head or both, until she let go. Then the strength I had thought depleted grew as I kept on moving.

"Lowra!" she called out. Her voice was not as strong as usual, but to me it felt as forceful as an elephant. I moved quicker, unsure if she was behind me or not, feeling her presence anyway.

I reached the front door of the house, the two statues either side of me, and I could see Miss Jennings walking further and further away. I stepped forward way too slowly, as if I were trudging through a vat of treacle. I heard something or someone behind me. A gust of air hit my face; I'd forgotten what that felt like. I opened my mouth to call out to Miss Jennings, but there was only silence. Why couldn't I speak? I moved onto those steps, one foot at a time until I felt my entire body jerk forward, tumbling down each of the steps until I reached the bottom.

I looked up and she was standing at the top of the stairs.

"Lowra!" she called.

A man and a woman crouched down beside me and my body started to shake. I couldn't stop it.

"Are you OK, love?" said one of them. I nodded my head as I heard the door slam shut. My tummy curdled. Was she here?

I could only hear the unfamiliar voices of the woman and the man.

Did I live here? Did I need them to press the bell?

"No. No, I was just passing. Wanted to look at the statues. I don't live here." And there was that strength again; the forcefulness in my voice and that absolute determination.

They helped me up to my feet and the shaking didn't stop, even when I realized she wasn't there.

"Let's at least get you to a hospital," said the lady.

"No, but thank you," I said, limping away from that house, the heat in my steps pushing me further and further away.

I knew exactly where I was going.

When I believed I was as far away from that house as possible, I sat at a bus stop and realized at some point along the way I'd stopped shaking. I kept looking up to see if she was there, ready to run again, but she wasn't. I did wonder if she'd called the police to come and get me, but then she wouldn't because there was always the chance I'd tell them what she'd done to me over the past four years.

I had nothing except the clothes on my back. That hideous 1950s dress, yet I still looked better than I usually did because of the inspector's visit.

A woman sat beside me.

"Long day?" she said.

"Something like that."

"I know that all too well."

"I'm hoping you can help me . . ." I began to shake again.

"What is it? Are you all right? You're shaking like a leaf."

Little did she know she'd done me a favor all those times she'd threatened to call social services to take me away and put me in a home.

"Can you tell me where social services is?"

"You mean the council offices? It's not far from here, but you'll need to take the eleven bus."

I opened my mouth to speak.

"Don't worry, love. I'll pay your bus fare," she said.

The kindness of a stranger had restored my hope—to the size of a grain of rice, but at least it existed.

The signage of Ranklin Council looked like a mirage, a figment of my overused and tired imagination. The board beside it listed a number of departments and I focused on the one I needed immediately.

"Can I help you, love?" said the woman behind the counter.

"I'm fifteen years old and . . . and I need a place to stay."

"Runaway, are you?" she said with disinterest.

"My stepmother . . . she . . . she . . ." That was all I had, which took all the strength left running through my body. If they refused to believe me, if they didn't care, I would walk the streets until I dropped. I'd already seen the worst life had to offer and death would probably be the best step.

The woman quickly walked out from behind the desk and asked if I wanted a cup of tea. She looked me straight in the eye as she spoke. And just in that one moment I felt everything lifting from my entire body. No one, especially her, had ever done that. The education inspectors never did, and when my grandma had, it was never me she saw. But this woman, she saw *me*, and it was then that I allowed myself to believe everything was going to be OK.

1993

"Did Nina get prosecuted?"

"Not at all. It would have simply been my word against hers and I'm not sure things were that great in the late seventies—they're not even brilliant now when it comes to children and safety. But they took my word for it and drove me to a children's home that very night."

"I'm so sorry."

"Why? I had a warm bed and hot food three times a day, which all the kids complained about but I thought was the most delicious food I'd ever tasted!"

"I get it," said Monty.

He didn't. And there was no way Monty could understand anything of what I'd just told him. Just as I couldn't know what it was like to walk in his shoes, it would be unfair of me to expect him to understand what it was like in mine.

Chapter Thirty

Lowra
1993

Thankfully, there was no real time to process what I'd done by telling Monty the truth, because the next day my intercom sounded unexpectedly.

"I had to tell you this in person, Lowra."

We both sat down.

"Remember the acquaintance who works at the Smithsonian?"

"The handwriting expert?"

"He got back to me concerning the photocopied words from the piece of paper you found in the attic."

"And?"

"The last two words, at least, are not in Swahili, as I had assumed, but may be from another language."

"Which one?"

"Apparently it's likely to be one of the two major Bantu languages, according to his contact at the Museum for Central Africa, in Belgium."

"Bantu?"

"Kiluba. Possibly. Plus, it's a language she—the contact—just happens to be familiar with. The modern version anyway," he said, ignoring my question. Sometimes Monty would assume my knowledge on such things matched his own, when it didn't. And never would.

"Well, that's good, isn't it?" I said, instead.

"The modern version may differ to what was spoken in, say, 1905 . . . so we can't be sure of a perfect translation, but they're working on it. They haven't finished with the other words yet as they're finding a couple of them a bit challenging, but he thought I'd like to see this."

He handed me the polka-dot notebook.

"There's a yellow sticker on the page and I've written them down."

I opened the notebook to the translated list of words.

Al??e
?????? away
Maybe?
??????
Ka?ili
Ma??
D?kem?e
Good child/boy
Help me

Chapter Thirty-One

Celestine
1908

At times, as I prepared dinner or breakfast or afternoon tea, it was easy to release bits of my spittle into a bubbling pot, or wipe a piece of meat on the floor just before laying it on Agatha's plate.

Therefore, at least I could describe cooking for Agatha and Cyril as joyful, while cleaning the rugs and Venetian blinds, which now had to be done regularly, was time-consuming, strenuous, and something I dreaded. Who knew that watching and conversing with Mrs. Cuthbert, Enid and Bill had been an apprenticeship? The wooden slats of the Venetian blinds at the window took longer than I had envisaged, as each had to be removed individually to clean. As I'd observed with Enid, I used the brush to beat the carpet, the strokes soft at first, then increasing in might as clouds of dust hovered over me. I no longer saw the rug as I struck it over and over again, until the cane brush gave way and snapped in two. I doubled over, my vision clouding as I slowly crumpled to the floor to join it. I didn't want to get up again, happy to stay there and just not move. But as soon as I heard her voice, I knew I had to.

Luckily, my chores tired me out so much I had no energy to truly take in the reality of where I slept at night. I always made sure not to drink too much water so the need to urinate was lessened during the night, but this just made me parched and weak.

I spoke very little with Agatha and Cyril. I did what I was told and this required not many words from me. So I was surprised one day when Agatha called me into the study with an unusual request.

She was standing in front of the mantelpiece where the few remaining artifacts of Sir Richard's collection were displayed. The photographs we had taken that day in London still remained on the wall.

"What do you think about these photographs?" she said, pointing to each of them. "Very modern, aren't they? So clear." As she moved along, her footsteps made annoying sounds against the floor. "This one in particular is very amusing." She pointed toward the photograph with me dressed in a piece of cloth around my waist. If only she knew—that my thoughts on that day were tame compared to the ones I currently harbored.

"Is this the type of clothing you are used to?"

I did not answer and could see no point in this exchange, except for my humiliation and her amusement.

She continued. "How much do you think they will fetch? Richard left a lot of debts that need paying, and I for one am very fond of this house and have no intention of moving away to help pay them off. So . . . do you think they will bring much money?"

"Yes, madam," I said, because I really didn't know what else to say. This was trickery because Agatha of course had no real interest in my opinion.

She persisted. "I mean, do you think they're worth anything substantial?"

"I do not know the value of such items." I only knew what they meant to me, and at this point I would not care if I never saw them again. Perhaps Agatha assumed her words would hurt me in some way, when in reality she was simply taking time away from the chores I had yet to complete.

"I must say, you're not being much help." Her eyes narrowed. "Is there nothing that will elicit an emotion?"

"That would depend on what type of emotion you are attempting to elicit, madam." The last word, I spat. On the surface, this exchange between us was civil at best, but I felt it.

I felt a darkness.

"Take them off the wall and make them ready for sale," she said as she flounced away.

Later, when Cyril and Agatha left for the evening, I walked back into Sir Richard's study and gently pulled the five photographs from the wall. I imagined breaking each and every one of them in two, before tossing them onto a bonfire. Images of that day were fresh in my head. The expression on my face that clouded a multitude of unsavory thoughts. I remembered it all clearly. It wasn't even that long ago and yet so much had happened since.

I slowly pulled out the pocketknife, my eyes scanning but not truly taking in each image.

Look up at him with adoration in your eyes!

Wear it, like you did back in Africa.

The words of the photographer were spoken in my mama's voice, and then my father's and then Kabili's, until I could take it no longer. I picked up the photograph—the one of Sir Richard sitting cross-legged on the floor as I handed him an empty cup of tea. A pose of servitude that had made no sense at the time, yet now illustrated my life in detail. I held the knife against the neck of Sir Richard, as I looked at the other photograph of him standing proudly with the gun I should have had the courage to turn on him that very day.

I squeezed my eyes shut. The image of my father's lifeless body, bloodstained, fresh blood pumping from the wound in his neck as he gasped his last, was clear as I made the first split across Sir Richard's neck.

I felt nothing.

Look up at him with adoration in your eyes!

The second slit, from his neck to his waist, produced more feeling, and more so as I stabbed at the picture deeper and deeper, the photograph ripping to sheds with each frenzied movement of my hand.

Wear it, like you did back in Africa.

Look up at him with adoration in your eyes!

The knife invading every part of him, just as he had done to my life; diminishing this image of him to almost nothing. When there was little left of the photograph, and with sweat dripping from my pores, I sat back, spent, my breathing escalated.

I didn't care about the consequences, or what Agatha would do to me. Surely locking me inside an attic for most hours of the evening and driving me like a workhorse meant there wasn't much else she could do anyway—but at least for those few seconds I'd felt empowered by a moment of victory.

"I know what you did," she said. I was on my knees scrubbing the kitchen floor the next morning, as she stood over me.

"What is it you are referring to, madam?" I stood up, and it annoyed me that I still only reached her eye level, even though I no longer fitted some of my trousers.

"I know what you did to the photograph. What I don't know is what possessed you to behave with such frenzied abandon. I hope this isn't a taste of you giving in to some type of animalistic instincts, because that would be a prob—"

"No, madam, there is a simple explanation."

"Go on."

"I am terribly sorry, but the frame was already damaged and it did not take much to tear the photograph when I tried to retrieve it from the wall."

Her expression, a smile, confused me. And when she brushed the tip of her finger against the top part of my left ear, I could only look up, not used to any physical contact from her.

"Don't worry, there are four more delightful images of you both which I am sure will fetch a pretty penny. I'm not sure who would be interested in such things, though. Frightful!"

"Yes, madam." Even her lack of sense must have been able to fathom that I had indeed used a knife to destroy that photograph, yet she'd not questioned me any further. Agatha truly believed I had ripped it to shreds with my bare hands. She truly thought me to be a raging beast!

"It can be our little secret," she said, smiling. "You may resume your duties." As she turned on her heel and headed toward the door, I exhaled, not knowing I had been holding my breath.

I'd sometimes open the door of what was once my room. There was no comfort in doing so, only a reminder of what else I had lost.

Then one day, I saw her. In my bed.

At first I thought this to be another waking dream, where the vividness of my imagination would rescue me from unsavory thoughts.

But this was real.

She was real.

Her skin was alabaster white like a mythical character. I watched as she slept soundly in the bed.

I shouldn't have been in there as this was no longer my bedroom. The attic was my domain now. But seeing this stranger in my bed was most terrifying at first, and perhaps what I deserved for sneaking a look at what had nothing to do with me anymore.

So, when I saw her again, this time standing right in front of me, I was confident this was certainly my imagination. A person, a girl. Her shoulder-length hair almost golden and dressed in a ring of little flowers which sat on top of her head. The same height as me, possibly the same age or younger, and most certainly not Agatha.

"Hello," I think she said. I had been hunched over at the sink, preparing vegetables and fighting to keep my eyes open.

She spoke again. "Hello?" Then a giggle. She was wearing a sky-blue embroidered dress with white socks pulled up almost to her knees. I noticed everything about this figure, this figment of my lonely imagination.

And then she was gone. As quickly as she had arrived.

When Agatha told me to prepare a third place for dinner, I assumed it to be for another of their friends. They sometimes had guests over; men and women who acknowledged me only when they needed an extra napkin or some more potatoes on their plate.

"This here is my niece, and we call her Tilly," said Agatha.

It was that figure again. The girl. And she was real.

"Tilly, this is Celestine. Say hello, Tilly."

"How do you do, Celestine?" she said, putting out her hand. I slowly went to shake it but caught Agatha's raised eyebrows just in time.

"My brother is very busy and a widower. Tilly will be spending a lot of time here and I will be teaching her the basics of how to become a refined and dignified young lady."

In my head, I scoffed as Agatha was far from dignified.

"Tilly insisted that she meet you."

"Thank you?" I said this as a question because the scene could not have felt more bizarre.

When Cyril walked in, it became even stranger.

"Ah, splendid, you have met our niece. Now, Tilly, you will have a playmate."

Agatha's eyes widened, her long fingers grazing her chest. "I beg your pardon?"

"The poor child does not want to be entertained by two much older people like our good selves. Besides, we have much to do today, Agatha. Do you not recall the errands we have to run in town?"

"Yes, but Cyril . . ."

"I am certain she will be in good hands. Doesn't Celestine already take good care of us?"

She cleared her throat. "Luckily for you then, Celestine, you may have the afternoon off to keep my niece here amused."

"Thank you?" Again I said this as a question, not that Agatha would notice. The absurdity that I should perceive this as good news was so shocking, almost laughable, that I simply had to question it. "It will be an honor to entertain Tilly."

"That's *Miss* Tilly to you," added Agatha.

That afternoon, I was left with this little girl named Tilly. I wasn't sure what I was supposed to do or say, when all I craved was rest, and perhaps to consume a hearty meal and not the stolen mouthfuls of potatoes and peas I had become used to.

"Why are you staring at me?" she said.

"I'm sorry, madam."

Her giggle hung in the air and just stayed there. "My name is Tilly. I am eleven years old. I am not a madam or a miss, silly."

In England, the only people I had talked to of my own generation were Bill and his odious friends, and I felt unsure of how to interact with this strange girl, while not even sure I wanted to.

"Come on, let's go and play," she said.

I had no time to play as there was so much to do, yet I didn't want to offend her.

"Would you like me to help you finish your work?" she said.

"Why would you do that?"

"Then we can play."

"I am not sure there is time for that . . ."

"My aunt said you didn't have to do any work today. So we can play."

I had work to do, chores that would simply pile up if I let them. However, this girl with little flowers in her hair held the promise of something brighter. Play. Which meant to be free of work, if only for an afternoon.

That day I was introduced to hide and seek. I did think about hiding in the attic, but I didn't want her witnessing where I spent every single night. Instead, there were many little compartments that I used, like the cupboard under the stairs or even the pantry. What I thought was a very strange game actually turned into something that allowed me to experience my first belly laugh in so very long. Yet being with Tilly allowed me more than to simply smile; it also made me forget. To forget I had dinner to prepare in the evening and a mountain of chores that would have built up just because of this one moment. But I decided it was worth it. It was worth it for the simple unadulterated joy that being in her company had suddenly given me.

Tilly came back the following day and then the following weekend. Her weekly regular appearances in my life made the reality of sleeping in a dark and cold attic almost bearable, simply because I now had something to look forward to every Saturday; like listening to her talk excitedly about things I knew nothing about, such as the porcelain doll she had been gifted by her grandmother and the rocking horse she no longer rode but whose hair she still enjoyed plaiting.

"I don't like school very much," she said, sitting at the kitchen table as I peeled a bowl of potatoes. Weakness no longer felt prominent in my body because it was as if Tilly had given me a reason to be well again. I also now ate much better, thanks to Agatha allowing Tilly free rein to eat anything she desired—which meant more food for me as Tilly would insist we eat together. Much more satisfying than the stash of old fruit I'd gathered up in the attic, which at times a mouse would get to first.

"What about you, Celestine? Do you like school?"

"I did."

"You don't anymore? Why?"

"I'm not allowed to go."

"Why not?"

I shrugged my shoulders. "I don't know."

"You're not missing much anyway."

I knew what she was trying to do and it wasn't working.

"Do you learn Latin?" I asked.

"Oh no, the boys do that."

"Then what do you do?"

"Needlework. We also learn how to be a wife . . . a good wife."

"Do they teach you how to be a good person?"

"What a strange question, Celestine. Isn't everyone good?"

Chapter Thirty-Two

Celestine
1908

"Shall we go outside?" she asked one day. "We're so close to the sea and I used to love going there with Aunt Agatha."

"Madam will not allow me to leave the house."

"Why not?" Her eyebrows rose. I wasn't about to tell her that even if Agatha permitted it, I myself had no desire to leave the big house. As much as I despised every single wall and each stick of furniture, I had become used to its existence. What had started off as a feeling of confinement now felt familiar, with the outside feeling unsafe in its unfamiliarity. Indeed, I had once almost come to harm on that very beach with Bill and his friends.

"My aunt and uncle are out; they don't need to know!"

"I will get into trouble."

"We will leave them a note." Tilly began to spin around. "It's such a sunny day. We can stay close to the house and pick some daisies if you don't want to go near the sea."

She stopped and clutched her belly.

"Are you all right?" I asked.

"Yes, just feeling like I want to vomit!"

I truly wanted to ask why she'd engage in an activity that would result in her feeling unwell, but Tilly did what she pleased. Hers was the complete antithesis to my own life and yet I still couldn't help but love her. Whatever love meant. It felt much like the love I felt for my mama and my brothers; somewhat diluted, but love nevertheless. Yet sometimes, just sometimes, it became further diluted with something I hoped wasn't jealousy.

Tilly raced off in front of me and appeared moments later dressed in her coat.

"I can't go out, Miss Tilly," I insisted.

"Then I shall go alone. Oh, and stop calling me 'miss'!"

"I must call you this as it is your aunt's instruction. Also, she would not want you to be in any danger."

"It is perfectly safe!"

"Miss Tilly, I cannot allow you to do this! Miss Tilly, it is not safe." As soon as I said those words, I realized they were for me.

"It's just the sea. I'm not asking you to get in!"

I held my breath and then exhaled slowly. "Very well, Miss Tilly. We shall go."

Her smile should have made this perceived sacrifice all the more worthwhile, but then my mind shifted to what could be outside those doors. It had been so long since I had ventured through them. I'd lost track of the days, weeks and months as every day had blurred into one. Each day the monotony so stark and obvious that nothing outside it made sense to me anymore.

My gray wool coat was one of the few items I'd been permitted to keep and remained in the wardrobe of what used to be my room. So I entered, further than the door where I would sometimes stand and gaze in. This time I lay back on what used to be my bed, my tired bones sinking into the softness of the mattress. I did not hear the door open until she said my name. "Celestine!"

I jumped. "Madam!" I said. But it was just Tilly.

"Oh, Miss Tilly, it is you."

"Who else would it be? I wondered where you had got to. Are you sleepy?" Dressed in her coat, she lay beside me on the bed as I shifted closer to the edge to allow her space.

We both looked up at the chandelier above us. This felt nice, peaceful; it reminded me of those moments spent with Kabili under our tree.

"I was just thinking, Miss Tilly."

"About what?"

"Memories," I said.

"Of what?"

"Let's go to the beach if you still want to . . ." Part of me wanted her to say she had changed her mind, as the thought of venturing outside felt so incomprehensible. I had felt that way on the ship, not knowing what awaited me in England, yet here I was.

She sat up.

I could hear Sir Richard's booming voice telling me it was my duty as a man to face this task head-on. I hated that it was his voice and not my father's I chose to hear.

"We shall go," I said.

Downstairs, Tilly opened the front door, the sunlight attacking my eyes.

The half-human, half-creatures were as I had left them, now seemingly much less aggressive in their demeanor.

"Come on, Celestine!" she called, already at the bottom of the stairs. I rubbed at my eyes as I took one step down. My stomach constricted as I took another step.

"Come on!"

The presence of the house behind me felt almost consuming. Yet when I turned around to look at it, I realized it was just a house.

It was just a house.

But somewhere deep inside me, I craved the safety of it. The attic at night. The loneliness, somehow comforting. I was not ready for any of this, none of it!

"Celestine!"

My heart rate increased as I took another four steps down and then stopped.

"What is it?" she asked.

"I don't know."

Tilly ran up the steps two at a time, stopping beside me.

"Come on, I'll walk down with you." When she took my hand, I almost jumped with the shock of this act. To feel the skin of another against mine was to experience both exhilaration and fear all at once. Her warmth fought against the coldness I had built up around me. She spoke words of comfort with each step downward as I clutched her hand. When we reached the bottom, I felt as if I had achieved so much, yet in reality it was so little.

She ran up ahead and headed toward the beach. I had no time to even think of turning back as my main concern was for Tilly.

The sound of the waves crashing against the shore was at first terrifying and then, when I allowed it to be, soothing.

"Where is your family?" asked Tilly moments later as we sat on the pebbly ground. I was glad I had persisted and not stayed behind. I had experienced so much that was good already: the warmth of the sunlight on my face and the recent memory of Tilly's hand in mine.

I looked out at the sea and then back to her, speaking the names of my family members for the first time in so long. Hearing these names allowed them to sound real once again and not a figment of a past that sometimes felt imaginary. But I didn't want them to be real. I wanted, needed them to remain an enigma I was unable to touch, because anything else would just be an added disappointment that resulted in my pain.

"Kabili sounds very nice."

The name of my brother said out loud resulted in pleasure instead of the pain I had predicted.

"I have an older brother and I find him annoying!" she laughed.

"Is that why you come here, to the house?"

"My brother is away at school. I sometimes don't think my father knows what to do with me."

"Do you miss your mother?"

"Of course I do. Just like you must too."

Another human being had acknowledged not only my mama but the relationship we had shared—and I was unsure of how to take that.

We must have spent an hour by the sea, giggling and talking, but I soon began to feel a restlessness with the knowledge I needed to return to the house and start dinner. I also didn't want Cyril and Agatha to return home and find it empty.

Tilly raced me to the door and of course she won. It had been an incredibly uplifting day.

"I was just about to send a search party," said Agatha, waiting by the door.

"My sincere apologies, madam."

"Not at all. As long as my niece is happy."

That night I cooked a tasty dinner before happily waving Tilly off. I walked into the attic with a smile on my face, and even when Agatha turned the key in the lock it remained.

It was still there the next morning as I waited to be let out to start my day. When Agatha did not appear, I used the extra time to think about the lovely day Tilly and I had experienced at the beach. I must have reimagined the whole day a hundred times, and still Agatha did not return.

The sun must have risen on two consecutive days now. My secret supply of fruit was now consumed, along with the jug of water which hadn't been topped up in days.

I was no longer smiling.

I had no idea why Agatha had left me here this long. If not for the faint sound of voices coming from outside, I would have assumed I'd been left in the big house all alone, to face a long and drawn-out death.

Another day passed.

I was being punished again, and this time I had no idea what for.

I was unsure of how long I'd been inside this time, as counting the days began to feel pointless. Once my stomach stopped growling, my need for food turned into fear that I may not actually survive this. A slow realization that, at the age of thirteen, this darkened tomb with its stench of urine and hopelessness was where I would end my days.

The last time she'd left me in here for more than a night, it had been only two days; the week before, three days.

When Agatha finally stood in the doorway of the attic, I assumed this extended stay was about to end. Yet all I could hear were her mutterings: something about Tilly and the way I had looked at her. I tried to tell Agatha I had simply looked at her the way I did everyone, knowing this to be a lie. Tilly was the morning sun in my life, whereas everyone else only represented darkness. Of course I looked upon her differently!

She stood over me, saying something about learning my place, but I wasn't really listening, my need for sustenance, air, light, much greater. It would have been easier to have dealt with this prolonged isolation if Tilly hadn't shown me a different way of being. If I hadn't been reminded of the sun, the sea and the beauty of the fresh air.

Agatha told me to empty the "disgusting bucket" and get prepared for the day. That, I could understand. That, I could follow.

I realized it was Saturday because Tilly came to visit. Perhaps this was the only reason Agatha had opened the attic door. Perhaps I'd still be languishing inside if not for her scheduled weekly visit.

"You look frightful!" she said as I stood over the kitchen sink.

I changed the subject. "How was your week, Miss Tilly?"

"I went horse riding after school and I did not enjoy it. I'm glad to be here."

"I am glad too."

"Celestine, are you all right?"

I nodded my head.

"Would you like to play outside? We can go to the beach again."

"Not today, Miss Tilly."

Her eyes narrowed. "Is it my aunt?"

"What of her?"

"Did she get angry about us going to the sea?"

"No, Miss Tilly. Why would you ask this?"

"Does my aunt treat you well, Celestine?"

I turned to her. Her eyes were alert and full of so many questions, while mine felt sunken, drawn and tired. I wanted to tell her I had been locked in an attic, this time for a week. I wanted to tell her everything that had happened to me since the Mayhews had moved in. How Agatha ruled the big house with venom and cruelty, while Cyril sat by and pretended not to notice. I wanted to plead with Tilly to help me. To please help me!

Yet what could she do? At eleven, she was younger than me and yet with more power than I could ever have, while at the same time with no power at all.

I turned my face away so she couldn't see my eyes anymore. "Yes, yes, she treats me very well indeed," I began. "I have merely been unwell, but I have recovered now."

Tilly appeared satisfied with my answer, as she began to talk about what was coming up for her next week. More riding lessons and a visit from a great-aunt. As I listened, so many questions surfaced on my own lips, one of them being, why was this happening to me? Not just the prolonged confinement, but all of it. I had successfully blocked out such thoughts yet today they had resurfaced.

Tilly continued to speak, and I skillfully muted her voice and even her presence. Now in that kitchen it was just me, surrounded by a spiral of events, items, and faces from the past that whizzed around me as I stood there alone and with no place to turn.

Chapter Thirty-Three

Lowra

1993

Celestine had been there.

In that attic and locked away.

I felt it in every inch of my body and mostly in my heart, the note simply confirming it.

Help me.

Like me, he'd been locked up all alone, an abandoned little boy already torn away from his family. How scared must he have been?

How scared had I been?

My mind felt weighted with so much information. I no longer knew where his experience ended and mine began. What I felt sure about was that Celestine, a little boy, was locked in an attic by someone from my own bloodline. He'd left messages as well as probably the most precious thing he owned—the necklace—an item connecting him with his tribe, his past and his family, to whoever would find them.

What about the carving in the wall? I was certain this had to be from Celestine too. A message he'd left a century ago, so that someone would find his precious items.

He'd wanted *me* to find them.

I may have let him down the first time I discovered them under those floorboards, but I wouldn't be making that mistake again.

This new determination to do right by Celestine mixed in with feeling so much lighter since telling Monty the truth about me and that house.

Perhaps that's why it felt easier this time to be standing in front of it with Monty, looking up at those steps leading to the two statues. Perhaps that's why my breath refused to come in spurts at the thought of walking up and into that attic again.

Inside, I still had to make sure the door remained open, in case I needed to make a quick escape. Monty asked me every two minutes if I was OK, so much so that I had to tell him to stop. Rushing to the space under the window, the floorboards still loose from where I had rescued the items responsible for starting this journey, I fell to my knees and immediately began to trace my finger over the shapes and lines etched into the wall.

"What are you doing?" asked Monty.

I could feel the letter M but that was it. Perhaps because it has such a distinctive shape, or I was kidding myself and this wasn't a message after all.

When I stood up and Monty did the same, he insisted another letter could be an A or a U, possibly a B. It was just too difficult to tell.

"I can't really be sure what the letters are or if they even mean anything. The good thing is, they led you to the items, so I suppose the message has already been received. I'll write them down anyway."

The stuff in the boxes wasn't of much interest: journals; old watercolors, including the one of a butterfly I'd spotted on my previous visit.

Just as I was beginning to think this was a colossal waste of time, Monty called out to me.

"I think I've found something!"

"Let me guess, another butterfly drawing?"

"Seriously, Lowra, take a look at this."

He lifted a small box onto a chest, opening it to reveal . . . well, papers.

"Shall we . . . shall we take it downstairs and take a closer look inside?" I said.

Of course, downstairs could never be in any part of that house and we simply ended up outside on the steps, beneath the half-lion, half-human statues. The site of my escape all those years ago.

Inside the box were mostly papers, important ones like deeds to the house, dated 1907. Some had survived the years while others were impossible to make out.

"Mr. and Mrs. Cyril Mayhew, it says here on the deeds," said Monty.

"Is there anything we don't know in there?" I said dryly.

"Oh, wow," he said, unfolding a piece of paper.

"What is it?"

"A document. The letter heading reads: National Incorporated Association for the Reclamation of Destitute Waif Children, otherwise known as Dr. Barnardo's."

"Isn't that the children's home place?"

"It is indeed . . ."

"What does it say?"

"Hold on," he said. I wasn't going to do that and instead stood beside him as the faint light from the sun hovered over the letter.

National Incorporated Association for
the Reclamation of Destitute Waif Children,
otherwise known as Dr. Barnardo's.

To Whom it May Concern,
We will require you to sign the enclosed agreement form and
shall be much obliged if you will kindly return it to us here.
This being done, we shall proceed accordingly.

Signed,
Charles Smythe
Honorable Secretary

"These agreement forms are blank and are a bit ambiguous," said Monty, unfolding two sheets of yellowing paper from the same envelope. They had been folded separately and had faded so badly over time they were impossible to read.

"This doesn't tell us much," I said.

"Actually it tells us a lot. What's the date on the letter?"

"1909."

"Yes, the year Caroline Mayhew was born."

We decided to regroup back at my flat in London, but I'd been in my room ever since we'd arrived twenty minutes ago, processing, thinking about Caroline, and, of course, Celestine even more than usual.

Help me. He'd written "help me." I couldn't get those words out of my mind, nor this feeling of powerlessness that had followed.

"Lowra, are you OK in there?" called Monty. I'd never left anyone in my home unattended.

I emerged from my room and he stood up. "Lowra."

"Sorry about that."

"Don't be. I just want to make sure you're all right."

"I'm OK, really."

It was strange seeing my behavior through someone else's eyes. Shutting myself away in my room for hours on end wasn't really unusual for me because it was where I felt safe.

"I hope you don't mind, but I used your phone a few times and one was long distance. I've left some money on the table."

I sat down.

"I've just spoken to my guy at the Smithsonian again," he said.

"What did he say?"

"He faxed through some more translations to my office—you know, from the paper—and he believes, as I suspected, that the third word is Mayhew."

I swallowed, further proof that this *couple* were responsible for Celestine's misery, just as Nina had been for mine.

"The third from last word is Dikembe."

Monty spelled the name phonetically.

"What does it mean?"

"According to his contact in Belgium, it's a name from the Congo, which would make sense because of the necklace and the language identified."

"Is he sure that's what it says?"

"We can't be one hundred percent sure about anything, but there's a possibility it could have been a name of a loved one or even Celestine's real name."

Why was Monty talking about names? A young boy had been locked in an attic for who knows how long, and he was concerned about names.

And then it hit me.

"The writing carved into the wall in the attic . . . D and M . . . and possibly B, you said. Dikembe!"

"Bit of a long shot, Lowra."

"It's him, it has to be." I wasn't quite sure if I knew this with real certainty or just wanted it to be so.

"Now we have the name Dikembe, we can at least look for that in our search—you know, census forms and suchlike."

I shook my head, still stuck on the realization of what had happened to him. To us. I was still on that.

"Can we call it a day? I'm really tired." My voice sounded like a deflated balloon.

I sometimes hated myself for feeling like this, especially when I thought I'd turned a corner.

When Monty placed his hand on my arm, I didn't flinch. "Take as long as you need. I'll be here when you're ready. In the meantime I'll go away, make some more calls, and maybe head back to Ranklin to see what I can come up with."

"And don't—"

"I won't go to see Ranklin's oldest resident, Matilda Ainsworth, without you. I am a man of my word! I will go back to the library archives, though. See what else we can conjure up."

"I'm sure Jean will be most helpful!" I said, with a tinge of something I didn't recognize.

That night, I dreamed of a little girl sitting in a dark room on a cold, hard floor. She wasn't alone for long because someone else would join her, me or whoever; together in our misery and loneliness.

I woke up with a start, the streetlight through the window allowing me to make out my shadow as well as cast a shine on that doll. Her glassy, emotionless eyes stared back at me. Was it Celestine's doll? And if so, who had given it to him and why? Had he written that message on the wall? Where did Caroline fit into the story? Or my mother? Who were the Dr. Barnardo's papers for?

"You look like death warmed up!" smiled Marnie. I had never appreciated her wit, but comparing me to a dead body was ironic. Because if we did the sums, the little boy who I hadn't been able to stop thinking about since that moment in the museum was most likely dead by now, and I'd never get the chance to return his things to him.

Or to tell him he was not alone.

"A couple of late nights," I said.

She looped her arm into mine and I stiffened. Even though Monty could be free with his affections, like patting my arm and once helping me up from my own sofa with his hand, that was as much as I could take.

I extracted myself from her grip.

"Tell me more. Who is he?" she said.

"It isn't like that . . ."

But as Marnie started on a conversation she really didn't need me to be a part of, I turned to her.

"Can you do me a favor?"

"Anything."

"Can you take over a few of my shifts? There's somewhere I need to be."

"For how long?"

"Indefinitely."

"The lady at the nursing home said to come after lunch, so we have a bit of time to spend with Jean until then. She's been very helpful," Monty said as we headed toward the library back in Ranklin.

"Love the new hair color," said Monty, a bit impatiently as Jean stood over him at the microfiche machine.

"Thank you. A bit of color always goes a long way," she said.

"Yes, it does."

"I have everything you requested in your phone call. I must say, this is all very exciting, Mr. Montgomery."

"As I said, please just call me Monty."

The insanity of this conversation drew me out of myself for a moment, giving me the amusement I needed.

"When you tasked me to search the *Ranklin Gazette* for stories or pictures of any Black residents besides our hero of the hour, Celestine—well, it was a task I took on with pleasure."

"As I know you would, Jean."

A giggle. "What I found seems to match what you found with the census records—I just couldn't find any other Black people who may have resided here in that time or within a twenty-year period after that."

"The census records of that time never referred to skin color or ethnicity when listing people, so we still can't really be sure."

"And people may have been a bit transient, coming into the area to look for work and not actually settling. Anyway, I took the liberty of taking another look at our archives and, well . . . you can see for yourself." She pressed a button and an image of the newspaper appeared. "Here we have the *Ranklin Gazette* again. Apart from the endless cats up trees, it never really says much, but in those days it was mostly about the affluent folk in the area, as you know. Sir Richard was always throwing fund-raisers and dinner parties, especially in the early days. Yet strangely enough, when the Mayhews took over the house, they didn't entertain or give as much to charity as Sir Richard—I don't think they were that well off, if you ask me. But in 1921, Mrs. Mayhew did put on a benefit for the soldiers who couldn't get work after coming home. Anyway, here they are. The picture isn't great but it's a lot better than the early ones. Better technology by then."

Our eyes remained fixed on the screen, as Jean pulled up a chair for me to sit beside Monty.

"That's Mrs. Mayhew, right there," said Jean, pointing to this woman, this woman married to a blood relative of mine, a woman who to me was no better than *her*.

Dr. Raj would have said I was projecting, but what we did know was that she and her husband lived in that house at the same time Celestine wrote that note, so they . . . *she* was complicit. The self-satisfied smile was a cover-up for all that was really going on in that house.

"Is Caroline there?" asked Monty.

"All the names are captioned underneath the photograph," said Jean, as if she knew the answer already.

I shifted in closer to the screen.

Under the image of a girl was the caption "Caroline."

"Monty, zoom in at the side," said Jean. I was a bit taken aback by her familiarity, but that didn't matter once the young girl on the screen caught my attention.

Half of her body may have been out of shot, but when Monty magnified the picture, her features were clear: her thick coiled hair and her smooth dark skin.

I gasped as it finally hit me.

"It all makes sense now," said Monty.

"Do . . . do you think . . ." I said.

"That she's mixed race? Without a doubt."

"Then the father . . . ?"

"Could be Celestine? Yes."

Chapter Thirty-Four

Lowra
1978

"Is it OK if I make a call?"

"I don't think calling home's a good idea without a social worker present. You've been here for three months now—you know the rules, Lowra."

"I want to call my grandma. She's in a nursing home."

"You've never mentioned calling before."

"She's not been very well. Can you help me to find the number in the phone book?"

"Surely you're able to do such a simple thing?"

"I've never done it before. I can hardly remember how to use a phone."

"You poor thing. Of course I'll help."

Minutes later, I was on the phone and being told by a voice at the end of it that my grandma had died.

"Are you still there?" said the voice. "Her daughter-in-law assured us her relatives had all been told."

In that shockingly unexpected moment, I wasn't sure how to feel, so I simply replaced the receiver.

A mixture of grief and relief followed. The relief was stronger. Relief she was finally out of all the pain that losing her son had caused. Relief at no longer having to worry about anybody else, because now it was truly just about me.

Lola Jaye

1993

We approached the Winter Pines nursing home having not said much to each other.

Finding out Caroline was of mixed race and possibly Celestine's child was enough to keep us in our own little worlds. Now, heading to the very place my grandma had spent her final years, mourning the son she'd never see again, it felt like a multitude of emotions were fighting for space inside me.

Winter Pines wasn't as I'd imagined it all these years. It was set behind an expanse of shrubs and inside it smelled of freshly cut lavender. I waited by the electric double doors, which kept opening and shutting each time I took a step backward.

As Monty went up ahead to speak with the receptionist, I quickly turned my gaze away from the watercolor of a butterfly, choosing instead to read the various laminated certificates of excellence on display.

A healthcare assistant named Cathy—according to her badge—showed us to a door decorated with stickers of flowers and Barbies.

"These are the two visitors who have come all the way from London to see you." Cathy's voice had suddenly switched to a childlike tone, and I wondered if that was how they'd spoken to my grandma.

Matilda Ainsworth was sitting up in an armchair beside her bed, her gray bouffant hair prominent and with two curled waves at the front. Her eyes narrowed a bit as we moved closer.

Cathy closed the door behind her. The first question I wanted to ask was if she'd known my grandma.

"So what do you two want?" said Matilda. I wasn't expecting her voice to sound so abrasive. Monty just looked on, amused.

"Straight to the point, I like that," he said.

"There's no other way to be, is there? These people talk to me like I'm the same age as my great-grandchildren."

"You have great-grandchildren?" I said.

"Yes, three of them. The little bastards insisted on putting all that sticky paper on my door. It's a bugger to get off."

"I bet it is," I said.

"You two look like you've come to finish me off, standing over me like the mafia. Take a seat on the bed. Don't worry, it's clean."

We both sat down on either end, and Monty explained he was a historian attempting to find out the history of 109 Ranklin Road.

"The most excitement you get in here is when someone keels over, so I am rather glad you decided to look me up. What led you here, to me?"

"You're a bit of a legend in Ranklin," aid Monty.

"I'd have preferred you said 'in Las Vegas,' but we can't have everything."

"Don't we all, Mrs. Ainsworth. So, what do you remember about the house?" he asked.

"To a child, it was this rather big and imposing lump of bricks—and don't get me started on those vulgar creatures either side of the door."

I smiled knowingly.

"I won't be able to help much regarding its most famous resident, Richard Babbington, though. He was before my time, I'm afraid."

"That's OK. There's plenty of info on him. We're more interested in the less famous occupants over the years. Like Cyril and Agatha Mayhew."

"Oh, well, that's easy. They were my aunt and uncle."

"They were?" I looked toward Monty.

"Close your mouth, a fly might fly in!"said Matilda.

I did as I was told.

"I used to go there on weekends or when there was a break in school. It was a bit dull at first, but Daddy always insisted. I think he just wanted me out of the way, and as my aunt and uncle had no children, well, it seemed like the perfect arrangement to thrust me upon them. They weren't the most exciting of people but when they moved into that house, things suddenly became interesting. And I made a friend!"

Monty and I looked at one another, anticipating what she was about to say next.

"I could tell my aunt and uncle didn't want me to play with him because he was different, but nobody told me what to do. So from that day on we became the best of friends. Oh, what a joy he was, indeed."

"Do you remember his name?"

She looked toward me as if seeing me for the first time. "Why yes, his name was Celestine."

I exhaled. This was unbelievable. Someone who'd actually met Celestine was here and sitting in front of us!

"Are you two married?" said Matilda in the silence that followed.

"No, we are not. So, Matilda, this Celestine . . . what can you tell us about him?" said Monty.

"Oh, he was delightful and like no boy I had ever met before. Not that I had ever cavorted with any boys during that time! It's just that now at this old age, I can definitely say he was the best of a not very good bunch!"

"So you two had a friendship?" I said.

"We did everything together, and I mean everything. Mostly in the house but sometimes we would even go outside, though not much—I don't think he liked it very much. I didn't realize it then, but I suppose people would stare. Look, this was a very long time ago and there's not much I can remember, but he was and remains very dear to me. When I was sent away to some awful boarding school for girls, I never saw him again."

Her eyes became glassy. "It felt like I had been punched in the gut, to be honest. Losing him."

"I'm sorry, Mrs. Ainsworth." I looked toward Monty and felt instantly connected by a thought: that this childhood friendship was more than Mrs. Ainsworth was letting on; that maybe Agatha wasn't Caroline's mother at all, and the agreement papers were for Tilly and Celestine's child, Caroline. Perhaps Agatha had thought to arrange for her niece's illegitimate, mixed-race child to be adopted and then changed her mind, taking her on as her own. I wasn't sure how to frame the questions that were racing through my head.

"Could you do me a favor?" she said.

"Anything," I said.

"Stop calling me Mrs. Ainsworth? I sound like an old woman."

"What would you like us to call you?"

"My full name is Matilda. But anyone I like calls me Tilly."

Chapter Thirty-Five

Celestine
1908

My life began to settle into a somewhat tolerable routine, with Tilly filling the void that had grown ever since the arrival of the Mayhews.

As usual, I cleaned, cooked and waited on Agatha and Cyril, and would fall asleep exhausted; sometimes with anger, other times with happiness at having spent some of my time with Tilly. She was my closest and only friend, a ray of light that illuminated the darkness of the attic, even though she'd never once set foot inside.

Until one day I decided to let her.

"This is your bedroom?" she said.

Suddenly, I was awash with shame. What I'd made into my own little home was a space of squalor to others.

"It's horrid, Celestine. I mean, how do you see?"

I wanted to tell her I'd learned how many steps it took to get from the door to where my blanket lay. I knew where I had carved out my name, which was just above the loose floorboards, and had even placed my father's beloved necklace under one, for safekeeping. The Mayhews had already sold all of Sir Richard's African pieces for a princely sum, and I couldn't be sure they wouldn't do the same with the necklace.

"When she opens the door for long enough, I can look around and see where everything is," I said with some pride.

"Can we go downstairs now?" Her voice had changed in tone.

"Of course."

"You shouldn't be living in there," she said.

"It's not that bad, really."

She narrowed her eyes. "You can't actually like it in there."

"I didn't say I liked it." My words sounded confusing even to myself. What indeed was I saying? I hated the attic. It was a cold, dark and lonely place, yet I had just defended its existence.

I was glad when Tilly left that day and the questions stopped.

The following evening, as Agatha and Cyril ate dinner, I stood behind them as they preferred.

"Tilly tells us your room shouldn't be so dark,"said Agatha.

"She did?"

"We will place a candle inside, so that you can see. Cyril has organized this, haven't you?"

"Indeed, I have."

"Thank you, sir, madam," I said.

"The real question is, what were you doing in the attic with Tilly?" said Agatha.

"She wanted to see my room, madam."

They both looked toward each other with an expression which made no sense to me.

"I told you, Cyril!"

"Calm down, Agatha."

"I will not!"

"Celestine, you may resume your duties in the kitchen," he said, shooing me toward the door. I stood behind that door and continued to listen.

"I warned you this would happen, Cyril!"

"Nothing has happened."

"Yet! But how long will it take?"

"He is just a boy!"

"He is, well . . . You know what they're like!"

A laugh from Cyril. "I know what I was like at that age . . . too afraid to even look at a girl."

"The likes of Celestine are not this way. He could rip her apart without a moment's warning."

"Oh, darling . . ."

"This is not a joke, Cyril. You married a learned woman and I have read books. I have also seen what science has proved. The photograph he claims not to have vandalized, for one."

"It was probably as he said—"

"At times he may appear docile and compliant, Cyril, but it will not take long for his innate and beastly desires to be fully unleashed upon poor Tilly, and—"

"Then in that case, my love, we'd best be rid of him sooner!"

My heart briefly filled with horror that they may be plotting my demise.

"You should not joke about this, Cyril. I am not afraid for myself, just my niece, and you should be too."

Agatha had been true to her word, and my room was now illuminated with candlelight, allowing me to clearly see the attic I had spent many nights in. She appeared proud of herself for providing me with the candle, but all it had done was shine a light on the various boxes covered in a film of dust that hovered around me like a circle of death.

Hence, the light had supplied no real surprises. I'd long since felt the sloped roof on my head, seen the window boarded up so no one could see out of it. The only difference the light made was the possibility of sifting through the large trunk, which I hoped to be able to open one day with my pocketknife.

I bent down and picked up a pen which had rolled in between

the trunk and the wall. This was possibly the greatest of finds. Having not had access to Sir Richard's study in so long, such luxuries had been out of bounds. The piece of paper I pulled out from behind the trunk was also a magical find, but when I ran the pen across it, nothing. It required an inkwell and was not like the Parker Sir Richard had gifted me; the same pen I had seen Agatha using many times.

I would ask Tilly to bring me a pen and also thank her for arranging to have the light placed in the attic. There was so much I wanted to speak with her about, but when she arrived I'd no idea it would be for the very last time.

"Daddy would like me to attend a new school."

"That would be very nice." I said this with a touch of envy. We were sitting by the candle in the attic.

"It's a boarding school and we will be going next weekend to visit."

I was unable to see past the fact I wouldn't be with her next week, unable to truly comprehend the words "boarding school' and what this would truly mean.

"I'll have to go home soon," she said. This part of the visit I always dreaded: just before the driver turned up to take Tilly away from me. The goodbyes reminded me a little of past ones. Yet Tilly always made sure I had prior warning, as if she dreaded that time too.

"Will you be able to come back after your trip?" I asked.

"I can't see why not."

"What if you don't?" I said, suddenly fearful. Tilly's visits had been consistent and in that I had felt a sense of security. Suddenly it was all about to change and, in my experience, that usually meant only one thing.

I brazenly touched her hand with the tips of my fingers, as if trying to soak in every part of her, consume her aroma, her essence . . . just in case.

She squeezed my hand, stopping me in my tracks. Her smile allowed me to enjoy how this felt, and gave me hope it would never end. “Celestine, we must make this day extra special. Just in case these are our last moments together.”

Chapter Thirty-Six

Lowra
1993

"There was a child."

Monty was quick to bring us back to the reason for our visit to Winter Pines.

"A baby. Caroline," I added.

Tilly's eyebrows rose quickly. She knew something.

The smile quickly disappeared, replaced by a seriousness in her tone. "A child?"

"She was of mixed race and we think—"

"I don't care what you think," she said.

I looked toward Monty, surprised at how quickly this conversation had turned.

"Tilly, are you OK?" I said.

"I don't know what you are implying." Gone was the cantankerous-granny vibe; in its place, a red face and pursed lips.

"We just wanted to know if you knew or met her. As you said, you were a frequent visitor to the house."

"I think you should leave."

"Tilly, what is it?" I asked.

She must have pressed the emergency button without us realizing, because Cathy was back.

"These two are just leaving," said Tilly.

"Tilly, I know Celestine meant a lot to you. I can see it in your eyes."

"I said, leave."

"If you remember anything else, please give me a call," said Monty, placing his card on her side table. "Anything, big or small. We didn't mean to cause you distress."

She made no attempt to respond as she quietly turned her gaze to the side.

I placed a piece of gum in my mouth as we headed out.

"So are we presuming Tilly was Caroline's mother? An unmarried mother at the turn of the century . . . Do you think Agatha took pity on her as she didn't have any children of her own?"

"It's a leap. But clearly the birth certificate is a lie or was forged in some way, as she can't have been Agatha and Cyril's natural child. But why would they take on a mixed-race child?" Monty questioned. "Sorry, this doesn't make any sense. Also, why is there no mention or picture of Agatha's husband in the *Gazette*? He just simply disappears!"

"What does make sense is that Tilly Ainsworth is hiding something."

"I guess this is a dead end, unless you want to dress up as a nurse and go back in there," he said.

"I don't give up that easily, and yes, I'm sure I can borrow a uniform from somewhere . . ."

"Are you kidding?"

"Yes, I am. But I'm a little frustrated . . . we're so close."

Inside the Flamingo Club cafe, the enlarged clipping of Caroline rested on the table as Monty went to the phone box to make a call.

In some way, this young woman was possibly related to me. If so, distantly, but related—and that thought alone amazed me.

Staring at the picture wasn't going to give us any answers, yet there was no doubt in my mind that Tilly Ainsworth knew more than she was letting on. Caroline had been named as Agatha and Cyril's daughter on the birth certificate, but why then were there papers drawn up with Dr. Barnardo's, even if they were incomplete? Was Agatha or Tilly her mother? And who was the father?

"Lowra, we have to go!" said Monty, rushing back inside.

"I've just ordered a fresh cup!"

"Leave that. Tilly just called my office. My assistant said she wants us to come back to the nursing home."

Chapter Thirty-Seven

Celestine
1908

"Keep your eyes closed, Celestine."

"But the room is rather dark anyway."

"Please, just oblige me!"

I felt the sensation of something cold in my hand, and when I opened my eyes the candlelight illuminated a face. I jumped back.

"Careful, you'll drop her!"

"What is this?"

"It's a baby. This way, you'll never be lonely in here because she's yours now."

The round bisque head had blonde hairs growing out of the top, porcelain-white skin, and glassy eyes staring blankly at me, dead yet lifelike. It was the most terrifying object I had ever seen, and now it was mine?

"She's my favorite doll in the whole wide world. She was my mummy's."

"Didn't she . . ."

"Yes, she died. But I want you to have it."

"I can't take this!" This I meant. With its lifelike features, I wasn't sure if it had the power to come alive at any moment!

"You can give her back to me when you see me again. My daddy says she looks just like me."

I looked once again at its face, the only true resemblance perhaps the hair.

"When you feel lonely, just hold her close. Until I get back."

She looked hopeful, and after everything she'd brought into my life, I wanted to please her. "I'll name her Tilly," I said.

"That would be splendid."

"You will be back, won't you?"

"Yes, of course, but not as often." Her face reddened.

I placed the doll on the trunk, suddenly feeling pressured to return the sentiment.

"You don't have to give me anything, Celestine."

"How do you know what I am thinking all the time?"

Her giggle filled the attic and I wanted it to go on forever. I twirled my father's necklace in between my fingers, the most precious item I owned, pondering whether I should give it to her while knowing deep in my heart that I could never be separated from it.

Chapter Thirty-Eight

Lowra
1993

We were back in Tilly's room.

"You'd better take a seat," he said. A small brown vanity box sat on the bed, which she moved so Monty and I could sit down.

"Is it OK if I take notes?" said Monty, waving his notebook in the air.

"If you must. I'm only going to say this once. But first, I think you'll want to read this."

Reaching into the vanity box, she pulled out an envelope. It was addressed to Agatha Mayhew, postmarked 1909.

Dear Agatha,

I have received various correspondence from you and apologize for waiting until now to respond. This has been a very difficult time for me, and although I have been guilty of my own indiscretions, which you have forgiven, this one predicament you have presented to me is something, as a man, I am surely unable to forgive.

I believe none of this is of your own doing. To be taken advantage of by someone we trusted and gave a home to is unspeakable, and for that, my darling, I am truly sorry.

Perhaps I would have returned, if you had not kept the result of this misdemeanor for all to see.

I will never know why you did not see fit to place it elsewhere, as there are many good homes where it could have been left. However, you made the decision to keep it with you, even going so far as to proclaim this bastard child mine on a birth certificate.

It is for these reasons that I can never return.

I rue the day we ever occupied the house of my cousin Richard. It has been a source of misery ever since.

Please do not contact me, now that we have completed the divorce. I have found someone who will eventually provide me with an heir once we are married.

I do not proclaim her to be the love my life, because that was you. However, this is where I choose to be.

I trust you will accept my generosity in allowing you to keep the house, which rightfully belongs to myself and my future offspring. It is the least I can do for you, and I never want to set foot in that house again.

Yours,

Cyril Mayhew

"I always found it strange that my father went from insisting I go to Aunt Agatha's every chance I got to saying I should never see her again. It wasn't until I was a little bit older that I defied him—I must have been in my very late teens—and I went back to the house to look for my friend, for Celestine, desperate to see him again."

Her eyes were glassy.

"Instead, I saw the strangest thing. A little girl running about the place. She must have been around six or seven years old. When I asked Aunt Agatha about her, she just said she'd taken pity on this child and adopted her."

"We did find some old papers from Dr. Barnardo's, which we

couldn't read but may have been something like an adoption agreement," I said.

"I wouldn't take any notice of those. She probably wanted to forge something and thought better of it. I mean, who would believe she'd adopted a colored girl?"

"Why did you get so upset earlier?" I said.

"Slow down with the questions, child. My brain isn't what it used to be."

"You did get really angry, though," I said.

"What you have to remember, young lady, is that this was a very long time ago. It isn't like nowadays when people care less about such things. Just look at you. Upstanding young man, no doubt," she said, looking toward Monty. "The shame it heaped onto our family hasn't gone away, just because society has changed a little. That's why I reacted the way I did."

Monty sat back in his chair.

I waited for him to ask a question but he didn't. I spoke instead. "So you're saying Agatha was Caroline's mother but you don't know who Caroline's father was?"

"Could have been anyone, I suppose . . ." She turned away.

"Celestine?"

"What? Never. He was just a boy. And he wouldn't do anything like that, whatever that letter implies." She shook her head vigorously and then slowly, as if weighed down by some sort of realization. "But what do I know? We were all but little children when we were friends. I have no idea what he could have grown into over the course of a year or so. No one does, do they?"

Monty's lips were pursed, as if trying to prevent any words from coming out.

"So you're saying you think Celestine may have fathered Caroline?" I said.

"That's not what I said. Either we talk about what I do know and was witness to, or you leave!"

"Of course, I'm sorry."

Monty had moved away. Not physically, but he no longer felt present.

"I felt sorry for the poor little thing. My aunt didn't always treat her well and she never mixed with anyone."

"Was she . . . ?" I didn't want to ask the question but I had to. "Was she put in the attic?"

"You mean like Celestine?"

"You knew about that?"

Her eyes clouded over. "Of course I did, but what could I do? I was just a little girl myself."

I let out a quick breath. Although I knew he'd been there, this confirmation felt like a blow.

"I only visited once a week for a matter of months."

"How long would he spend there . . . in the attic?"

"You do realize I am ninety-six years of age, don't you? There isn't much I can remember."

It seemed whenever we asked something uncomfortable, Tilly would mention her age.

"I'm not judging you, Tilly." Perhaps a bit of me was judging her.

"Back to Caroline, then," said Monty, suddenly returning to the conversation.

"She never really had any friends or acquaintances—not just because she was colored but because . . . well, because she was mute."

"Caroline couldn't speak?" asked Monty.

"That's what I said. She was born that way, and even though my aunt kept her close, it didn't stop her from cavorting with anyone she could find, did it? In no time at all, she too was in the family way. No, actually, that's not true, she would have been in her midtwenties."

"Caroline was pregnant?" said Monty.

"Indeed. Like mother, like daughter," said Tilly. "For years,

Agatha had carried the shame and the burden of having Caroline, even prepared to lose her own husband. Kept saying it was her punishment or something like that, so she got on with it. It helped that Caroline was never any trouble. Mostly she just played chess with one of Aunt Agatha's friends, and that was it. I presume he might have fathered Caroline's baby, or maybe it was one of the servants . . . Anyway, when she too was carrying an illegitimate child, well, it was as if everything changed for Aunt Agatha. I remember her saying to me—not these exact words, of course—but something about the shame no longer being hers and that it now belonged to Caroline."

"That's awful," I managed to say.

"I suppose for Aunt Agatha it set her free of the burden, so she felt no guilt about sending Caroline away to have the baby. I remember going to visit one day a few months later and this new baby was there. I mean, I thought they'd have sent it to the Foundling Hospital or something like that, but no, there she was in the house, clear as day, her skin as white as mine."

"What about Caroline?"

"Nowhere to be seen."

"She was gone?" said Monty.

"That's right."

"Did you ask Agatha where she was?" I said.

"Of course I did! She said Caroline's condition had worsened since having the baby. Although she still never spoke, she was now prone to hysterical behavior or something like that. In other words, she wasn't fit to look after a baby and was now living in an institution more equipped to deal with her *situation*." She whispered "situation" as if it were a dirty word.

"Do you know the name of this institution?" said Monty.

"This was decades ago, young man. I'm surprised I remember as much as I'm telling you now. So, no. However, it wouldn't surprise me if it was an asylum of some sort."

I closed my eyes.

"You all right over there, young lady?" she said. It took a moment to realize she was talking to me.

"Is there anything else you can remember? Something Agatha may have said when she gave you the letter?" I asked.

"It wasn't Aunt Agatha who gave me that letter. As one of her few living relatives, I inherited some of her bits in the will, including this vanity box. The letter was tucked into the side pocket."

"So who inherited the house?" said Monty.

"Well, I suppose Caroline would have if . . . well, you know . . . if she wasn't mad, and . . . well, you know!"

"Yes, we know!" said Monty abrasively.

"So it passed down to Caroline's daughter," said Tilly.

"What was her name?" I said.

"Oh, drat, I can't remember. At my age you forget a lot of things."

"I'm sure Monty and I can look at land records or something . . ."

"No, no, there's no need. I'll remember in a minute. I should know this, considering the name happens to be associated with one of my favorite movies of all time."

"Tilly, it's OK . . ." I said.

"*Gone with the Wind*!" she said, her finger pointing in the air. "The actress!"

"Hattie McDaniel?" said Monty, with a look of disbelief on his face.

"No, the lead. Vivien Leigh!"

The word stopped, as did my breath.

The room began to spin.

"Vivienne?" said Monty, before I could even utter my own mother's name.

Chapter Thirty-Nine

Celestine
1908

Two weeks in a row, I waited for Tilly to visit.

"She isn't coming," said Agatha, who appeared to be walking around with an air of triumph.

"Is she unwell?"

"She looked very well when I went to visit my brother last week."

"Is . . . is she coming back?"

A tiny smile remained on Agatha's lips. "Don't you have work to do?"

"Yes, madam. I would simply like to know when Miss Tilly will be returning."

She ignored me but I knew the answer. The answer was always the same. Now, that doll was all I had left of her. This lifeless thing, all I had left from my only friend who was now lost to me forever.

I ran my fingers over my name carved into the wall, and then placed the doll under the floorboards for safekeeping, along with the necklace as I couldn't risk Agatha or Cyril finding it.

The chores began to feel much more laborious. At least before, with the promise of a visit from Tilly, they had been tolerable.

Now, it was once again a cycle of never-ending work without reward. My life was tinged with a growing pointlessness, becoming harder and harder to shift.

If Cyril was the kinder of the two, or at the very least indifferent, I knew he'd be honest with me.

"She's gone," he confirmed.

Alarm shot through my entire body. "Miss Tilly has died?"

"No! She's gone to a boarding school. Didn't Agatha tell you?"

I slowly shook my head as I remembered Tilly mentioning the school, and how quickly I had placed the possibility into a box, never to be opened.

"I don't suppose she would have."

I felt glad that she was alive, existing somewhere without me. Attending a school and having lessons I would never have a chance to even observe. I not only missed my friend but also envied her, and such feelings confused me.

"She will not be there all the time, will she? What of—"

"You really have to talk to Agatha about all of this, she's *her* niece." He placed a pipe in his mouth and I was momentarily reminded of Sir Richard.

"I'm sorry, old chap," said Cyril. "I know you were incredibly fond of her. Maybe that was part of the problem."

As he left the room, I caught sight of my black Parker pen on the floor by the door, quickly picked it up and placed it in my pocket where it rightly belonged.

I sat on the floor of the attic, pondering Cyril's words. Liking Tilly was the problem? I had no idea what he meant by this—how could liking another person be wrong? Yet no amount of pondering could change the fact that Tilly was gone and likely never to return.

I ran the pen over the paper, feeling an instant release as the words left my head and transferred themselves into reality.

Breathe.

Footsteps.
Is anyone out there?
I hope not.
Happy to stay here.
Forever.
If that's what it takes.

I screwed the paper into a ball and started again on a fresh piece.

Alone
Locked away
Mayhew
Lonely
Kabili
Mama
Dikembe

The few words—and perhaps the most important—I had managed to memorize from *A Dictionary of Languages as Spoken in Various Areas of the Congo Free State* appeared in my head.

Mwana Muya
Nangula

I held on to Tilly's doll on nights when the weight of loneliness became overpowering and not so easy to brush off. Even though it provided only a false comfort, at least it existed and was someone to talk to about my plans.

Losing Tilly meant I was back to thinking about the future and less focused on the present. By now I should have earned enough money for my labors even if I was never to see any of the funds Sir Richard may have left me in his will. It was the done thing, after all, to be paid for goods or services rendered. I knew that basic fundamental fact and yet I'd never brought this up with the Mayhews. Perhaps I had been hopeful they'd do the honorable thing and pay me now it was clear that Sir Richard had lied about leaving me money in his will. It was not the first lie he'd told and I was a fool to have believed any of his hopeful words.

Had I not learned?

I was older now and some would say wiser. I knew the value of what I brought to the house and felt the time was now to present this issue.

"May I speak with you, sir?"

"What is it?" Cyril was in Sir Richard's chair in the study.

"Sir, I took the liberty of asking some of the service people who attend here about . . . about . . ." The words appeared stuck on the tip of my tongue. "A fair wage."

He raised an eyebrow. "Is that so?"

"Yes, sir."

"What did they say?"

"The pay range varied, but perhaps with what I do, I should be paid twenty pounds per year." Indeed, with everything I did, I should be earning double that amount.

He stood. I'd shot up in height recently and we were now neck and neck.

"Done your research, I see."

"Yes, sir. I mean, I was just trying to help you . . . so as to know what to pay me."

"That is very helpful, young Celestine."

"Thank you, sir." Part of me was suspicious that this was going too well. Cyril, although the fairer of the two, was still allowing this to feel too easy. But I was being more than fair in not even asking for backpay, simply content to receive payment from now on to go toward my future. Agatha and Cyril could not keep me here forever.

"Would you be requiring backpay?" he said.

"No . . . no, sir, I am happy for my pay to begin as of now."

"That is very gracious of you."

I felt a rush of good feeling between us. Cyril never said much in our day-to-day dealings, but he was a fair man; that he had just proved.

"I am to start dinner," I said as a well of hopefulness swam through my body, staying with me as I partook in my chores. I even hummed my mama's song, something I had not dared do for some time now. Tilly had left me with the greatest of gifts—the need and desire for more. To one day be out of this house, on my own and enjoying a life outside it. Outside the attic. I could do it, I knew I could.

The next morning when the key turned in the lock, I was surprised to see Cyril and not Agatha standing there.

I jumped up, suddenly ashamed of my surroundings as the candlelight illuminated the space. He'd never set foot in here before.

"After you prepare dinner tonight, we are to go out" he said, adding, "You are to look presentable."

He shut the door behind him but didn't lock it—a noted and positive difference already taking place. Perhaps like with Sir Richard, our trip would involve some sort of adventure. Instead of the tailor's or a photographer, a visit to the bank!

Dinner as usual involved Agatha complaining about the potatoes being too hard, with Cyril saying nothing about what was to come.

I waited expectantly by the front door, less apprehensive about going outside now thanks to Tilly. It was getting late, though, and I couldn't be certain if the bank would still be open.

"Where are we going, sir?"

We reached the bottom of the steps, and he grabbed my arm so tightly I felt it would leave an imprint. A chill quickly crept up my body; not a result of the slight wind, as we walked along Ranklin Road. Once further away, he let go of my arm as we headed in the direction of Ranklin High Street. We were walking for what could only have been minutes but felt like an hour.

Although it had been some time since I had ventured here, I was certain of never once turning into this side street, where an abundance of unkempt persons were scattered around at a time they surely should be in their homes. Men, women and even children, dressed in what could only be described as rags, sat on steps by candlelight, some drinking from bottles, others barefoot and without shame. A beggar sat cross-legged on the littered floor, shaking a dirty cap with the sound of only a scant few coins. Clean washing hung from lines across the street and the stench of the gutters rose from every corner.

Was this really England? The one that had often been sold to me as so regal and civilized, and in many ways better than my own country? In a silent but obvious way, perhaps I had been in agreement with the popular view, yet the behavior of those surrounding Cyril and me showed that absolutely anybody could be a savage. Weren't even Sir Richard and the Mayhews savages in their own "refined" way?

The pail of dirty water thrown across the street just missed my freshly polished shoes, a secondhand "gift" from Cyril which were still too loose, shaking me from my thoughts. We moved up onto the steps of a large building that gave us a wider view.

"You see these people here?"

"Yes, sir."

"These are the stain on society. The poor and the wretched."

My face ached with confusion as I turned to him.

"Look at them!" he roared. I had never once heard Cyril raise his voice to me or to anyone.

I turned my face back to the scene below. Even from such a high view the putrid smell rested in my nostrils.

"Look at them properly!"

The smell was now unbearable.

"A lot of them will be riddled with disease, and many will die young from ailments like diphtheria. Have you heard of that?"

"No, sir."

"Even the smallest of children will have to crawl into textile mills to earn a living. Some of these people will die of starvation. Whereas you seem to forget how lucky you are living up in our home."

I nodded my head because to open my mouth further would be to invite the smell of rotting food and disease.

"These people here are white and even they live like animals."

I nodded my head.

"This, Celestine, is what will become of you if you continue to misbehave with us. Is this what you want?"

I shook my head quickly.

"Then you must do as you are told. Do you understand me?"

I nodded my head again.

"Your duties, as always, require you to stay in the house and its grounds. But on the odd occasion I or Mrs. Mayhew need you to run an errand, I would expect you back at the house within a reasonable time. Is that understood?"

"Yes, sir."

"It is unfortunate that I have had to reiterate your place with us, but you gave me no choice. At least now you are clear."

Cyril continued his speech as my eyes became transfixed by a man sitting on a step and biting into what looked like an apple. I had seen not one Black person in Ranklin, so he was easy to spot. He looked up once and it was then that I knew. I knew who this man was.

But as quickly as this image had appeared, it disappeared again as the man walked through an open door I would think about for the rest of that night.

Once Cyril was satisfied I had learned my lesson, we headed back to the house where he proceeded to speak and I continued not to listen, unable to erase from my mind what I had seen. Not the squalor or the deprivation but that quick image of that man.

The implausibility of it mixed with endless possibilities that I had not been mistaken.

The man I had seen was my brother Pako.

So, despite Cyril's best efforts, that glimmer of hope returned.

Bill being off sick for a second day in a row was a stroke of luck, as I was tasked with collecting the vegetables and bread. I headed outside for the second time in as many days, this time fueled by a power and determination not felt in so long.

I retraced my steps from the night before and stood looking at that door once more. In the artificial light of the streetlamp the door had looked blue, and now in daytime the splinters were more visible, but it was certainly the same one. My heart rate accelerated in what I could only imagine was excitement because I might be inches away from where Pako, my brother, resided. He could actually be inside that building! I ran down into the street and to the door, my fists about to pound on the wood just as it opened.

And there my brother stood before me.

Everything around me ceased to exist. It was just me and my beloved eldest brother Pako. His nose was slightly wider than mine but with a mark on the bridge, just like our father's. His eyes, not as bright as they once were, narrowed. A large bruise dominated the side of his face, his hair slightly unkempt.

"Pako," I said.

"My name is Malcom. Malcom Sandersfield." His voice was just as I remembered. Deep and sounding just like our father's, I think. Although I could not be sure because these words were in English. Perfect English, as if he had lived here his entire life.

I stepped closer. "It is me, Dikembe, your younger brother."

He stepped back. "Stay away."

"I am not going to harm you."

"I have no idea who you are."

I had not envisioned this standoff. In my thoughts of what this reunion would look like, I had run into my brother's arms, reminisced and made plans for the future. Nothing resembling . . . this.

"Leave," he said. But his words were far from convincing and this only assured me of who he was . . . my brother. The eldest one and not my favorite like Kabili, but my kin all the same.

"Pako," I said.

"I have no idea who you are referring to, young man."

"You are my brother . . ."

"So because I am colored you assume we are brothers, or do you mean in the sense of us being kin of the Empire?"

He laughed harshly and shook his head as he brushed past me.

"Wait!" I called out, following closely behind him. I refused to believe this wasn't my brother. This was him. It had to be.

His strides were long and determined, so when he stopped and turned to me, it was a relief because I couldn't afford to lose him again. Not after the first time, when I had left him standing in line during my farewell.

"Pako, it is me. Do you not recognize me? I have grown and now I speak impeccable English. Perhaps if we spoke in our language . . ."

"My name is Malcom, the only language I know is English, and I have never seen you in my life. Leave me be, young man!" His nostrils flared, and he turned and began to walk away.

"Do you remember our mama?" I said.

That was when he turned to me and the corner of his mouth twitched. I saw a past in his eyes and the people who had occupied it. I saw a longing for something more. I also saw fear.

I continued. "My home is in a village with my mama, my daddy and my four brothers. You are the eldest. You would accompany our father and brothers when you worked away, and I would stay home and wait on you all with our mama. One day they took him from us and you wept like a baby. As did we all. You remember, Pako! You remember!" I could not help the tears falling down my face, even though I'd vowed never to shed them again. I was desperate for him to hear me, to acknowledge we were brothers. There was no way he could deny this. There was no way.

He wiped his eye. "Your story does sound familiar."

I stepped closer. "It does?"

"Of course. Is that not the story of any colored person in this land?"

"But . . ."

"I am not who you seek. I am sorry."

"Pako!"

"My name is Malcom Sandersfield," he repeated. "Please stay away from me because I know nothing of the people you talk about!" The emotion in our voices had begun to attract attention. There was judgment in the eyes of those dirty faces as they stared suspiciously at my cleaner clothes and upright demeanor.

By the time I turned back to Pako, he was walking away again.

I caught up with him and placed a firm hand on his shoulder. I possibly made him jump, because his response was to swiftly spin around, and with two hands he shoved me onto the rough floor. "You will never lay your hand upon me again!" he roared. Pako had always possessed a boisterous flare, but never like this. My mind refused to believe it wasn't him, though. Time away changes people. It had already changed me.

I watched him rush off, but that was of no concern because I knew where he lived. I would go back until he listened, until he accepted we were brothers.

I almost forgot to collect the food, but I did so with an extra weight leveled upon me, hoping Cyril had not timed my absence. I wouldn't give up on Pako. For reasons I was not privy to, he had denied me. Perhaps he was being held in much the same way as I and was scared for his safety, yet also scared to run.

Bill was still off with sickness, so I was able to return the very next day, only to be told that the "blackie" who lived there had moved on.

That night when Agatha locked me inside the attic, I actually welcomed the sound of the key in the lock.

Cyril and Agatha were quick to mention how obedient I had become since the trip to visit the town slums—and they were right. Unbeknownst to them, the trip had achieved the desired effect, but in a different way. It had allowed me to find and once again lose my brother, and in doing so my entire family, highlighting that there was nowhere for me to turn to, with not even my dreams affording me a way out.

The flame of the candle flickered as I sat on the floor of the attic. The doll remained under the floorboard, along with the necklace and a piece of paper I had written on just before the black Parker pen had stopped working.

I had nothing to lose now. I could topple over this candlestick and watch as the entire house burned to the ground. With Cyril away, I could even go downstairs now and put Agatha out of the misery she constantly caused me, just by existing.

How I hated her.

Chapter Forty

Lowra
1993

My mother. My beautiful mother Vivienne had been Caroline's little girl.

I knew in my heart that when my mother's birth certificate finally arrived from St. Catherine's House, it would confirm this.

Mother: Caroline Mayhew.

Father: unknown.

Which meant my grandmother was Caroline Mayhew. But was my great-grandfather Celestine?

Over and over again, Monty kept saying he did not believe it.

Yet, I did.

"Do you remember much about the little girl, Vivienne?" We'd returned to visit Tilly at the nursing home but this time a blanket of warmth washed over me, because for the first time as an adult, I was speaking with someone who'd actually met my mother, and who was in fact distantly related to me too.

"Only that she was rather spoilt—Aunt Agatha saw to that! Vivienne was the child she'd always wanted, I suppose."

"Please, tell me everything."

"Oh, do calm down! I hardly visited Ranklin by then, especially after I married my second husband. We were traveling all over as he was some type of international playboy, you see. Well, he thought he was. Unsightly fellow, big teeth. I'm sorry, my dear, but there isn't much I can tell you about her."

My excitement, although a little watered down, remained and it wasn't going anywhere. I explained as simply as I could to Tilly that Vivienne had been my mother, Caroline my grandmother. We tried quite unsuccessfully to work out how we were related and settled on the fact that Tilly and I were really distant cousins.

"If it makes you feel any better, your mother never wanted for anything except a father. Boys don't seem to run much in this family; no wonder the men always appeared wayward as they searched for that elusive son. However, it sounds like she found something good in your dad."

I swallowed and noticed that Monty had scooted closer to me on the bed, his hand landing on mine.

"I know she died young and that's appalling, but from what you've told me, even in her short life she managed to find true love. At the age of ninety-six, I've never managed it. Equally tragic, you may say, but I've had a lot of fun along the way."

Monty's hand remained on mine as Tilly continued on a bit of a tangent about herself.

Once again, I enjoyed the warmth of his touch and it didn't feel as awkward as the first time he'd shown this type of affection.

"Sometimes what you're looking for is right there in front of you,P "illy said, lost in her own memories.

Monty squeezed my hand tighter.

"I bet you didn't think when you were on your way to Winter Pines nursing home that an old woman would know so much."

"I must admit, we did put off coming to see you."

"Exactly. Yet sometimes we find things in the most unexpected of places. Just like when I inherited that tatty vanity box—the last thing I expected to find was a letter tucked in the side. Now just look at where an old doll I can't even remember, a necklace and a piece of paper have led you. Now you have little old me as a relative! Who knows what else is buried in that old house! You have a lifetime to find out, I suppose."

"I won't be living there, Tilly."

"I see. As you wish. Just find a way to keep hold of it."

That afternoon, I left Winter Pines feeling more alive than I could remember.

Having felt connected to Celestine right from the moment I had first set eyes on him in that museum, every piece of information thereafter had simply brought us closer and closer together. Finding out my mother, who I hardly knew anything about, was at the center of this . . . words could not describe it.

It was Monty who decided to pierce my bubble of happiness as we stood facing the sea, with something we'd both been dancing around ever since walking out of the Winter Pines nursing home.

"We still don't know who Caroline's father is," he said. "Despite what Cyril's letter implies . . ."

"I suppose we have to look at the possibility . . ." I began, because he wouldn't.

"No, actually, we don't. Celestine was a boy, for a start, if we look at the date on the photograph with Babbington. So at the time of Caroline's birth he would still have been a child, Lowra."

The waters were choppy, making unwelcome sounds.

"We don't actually know his date of birth, only . . ." I began.

"Why is it so hard for you to see a child when you look at him?" Monty's expression contorted into a mixture of emotions, like on the train during that awkward discussion, but this time much stronger with the added effect of an angry sea.

"That's not what I said. It's obvious he was a child. What's got into you?"

He moved closer to the water and I followed behind, the wind singing in my ears, the taste of salt on my lips.

"I can't expect you to get it, just because we had a deep and meaningful conversation on the train."

"That isn't fair. You talked and . . . and I listened."

"This isn't a onetime thing for me, Lowra. It's constant, and when you start celebrating your newfound heritage you won't have to ever deal with the consequences that go with it, because you look like this." He waved his hand in my direction and I turned away.

"Your experiences will never and can never be the same. I mean—and I'm sorry to bring this up, I truly am—even when you got ill, the treatment you received wouldn't have been the same for everyone. Even then it's still . . . different."

"What's that got to do with anything? How could you even bring that up?" I felt exposed.

"I am sorry to do that, Lowra, it was a low blow . . . I just wish you understood, truly understood. How we are seen is not the same, and even more so for Celestine, who now, decades later, is still being judged. Now he's a fucking rapist!"

"I never said that, Monty. Not once did I say that."

Although this conversation was going in a direction neither of us had planned, it started to feel necessary.

We sat on a couple of large and uncomfortable tree barks which had overturned on the beach.

Monty closed his eyes slowly, then opened them up. "When you referred to the man at the Rinchester estate as my friend, I had to laugh. I am part of a profession made up of old white men, and anyone like me or darker is usually subject matter to be regarded with either pity or contempt. Nothing's ever said outright, but it's there. You feel it in every fiber of your being, but carry on regardless."

The sea made a loud swishing sound as the tide moved in.

"Since you and I started this, I don't know, quest to find out what happened to Celestine, it has constantly brought up horrible memories, feelings, you know? Of course you do, because it's the same for you . . . but in a different way. Doing this type of work puts me face-to-face with a past that is dirty, unjust and downright despicable."

I shifted closer to him, not just to hear him better but to offer a presence. Anything.

"Babbington's book conveniently leaves out the slavery and the people of the Congo being forced to work or face the consequences. He left out the part about the frequent whipping and beatings. Entire villages being burned down to nothing. The repeated rape of women and children by the Belgians and their allies. The forced incest . . ."

A gasp leapt from my throat.

"Yes, mothers and their sons forced to . . . I can't even say it, Lowra. I can't."

He bent down and picked up a pebble. "The severing of heads and limbs—of babies. Sir Richard left that all out of his fucking books." He launched the pebble toward the sea. "So whether it's looking at very clear pictures of the mutilated and battered bodies of Celestine's people, my people . . ." Monty's voice began to break. "It's a lot to take in and still be me."

I had not expected this. This vulnerability. I wanted to say something to soothe him, yet hadn't a clue what. My hand brushed the tip of his fingers as our gaze turned to the sea and the incoming tide. Being affectionate did not and would probably never come naturally to me. I only had words, but in this instance they weren't really enough, even if they did remain in my head.

He placed his hands to his face, effectively moving them away from mine. I felt relief.

"This is twice I've broken down in front of you."

"We're even, I think." Hopefully it wasn't too soon to make light of something we both knew wasn't funny. But in all honesty, I was glad this being vulnerable thing wasn't one-sided.

Since Dr. Raj, I'd never told anyone about the attic until Monty.

"I blame myself," he said.

"What does that mean?" The side of my knee was touching his now. This human contact was far from threatening, but OK. Yes, it felt OK to be this close to another human being. To Monty.

"I was always good at math, so I should have become a mathematician as my mother suggested. My father reckoned I chose this subject to overcompensate for my lack of Blackness, as he called it!"

I felt a swish of relief when he let out a small laugh.

"This type of work excites me, Lowra, but at the same time it devastates me."

Before embarking on this journey, I hadn't known much about the world Monty talked of. I'd been blinkered, yes, and I suppose being locked away in the attic had made sure of that. Similarly, after I ran it was easier to carry on in much the same way, my eyes facing forward and making sure to block everything and everyone out.

Was that enough of an excuse, though? For me, it had been. Until now.

Now, it was as if I'd placed on my face a new pair of glasses. New, smudge-free lenses, as we headed to the Flamingo Club cafe, walking along Ranklin High Street. It wasn't my imagination when this person or that kept turning to look at us; some a bit curious, others with their eyebrows all in a knot. Now I recalled the man in the bookshop, questioning Monty's credentials and not bothering with mine; and in a different way, the ticket inspector letting me off on the train, and the suspicious way the police had reacted when Monty tried to let himself into that house.

My heart ached for Monty, but more for Celestine. If this could happen in the 1990s to an educated, grown man, then what had a young African boy gone through in the early 1900s? Whether he was my great-grandfather or not, he was also a child. A little boy who deserved so much better.

I didn't want to think only of the pain he'd felt, losing his home and his identity and living in an attic, but all of it.

I understood what it felt like to be grieving for a family you would never see again and to be locked inside a dark room, wishing your life would just end and that tomorrow would never come. But the other stuff—that would never be known to me.

Celestine
1908

I wasn't sure if it was even my name being called at first, but after the second screech it was obvious.

"Celestine!"

I raced to the door of the room and it was open, just as it was every morning. The bed as usual was unmade and the room untidy—yet another job that awaited me after finishing the kitchen and dining room. Then there would be the cooking, because even dinner for one required an elaborate meal, apparently.

"In here." Her voice came from the adjoining bathroom. The sound of slightly splashing water signaled that she was in the bath.

I stood respectfully outside the door. "What may I get for you, madam?"

"Come inside, you silly boy!" Her voice was full of amusement, which was not usual for Agatha.

I opened the door slowly. The tops of her shoulders were visible, my gaze remaining at eye level.

"Come closer, Celestine. Where I can see you."

The claw-footed bath now looked smaller with her in it, and I wished it was bigger. Big enough to engulf her entire body, so all I had to see was her face as I pushed it deeper into the bathwater.

"Yes, madam, what can I get you?"

Thankfully, the water covered her nether regions and her hands were draped over her chest.

"As you know, Cyril is away visiting his brother, who got himself injured in British Somaliland."

Cyril had been gone a month now.

"What was his brother doing there?"

"Do you know of the place?"

"I have seen it on the map, madam."

"Well, we never question what we do for the love of the Empire."

"Shouldn't everything be questioned?"

She didn't like it when I talked like this, and I chose my moments carefully. For me, it was like a sport with no real prize, and I only tried it when Cyril was away because far from being the weaker of the two, he was the strength that assisted her evil. They were indeed the perfect match.

"I am not interested in all of that. It's just rather unhelpful he's going to be away for so long."

She moved one of her hands from her chest, revealing a breast which shook upon its release. I turned my face away promptly. This was not the first time I had seen that part of her body, as since Cyril's trip, she'd called me into her room more than once to assist with dressing; once, apologizing when her undergarment slipped to reveal her chest. Agatha was not one for apologizing so had clearly felt as mortified as I had that morning.

This was the first time she had asked me into the bathroom.

"One thing he did an excellent job of was washing my back." She handed me a long-armed brush. "Can you do it?"

Of course, this was not a request but an order, so I took the brush from her tentatively, feeling as if yet another line was about to be crossed.

I smoothed the brush in a circular motion on her left shoulder.

"Somewhat stronger than that. Come on, boy!"

I hated when she called me *boy*.

"That's better," she said.

At the age of fourteen, my arms had strengthened with the heavy lifting and laborious daily chores. Yet at such an angle my arms quickly began to ache as I rubbed the Pears soap into her back.

In my mind's eye, I imagined the wooden brush rising up high above her head before landing over and over again on the base of it, until blood splattered the walls and dripped into the bathwater, her cries drowned out by a gush of water entering her lungs, causing her to choke until she breathed no more.

"A bit firmer," she requested. I obliged, moving the brush up and down her back.

Without any warning, she stood up, her back toward me, splashes of soapy water falling to my feet. I blinked rapidly. I had never seen a naked woman before in my life, and when she turned around, my entire body stood catatonic for what felt like an eternity.

Her smile did not seem appropriate. Indeed, nothing about this moment did.

"Well?" she said, one eyebrow raised.

I was supposed to say something but could not think of one word. Luckily, her laughter drowned out any expected response.

I hated myself when my eyes traveled to the furry center between her legs. I had never seen anything like this before and it appeared unreal to me, yet tangible. I turned away but it was far too late, for I had already looked, had already felt the heat brimming between my own legs.

I ran to the door and raced up into the attic, where I was safe and away from what I had seen and did not understand. Yet as I lay down in the fetal position, trying to erase it all, an unnamed intruder remained. It was more of a feeling, an ache that existed in between my legs. A hardening of my appendage that I had never experienced before.

What was happening to me?

The next morning, I was more careful than ever not to make any eye contact with Agatha. My embarrassment was not matched by hers, though, as she appeared unchanged since what had happened just one day before. Perhaps to her it did not require discussion or any form of embarrassment, and I was making this bigger than it needed to be. This was what I explained to myself as I scrubbed the floor that morning and baked the potatoes with extra crisp, just as she preferred. When I served dinner for one, I stood over her as an unidentifiable energy hovered in the room.

"The food is exemplary today. I am not one for meat, but these vegetables are exquisite and flavorsome." Her words sounded false and contrived, as if she knew that what had happened yesterday was so utterly wrong.

When an older man made the food delivery, I asked after Bill. He was at times a menace and would say the most hateful words, but I had started to feel a level of claustrophobia with it being just me and Agatha in the big house, more than I'd ever felt locked in that attic.

He stooped as he stood. "He's only gone and got a job at the local pit. They have a new law that says they can only work eight hours at a time. That lazy oaf wouldn't have gone near them otherwise!"

As I placed some of the items in the pantry, a small knot

appeared in my stomach. I didn't like change. The many months since Sir Richard had died had been spent knowing what I had to do each day and where I would sleep at night and who I would encounter during the day. Bill was part of that consistency and now he too was gone.

When Cyril returned days later, this brought some normality back into my life, albeit temporarily.

I served dinner that night to an angry Agatha, her eyes bloodshot, her mouth in an angry knot. Luckily I was not the recipient of that anger.

"My family need me, Agatha!" said Cyril.

"What about me? I need you!"

"My brother will need months of rehabilitation, and I have to preserve the family business and make sure his children are taken care of. I don't have any of my own, and they look upon me as a second father figure."

"Is that another dig at me then, Cyril?"

I had never witnessed such a brazen exchange between the two before.

"No, my dear, I am just stating fact." He looked up as I bent to place the gravy boat on the table. "Celestine, I am leaving my precious wife in your capable hands."

"How long for, sir?" I interjected, with glee because I knew this was hurting Agatha. Then I realized this would mean being left alone with her again.

"I need you here with me, Cyril!" she whined.

"They need me more right now, and it is only for a few months. You can make the trip to visit."

"What about me?" said Agatha.

The moment Cyril left, Agatha took to her bed immediately. Over the next few days, she instructed me to leave food and drink outside her room at set times. Of course, I did not miss her presence around the house or wish there to be a repeat of that naked encounter, which seemed to hover between us like an unspoken threat.

With my daily tasks completed, it would have been easy to take more liberties than I did. I cooked more food than was needed, taking the extra upstairs with me just in case Agatha decided to leave her room and resume normality, which could include withholding food. I even sneaked into my old bedroom a few times and tried sleeping in my own bed. But there was no way I could settle, the fear of Agatha discovering me all too real.

I could also have left the house.

But I didn't. I couldn't. I had no money and indeed nowhere to go, and the shame of this reality simply added to my distress. This house was all I had known in this country—good and bad. It was familiar, and in that familiarity was a safety which felt better than the unknown, which was really all that awaited me outside.

Chapter Forty-One

Celestine
1908

Cyril had been gone one whole month, and Agatha now required dinner to be brought to her as she sat up in bed.

"There's a problem," she said.

I gazed down at the food she'd requested for dinner. Everything was in its place.

She patted the space beside her on the bed. "Sit down."

I was instantly reminded of how wonderfully soft these beds could feel. Once, not that long ago, I'd regularly occupied my own bed, swamped in cotton sheets and the softest of pillows. Now, I could only steal moments on that very bed which had once been mine.

"Would you like to stay in here tonight?" she said. Her thin mouth curved into a smile.

"But where would I sleep, madam?"

"In here. With me." Her forehead wrinkled as if the words spilling from her mouth did not match her thoughts. And although this felt confusing, it was also enticing, as my thoughts overflowed with how it would feel to sleep in a real bed without any fear of being discovered. Maybe then I would experience the full night's sleep I so desperately craved.

I opened my mouth to speak, but she placed her finger on my

lips as if to silence the words. It was then that I realized she was dressed in a flesh-colored nightgown and I was unable to see where the pale fabric ended and her skin began.

"Come on." Her voice was softer than usual, yet still commanding. She lifted the corner of the sheet and a waft of warmth with the promise of comfort flew into the air, reminding me of just how cold the attic would be tonight, my lone blanket inadequate in its quest to keep me warm.

"Madam . . ."

"It sounds like you prefer the floor of the attic to a nice warm bed. If that's so, very well, " she said, slowly lowering the corner of the sheet.

"No, madam. I mean, yes, I would like to . . ."

"Then do so." There was that tender tone again, which I did not know could be trusted. Yet my body held no such questions, simply aching for the comfort and warmth only the inside of that bed could offer. I slowly slipped out of my shoes, a feeling of both acceptance and fear creeping over my body, a mixture that made no sense as I climbed inside the bed. She pulled the cover over us both and I was unable to describe the feeling of joy which immediately cascaded around me.

"Feels nice, doesn't it?" she said. The softness of the pillows felt like nothing I had experienced, even though it was something I had once had at my disposal. Agatha's body heat only made the experience more vivid, transporting me to a place of beautiful memories, of happiness—as long as my eyes remained closed.

"Goodnight," she said, turning her back to me. I'd be asleep very soon but resolved to stay awake long enough to enjoy how this felt. The heat that radiated from her body reminded me of my mama when she had held me tightly as we lay on a mat; or when she'd embraced me minutes after an insect had bitten into the skin on my wrist. If I squeezed my eyes tight enough, I was with her again, could smell her, the scent of her cooking and the sweet aroma of fruit which lingered on her garments.

I wasn't sure if I was awake or asleep, but I could feel my mama's arms around me as I drifted off into what would be a deep and wondrous sleep. I was with my mama again. I was Dikembe once more, and this was the best I had felt in so very, very long.

Morning arrived; I opened my eyes but Agatha was not in the bed. My eyes felt heavy, as if I had slept for only an hour.

"Did you sleep well?" Her voice made me jump. She was sitting by her dressing table and running a brush through her hair.

I shook my head, and slowly images began to appear in my head, as well as unfamiliar sensations . . . and then her voice: "This can be our little secret," she'd said.

Like when I had destroyed the photograph in Sir Richard's study. When I had done something wrong.

This can be our little secret, Celestine.

"No need to begin your tasks, you can start on dinner later."

"Thank . . . you," I said.

I stepped out of the bed very slowly as Agatha ran the brush down the strands of her hair. I looked down at the space where I had lain my body the night before, which had begun with beams of happiness and comfort at Agatha's rare show of kindness at allowing me to sleep in her bed. Then that unfamiliar pleasure I had felt, that urgent hardening in my groin and that first touch of her hand, which I had assumed had been by mistake. The second touch told me the first had been purposeful.

And now my shame.

I looked down at the ruffled sheets, now a disgusting reminder of what had occurred just hours before. The obvious soiling screamed at me, covering me in its filth. Mounds and mounds of guilt rose up in my belly, as I quickly pulled at the sheets and bundled them into my arms.

"Whatever is the rush?" she said.

I could see her in the mirror, smiling—at me or her reflection, I did not know which.

I moved to the door, the soiled sheets covering my clothed body, yet still I felt naked. "I must wash them."

"Do as you wish. They will have to be washed at some point."

I could not look her in the face, but I wanted to. Perhaps then I could see some clue as to what had happened last night. As if her expression could confirm or deny the images now living in my head. Instead, I rushed out of Agatha's room, and minutes later was scrubbing the sheets clean in the basin and then attempting to squeeze the shame out of myself as I pulled them through the mangle.

Yet nothing worked. I myself remained stained, tainted. I had committed an unforgivable act and I was no longer the Celestine who had walked into that room the previous evening. I didn't know who he was anymore. Only that he was dirty and weak. So weak to have let it happen. My body had betrayed me when what I should have done was leave that room last night and lie on the floor of the attic. Just as I did every night. Yet I hadn't done that. I had stayed. After which I'd fallen into a slumber, perhaps with the assumption that when I woke up, it would all have been a dream, a nightmare.

As each hour passed, shame grew inside me, just as strong as the feeling I had somehow turned into something grotesque. A creature. Voices from the past adding to this new belief that I was indeed a beast, uncivilized. Such words formed in my mind like some type of absolute.

Therefore, if I were a beast, a monster, then it was quite understandable that I had behaved like one. Perhaps those angry, murderous feelings toward Sir Richard had simply remained dormant and I was indeed capable of atrocities. Maybe . . .

There was only one thing left to do and this time I had to do it. Either that or I stayed, and one of us would die.

That afternoon, I left the big house with a small bag filled with food and a change of undergarments, and headed first toward the greengrocers, next the ironmongers, and then further up the high street until the big house was no longer visible. I got to Lyles Coal Merchants and then I stopped.

My heart beat rapidly in my chest.

Ever since I had arrived in England, I had been living under the protection of the big house. The beginning had been frightening, and then I had experienced a semblance of happiness with Tilly, and now life felt bleak again. Throughout it all, the only constant in my life had been the big house and I wasn't sure I could actually leave it. Where would I go? Who would I turn to?

I spun on my heel and headed back in the direction I had come from.

Within minutes, I was back at the big house.

Chapter Forty-Two

Celestine
1909

I was finally to be free of the big house. This I told myself daily, ever since attempting to leave that first time.

But I needed to be meticulous with my planning; I had no intention of ending up like Pako or those other poor wretches soaked in poverty and hopelessness.

I just needed a little more time.

The candlelight gifted to me in place of Tilly, which I used to resent, now assisted me in exploring the contents of the trunks and cases stacked inside the attic. I'd often been too exhausted to riffle through them, but my lighter workload these days meant taking advantage of my extra vitality. One of the items I recognized as one of Sir Richard's antique leather steamer trunks. They—Agatha and Cyril—must have packed what they had no need of inside it.

Among the large haul was Sir Richard's doodling. He was a writer of some sort, yet never allowed me to read his work.

A small stack of typed papers also caught my eye: orders for goods, services and wage slips. I swallowed. Sir Richard had paid his staff well, but even what they'd earned was nothing compared to what he'd spent on my schooling, clothing and food. But this was not the time for ill-spent sentiment—I had more than paid it back with the labor I had endured since his passing.

I continued to riffle through the papers, determined to find something, anything, berating myself for not having done this sooner.

My efforts appeared pointless, though, as I found nothing of significance.

The next morning Agatha announced she would be out until the afternoon and, fueled with a desperation which had not tempered during the night, I headed to her room, feeling not one speck of guilt at rummaging through her chest of drawers and searching behind the dressing table. I was even prepared to search under the bed if I needed to, though my eyes had so far refused to look at it.

Inside the wardrobe, covered by the hems of her many dresses, I spotted a leather vanity box, pulled it out, and under four empty bottles with silver-plated tops I found a small wad of papers.

Luckily, my knowledge of words and meanings was as sharp as ever. I'd once asked Sir Richard if it was possible to forget how to read and he'd laughed, and simply said, "No, dear boy, that is an impossibility. Once you become soaked in the nectar of education, it stays with you forever and is the best investment a man can make."

Now, sitting on the floor of Agatha's bedroom in front of her wardrobe, my education had led me to understand the significance of what I now held in my hand; the document I didn't know I'd been seeking. A piece of paper with the power not only to breathe new life into me, but salvage what was left of it too.

The key to my escape had been here all along, resting alongside me and waiting for the time to make its appearance at the very moment I would need it.

Documents with both Sir Richard's and Mr. Roger's signatures.

An amendment to the last will and testament of Sir Richard Babbington.

*

That night I served dinner with no words. Cyril had come back and Agatha appeared more engrossed with him than ever before. Apparently his return was temporary but his appearance was a relief for me, because at least Agatha would not be asking me back into her room. Since that night almost three days ago, the incident was never once referred to, with Agatha behaving as if nothing had happened. But something *had* happened. And whether I allowed myself to acknowledge that or not, it had propelled me into finally taking the action needed to be rid of this house forever.

"Bring more water," said Agatha.

"Certainly, madam," I said.

Once I had rushed in and paid a price. This time, I would be more calculating, just like them.

This time, I had legal proof Sir Richard had wanted me to have an inheritance all along. I also had the name of a man of good standing who could help me. One way or another I would extract what was mine, nothing more and nothing less.

It was only a matter of time.

It was simply like any other morning, but it wasn't. This time I knew that once I stood in between the two half-man, half-creature statues, I'd never return.

Everything I needed was tucked inside my pocket. One document. The possible key to everything.

"I am going to collect some essential items as we have run out of bread, among other things." I sounded as convincing as I ever had.

There was no response from anyone, as I'd known there wouldn't be. Cyril had left for his brother's the previous night and Agatha had immediately taken to her bed, crying that her husband no longer loved her.

I stood in between the statues, recalling the first time I ever saw them. My breathing accelerated as I moved down the steps and further and further away from the big house, past the beachfront, the sea and then into town, past the slums and buildings which served the people: coal merchants, greengrocers. Past the children with dirty faces and beggars with walking sticks. I stopped outside the baker's. We needed bread, that much was true. I stood staring at the door for perhaps a minute and then I moved on, my pace quickening. I had no idea where I was now, only that I began to stand out even more. My clothes—mostly Cyril's hand-me-downs—may have been tidy, my shoes shined, yet I felt as different as could be.

A man in a tall black hat stood before me. "Are you lost?"

"No, sir. I am looking for this address." I pointed to the words at the top of the precious piece of paper, which, if I allowed myself to believe it, could change the course of my life.

"The street up ahead and to your left," he said.

"Thank you, sir."

As I turned away, I could feel his eyes watching me, catapulting my body back to that house with the two creatures, three if you counted Agatha.

Yet wasn't that where I truly belonged? Even this stranger could see I should not be here in this smart street, with no one to tell me what to do and who to be.

I exhaled softly at the door with the sign R. MAITLAND AND SON, and as it opened, he recognized me immediately.

"Celestine?" His facial hair may have been dotted with specks of white I did not recall, but this was undoubtedly Sir Richard's closest friend and confidant, Mr. Roger.

"What are you doing here?" His concern felt soothing, as did his familiarity.

He gestured for me to take a seat inside his office, and without warning, my hands, my wrists, my entire torso and head, began to shake as a stream of silent tears fell from my eyes. I had not planned any of this and its lack of warning alarmed me, as did my lack of control.

"Oh, Celestine," said Mr. Roger, his expression now one of alarm. Yet I could not stop; it was as though this avalanche of emotion needed to leave my body before I could even begin to utter a word.

Mr. Roger sat me down and handed me a handkerchief, which I shakily used to try and wipe at my eyes. And yet the movements did not stop, along with every ounce of emotion rushing out of my body: fear, anger, grief—a multitude of words to describe feelings I'd thought buried deep within, yet now betrayed me with their violent presence.

Yet still I was silent, true to the silent pain I had endured since the day my father had died.

"Whatever has happened? Should I send for a doctor?"

I banged my fist onto his desk.

"As you wish. We shall sit this out," he said. At last someone was listening, and without me having to say a word.

In time, the tears subsided; my body began to comply and embarrassment came in their place.

Mr. Roger's eyes shone with kindness, even though I could not trust them. Not ever. "Take your time, Celestine. Please."

I hated his pity yet welcomed it. His typist had prepared me a cup of sweet tea which felt warm and comforting against my tongue.

"I would like some assistance, Mr. Roger."

He studied the documents I had given him moments before, his forehead wrinkling. He leaned back against his chair and sighed. "I have read the document, this codicil, and recall drawing it up for Richard . . . I just assumed he had never got round to completing it. However, I see here that he had a Jonathan Talbert and Daphne Meyer as signatories."

"I do not understand, sir. If you recall producing this document with Sir Richard, why did you not question the will when it was read? Why did you not think . . ."

His face turned a bright crimson. "Celestine, people change their wills all the time and Sir Richard could be unpredictable, especially with the drinking, which seemed to get considerably worse over time."

"I see." I did not.

"I am clearly at fault here, as I should have at least sought these papers out and verified them. You say they were in the—"

"Attic," I said bitterly. Of course, I would never reveal my presence in Agatha's bedroom. Yet I also wanted him to be splattered with venom from each of my words. I wanted him to feel what the word "attic' truly meant to me. My prison. My potential tomb.

"He clearly wanted you to be looked after." He narrowed his eyes. "Have you been looked after?"

I hesitated before I spoke. "I was fed and clothed, sir."

"Then that's good." He no longer made eye contact with me, his eyes shifting from side to side; to the wad of crinkled papers on his desk, to the floor.

Something inside me turned and I made the decision that today, in this very moment of mounting fury, would be the first and last time I ever told anyone about what had really happened to me in that attic.

"Mr. and Mrs. Mayhew kept me locked away inside that attic, only removing me for toil worthy of three grown men, which I completed daily and sometimes without a grain of food in my stomach. Hungry or not, I slept on the floor of an attic for a few measly hours, only to have to get up again before sunrise to do it all over again. All for no pay."

"What?"

"And even with all of that, the worst part was when . . ."

He looked up. Finally, his eyes connected with mine. "Celestine?"

"The worst part was . . . Mrs. Mayhew . . . when . . ." I swallowed. I would never say it. Never would those words leave my mouth. Yet the memory of it had started to form in my head the minute I had walked into this office. A memory I had disputed daily yet could no longer deny.

"The worst part was hearing the key turn in the lock every single night I was locked away, not knowing if she would come for me the next day or the next week! Sometimes she would leave me there, cold and hungry, especially if she believed I had been uppity that day. A way of teaching me a lesson, she said."

His own eyes had watered and I wondered if, when he looked at me, he could see the disgust I felt.

"Celestine, I am so sorry. I did not know—"

"I do not need your apologies or sympathy, I simply require what is mine. Yes, Sir Richard did provide me with a good life, yes, he did feed and clothe me, but that really isn't the point, is it?" This familiar anger simmered. "I simply want what is owed."

He smoothed out the wrinkled pieces of paper. "Celestine, I will do whatever it takes to help you. It won't be easy because, well . . . it's unprecedented, what we are going to do."

"No one has ever sued over a will before?"

"Not that. I mean . . ." He cleared his throat. "A colored man suing a white man for—"

"I just want what is owed to me, so I can begin the rest of my life."

"We have work to do, but we shall get on with it. Come and see me tomorrow and we will make a start."

"Yes . . ." I said with hesitation.

"Celestine, do you have somewhere to sleep tonight?"

My bravado was fading. My breath came in spurts, too fast for my words. "I will not go back there, not ever!" How I hated myself even more for that. To display such weakness.

"Then you shall come home with me."

I began to feel calmer, though on the tip of my tongue was a quick refusal. Yet this man owed me so much more. If it were not for his indifference, my life since Sir Richard’s demise would not have been the horror it was. Therefore, I would allow Mr. Roger the chance to exorcise his guilt. I cared nothing for him as a man because to me, he’d been complicit in everything.

I greeted Roger’s wife with a politeness I had to force out of me.

“This is Richard’s boy, remember?”

“Yes, I do,P ”he said.

“I am not Richard’s boy. I am Celestine.” I spoke robustly.

“Yes, of course.” He scratched his head as if his hair were a source of great inspiration for what to say next. “Darling, could you also prepare something for Celestine? He is famished, I’m sure.”

Minutes later I was standing in the small kitchen.

“What are you doing?” Her voice was shrill, causing me to drop the glass of water I was carrying.

“What is it?” asked Mr. Roger, running into the kitchen.

“I was simply about to prepare the table for dinner,” I said.

She placed her hand to her chest as Mr. Roger began to chuckle.

“This isn’t funny, Roger,” he said.

“Celestine, you don’t have to serve us dinner. Mrs. Maitland has everything in hand. We aren’t so grand here as to need a servant.”

We ate mostly in silence, but Mrs. Maitland’s eyes spoke so very much as I chewed each morsel of her pie, the pastry not as crisp as mine.

That night, I sat on the bed in a proper bedroom as their voices echoed through the walls. I sensed that I was the subject of their conversation.

I moved out of the room and closer to the voices.

“That is our son’s room!” she hissed.

“A son who has not slept in there for over five years and has a family of his own!”

I was unconcerned about this bickering because I did not intend to overstay my welcome. As soon as I received what was rightfully mine, I would be gone, never to be seen by either of them again. For now, I had a bed for the night—albeit one I could not use, simply because the last time I had been in one . . .

The floor offered a familiar safety, and that was where I lay until the morning.

"I am not comfortable in my own home. There's something in his eyes and it scares me. Quite beastly, in fact."

Mrs. Maitland wasn't saying anything I hadn't heard before from Agatha or Daphne. I had to wonder if either had ever seen a beast before in their lives! If it was anymore than the pictures formed from books and then conjured up in their imagination of what a boy of my hue was really like, underneath the demeanor of a human being. Because that's what I was—a human being, just like her. Yet according to my experience thus far, not everybody in the world shared that view.

Why was it that back home, with my family in our village, the presence of a white man brought wonderment to me but never suspicion—until they hanged my father?

I ate my third breakfast at the table with them in a silence punctuated with so much, each chew scrutinized by Mrs. Maitland. Who knew that placing the glass to my lips would be such a major event, one worthy of full examination? Out of habit, or perhaps just to scare her, I gathered up the crockery and took it to the kitchen. The whispering began almost immediately.

When I returned, I spoke first. "I understand, Mr. Roger. I know I must leave now. I just don't have anywhere to go. I have no family here . . ." By saying this in such a pathetic way, it was my hope he'd forgo waiting for any payout from Agatha and simply offer me money from his own pocket. Instead, he said,

"There are some cheap lodgings not far from here. I do some work for the owner and I can speak with him. The closer you are the better, just in case we need any extra information. Of course, I will pay."

Of course.

"I shall be visiting the Mayhews tomorrow, now I have a good case against them. Let's see what they say—although I'm sure you will appreciate, Celestine, that we cannot expect results right away."

I felt a wave of disappointment, impatience gnawing away at me. I needed something to change, and soon.

The owner of the lodgings was a stooped-over man with a kind face. He nodded his head as he reeled off the house rules, to which I wasn't really listening.

Inside the small room, a chill immediately hit my bones. Yet this was of no concern because I was used to the cold. I plumped up the pillow on the bed and this time managed to lay my body onto it.

I squeezed my eyes shut. That first night at Mr. Roger's I had fallen asleep on the floor straight away, helped in part by the exhaustion of the past few years. Now, with my body slightly rested, sleep refused to come quickly.

I sat up and then it came to me.

While Tilly's doll would at times offer comfort, it was nothing like that of my father's necklace for times such as this. Yet both remained under the floorboards in the attic of the big house, because in my preoccupation with leaving I had forgotten to take them.

I ran my hand over the contours of my neck, naked and bereft with the absence of the only object in the world that mattered to me.

I could never go back to the big house to fetch it, nor could I ask Mr. Roger to do so, as I had no way of knowing what Agatha would do with it out of spite or greed.

The necklace would have to remain in that cold and airless space, never to be seen again. The final resting place for all I had left of my family.

Chapter Forty-Three

Celestine
1909

"Celestine, I have some good news," said Mr. Roger.

I rubbed at my eyes, weary at this early morning visit to my lodgings.

"Mrs. Mayhew has agreed to pay you."

"She has?" For a moment I believed this to be a dream.

"A tidy sum of two hundred pounds."

The words sounded real enough, but I still couldn't be sure.

"Mrs. Mayhew has flatly refused to give you what Richard had bequeathed to you, which was four hundred pounds, but half is better than nothing. Also, due to his debts, you wouldn't have got that much anyway."

Two hundred pounds.

"Mr. Mayhew is away and Mrs. Mayhew doesn't want this to go to court, so . . . Are you agreeable to this?"

"I expected more of a fight from her."

"I couldn't believe it myself. I will collect it at the end of the week."

"Collect what?"

"The money."

A cloud of disbelief still hovered over me.

Two hundred pounds. A fortune.

"Celestine, this is a lot of money. Enough for you to start again somewhere and live well."

As he spoke, the words began to slowly sink in.

"I am grateful for your help," I said eventually. "How much—?"

He shook his head vehemently. "No, Celestine, I won't hear of it. I have failed you and Richard enough. I will not even think of charging for my services."

"You are very kind," I said, not really meaning this. Even with the news he had just given me, I still felt a well of resentment flaring up inside, unable not to imagine what my life would have been like if he had ensured that Sir Richard's wishes had been upheld from the start.

Or if, indeed, I had searched the house sooner.

I was just as much to blame.

"If you need any help, Celestine, I am here," he said. Of course that offer would expire soon, especially if his wife had anything to do with it. But it was my intention to gain as much knowledge from Mr. Roger as I could; my next move needed to be made with precision.

A week later and I was staring at a stash of money strewn on the bed of my lodgings; money that belonged to me.

Agatha and Cyril had turned me into a workhorse whereas a school like Ranklin was where I belonged, before heading to a good college and life as an English gentleman. They had robbed me of a future I'd certainly been on the verge of experiencing. Though hadn't Sir Richard robbed me of a different future when he headed to my village just four years earlier?

All of them were as bad as each other.

This money had not suddenly filled me with joy—that part of me was gone. It did allow for a necessity to grow, a need to become someone in this life and never be at the mercy of people like Sir Richard or the Mayhews ever again. I was under no illusion about how wealthy I now was. Two hundred pounds was a sum the likes of Bill and Enid would never see in their lifetimes. It would be so easy to find out how much a ticket would cost to sail back home and do just that—but where would I start once I got there? I did not know the name of my village, let alone how to reach it. What if Sir Richard had been right and it had burned to the ground? Had I really seen Pako that day, or someone who simply resembled him? Did I have any family to return home to?

Perhaps it would simply be sensible to make a life for myself here in England. A place of certainty and a degree of familiarity. To make something of myself and *then* find a way to get home.

My mind overflowed with possibilities, something I was not used to having in my possession. Along with all that money, it meant I had to be careful and not frivolous, like Sir Richard.

The money wouldn't last forever, of course.

I just had to find a way to make sure it did.

With a bag full of cash, clean clothes on my back and a head full of knowledge, I headed out of the lodgings and on my way. Everything about my life was going to change. An adventure, some storybooks would call it.

And yet, after everything I had already encountered at the age of fifteen, why did this now feel like the most terrifying moment of my entire life?

Chapter Forty-Four

Lowra
1993

I was back in London, home of the familiar, and yet everything had changed.

The world I'd lived in before discovering the necklace, the doll and that piece of paper no longer existed to me.

I would never be the same again.

And that was OK, because that other life had mostly been spent sitting alone in my flat waiting for a call from either an employment agency or a cold caller. Or working, or thinking about work and ways in which to just exist and not get ill again. My life really hadn't consisted of much else, yet I'd convinced myself it was all I needed. Little did I know that when I had gone to that museum exhibition, unable to take my eyes off a photograph from 1907, I was possibly looking into the eyes of my own history.

Not only was this child possibly my great-grandfather, he'd also experienced a similar childhood to mine, even though we were born on different continents, a century apart.

Celestine and I were connected in a way I could never have imagined.

While I might not have proof, in my heart I knew he was Caroline's father, the baby no one wanted and whose own baby—my mother—had been taken from her before being sent away herself. To an asylum, Tilly had said. *Just like me.*

Monty still went back and forth over the notion of another Black person having possibly lived in or passed through Ranklin around 1908–1909 who could have been the father of Agatha's baby. A part of him refused to believe a woman capable of abusing a child sexually—and that's what this was Celestine had been a child and she an adult. It was abuse. Not only locking Celestine away at her will and against his, she'd also taken whatever else she desired from him.

Monty found it easier to believe this of Richard Babbington, especially considering the ambiguous stuff he'd written in his book. But I knew differently.

"You have no idea what women are capable of," I said.

1975

It was one of those days.

One of those days when trying not to think of my dad wasn't working.

"Could you . . . bring one of the photo albums up? Please?"

"And I said, would you like a magazine? How about another copy of that *Jackie* you like? I bought a few and I think you have earned one—"

"I don't want a magazine!"

She stood up slowly and patted down her corduroy skirt. "You might want to tone down your voice. I came in here with good intentions."

I hated when my tears came. I didn't want to own them or for them to be mine, because it meant I wasn't pretending enough.

Then the anger would come.

Mine.

Last week, or last month, had been one of those times. I actually told her to "fuck off," a phrase I'd never used before. She'd got so angry she cried—while pushing a large nub of Shield soap onto my tongue, pushing my chin up, shouting at me to wash the words right out of my mouth as I coughed and spluttered into the air.

"I just want to see the album," I said slowly.

She didn't say another word as she locked the door behind her.

I have no idea how many days later it was, but when she knocked on the door I did think it was weird. Even weirder when I saw the door wasn't locked and there on the floor was a pile of charred books, with a burnt aroma wafting up from them. I bent down for a further look, hoping it was my school textbooks; algebra would have been great. Instead, all I could make out was the disjointed lettering on one which read: FAMILY ALBUM.

1993

There'd been no one around to acknowledge what had happened to me in that house, that attic, and if I could do nothing else, I would acknowledge what had happened to Celestine.

When Monty insisted we take a break I agreed, even though I was fired up and ready to just get on with it and keep digging. Yet it was clear to me that it was Monty who needed the break.

"I have to step away from all this and look after me for a bit. You know, go meet friends again, take in the theater, have a drink, visit my folks, do a food shop. My head's all over the place. It's been . . . a lot."

I told myself this was a good idea and decided to attempt something different by inviting Marnie to the cinema, much to her surprise. I figured this was enough, plus I wouldn't have to make much conversation the entire night. When she suggested we go for a drink afterward, I quickly made an excuse and then went anyway. This was supposed to be a moment of change and I would just have to embrace everything that went with it.

I ended up having a good time, even if most of the night was spent thinking about Celestine.

When Monty finally pressed the intercom to my flat, I felt a surge of relief . . . and excitement. The short break had clearly done him good. Having not seen or heard from him for two weeks, I noticed the change in his face. No bags under his eyes, his skin notably brighter.

Also, I had missed him.

"Are you sure you're ready to go on with this?" he said.

"Very sure," I said.

"Good, because I can't stop thinking about it all. Caroline, Celestine, the necklace—all of it. We've got to see this through, haven't we?"

"Of course we do. We have to find out what happened to Celestine."

Chapter Forty-Five

Celestine
1909

This time I was in London on my own terms.

On the train, I kept holding my breath during the first few minutes of the journey out of Ranklin, as it receded from view. Only when I believed the town, the big house, the half-creature, half-human statues were all truly gone, did I dare to exhale, allowing my eyes to draw in the sunlight as it caught the tops of the trees.

Ranklin was no longer a part of my peripheral vision, and hopefully my memory too.

Now, back in London, I was unable to find any emotion associated with my first visit. Surrounded by a plethora of people walking in opposite directions and with the exact same expressions, it seemed, I felt nothing mirroring what I had that first ever day in London. That promise of an experience which would outshine everything else; at least, that was the way Sir Richard had sold it to me. Now, London just seemed like the logical place to begin, simply because apart from Ranklin, it was the only other area in England vaguely familiar to me, yet big enough, I assumed, to allow me to get lost in the throng. A chance to truly disappear and run away.

Perhaps even from myself.

Out of instinct, or a need for the familiar, I followed the water.

It looked and felt nothing like the beach in Ranklin but was darker in color, with a cloudy and heavy mist hovering over it, eerie and uninviting. Men smoked cigarettes as they congregated around it on a bridge leading to a floating pier, with rickety rowing boats moored on the river beneath. Unlike the area in and around the Sapphire Hotel where I had previously stayed, this was full of squalor and odors I did not care for.

I headed into yet another street where litter lined the curbs and little children played among themselves.

The children were both Black and white, some sitting on the pavement while others were throwing a weathered ball against the wall. There appeared to be a togetherness as they gathered, dressed in their rags and with smeared faces. In Ranklin I had only ever seen one person with my hue—the man I had thought was my brother Pako—yet here, while I was still in the minority, I was not alone. This was something I had never seen before in England, and deep inside me I felt a pull to this road, this area, while another part of me knew I could never live in such squalor.

I wandered away from the water and into a street with shops and names I could not pronounce. A horse and carriage trailed past carrying boxes, and beside me a man nodded his head. He was Chinese. Indeed, so were the men standing in line outside the shops.

This area confused me with its contradictions, but it was about two streets away from where I would find my first paid employment.

Raif was a skinny man with an accent I couldn't place, whose bones jutted out from his threadbare jacket. Not that you would know it to look at him, but he was financially comfortable enough to own a small drinking establishment not that far from the Sapphire Hotel in walking miles, though it could not have been further away in class. The public house named the Tavern was unkempt, serving rowdy men who spilled drinks onto the floor as they sang, but it was the only one with a HELP WANTED sign.

"I used to run a place up north where I'm from, but fancied me chances down south. I run a good establishment here," he said, chewing on something unidentifiable. "Not like them Chinese with their gambling dens and taking all that opium."

"Opium?" This I had never heard of and would have to look up. I prided myself on knowing most things.

"You can work mostly out back, but if we need you to collect glasses and clean up front, you will do that too. That good with you?"

I nodded my head as excitement began to build up inside me. I was to be paid for this work, which meant for the time being living modestly and not touching any of the money in my possession, until I could concoct a firm and sensible plan. Having sacrificed so much of my life up to this point, this was my one chance to get it right.

"Can you start tonight?" he said.

It was difficult not to feel overwhelmed by the strong aroma of alcohol and tobacco—smells I could only associate with Sir Richard. "Yes," I said.

"Welcome to the East End, then," said Raif with false joviality.

By nightfall, the public house became filled with men too drunk to care about my presence. Once or twice I even spotted a couple of Black men. The three of us made eye contact in a way that spoke of a kinship not bound by blood, but a knowledge of a shared experience.

The work was repetitive but not taxing. Having been used to much harder over the last two years, I accomplished it easily each day. I even got used to the small, stained mattress on the floor of my new room at my lodgings near the public house. The various loose floorboards were useful places in which to hide my money—in separate slots, of course, just in case. Now in paid employment, I didn't need much of it for day-to-day living, but I made sure to check each amount daily. Even though the other boarders never entered my room and I slept with the door firmly locked, I remained vigilant.

None of the other occupants of the house really bothered with me, and I rarely spoke with them unless it was to say hello. My manners had not escaped me.

One day I would own a house grander than Sir Richard's—as well as the funds to actually maintain such a building. It was easy to see how he'd been living far beyond his means, what with his trips to Africa and the endless bottles of whisky.

This current situation would not be my life forever, but for now, it suited me.

The Tavern continued to be full of the liveliest and loudest men I had ever met. There also didn't appear to be anyone befitting the role of English gentleman, or if there were, I didn't see them.

These men, mostly sailors or the odd soldier, were both friendly and great sources of information, and like the children I had seen on my first day were a mixture of nationalities, accents and languages. From what I was able to ascertain so far, people of my color generally lived in this area, with a larger concentration around Limehouse.

One evening, Raif decided to join me on my break, which I always spent outside in the backyard in the hope of fresh air. In reality, I sat with the stench of sewage and a friendly rat who stood alert for leftovers.

"What is it with you?" he said.

I bit into an apple. "Whatever do you mean?"

"You speak like a . . . well . . . like one of those toffee-nosed buggers. I've met my fair share. Sometimes they like to come in here with their floozies so they won't get recognized. It's like you don't belong in that body of yours."

I wasn't quite sure what Raif was trying to say to me, but

generally he was intoxicated with alcohol, which meant he slurred his words at the best of times.

"I have attended one of the best schools in the country, and for a short while I was far more learned than the majority of my class. I suspected my peers merely sat around as if they were passing time."

"Is that so?"

"I also had an excellent private tutor." I placed a palm to my mouth and quickly looked toward Raif. Agatha and Cyril would not have liked me talking this way. They would have referred to it as "getting above oneself."

"I mean . . . I was fortunate to have learned a great deal thanks to the generosity of Sir Richard Babbington."

"Never heard of him."

"Sir Richard would not have frequented your establishment—he much preferred to drink alone in his study. You wouldn't have met."

"You are a comedian, aren't you!" He clutched his stomach and continued to guffaw with exaggeration. I simply smiled. "I like you, Celestine."

I smiled, hoping he would leave me and the rat alone.

Working evenings meant that daytime had to be filled with an activity of some sort, or else a restlessness would grow and irritate me until I did something. My idleness often felt like a burden, so I began to purchase books I could read in the park. My favorite by far was *Robinson Crusoe* by Daniel Defoe, which I had begun at school.

I was simply desperate to sink into a book that was not about science, eugenics and the differences between men, and the premise of this particular book had always felt appealing—especially as one of the main characters was a Black man.

I read and studied the book hungrily. My elation at visualizing this character was at first thrilling, until similarities with Sir Richard started to trickle from the pages and into my consciousness. The more I read, the deeper my sense of humiliation. Soon after, and I am unsure why, I purchased one of Sir Richard's publications, *The Trek to Africa*, even though I would never open it. His smiling face on the front cover was enough to set me on a path to search for other books on similar subjects.

It was easier than I thought to find books and articles centered on what Sir Richard and every other writer, it seemed, referred to as the Congo Free State. I had not grown up in a village or a country named the Congo Free State. That term sounded most odd to me.

Then there were other books, like *King Leopold's Soliloquy* by Mark Twain, which made me see a truth I hadn't wanted to see: that the country I called my own had been in crisis throughout the time I had lived in it.

Finally I had the space to truly ponder how I, as a young child, had been sheltered from the brutal injustices, the killings and the carnage. How my parents, my mama and father, had truly saved me. It was when I read E. D. Morel's *Red Rubber: The Story of the Rubber Slave Trade Flourishing on the Congo in the Year of Grace 1906* that the macabre truth of what was occurring finally became real. The year of my leaving was not coincidental. My mama and possibly even my father, before his demise, had planned it so that I would not fall into the same fate as everyone else in my family, my village and the entire country. My parents had protected me, shielded me from the forced work, the beatings and the sheer torture inflicted upon them on a daily basis.

My memories began to make sense. Never seeing anyone else apart from my family and Ina Balenga. Shunted away from the rest of my village.

My memory failed me, yet my reality did not.

Was this because I was a good and special child?

It seemed immoral to hide behind such a term and yet everyone around me ensured I had been treated as such. As if my brothers were "bad' and I good. And even though I knew this was not the intended meaning, the result felt as much.

Words I'd once said with pride were now tarnished, since finding out what this had truly meant for everyone else.

What it had truly meant for my brothers.

It was some time before I read again. No longer thirsty for stories that claimed to reflect me, I preferred instead to read books about trees and wood types which were not so easy to come by. Sometimes, if I couldn't sleep during the night, which was often, such a book would offer a soothing comfort, and also wash away some of the guilt at having left my father's necklace in the confines of the big house.

As months turned into years, it became easier to remain anonymous living in an area where there were other Black men. In Ranklin I had been an anomaly; here in East London I was one of more than a simple handful! My neighbors still appeared fascinated with me, though, often referring to me as "the one who speaks well." Some of the men had arrived from far-flung parts of the world or just from outer London, looking for work now the Olympics had brought in an influx of people. Many of them longed for fluency in English or simply to read, and I'd find myself slipping into the easy role of tutor. A more smiley Mr. Lattery, I suppose, but no less efficient.

As word spread of my makeshift classes, I quickly found myself with three students joining me each afternoon on the steps of my lodgings, pen and paper in hand. This gave me something to do and avoid the idleness that threatened to creep up on me if I let it. An idleness that sometimes led to thoughts of anger and regret; pointless emotions that could only lead one way.

I soon became the go-to person for free tutoring. Of course, I could have charged a fee, but I never would. Seeing the men as they sat on my bed or on the floor, heads down in books I had paid for, gave me a sense of purpose. It also felt like I was repaying a debt I'd no idea had existed.

By the time I was nineteen, I had been living independently in London for four years and had a bank account which only housed a fraction of my money. There still existed within me a deep-seated fear of needing access to it at a moment's notice—just in case. I was never sure what the *just in case* was.

I kept up with private tutoring while continuing my work at The Tavern. It had taken all this time to assimilate myself into independent living, which had not been easy. Neither was living with those images that regularly visited during the nighttime as I lay in my bed or on the floor beside it: those of my father and what he must have experienced during his last moments. Added to this was my fear that Agatha or Cyril would reappear, demanding I return to the big house.

My plans to make something of myself had never gone away and were mostly jotted down on endless pieces of paper, with the assurance they would one day become a reality.

In the meantime, The Tavern and tutoring continued to be the learning curve I had needed in order to survive in "the real world," supplying me with the tools I had lacked since the day I was born.

I had begun to charge some of my less impoverished students, not least to keep up the appearance of needing extra money. Now I'd moved into more spacious lodgings which were certainly more private, I relocated the classes to the backyard, where I mostly taught English with a bit of mathematics for those who wanted to learn.

I used some of my daytime hours to search for work, as it began to feel as if I'd grown out of the rowdiness of Raif's public house.

My search was sometimes met with scorn, being totally ignored, while some shopkeepers were happy to tell me to come back another time. My system of recording all the places with HELP WANTED signs that I had spoken to was useful in avoiding duplication, as "shut the door on the way out and don't come back" was a sentence I had no desire to hear more than once!

Little did I know just how important such a system would be to my life and that of countless others.

1913

Dele, a young man who lived in one of the rooms in my building, greeted me with a nod. I wasn't one for casual chat, but he was friendlier than most and I was curious about his name—a strong African name, I gathered, chosen by his parents and not a stranger.

It reminded me of Dikembe. A name I had not heard from anyone's lips in many, many years.

"Ever since the Olympics ended, work has been scarce. I'm not sure how long my money will last." Dele spoke with a slight accent, as well as a lisp.

"What happened at your current place of employment?"

"They have enough staff apparently. I just don't know what I'm going to do, Celestine."

"What about your family? Are they back home?"

"This is my home."

"I do beg your pardon. It's just, your name . . ."

"I'm here in the mother country now, where I intend to stay."

I had no inclination to debate this further, but my mind did turn to the stash of money I had dotted around my lodgings, with which I could help Dele in one fell swoop. But this wasn't the answer.

"If I hear of something, I will endeavor to let you know," I said sincerely as my brain ticked loudly in my head.

When Dele had left, I unfurled the piece of paper from my pocket, smiling as I did so.

I returned to the teahouse I had been to just the day before.

"Excuse me, madam."

The woman with the enormous purple hat and raised eyebrows stared toward me. "What is it?"

"Yesterday, when I asked about work, you said you only had enough for after hours, clearing up and so forth."

"That's what I said."

"What if I found someone who could work for you? A man. A hard worker."

"Send him to me then."

"Yes, of course, ma'am, but may we discuss his wage first?"

"You're not all about that union rubbish, are you?"

"This is another matter."

An hour later, Dele was grabbing my hands wholeheartedly and with words of gratitude.

"How can I thank you enough?" he said.

"No thanks needed. I'm happy to be of assistance," I said. "Besides, I'm being compensated for my efforts."

"So you will take money out of my wages?"

"Just your first set. Like a . . . a finder's fee."

I could almost hear the cogs of his brain working, weighing up if this was worth it. I wasn't overly proud of myself for what I said next, but did so anyway. "It will not be long until you're thrown onto the street. Isn't it better just to part with a small amount now and reap the benefits of full employment later?"

I had already made the agreement with the teahouse to give me a percentage of his first set of wages directly, having negotiated a fair and good wage. I was desperate for Dele to agree or else my new venture would disintegrate even before it had begun.

"I shall do it. Thank you, Celestine."

I hoped he was as good a worker as I'd promised. There were so many variables that could make this fall to pieces, and if it did, that would be fine. I still had the money stashed away; I would be able to survive. But I, for one, was tired of simply surviving.

A fire burned inside me: to be more than what the likes of the Mayhews or even Sir Richard expected. Never would I answer to another human being again. Never would my life be determined by the actions of another. It would not be easy, but nothing so far had been and yet here I stood, alive, breathing and utterly hopeful.

"That bugger has let me down again," said Raif as I swept the warehouse at the back. He hadn't asked me to do so, I was just fighting idleness, while Raif saw this as me being a conscientious worker. Over the last several weeks I had replicated what I'd done with Dele by matching a handful of men with employers. I had enjoyed the challenge and earned a healthy percentage in the process.

"You mean Tom? Has he not been well?" I said.

"He's a lying little runt. Sick, my foot! We're expecting a crowd in tonight. The ships have docked and those sailors drink like fishes. How am I supposed to get the extra staff by tonight?"

My mind rested on the number of people who lived close to my lodgings, destitute and hungry.

"I may have someone in mind."

Raif eyed me with suspicion, something he did to everyone because that was his nature. Yet over the years, he'd developed a trust in me that would never, ever be reciprocated.

"He's colored," I said, searching his expression for the usual astonishment followed by disappointment and finally acceptance. I was learning fast. He did not disappoint.

"I don't care what color he is, if he can work tonight."

Albert, the employee I provided, worked harder than Tom ever did. So when Tom returned the following week, Raif behaved decently by keeping them both on. My estimations, although already low, had crept up regarding Raif—until I overheard a conversation between him and Tom.

"Do you think I'm going to pay you for being off, Tom, is that it?"

"I was really sick. Ask anyone."

"Get out of my face!"

"I'm just asking for a sub. Go on, just a sub. Until next week. You know you weren't paying that colored boy what you pay me, so you saved a bit!"

Raif had often praised himself for giving "certain types" of people a chance. As well as me, he'd hired other Black men over the years. Yet after a short conversation with half of these men, it would appear that Raif paid the Black men—including myself—a third less than his white male and female workers. As this realization began to sink in, it took everything I had not to march into his pub and drag him out by the collar. This was not gentlemanly behavior, but my mask was slipping. Perhaps thinkers like Arthur de Gobineau or even Roger Maitland's wife were correct, and I was simply a beast ready to unleash his animal desires onto everyone.

I allowed my anger to decrease, but only after acknowledging that it was justified. What Raif had done was immoral and unjust, and unlike when I held no power locked inside an attic, this time I endeavored to do something about it.

"You haven't got a leg to stand on," said Raif when I brought my grievance before him.

And he was right. None of the new labor laws really applied to non-white people, it seemed, so the only course of action was to hit Raif where it would challenge him the most—in the pocket.

Albert was the first to refuse my challenge of a walkout.

"I can't risk it, brother. But I do appreciate what you are trying to do, just as I appreciate everything you have done for me."

"The more of us who walk out, the more Raif will see that—"

"I can't do it! I have a family to support."

The response from the others was very much the same, so it was just I who stood alone, a protestor on the path to nowhere.

I had been waiting for the summons and when it came, Raif gave no surprises.

"I hear you've been causing trouble, lad."

"I do not think it is fair that some men here earn more than others."

"I used to think you were a good one. After all I did for you, here you are trying to mess with my livelihood."

"Not at all. We just want what is fair."

"We? Look around you, you're all alone."

He stood close to me.

"Anything to say in that fancy accent of yours?"

I stepped back. I would never allow Raif or anyone else to intimidate me ever again. "I have made my feelings clear. I would like to know what you are going to do about it. We are just asking for fair pay. That is all."

He wasn't listening. "I liked you because unlike most around here, you spoke and dressed well. I should have known you were just another one with ideas above your station. Wanting more than you're meant to have."

I did not say a word as I passed the apologetic faces on my way out of the building. I couldn't really blame them for not supporting me. I had options. I'd always have options.

The night I left the Tavern for the last time. The rain had made the street slippery and as I turned into a dark road, the air became punctuated with voices behind me.

"Oi, you!"

My footsteps quickened.

"I'm talking to you. Yeah, you, you Black bastard!"

I had never heard this term directed at me before; I was

certainly not a bastard, but the son of a proud and brave man. I thought it best not to converse with an angry mob, though, as my pace quickened further, their footsteps following behind.

"Oi, we're talking to you!" Another voice. This time I recognized it as Tom's.

I turned to face him.

"Yeah, it's me. Trying to get all the other Blacks to rise up against us, weren't yer?"

"Not at all." My street was just another five minutes away. Just five minutes.

"So what was all that with Raif about then?"

He was joined by two others I did not recognize.

"Gentlemen, I would just like to be on my way." I thought about the money tucked into my sock. It wasn't much but perhaps it would convince them to leave me alone. I had to make a quick decision, but decided it was pointless reasoning with buffoons, so I turned and quickened my pace past the small theater on the corner, regretting my decision to leave the pocketknife at home where I slept with it under my pillow.

My heart was beating much faster than it needed to as the footsteps behind me sped up again. The last words I heard as I turned to them and felt the full force of a fist smash against my cheek were "Get him!" followed by a ringing in my ear, my body pulled limb from limb as the tips of two pointy boots embedded themselves in my abdomen, shins and buttocks. The salty taste of fresh blood ran from my mouth and trickled down my chin.

Pain and then a blinding light and then my mama's face.

I hadn't seen it in a while.

Then Kabili's and each of my brothers' faces.

When my body became elevated by the scruff of my neck, it was my father's face that I saw as my head connected with something hard and I heard a crack.

I lay on the floor and my father was standing in front of me, tall and taut. There was no mark around his neck where he'd been hanged from a tree, no bullet holes. I had never seen him look so relaxed and happy, his smile wide and free. He was calling my name with his arm extended and his palm opening and shutting.

"Dikembe," he said softly. The light did not affect his vision as he stared toward me clearly.

I raised my arm. I was ready to go now. To leave everything behind. This sense of peace descending over me felt like no other.

I floated up into his arms, and I felt warm and above all safe as I left everything else behind; all that pain in my body, in my head and in my heart. I let it all go and was ready to connect with my father again. To go wherever he wanted.

"Dikembe," he said.

*

Nobody ever told you
You were missed.
You were loved.
I wish I'd been there
For you.
I wish you'd been there
For me.

It is too late.
We are separated.
Apart.
By a lifetime. By a mortality.
If only they allowed you to live.

Lowra

PART THREE

Chapter Forty-Six

Lowra
1993

BLACK MAN FEROCIOUSLY BEATEN TO WITHIN AN INCH OF LIFE

Celestine was gone.

Disappeared off the face of the earth.

I wanted to cry for Celestine, to grieve, yet the emotion wasn't there. Not because I'd never met him—no, our bond was stronger than ever. There'd be no tears because I still needed to believe he had survived this. That after everything he'd been through during his short life, it hadn't ended in such a brutal way.

Since the moment we decided to take this journey, Monty and I hadn't had much to go on, even though his picture hung in exhibitions alongside one of the country's most famous explorers of that time. So the discovery of a local newspaper gave us hope, in a bittersweet way.

It was Monty who'd suggested we stick to searching local newspapers in "typically Black areas" of that time, which happened to be those located by docks like Liverpool, Cardiff and Canning Town in East London. Monty was convinced Celestine would have headed to one of those, and the easiest place to start looking was London.

"*The man, known locally as Celestine Babbington, was left for dead outside the Motif theater in Critchley Road. Little is known of his condition, although he is not expected to survive,*" I read.

"I think this story was only reported in the newspaper because of the proximity to the theater," said Monty. "At least we know he kept Celestine Babbington as his name, so we can stop looking at the variations we'd conjured up with Dikembe."

"I don't think that's a good idea, Monty. What if the name Dikembe fits in somewhere?"

"But we've looked for Celestine Dikembe and all sorts of variations, and nothing. Not even a census entry!"

Monty was right: the trail was cold even if I refused to admit it. Despite Monty tapping into the resources of his historian acquaintances, museum curators—anybody—we still didn't have much. We'd spent hours leafing through eighty-year-old records belonging to the Strangers' Home for Asiatics, Africans and South Sea Islanders in Limehouse, which was a long shot because Celestine had never worked at sea, but he could have gone there for refuge. Yet, still nothing came up in their recorded ledgers, although we couldn't be sure all the names were listed anyway.

"Where would a young man under the age of twenty end up?" said Monty.

"Begging?" I didn't want to think of Celestine doing that.

"He could have enlisted."

"Would he have been allowed?"

"There were thousands of non-white soldiers, so certainly."

Another piece of history I knew nothing about.

"So how do we find out?"

"Service records, perhaps. Or we can look at records of medals. I mean, we have a name that probably isn't that common, so—"

"Sounds like a good plan."

"I know someone at the Imperial War Museum who may be able to help, but I'm not hopeful that's the route to take."

"Why?"

"The date of the attack was just a couple of months before the First World War broke out."

"So . . . ?"

"So if he was as badly beaten as we believe, there's no way he would have been in a position to enlist—even if he'd wanted to."

"What about later?"

"We're assuming he was alive by then, and I know that's what you want, Lowra—what we both want—but we have to think about the possibility he died in the attack."

Beaten to within an inch of his life, the report had said. All alone, and far away from his family and everything he'd known for the first half of his short life. Any potential he'd had, snuffed out.

In thinking about all he could have been, I admit, for the sake of this moment, I romanticized it all. Yet who were we to know how his life would have turned out?

If only they allowed you to live.

Monty shook his head, closing the notebook. He took his glasses off and I noticed his eyes were bloodshot.

"We have to check out the area around the Motif theater, see what's there now. Maybe Celestine lived in that area. Dead or alive, I need to know how he lived, where he walked, what he saw," I said.

"Already thought of that, but it's my mum's birthday this weekend, so I'll be off radar. You know how it is."

I didn't, of course.

"It's a big one, so I'll be consoling her with the merits of old age, while fending off relatives I haven't seen in years who feel the need to ask why I haven't yet acquired a wife."

"Oh, OK," I said, hoping my disappointment was hidden. I'd got used to seeing Monty almost every day of the week since resuming our search after the "break." It was surprising just how easily he'd slotted back into my life and the joy I felt being around him; something weird in itself, considering the subject matter was far from joyful. Yet it was as if we bounced off one another, and more important, I felt supported by him at times. I hoped I did the same for him. Especially now I was becoming better at seeing his point of view on things that really mattered to him.

I wasn't used to such a close friendship. Growing up, my only pal had been made of porcelain. With Monty and me—the words "Monty and me" even sounded odd—I couldn't work out if it was romantic or just . . . friendship. Either way, I would miss him this weekend.

"Have fun," I said halfheartedly.

I was now used to climbing into bed at night with that doll and her glass eyes staring at me, the necklace in pride of place on my dressing table and the piece of paper safely tucked inside a plastic sleeve Monty had given me. Regardless of my blood ties to Celestine, I deserved none of these items and they needed to be back with his direct family.

My family.

I closed my eyes and exhaled. The time for honesty was now. Even if Celestine had survived the attack, chances are he'd now be close to one hundred years old and unlikely to still be alive.

There, I'd said it. Celestine was dead. Either after the attack or sometime later, but dead nevertheless.

But in finding Celestine's relatives and descendants, I'd also be finding my own, and that, I had to admit, remained the biggest pull of all.

As soon as I stepped off the bus at the corner of Critchley Road, I felt something.

I stopped for a moment, trying my hardest not to imagine what Celestine must have felt being set upon by a group of thugs on this very street. Had he felt like me, when Nina had rained blows on my face and head for no apparent reason other than her rage, which really had nothing to do with me? Had he called for his mum just as I'd called for my dad?

I had never felt closer to a person in my adult life than I did to Celestine in that moment, standing outside the now derelict Motif theater.

We were two children born in different centuries; lost and alone, yet connected by a set of experiences I wouldn't wish on my worst enemy.

A wave of emotion hit me and a floodgate threatened to open up. This wasn't an "episode," as they called it at the hospital. This was real. I wasn't chasing a ghost. He was gone, yes, but to me he was real. So incredibly real.

I moved along the street and well away from the theater, tears blurring my vision.

Much of the area consisted of run-down and neglected buildings, but I was pleased to spot a library on the corner and really hoped it was just as comprehensive as the one in Ranklin.

I wasn't disappointed.

As soon as I mentioned the name Celestine Babbington, the librarian began to excitedly press a number of keys on his computer, and within minutes I was in front of another microfiche machine staring at a newspaper cutting about Celestine Babbington, a local businessman whose business had burned to the ground after race riots in the area. It was dated 1919.

"He's alive!"

"Would that be the man you're looking for then?" The librarian's teeth were yellow and he showed them off enthusiastically as he smiled.

"It is," I said, a little more sombrely.

"So, why so sad? This is good, isn't it?"

I thanked the librarian and fled outside. The cool air hit my face, already soaked with tears.

Once again, Celestine had shown up to tell us his life had taken yet another crappy turn. Having already been through so much and now trying to make something of himself, there he was being shot down yet again.

Why did this keep happening to him?

My life had been one big letdown after the age of eleven, disappointment after disappointment. This had happened so much I never actually felt it anymore. I could only hope Celestine was like that too. That no matter what disappointments he faced, he was always able to rise again.

The only good thing I could take away from this discovery was that in 1919, Celestine was still alive.

When I told him, Monty was of course pleased with this news, and just two days later called with even more to share.

"As you know, we've been searching the electoral and census records for Celestine Babbington, which made sense considering that's the name he'd been given, and as you found out, still used for his business."

"But we've never found anything official in that name beyond the newspaper clippings."

"Exactly. Anyway, the guy at the Smithsonian—well, he took another look at the so-called doodlings on that piece of paper, because if you ask me, he's been a little obsessed with it since I gave it to him."

"And?" I hated when Monty did this. "Can you just get on with it?"

"After a lot of debate, he's decided that one of the words is Kabili, which is also a name. And when we put the names together with the others we know—Celestine, Kabili and Dikembe . . ."

My heart raced.

"So I went back to the census and found an entry for the name Dikembe Christopher Kabili."

It suddenly felt hard to swallow. This was it, we'd found him. He'd changed his name; this was him.

"It's not him, Lowra."

I swallowed.

"This man is only fifty years old, whereas Celestine must have passed years ago . . . You know this."

Of course Celestine wasn't alive. I knew that.

"This guy may be a distant relative or have nothing to do with him, but we have to pay him a visit. Now."

All the other name variations had led to dead ends and phones being hung up, so there was no reason this should be any different.

But it is.

I felt it in every cell of my body: Dikembe Christopher Kabili was about to unlock everything we needed to truly find out what had happened to Celestine.

Chapter Forty-Seven

Lowra
1993

Number 6 Shirley Avenue was on a smart road located in Highgate Village, North London; the part that could pass for the countryside yet was only a tube ride away from the city. It was elegant and leafy, with rows of large pastel-painted houses with no curtains and spacious lawns out back, spotless roads, and a huge park full of strollers and little dogs running toward tennis balls. Whoever this Dikembe Christopher Kabili was, he had money and lots of it.

It was Monty who knocked on the door, while I looked around the graveled driveway, home to a large Mercedes. There was an empty spot beside it, meaning there might be no one home.

I cleared my throat and balanced on my heels, for no apparent reason other than nerves.

When the huge dark green door finally opened and a waft of a generic air freshener flew into my nostrils, I realized I'd been holding my breath.

If this man was in his fifties, it didn't show. His unlined dark brown skin actually glistened against his gray New York Yankees shirt, his eyes a little suspicious behind a pair of glasses, a small mark on the bridge of his nose.

"Can I help you?" he said.

"Yes, hopefully," said Monty. "I'm Monty Alburn and this is Lowra Cavendish. We are both looking for a Dikembe Christopher Kabili."

"Bit of a mouthful there," the man said with a wary smile.

"So that isn't you?"

"I didn't say that," said the man. "Can I ask what it's about?"

That's when Monty looked toward me, and I looked back at him without saying anything. In all the excitement we hadn't actually thought about what to say, if we came face-to-face with this person!

"My name is Lowra Cavendish and I grew up in a house in Ranklin. It's a seaside town . . ."

"I've heard of it."

"Of course. Sorry. It's just that there are some items I came across there . . . old things that I believe, *we* believe, belonged to someone called Celestine Babbington, who we're hoping is somehow related to a Dikembe Christopher Kabili. Those items led us here, and we hope you can help us."

He looked me straight in the eye and then smiled. It was a warm smile. "I'm Dikembe Christopher Kabili. But everyone calls me Chris."

Now I didn't know what to say and was grateful for Monty. "Do you know of a Celestine?" he said.

"These items . . . valuable, are they?" asked Chris.

"Just a doll and a necklace," said Monty, deliberately playing it down.

"A doll? And a necklace, you say?"

"Yes," said Monty.

"Well, as intriguing as all this sounds, I'm afraid it has nothing to do with me." He actually began to step backward, his hand on the door. I couldn't allow that door to shut on us because this Chris, he knew something.

"The things, they may actually belong to this man Celestine, and it would be nice to get them back to one of his descendants. That person could be you," I said.

"Really. Just by my name, you can tell?" he said.

I thought back to the three photographs of Celestine and could see a resemblance in Chris. Or perhaps that was just wishful thinking because there's no way I could be sure.

"Do you know of a Celestine in your family?" said Monty, clearly getting annoyed.

"Sorry, I don't."

"You have quite a distinctive name," said Monty, not willing to let this go, just as I wasn't.

"Not really." He moved further behind the door. "I don't think I can help you."

Monty continued. "If you could ask around your family, whether they knew of him, we'd be very grateful. I'm a historian. Here's my card."

Chris took the card, nodding his head. "I'll ask around."

We headed toward a nearby bench and sat down.

"So that's that then." My voice might have sounded a bit defeated but I was far from it. If anything, finding myself face-to-face with this Chris had left me energized.

"Something just doesn't feel right," said Monty.

"I feel the same. That name . . ."

We wandered back toward the train station, despite wanting to turn back and knock on that dark green door again. Our footsteps slowed and then we stopped so I could buy more gum.

"How do you get through so much gum?" he said.

"Nerves," I said truthfully.

We were almost at the station when we heard a voice: "Wait!"

We both spun around at the same time.

And there was Dikembe Christopher Kabili, standing right in front of us.

*

When he told us to follow him, we did. The walk back to the house felt longer somehow, Monty and I like two kids being led away into a fantasy world we couldn't wait to inhabit.

When we finally got back to that dark green door, he told us to go inside.

The corridor was bright and airy, with circular spotlights slotted inside the ceiling. Pictures on the right-hand wall showed two beautiful children hand in hand. The little girl had three large plaits on her head and an even smaller boy stared at the camera with the hugest of smiles. Chris opened the door to a long, narrow lounge which I think would be described as minimalist, and far beyond, a large garden with a plastic slide and a pink bike lying beside it on the grass. The leather sofa was cream, and all I could think of was how it could stay that way with two small children about.

"Please sit down. I'm sorry about before. I can be a bit protective of my family, but yes, I do know the person you're looking for."

My breath caught in my throat. "Are you serious?"

"You're looking for my dad."

The silence felt as long as an eternity.

I couldn't quite believe what he had just said.

"I was named after my father who was called Dikembe Kabili, and who you know as Celestine Babbington."

I sat down because I needed the support.

"It was a bit of a shock hearing the name and I had no idea who you were, so I called the number on the card and your assistant verified you were indeed a historian. I'm not sure why I did that; I guess I watch too many detective shows. I'd seen you both sitting on the bench so I figured you couldn't have got far."

No part of me could believe I was sitting in the house of Celestine's actual son. My fuzzy mind was unable to decipher who he was to me, but if we were related, that in itself was amazing.

I had family. Closer even than Tilly was.

"Wow. This is something . . ." said Monty, for once at a loss for words.

A limitless set of questions sat on my tongue but nothing appeared.

"What do you know about your dad's early life in the Congo, now known as Zaire? I mean, did he tell you much about his past? We did find out quite a bit, so maybe we can sit with you sometime and cross-reference. Go through it all with you . . ." said Monty.

"Do you have any siblings?" I said finally. Of all the questions I could have asked . . .

"No." His mouth made an O shape and he let out a breath. "This is a lot."

"I know," I said. My eyes searched the room for pictures of Celestine, but unlike the hallway, the walls were blank save for a painting of three women in large colorful hats.

"It's been a long and revealing journey so far, but we hope you can fill in a few pieces," said Monty.

"I don't have all the answers, I'm afraid." He stood up. "But there is somebody who does."

"Who?" I said.

"My dad."

"Sorry?"

"My dad will know."

"Celestine is alive?" I said, not believing my own words.

"Yes, and he's in the next room."

The silence felt intense, with only the sound of our footsteps as we padded along the hardwood floors which led to an old man sitting on a chair in a sun-filled conservatory, dressed in a brown cardigan and velvety brown slippers.

And he was real. Surrounded by bright sunlight along with a

couple of large exotic plants, his hands clutching a mug that read GRANDAD.

"Dad?" Chris called out.

"Last I checked, I'm still here. Just about anyway."

"Dad, don't joke about stuff like that," said Chris, before making the introductions.

"My boy needs to come to terms with the fact his father is one year away from a telegram from the Queen. I'm not going to be around forever. Every day after ninety is a bonus. Anyway, how do you do?" He sounded like a voice on one of those old-time newsreels Monty and I had watched one day during a lull in the search.

"Excuse me for not getting up—it does take some time these days."

"No, that's OK," I said.

Chris shook his head. "I'll go and get the teas."

"None for me, this is still warm," said Celestine.

Was this truly him, though? I sat down in one of the chairs opposite, and I knew as soon as I looked into his eyes that he was the same man as the boy in the photograph.

Despite the skin which had sagged with time and the odd scraps of facial hair, I could see in the whites and browns of his eyes that this was undoubtedly Celestine. These were the eyes I had stood and searched in that exhibition, and seen in my dreams so many times afterward. The eyes I had thought about daily ever since.

I'd recognize them anywhere.

This was him. This was Celestine.

Monty was quiet. Sitting in the other chair, he looked a bit like a rabbit caught in headlights. All that searching and digging and traveling back and forth to Ranklin—in all that time and effort and emotion, he'd never for one moment thought he was alive.

"So . . . Mr. Kabili," began Monty.

"According to my son, you seem to know a lot about me, so I think we can dispense with formalities. Call me Dikembe. That's my name—Dikembe Kabili."

Dikembe Kabili.

I could almost feel the relief from Monty. Celestine had changed his name from Babbington and this meant everything.

"So . . . ninety-nine. You look good for it." I said this out of nerves, nothing else.

"Apparently I can pass for eighty on a good day. However, I am not sure that's enough of an advantage. I mostly sleep throughout the day. Alas, when you first knocked on the door I was indulging in my favorite pastime and oblivious to what was going on. However, I wake up before the sun each morning, much to my son's annoyance!"

"I can imagine!" I said.

"My appearance is probably down to good genes, although I won't be able to substantiate that claim considering I haven't seen my kinfolk in almost ninety years."

The mood in the room changed; a reminder that this was about more than niceties, good humor and compliments—however heartfelt. This was about so much more.

Chris walked in with a tray balancing a teapot and three cups.

"At last! Tea is my tipple of choice, while my son here prefers a glass of wine."

"There's nothing better," he said, smiling toward his dad. They clearly shared a wonderful bond.

That day in the bright conservatory of a North London house, we sipped hot tea as I relayed the abridged version of the story that had led us there. Monty's interest as a historian was clear, but I found myself a little tongue-tied when it came to explaining *my* involvement, so I just told the truth. Well, part of the truth. The palatable bits.

"It started with the message."

"A message?" asked Dikembe.

"Words, I think, on the wall just under the window. We couldn't make out the letters—"

His eyebrows squinted. "My name. I had written my name," he said, now smiling. "Dikembe."

"That message led me to the loose floorboards and these items which became so precious to me as a child. I always felt they had been placed there just for me to find."

Dikembe cleared his throat. "Were you playing hide and seek in the attic?"

I looked at Monty, feeling a surge of support. "Something like that."

As father and son listened intently, Monty went on to explain the process of tracking him down through the years.

"You never appeared on any electoral register. During the First and Second World Wars, these registers were patchy to say the least, so we lost track of you . . ."

"I don't believe I was ever registered by Sir Richard, and in my adult years . . . let's just say it wasn't hard to stay off the radar in those days, so to speak. Now, of course, my son is the owner of this house, so there is no need."

"That makes sense," said Monty.

"Do you have any photos? Of the necklace?" asked Dikembe.

I shook my head slowly. Thinking this may have turned out to be another dead end was not enough of an excuse; I really should have brought along the Polaroid. When I said as much, Dikembe simply took my hand as if to quieten me. And as our skin touched, I felt it: that connection I couldn't articulate, with the room suddenly feeling empty except for the two of us.

"It's been almost a century since I last saw them, never truly believing I ever would again—a short while longer won't hurt."

The moment I began to describe it—the contours, the smooth texture and its beautiful clawlike design—the face of this man

Dikembe shone with such happiness, such light, confirming it was even more precious than I could have imagined.

It was everything.

Another set of teas was brought in.

"So you wish to know what occurred after 1913?"

Monty pulled out the polka-dot pad. "If you don't mind me writing stuff down, that would be great. Never in all my years as a historian have I been able to personally interview a subject."

"I hope I am more than a subject," smiled Dikembe.

"That you are, sir. That you are."

I'd never seen Monty like this, all fidgety, a bit like an excited kid.

"Obviously recording your own voice and your exact words would have been better, but I truly didn't think . . . Wow. I still can't believe we're here, you're here," said Monty.

"Perhaps you could bring one of those Dictaphone things next time and I can do just that."

"You'd like us to come back?" I said.

"Of course! We have almost a century of life to get through. Besides, I'm not the fastest talker, as my son will testify. It can take me some time to get to the point."

"Tell me about it!" said Chris. "Seriously, though, when he first sat me down and told me his story, well, I was blown away. It's worth the wait."

I felt warmed at Dikembe's invitation for us to stick around and come back tomorrow with a Dictaphone. What was said needed to be in his words because this, after all, was *his* story.

Also, for me to even begin to put the final pieces of my own story together, I needed to know his.

"You'd better sit back then," he said, doing just that. "Because what I have to tell you may take some time."

Chapter Forty-Eight

Celestine
1914

I'd seen hate in the eyes of the boys who had beaten me that night, and now in the faces of everyone I met.

It was a rude awakening for someone who believed himself different from the Black people depicted in books, and even those I'd encountered at the lodgings and the tavern where I had worked. Unlike me, they were unread, some uncultured, and deep inside I had the audacity to believe I was above each and every one of them. It was there in my actions, in the way I spoke and even when I taught.

That changed the day I was beaten half to death outside a theater.

The blows that rained down upon me that night had left behind physical scars that would take months to fully heal—but the emotional ones were much more far-reaching.

With every kick I was told I was nothing, scum, a stain on society. With every punch, words like "coon," "golliwog," "nig-nog," were spat at me with venom. These were terms I had never been called. In books, I'd seen the words written, but they'd never been spoken directly to me.

Now, at the age of twenty and with this extra layer of experience, the giant pot of anger stirring beneath my surface had only grown. The "smile" I'd perfected when serving Agatha and Cyril stayed in place, my demeanor now sprinkled with touches of humor to show everyone I met—Black and white—that I was of good moral character and far from what popular thinkers believed me to be. Yet inside, sometimes, a raging beast longed for its moment to unleash its pent-up rage onto the world.

I sometimes fantasized about what it would feel like to have that sense of freedom running through my body. A freedom to enact whatever I wanted on whomever with a lack of consequence. How would that feel? Liberating, that's what.

But I often struggled to know what that would achieve.

Vengeance, for one. I should at least find the men who'd beaten me, and one by one, unleash a prolonged pounding of terror onto each of their white bodies as they had done with my Black body.

I'd of course be thrown in prison, and if they died, I would be hung up high at the request of the law, my life brought to an end before it had a chance to truly flourish; a moment of pleasure eclipsed by the most final of consequences.

Prison, of course, I could have endured, having already done so for four years of my short life.

It was taking a number of weeks to reach the milestone of being steady on my feet for long periods and being able to move around without debilitating pain. I hated being idle and reliant on others like Royston, who lived in the room next door. He'd clean the house and ensure I had food to eat. I was grateful for his help, even though I also resented it.

Since I could not work, I was forced to dip into my inheritance to pay for food and rent, much to my landlord's relief.

I owned a stack of unread books, including those on trees and fine wood which curbed the feeling of being idle. I also read and reread autobiographies on great men like Ignatius Sancho, which simply fed my desire to get out and achieve. Not only was I more determined than ever to make a financial success of my life, I couldn't imagine doing so without helping others. So, as I healed physically, I was able to resume reading classes with some of the men, including Royston and even those who had not supported me during the ill-fated strike at the Tavern. I held no malice for my people. We were all just trying to survive in this country. That much I now understood.

One surprising result of the attack was finally being able to sleep in a bed again, having been forced to while in so much pain.

My desire to place young men into work while teaching some to read no longer felt like enough. Directing my own people into servitude was never the legacy I wanted. Yes, they needed financial security to succeed, but one thing I had learned was that the security of education was something nobody in this world could ever beat out of me, and I wanted to instill that confidence in others, if they so wished. Instead of simply teaching them to read, I would also include subjects like bookkeeping, money management and others.

My moment of recuperation also became a time to plot, plan . . . and wait.

The war had brought with it hope and then hopelessness as everyone realized it would not be over in mere months, as many had first predicted.

The limp I had developed thanks to the beating at least stopped people from referring to me as a coward, as anyone seen to be eligible to join the war effort was expected to do so.

My small enterprise lining up workers with employers died a temporary death during the war, but afterward the situation began to improve. Many of the returning soldiers were without work and it was even harder for Black men. This was where I came in. I rented a shop, still in East London because I was determined the attack would never curb the love I had for the area. The feeling of intense pride as THE EMPLOYMENT REGISTRY was neatly painted above the window was unmatched by anything I had felt up until that point.

My work required a good memory and a lot of guesswork. Matching a particular employee to a certain employer demanded a specific skillset as well as an abundance of common sense. With a small roster of local traders already on my books, as well as men waiting to be matched right away, my business was profitable within a month.

The business not only financed the study books and other tools needed for my *underground* school—for want of a better name—but also paid the rent for a larger home for myself, this time located further north of London in a handsome area with wide roads and an abundance of trees.

I filled each large room of that house with everything I needed to live a comfortable life. It served as a functional space for me to retire to after the majority of the day spent at the employment registry.

The back room of the shop became my classroom. My new home and its grounds were no longer open to anyone but myself.

As a boy, I had only occupied a classroom for a matter of months, but that was long enough for the experience to have left its mark in perhaps the wrong way. Now, sitting inside a room full of impassioned human beings, I fed off their thirst for knowledge and it felt thoroughly intoxicating. For the first time, I felt alive with purpose.

Lowra
1993

"Giving is so often seen as a selfless act, but in this case, it was selfish," said Dikembe.

"You taught for no pay and used your own time and resources. How is that selfish?" I said.

"What it gave to me in return . . . something to focus on which wasn't anger or . . . regret and what I couldn't change. It gave me everything I needed at that time, as well as joy when one of my students succeeded—this can only be selfish."

"I get it," said Monty.

The more Dikembe spoke, the more conscious I became of the dimming sunshine as the light in the conservatory began to fade. I always knew when Monty was ready to leave somewhere because he'd start shuffling his notebook and pen, and whatever else he could find—but I wasn't ready yet.

I may have only been alive for thirty years, but it felt like I'd been searching for Dikembe for over eighty. I suppose I had been—through my grandmother Caroline and my mother Vivienne. Perhaps we'd all been in some weird "missing family" relay race, and now I held the baton, I wasn't quite ready to let it go.

I wasn't ready to let *him* go.

Celestine
1918

I had to close the employment registry briefly, as many areas in the East End had been damaged by enemy attacks. I was one of the lucky ones, managing to live within a comfortable cocoon in my home, sometimes not leaving for days on end; not really needing to, as I had everything I wanted at my disposal and made no time for socializing or fraternizing with anyone.

Of course, this wasn't sustainable. When a school full of children was bombed in an area not far from my employment registry, I mourned with the rest of the nation because I wasn't devoid of emotion, however much I believed myself to be.

It may have been a relief when the war ended, but by 1919 a new one had started.

"It won't be long until it gets here," warned Royston, referring to the riots which had already consumed Glasgow. "They may be targeting the Black sailors, but we know they're not going to be asking for credentials before they bash your face in!" he said. As well as being someone I could actually call a friend, especially after his help during my recuperation, Royston was a gifted student who often assisted me with the others.

"I feel like I should just take myself back to Barbados. Take yourself back to Africa, why don't you?"

I dismissed Royston's joke with a smile.

"They're having a go at anyone they can find who looks Chinese, Indian or Black. A bit of a worry," he continued.

A chill ran through my body as I recalled my own attack and the possibility of it happening again. I may not even be a sailor—supposedly the intended target—but a man enraged with his own insecurities, inadequacies and misinformation would never see beyond that.

When rioting inevitably broke out close to the area, I took it upon myself to announce the temporary closure of the employment registry and the school once more. The men were disappointed but understood I was not prepared to risk their safety or my own.

As I ran the broom across the floor, I felt a sadness at having to close up once again. Financially I'd be taken care of, as my inheritance from Sir Richard remained substantial enough and I had added to it over the years. My sadness was more for my students: without the classes, what would they do?

As I locked up that evening, I promised myself it wouldn't be long until the registry and school were up and running once again.

An hour later, the employment registry had burned to the ground.

It was Royston who'd banged on the door of my home and walked with me back to Limehouse during the early hours of that morning, arriving in time to watch scores of people standing by my business, pointing at the embers as they flared up into the sky to wait for the sun. To them this was just a burnt-out building. To me, it was a business I had built up with pride, one I was financially rewarded for while at the same time assisting others to one day achieve the same.

Now it had all but disappeared in an act of cowardice.

The shops on either side were left untouched. No doubt my being a Black owner and the nature of my business, considering the current climate, was intolerable to some.

"I can't believe this!" said Royston with tears in his eyes.

I wasn't listening.

"I'm sorry," he said, as I simply turned on my heel and began to walk away from it all.

More people had gathered but I no longer saw them as I pushed past, could no longer hear them. Walking into the throng of what could only be the aftermath of destruction, I found a small wall to sit on, watching those I assumed to be participants in these riots scattering away with the imminent arrival of daylight. Though I was outnumbered by them, this did not concern me. I willed them to accost me—someone, anyone—so that I too could unleash my own anger just as they had.

My eye was caught by one of them, at random. His trousers were torn at the side. He and his comrades were laughing about something or other. I couldn't be sure it was about my registry, but I did not care, because in that moment their laughter was about me.

Lowra
1993

"What did you do?" I asked.

"I let them be," said Dikembe.

Celestine

1919

I jumped off the wall as the man with the torn trouser leg walked away in the opposite direction. His lopsided movement reminded me of Bill's.

I followed.

He stopped to light up a cigarette, I think. I stopped too. Then he continued down an empty road.

I increased my pace, catching up to him quickly.

"What do you want, Black boy?" he said, swiftly turning to me with an expression that told me the bravado had gone, along with his friends.

I said not a word, grabbing him by the scruff of the neck so hard I'm sure my nails made imprints.

His voice was quiet as he struggled to speak. "What do you want?"

I found it quite funny he'd asked what I wanted. I know what I wanted: to end that miserable existence he called a life, one that was filled with hatred for people he'd never even met, based on a view so irrational it beggared belief. But first I wanted him to feel the terror I'd felt on *that* night. For him to experience the humiliation I had endured on a daily basis during the latter part of my childhood, thanks to people who thought like him.

"I haven't got any money . . ." His voice was now a rasp thanks to the pressure of my hand, making him sound just as evil as he was.

With just a little more pressure I could make that voice go away forever.

With my free hand I felt for my pocketknife—the one I'd carried with me ever since that moment on the beach. It was the most ungentlemanly thing about me, something I told myself I needed simply to make me feel protected.

"Go on then, do what you're going to do," he said, now realizing what was in my free hand.

Voices unleashed themselves in my head.

"You must always be like Mbidi," said my mama's voice. "You must always be the Black king."

But what if, for just this once, I wished to be the red king, Mama? The color of blood. What if just this once I wanted to do what was not right in the eyes of some, but felt absolutely right in this moment? What if I was fed up of being trampled upon, being told what to do and who I was, Mama?

What if I no longer wanted to be the Black king?

I felt the blade between my fingers, now where he could really see it. I wanted him to feel every last piece of terror that I had ever felt.

I pressed harder on his neck. In his face I saw Cyril, Agatha, Bill and his friends, and even Sir Richard.

Sir Richard.

I used to believe he was my savior. At least, this is what had been drummed into me by people like the Mayhews over the years. And lying on the floor of the attic definitely reinforced that, because he'd never have treated me that way. He had sent me to the finest school and draped me in the most beautiful clothes, my feet dressed in shoes shinier even than his.

Now I knew better: he'd simply been the one to trap me first. To kill me with kindness—long before Agatha and Cyril Mayhew had thrown me into that attic.

Here, now, I wanted the pain to go away. The pain I thought had been buried for so very long but surfaced when I least expected it. The political climate of England now giving me an excuse and outlet for this pain to be realized.

And unleashed.

If I killed this man, his body would likely be discovered the next day; they might assume one of the seamen had done it in retaliation.

I squeezed a little harder on his neck.

But what if somebody got arrested for my crime? While unsure whether I could live with the death of this man on my conscience, I was certain I couldn't exist with the knowledge that an innocent man had been executed for my own deed.

I looked him squarely in the eye as he continued to struggle for breath.

Just a few more seconds and he would be gone.

I pressed harder, closing my eyes, and all I saw were their faces: not the Mayhews or Sir Richard, but my parents.

My eyes widened as the man fell to the ground.

"Please," he said. "I've got kids." His words bounced off me like a ball. They meant absolutely nothing as I placed the blade back in my pocket and curled my fists.

I picked him up again, and the first blow to his face took even me by surprise. The second one felt more real, as did the blood which trickled over my knuckles. The third blow, and the fourth and the fifth, took me into a rhythm that transformed me from subservient unpaid worker to self-made businessman, to angry savage thug, as had always been expected of me. The man whimpered as he fell to the ground again, his expression reminding me what fear was. I stood over his quivering body, my mind still contemplating as he slid backward slowly. It would have been very easy to re-produce that blade and put the animal out of its misery. Slit his neck in the way they had done my father.

Instead, I placed my hands in my pockets and walked away in the opposite direction.

Chapter Forty-Nine

Celestine
1919

I kept expecting to see a policeman at my door but it never happened.

I concentrated on finding new premises this time just outside East London, in the north—yet not too close to my home. My business had garnered a good reputation so most of my clients followed me to the new premises, which meant my first few months of trading were good. However, when some of my staff were offered repatriation schemes from the government to "go back home," some actually took them, while those who didn't remained in fear of what might happen next. When Royston asked if I was one of those living in fear, my mind became full of confusion. Once I would have done anything to return home, but now I no longer had any idea of what that looked like, or even if anyone I recognized would still be there. My home was here, and my standing in the community should ensure I wouldn't be on any government list.

As should the name Babbington.

The new policies did affect my business though, and once I found that some of the employers on my register were also aiding the government by firing a lot of my men, I made sure to blacklist them.

Nevertheless, I still managed to make a good living as well as continue with the free schooling. I tutored six men on a rotating basis, twice a week after I closed up shop. I taught everything from reading to arithmetic to bookkeeping—a skill I had taught myself—or whatever their particular needs happened to be.

My life had a rhythm again. This routine was both comforting and reassuring. Yet something changed within me at the age of twenty-five, having seen the destruction of a war, rioting on my own doorstep, and a flu which had wiped out thousands.

A new hunger emerged inside me.

"I went to visit my sister in Battersea," said Royston, during a lesson on simple arithmetic. The other five students were diligently working out their math problems; Royston was always the one to speak first and usually with such animation.

"That's nice, but I am struggling to see what this has to do with subtraction," I said, smiling.

"That doesn't stop old Royston," said Cuthbert, another of the students also used to Royston's interruptions. It was possibly time for a quick break anyway. They had been working flat out for an hour.

"Do you know they used to have a Black mayor?" said Royston, pulling up his chair.

"Don't be ridiculous," said Martin, a sailor from St. Lucia.

"It's true," said Royston. "A Black man and a mayor. John Archer is his name. He's still a man of power too, president of the APU."

"What's an APU?" I said, feeling quite embarrassed. I had read stacks of book yet didn't know what these three simple initials meant.

"The African Progress Union. I don't have much to do with it myself, but I've heard good things. They paid to defend some of the men caught up in the troubles."

"The riots?"

He nodded his head. "Apparently he's a great speaker too."

"Must be, to have convinced people to vote for him!" said Laurence, a warehouseman originally from Birmingham.

A collective laughter followed, while my pose remained stoic . . . and still disbelieving.

I shook my head. "This can't be. Are you sure? A Black man being elected into power?"

"It's true," said Gabriel, who I was more inclined to listen to as he hardly spoke during lessons, something I was grateful for because it was sometimes hard to decipher his Jack Tar lingo. This was one of the things his current employer liked about him apparently, his lack of words. A heinous comment which I'd ignored, knowing one day he would be able to afford his own business.

"Told you," said Royston. "He was elected in Battersea in 1913."

"What good did that do? Didn't stop this country burning when they wanted us out!" said Laurence. More laughter followed.

"I'm not really sure that's his responsibility," said Royston. "I'm just happy he exists because I never thought I'd see one in my lifetime, and they haven't even killed him!"

I knotted my hands together and listened as they sparred with words concerning this enigma, this real-life person. Having been so tied up with reading about great men from the past I was never actually going to meet, I'd failed to seek out the greatness happening around me.

I reached my destination with minutes to spare. The APU was attended by a slew of Black and white gentlemen, but I remained focused on the man leading the meeting. A well of emotion filled up inside me. Gabriel and Royston had been correct: this man's skin edged toward my own shade and his hair was as coily as mine—and he'd been a mayor! They had not been joking or mistaken; here, standing upon a wooden podium, was John Archer, explaining to those of us assembled that being the mayor of Battersea had only ever been part of his story, that he had so manymore political ambitions awaiting him.

The audacity!

I lapped up every single word he spoke; the tone of his voice, his mannerisms, delighting me, filling me with a power I did not recognize. When he came to the end of his speech, I was far from spent and craved so much more.

He quickly became besieged with well-wishers who stood in line to greet him. I hadn't formulated a speech in advance, perhaps due to not actually believing he existed until I saw him for myself. I waited in line anyway and before long, he was standing in front of me.

"Hello, sir," I said. "I wanted to say I greatly admire your work and position."

"Thank you," he said as he shook my hand. To feel this skin against mine was like a wealth of wisdom passing from his mind to mine.

"May I speak with you afterward, sir?" I asked as the line behind me seemed to increase.

"If you don't mind the wait."

"I do not." Because to be in a room with such smart-suited and obviously learned men, both white *and* Black, was exactly where I wanted and needed to be. This was like a utopia I never knew existed, having been confined—by choice—to my own little world, and only venturing out through reading when I should have been doing much more.

An hour later, when John Archer approached me, I felt a swish in my stomach. He commanded such respect, the likes of which I had not seen since I had stood beside my father.

"Thank you for waiting," he said.

"It is an honor to be in the presence of the first Black mayor in England."

"I would love to claim such a title, but that honor would have to be given to Allan Glaisyer Minns in Thetford, Norfolk, a few years back."

"I did not know this."

"Now you do."

I felt a splash of disappointment at my lack of preparation for this conversation.

"Are you intending to enter politics?"

"That is not my forte, sir."

"But you are hoping for something from me?"

"Yes, sir."

"And what would that be?"

I wanted to say wisdom, hope, inspiration . . .

"Well?"

I did not want to waste his time, but I needed to walk away with something . . . I just didn't know how to articulate what that was. Perhaps I didn't need to.

"All I require is hope, sir, and already you have given that to me, just by your existence."

His smile was warm, comforting. "By the sound and look of you, you seem to have done well so far for one so young."

"I am twenty-five years old, sir, and it is now my aim to do better."

"You will. Just be aware that sometimes the journey can become derailed by something or someone. It is never a straight line."

"It has never been a straight line for me, but even for you, sir?"

"I may have become a mayor but there were still many obstacles to overcome. Some may say they were even bigger than when I was attempting to get elected. Like the issue of where I was born being called into question so many times once I took up office, and even now!"

"I am from Africa, sir."

"I tell them I'm from Liverpool. They hate that."

It was my turn to smile.

Another smartly dressed man leaned in and whispered into John Archer's ear. I knew my time was up.

"Young man," he said, "I hope I have been of assistance."

"More than you will ever know. I hope I can also be of assistance to the union, by making a donation."

"But of course. Hopefully we will see you here once again."

"Yes, sir, most definitely."

He turned away and then back to face me again. "I would encourage you to read W. E. B. Du Bois and Booker T. Washington. Should put some fire in your belly."

"Are they Black gentlemen?"

"Yes, from America."

"Where would I find such books, sir? It was difficult enough to find the book on British Black men, let alone anyone else."

"I'm sure you'll find a way."

That short and simple meeting had given me the answers I needed, because just by existing John Archer had shown me what was possible, reminding me that even when you had supposedly *made it*, knives would still be drawn ready to cut you at any turn, and this was something I'd dealt with time and time again.

I was in no way unique in that regard.

What I also needed to remember was that nothing had defeated me, even when perhaps it should have. That night after the registry had burned to the ground, I'd been tempted to end my own life by ending the life of another.

Yet I had survived for a reason, a purpose, and was willing and ready to fulfill that purpose and continue to make my mark on this world by helping others. The day my mama had kissed me goodbye on the shores of my birth land and all that followed would never, ever be in vain. I would continue to be all my mama had wanted for me, while in some small way also making my father proud.

Chapter Fifty

Lowra
1993

The day I met him for the very first time, he told me to call him Dikembe. It seemed disrespectful somehow, to call a man of almost a hundred by just his first name. Especially when there was a chance that this man could be my great-grandfather. But that piece of information needed to be saved for later, because there was something he had to see.

When I returned the following day with the items that had started this journey, his eyes had already started to glisten as he sat on his "favorite chair" in the conservatory, his son standing beside him.

I pulled out the necklace and before I even looked up, he'd already extended his hand.

He kept his arm extended as he gently clutched the necklace within his fingers. His eyes closed and a single tear appeared from one of them. I found it difficult to hold my own emotion, feeling that Monty and I shouldn't be there, intruders in this very special and precious moment.

"Dad, are you all right?"

He opened his eyes and stared down at the necklace in his hands. "I cannot quite believe this is happening."

"Dad, it's beautiful."

"Yes, my son, this is . . . This is my father's necklace." His chest heaved with emotion and this almost one-hundred-year-old man began to weep gently, rocking back and forth with his father's necklace in his hands, and now close to his heart.

"It will be better if you come after the weekend," said Chris, when I suggested we leave and return the following morning. "I don't want to tire him out and he has a routine . . . and it's been the most extraordinary few days . . ."

"I can only imagine," I said, as we left the conservatory with Dikembe still holding the necklace.

"I am glad you're transcribing my dad's story. There's still so much I don't know and it would be great to look back on it, share it with my kids when they're old enough."

I wanted to ask about the children and his wife, but more about any other possible relatives. They were my family, all of them; I knew this, I felt this, yet for now I had to keep quiet.

"Dikembe's story is part of a forgotten history and we will not let it die. In all my years as a historian I have never heard a story like this firsthand. It's a dream come true for any historian, but for me, it's a privilege. I'm just so pleased he's still alive." Monty's voice broke but I didn't say anything. This truly was an emotive time for both of us, and so far listening to what his life had been like after the attack, when everything changed for him yet again, was incredible. His storytelling was without self-pity, full of humor, and so clear it could have happened yesterday.

That evening as we walked to the station, we hardly spoke. At least the tube ride gave me the chance to process what I had just seen and what Dikembe had said so far. I felt excited for the next day and the next . . . Indeed, for once I felt excited for the future.

The sound of young voices greeted us as we entered the conservatory, where Dikembe sat in his chair with a little boy nestled in between his knees on the floor, a slightly older girl sitting on the arm of the chair.

"These are my two boisterous children. Ammy, get off your granddad, please. You're ten, not two!" said Chris.

"Don't fuss! As long as I get away with no broken bones!" said Dikembe. The little girl leaned in and planted a kiss on her grandfather's smiling face.

"My wife, Sandra, is currently in the kitchen pretending to prepare lunch," said Chris.

"Sandra, come and say hello!" said Dikembe. His voice was low but she appeared to hear him because she walked into the room, waving at Monty and me. She was tall, slim, with her hair wrapped into a braided bun. She was possibly the most beautiful woman I'd ever seen.

"What do you mean, pretending!" she said, flicking a tea towel across Chris's arm.

The seven of us relocated to the large dining room, where takeaway boxes adorned the table.

"I thought we could have a very early dinner so you can join us in Dad's favorite—Indian food."

"This is very kind," said Monty.

"Not at all," said Dikembe, moving slowly into his seat with Chris's assistance.

This early dinner was a clear indication that Chris wanted us out by the early evening. But that was OK. I'd already decided to book into a cheap B&B, just to be close and on hand. Now we'd found him, I didn't want to spend another unnecessary moment away from him, so two trains and two tube rides suddenly felt like too much.

"You'll have me falling asleep after all this!" said Monty.

"If my story becomes a bit boring, at least I can blame the food." We all laughed at that, even the kids, who I doubted could understand. Aminata—who they called Ammy—was ten and little Justin seven. More pictures of them decorated the cabinet by the dining table. One with Dikembe, Chris, Sandra and the kids stood next to a vase of fresh flowers, alongside a black-and-white picture of a woman smiling closely at the camera, who I assumed was Chris's mother. I was happy for Dikembe but sad for my grandmother Caroline, Dikembe's other child . . . Nowhere to be seen because in this home, in this life, she did not exist.

"Aminata is a very beautiful name, I must say," said Monty.

"So is mine!" said Justin grandly.

"Don't be rude, Justin," said Sandra.

"We named our boy after Sandra's dad, as I insisted we name our first after my mother," said Chris.

Both Dikembe and Chris were smiling but I knew what grief looked like—and they both wore it in flashes. Even in a home so full of happiness and joy, it was still easy to see and feel.

Dikembe being part of a real family was something he utterly deserved after everything he'd endured, but I had to wonder if this could also have been my happy ending, or if I even deserved one. As I scooped spoonfuls of curry and rice into my mouth, I looked around me; all this life and laughter sat at the table, and it began to feel possible that I could be a part of this after all.

If I tell Dikembe we are related.

I brought the glass of water to my mouth, and decided there and then that Dikembe would have to know the truth.

Chapter Fifty-One

Celestine
1921

At the age of twenty-seven, my business and school were doing very well, and I found myself donating money to causes such as the African Progress Union and a number of underground organizations concerned with the advancement of Black people in London. It saddened me that I could never see myself as what was now termed an "activist," partaking in the revolutionary acts of people such as John Archer or Dr. John Alcindor. However, it was Royston who pointed out that my work in the community was activism in itself and that monetary donation to such causes was more than enough. It would seem that whatever I did, my own self-criticism was never far behind, but I was glad for Royston's opinion, even if his words failed to penetrate.

When John Archer chaired the Pan-African Congress in London, of course I attended, happy to see him again. We didn't get to shake hands or exchange words this time, though, and this was adequate—his input in my life had already been cemented two years before.

I bought a home big enough for two families, and I wasn't even sure why. Perhaps to keep up appearances as I had a respected name in my community to maintain. It was still located in Highgate Village and not too far from the previous one, yet this house was furnished with the sparsest (although costliest) of furniture. Apparently art deco was a popular style abroad, not that I cared; I had simply viewed it once and purchased it along with the furniture.

The staircase leading to the attic was something I hadn't failed to notice during the viewing, and I had made the decision never to enter that room. Ever.

I concerned myself with modern appliances like a vacuum cleaner. This at least would make life easier for Mrs. Markham, whom I employed to come into my home daily to cook and clean, which she did splendidly. Although I had the space, I was never interested in staff living in. Our relationship was a comfortable one that was neither quite friendship nor professional. Indeed, I often felt guilty at leaving the place in any sort of disarray, with Mrs. Markham complaining about not having enough to do. I paid her a good wage nevertheless.

I only really used the lounge on occasion, and of course my bedroom, but the rest of the house remained a stranger to me, though it was lovingly cleaned by Mrs. Markham. She'd sometimes joke about whether I was having company that night, to which I'd smile and maybe even shake my head with laughter. Other times she'd threaten to introduce me to her niece, a joke which fell back and forth between us like a tennis ball.

I was comfortable being by myself, and if this was how my life would remain forever, that would be fine. Of course, a man of my social and financial standing attracted women of all classes, and at times I took the liberty of partaking in their company. I was still alive, not dead, even if some of these ladies would beg to differ.

Lowra

1993

"Bit of a ladies' man, my dad," said Chris.

"That is not so," said Dikembe.

"You waited long enough to settle down, though!"

Monty and I could only smile.

"Don't be fooled, Lowra. He was ancient when he finally decided to settle down and have me!"

"Were you not in your forties before you had the sense to settle down with Sandra and have children?" said Dikembe.

"That's the done thing these days!" said Sandra, walking in with the children behind her. "Career women, right, Lowra?"

"I wouldn't really know," I said truthfully, my mind focused on Dikembe's reaction to the attic when he'd bought his new home. We had so much to talk about and yet it just didn't seem the right time to do so.

"Less of a ladies' man, more a preference to take my time when it came to huge life decisions. That was my reasoning, nothing more and nothing less."

"I was just kidding, Dad," said Chris. The mood had changed. I sensed Dikembe was uncomfortable. That, like me, he had things he didn't want to discuss.

"Let's move on, shall we? In fact, let's talk about something else. You must all be getting frightfully bored of all this talk of the past."

Celestine

1921

I am ashamed to say, but there were times I'd court a woman without any intention of taking things further than my bedroom.

My soul seldom felt awakened by an encounter with a woman, yet my body's desires remained intact, and this sometimes felt unwelcome, as if that part of me was unclean, while at the same time desperate to be satisfied. Sometimes, even during the act, I would stop halfway and tell her to leave, and if I didn't, I simply endeavored to endure each kiss, each caress, just as a way of moving closer to the end. Other times, I allowed myself to enjoy such moments, which would only be followed by a greater sense of worthlessness when it was over.

Sometimes I would be reminded of the past: moments that should never have been. The shadow of grief was also never far behind me. It didn't seem to matter how far I'd come, or how much money I made; it was always present, like an unwelcome friend. Once, I saw a pink flower in the park and it shone just like one of my mama's scarves. Then, an image of her embracing me during our hurried goodbye as we stood opposite that imposing ship; then my father smiling at me that last day, or Kabili and I sitting under the tree. The passage of time thwarted any real accuracy of these memories.

The longing would start with a dull ache in almost every part of my body, turning into a need to release what would only come when I opened my mouth and allowed a powerful sound to emerge: either a howl like a beast or a small cry like that of a newly hatched bird. Sometimes it would begin silently and during the company of a woman, as I summoned up the strength to wait until I was in the comfort of my own room and alone, where nobody could hear me. Where I could express all that I felt without judgment—because as a man, I wasn't supposed to cry. Yet I told myself it was permitted, because for those few moments I was not a man, but simply an eleven-year-old boy again.

At the age of twenty-seven I became close to a young woman named Della. She was described as beautiful by the announcer who introduced her set at a private gentlemen's club I frequented when I wished to unwind. The concept of unwinding was one that very rarely worked as I always needed to be doing something, whether it be bookkeeping or reading, as to be idle meant . . . thoughts. But Della managed, somehow, to engage me more than any of the others had. That night on stage, she wore a dress that sparkled under the ceiling light, carefully arranged curls stamped to the side of her head, her mouth almost caressing the microphone as she sang the words to "Dangerous Blues," her eyes resting on me and all the other gullible men in that hall. I was quietly mesmerized, though, half believing—like everyone else—that she could only be singing to me.

"Oh, I was singing to you all right," she'd said in that delightful American twang. Any American I'd met had always been upfront with what they thought of you, and Della was no different.

I felt tongue-tied around her. She wasn't about to fall into my arms just because of my custom-made shoes and gentlemanly manner. She required an effort I felt willing to exert.

"How did you pick me out of all those people in the audience?" I said.

"Come on, now. There aren't that many cats who look like you."

I wasn't sure what a cat was but I assumed it to be good. And it wasn't long until we were, for all intents and purposes, courting. I took her to some of the finest establishments in London, including a stay at the best hotels. But when she asked to come to my own home and I hesitated, she proceeded to tell me to "get out of my face!" I did just that, of course, believing I'd been given a way out. She'd clearly wanted more than I could give. Yet I was almost twenty-eight and had been courting women for some years now, my contemporaries acquiring families to fill homes much smaller than mine. I found it hard to see myself in any sort of romantic commitment, let alone as an actual husband.

Marriage happened to other people and it was something I wasn't even sure I had a right to.

After profuse apologies, Della permitted me to take her out to a beautiful meal at Kettner's, smiling when I explained that it had been opened by August Kettner who had been, no less, the chef to Napoleon III. She seemed impressed with such things and so I increased the frequency of our dates, hoping she wouldn't notice the gaping hole that she herself had discovered in me.

One night as we walked along the river, I noticed the wide smile on her face—that much I could see in the lamplight from the boats on the river. She looked beautiful.

"I find it crazy I've never even met any of your friends, yet I've introduced you to mine so many times."

"I know," I said, looking down toward my shiny shoes, because I didn't want her to see my eyes. Perhaps it wouldn't go down too well to tell her I only had one real friend—Royston—and the thought of introducing them had never even crossed my mind.

"Are you married, Celestine?"

I stopped and looked toward her.

"No, Della, I am not."

"Then what is it? Because you certainly ain't available."

I did not answer.

"It isn't just you not allowing me into your home or not meeting your friends . . . There's something else I just can't reach. It's like you're here but you're not and I'm tired of it, Celestine. I really am. I'm soon to be twenty-eight years old and I would like to be married. But how can I even consider marriage to a man who doesn't care to share any part of himself with me?"

I swallowed. "Marriage, you say?"

She began to walk away, her frame breathtaking in the light.

I caught up with her.

"Celestine, I've been offered a gig in Paris. A dancer named Josephine Baker is doing well there, so I think I can too. Some folks even say I look like her."

"There is no reason why you shouldn't do just as well."

Her sigh told me she did not want to hear this.

"Didn't you say it would be your dream to perform in Paris one day?"

"Of course you would know that, because I share all my dreams with you. I also tell you about my family, yet I hardly know anything about you. Just that you run an employment registry and you occasionally teach. Nothing more than that."

I felt a bombardment of disappointments flowing from Della.

"Shall I agree to it?" she said.

"Agree to what?" I was buying time, desperately trying to think of what to say.

Her eyes rolled. She was right to be angry because now I had retreated into myself, focusing on my own feelings.

"What I am saying is, shall I agree to take the job in Paris? If I do, I won't be back."

I knew what Della was asking.

To be true to myself, I told her to take the job, that these opportunities did not come by every day and that I would have taken it.

Of course, this was the wrong answer.

I chose the wrong answer.

The morning of her departure, there was still time to meet her at the train station and beg her to stay. Still time to ask for her hand in marriage before she left London, England and my life forever.

Of course, I did none of this. Instead, that morning I stayed in my home, not even attending the office. I remained locked inside my bedroom as Mrs. Markham cleaned the house that was already spotless.

My business continued to thrive, with now over two hundred businesses on my books as well as an endless flow of workers.

My bank account overflowed and I continued to give a lot of my money away to organizations which meant something to me, while continuing to dress in the best suits available from Henry Poole & Co.

Having this financial security did not take away the rush of emptiness I often felt, yet I didn't see this as loneliness, simply emptiness. I wasn't unhappy, and I wasn't happy. I was just *being*, and that was preferable considering I had lived through so much worse.

Then one day, something happened—or *someone* happened—because the moment they rushed through the door of the employment registry, my life was forever changed.

Chapter Fifty-Two

Celestine
1927

The moment I set eyes on her, I knew without any shadow of a doubt that Marjorie Cole was too good for me.

"Are you the owner of this establishment?" She'd appeared quickly, like a gust of the purest air, and had simply taken my breath away.

It was difficult to answer her question straight away or with any confidence.

"Well? Are you the proprietor of this establishment?"

Her skin was the darkest I had ever seen, glistening in the dull light of my shop. She had to be the most beautiful woman my eyes had ever had the pleasure of resting upon. With her thick coily hair pulled into a bun, her blue velvet skirt hiding what I could only imagine was further beauty, I was unable to speak. But it was the way she looked at me, her beautiful eyes narrow and challenging, which threatened to floor me in that very moment.

I hardly ever saw women at the registry, and none as lovely as her.

My mouth began to produce the correct order of words. "Yes, I am the proprietor. Can I help you?"

"My name is Miss Marjorie Cole."

A miss.

"How do you do?"

"Let's dispense with these pleasantries. My father and I own a very well-respected establishment and we have been using your agency for staff."

"Thank you for your patronage. I hope we have lived up to your standards."

"You run an exemplary business Mr. . . ." Her eyes searched mine.

"Please, just call me Celestine."

"We have no issues with your service to us."

"Then I am confused at your apparent displeasure."

"Do you have any women on your books?"

"Well, not really."

"Yes or no: do you have any women on your books?"

"Well, no, but—"

"There is simply no excuse!" she said.

"If you let me speak, madam, the reason I don't have any women on my list is simply because no women have applied here for employment."

"Are you trying to tell me there are no women who require employment? You live in an era where women work, and especially since the war—I mean, who do you think helped look after this great land?"

"I understand that, but I can't conjure up what does not exist."

"You're saying women do not exist?"

"That is not what I am saying, madam."

My forehead felt wet with perspiration. No one in my immediate circle would ever have the audacity to speak to me like this, yet here was this woman I did not know doing just that—and it felt strangely exciting!

"Do stop calling me madam—my name is Miss Cole."

Again she had told me she wasn't married, and perhaps foolishly, my mind stayed on that, straying away from her question at hand.

"Are you even listening to me?" she said.

"Yes, Miss Cole, and if you'd like to come into my office at the back, we can—"

Her bottom lip twitched.

"Or if you can wait five minutes while I pack up, I can invite you out for some tea and we can discuss this further."

"That would be preferable."

Minutes later, it still felt rather difficult to concentrate as she sipped tea from a gold-rimmed cup in a nearby teashop. Her eyes watching me, my insides were only able to respond with what felt like a thousand butterflies flying upward and downward. A most preposterous and unusual feeling! I had never experienced such sensations with Della or any of the other ladies I had spent time with over the years. This was different. Marjorie Cole was different.

Even as she continued to chastise me for the lack of women in my business, it was hard to tear my eyes away from her.

What I did understand was that Marjorie knew of two women looking for work, and I immediately agreed for them to be registered on my books.

By the end of that tea, I had a proposition for her.

"Why don't you be the first woman to work for me?"

Indeed, she would be the first ever *person* to work for me at the registry, as I had always preferred to handle everything myself—until now. Aside from her obvious beauty, I truly believed she could be an asset to the business and, strangest of all, I felt I could trust her.

This stranger.

"Why would you ask me such a thing?"

Her question was of course fueled with suspicion, and I couldn't really blame her. A woman of such elegance was perhaps used to unscrupulous men like myself propositioning her in various ways. But this was about more than me wanting to see her again—her ideas were good, and if she was right about the number of women I could get into the business, my profit could increase very quickly. Yet money was not my main motivator, I can admit. I wanted, *needed* to see her again.

"I think you would fit in well here," I said.

"Let me get this straight, you're offering me a job?"

"Yes."

"Do I look like I need one?"

"No, you do not. It's just that, after everything you've said today, I don't think I can afford to let you go." I wasn't sure if she'd understood the double entendre, but something in the way she looked at me told me she had.

Back inside the registry, she looked around and ran her fingers along the desk and window ledge.

"Is everything to your liking, Miss Cole?"

"Well, it is clean at least."

"Thank you." I wasn't about to add it was me who came in early each day to clean up before opening the doors.

"I could only work part of the week, as I still intend to devote time to my family business."

"Of course."

"We shall negotiate pay that is comparable to what you would pay a man."

"Of course, Miss Cole. Is there anything else?"

"This establishment does appear to be missing a woman's touch," she said.

Up until that moment, it hadn't occurred to me just how right she was.

Of all the women I had ever met, Marjorie was the most learned. I adored this side of her, just as I loved rereading back copies of the *Africa Times* and *Orient Review* and engaging in the healthy debates between us that followed. She confided that a friend had once said it was never good to appear too intelligent in front of a man. I scoffed at that, failing to understand why a man couldn't see this as one of the best parts of a woman.

"It's probably too much to hope for . . . for women to ever be seen as equals," she said.

"Nonsense! Wasn't it only a decade and a half ago that Emily Davison threw herself in front of a horse?"

"Indeed, but I am unsure if she was fighting for women who even remotely looked like me."

"I have never thought of this in such a way."

"Even though a lot has changed, like women receiving degrees at Oxford or being able to vote or taking a seat in Parliament, what hope does a woman like me truly have?"

All the hope in the world, I wanted to say, because I simply hated to witness her sadness. It was as if my empathy wouldn't allow me to see her sadness in isolation; I needed to be responsible for lifting her up, or else my day would also be ruined.

This was the effect that Marjorie Cole had on me.

Chapter Fifty-Three

Celestine
1928

It wasn't hard to see that Marjorie hailed from a long line of entrepreneurs, starting with her grandfather who'd arrived from Sierra Leone just over sixty years ago and started a thriving coal merchant business—because it showed in everything she did. We'd now been working together for three months, and the business had seen a surge in profit thanks to her simple suggestion to add women onto our books.

I wasn't sure how she felt about me, but I had fallen for Marjorie Cole in every way and was desperate to know if she felt a smidgen of the same. Sometimes, I believed she did, yet I assumed that someone with such a strong mind-set would have told me so.

"Your presence here has brought a much-needed brightness to this once drab shop," I said.

"It has?"

"Indeed. You are what it needed. Your radiance is bewitching." I immediately regretted such forward words, and I probably should have chosen a more appropriate moment than when she was stooped over the desk, filling in a form for one of our less literate clients.

"Why, thank you," she said, not looking at me. I was glad of this.

Later, as we sat in the office, she was more forthcoming. "It is most unusual to hear a man say such things to me nowadays."

"I find that hard to believe of such a regal woman."

"My royal lineage in Africa aside, here, I am a lowly spinster. Hence, my father is keen for me to spend as much of my time with you as possible."

"May I ask why?"

"I believe he has almost given up on me finding a gentleman interested enough to ask for my hand, at the age of almost twenty-nine. My father is aware you are a man of means and that is very important to him."

I hadn't expected any of these words from Marjorie.

"Why have you not married, Marjorie?"

"As a child, marriage was not something I wanted or felt I needed, simply preferring to follow my father into the business. That is what excited me, interested me. It also did not make any sense in my mind that my father would pay so much for my private education, only for me to squander it in the kitchen as I directed the cook on how to make my husband's favorite meal!"

Her words were unusual but refreshing, and this made her even more beautiful and even more unattainable in my eyes. I felt myself retreat. "Well, I'm sure any man will be pleased to have you on his arm."

I thought I saw her eyes flicker with disappointment. I hadn't meant to say that. Rationally I knew this, but I also didn't want to say anything that would encourage her either. I was far from worthy of such a queen, a woman with an identifiable lineage, when I didn't even know who I truly was, what with the name changes, the different countries, a home that wasn't really my home according to others.

Perhaps we were not a good match after all, and I had been fooling myself to even imagine myself worthy of such a woman.

After that day, something changed between us. A silent expectation had risen from Marjorie, meaning I now possessed the power to change everything with words and promises. Just as I had with Della.

We attended the teashop often. Marjorie smoothed cream over her scone as I stuck with just the jam, as cream did not agree with me in any way.

"Do you ever wonder . . ." she said. Her full lips moved so slowly when she spoke, yet her words were fast. I often wondered how she did that. "Do you ever wonder what it would be like to live in our ancestral country?"

Like a cloud quietly moving over the sun, the atmosphere changed.

I stiffened.

She continued. "I often wonder if our outlooks would have been . . . I don't know, different?"

My voice took on a harsh tone I suddenly could not control. "Sounds like a slightly narrow way of thinking, Marjorie. Are you saying there would be a lack of ambition and work ethic?"

"Why would I say such a thing? My grandfather was the hardest-working man I have ever met, my father just as much, so know that what you are implying is the furthest from my thoughts." Her eyes blazed into me and I turned away. Sometimes when she looked at me, it felt as if she could see right inside, and I didn't want that. I never wanted that because then . . . then she'd see all of me.

My onslaught of words continued. "If you ever bothered to find out, you would have known that I was born in Africa and I'm a very proud African despite the way I speak. It is possible to be both, you know." My words were ridiculous, especially in light of the fact that Marjorie and her family sounded just as British yet were very proud and knowledgeable about their ancestry—but that was the point.

My ridiculous tirade continued. "But I suppose everything needs to be about you."

Her eyebrows rose. She was too dignified to raise her voice in public, while I had descended into the gutter for absolutely no real reason.

I did not mean any of what I was saying. I had loved hearing about Marjorie's life, her childhood, and the love of two parents who doted on her and told her she could be and do anything she wanted in this life. It had allowed me to live vicariously through her stories with the purest of joy in my heart. But sometimes a word or a sentence would evoke a memory that would then feel like a shotgun going off in my head, with my heart and mind no longer willing to communicate.

"I should go," she said, standing to her full and glorious height.

"Yes, you should," I said. When she closed her eyes slowly, as if blinking back the threat of tears, my heart wanted to break. I so wanted to extend a hand to her, mutter an apology, but in that moment it would not have been sincere. I actually preferred that she left, just so I could be alone.

That night I went back to the shop and invented work to do. Anything not to have to think about what had happened in the teashop, my ungentlemanly behavior leveled toward a woman I admired greatly and could possibly grow to love.

After I closed up, I walked in the direction of my large, empty home. Then I turned back.

I had some apologizing to do.

It didn't take long to reach Yards Bakery.

The smell of freshly baked bread was intoxicating. The window signage also said: WEDDING CAKES.

I waited outside the shop and at 5:05 p.m. there she was, just as I knew she would be. She never stayed longer than she needed to.

"To what do I owe this pleasure?" she said. Her lipstick was bright red, accentuating her full mouth.

"Do I need an excuse to see you?"

"Not at all," said Ida, pulling her apron off and bunging it into her bag. Her body sang as she walked ahead of me and this was the first thing I had noticed about her—that and the clackety-clack of her heels, the night we'd locked eyes in Carnaby Street early last year. I hardly kept in touch and since Marjorie had entered my life, hadn't seen or heard from her. Ida understood the gaps in our communication and had never complained.

This was our familiar pattern. One I was comfortable with: where nothing was ever asked of me.

Chapter Fifty-Four

Lowra
1993

"Do you remember your first love?" I asked Dikembe.

"Yes, of course," he said with a smile tinted with sadness.

I was not a romantic but really wanted to fill in the huge gaps in Dikembe's story and needed them to be filled with love . . . and lots of it.

It was just Dikembe and me, what with Monty at a meeting and Sandra and Chris in the garden with the children.

Just the two of us, and an intimacy I couldn't explain. One born from a shared history . . . and a bloodline.

"Well . . . spill the beans!" I must have looked and sounded desperate, but he just smiled as Chris and Sandra walked in.

"Are you telling Lowra what a charmer you were in your heyday again?" Chris teased.

"Don't be so absurd," smiled Dikembe. "Your mother was the love of my life, and you know this."

"I know, Dad," he said, patting his father's shoulder. "The perfect blueprint for me and Sandra." The room fell silent as both men remembered the woman they had loved, who'd left them a decade ago. Sandra placed a supporting arm on Chris's shoulder and once again, I was struck at how beautifully close this family was; such an alien concept to me, it sometimes felt difficult to take in and digest. The only way I could understand it was through this burning feeling in my stomach, which I could only describe as sadness mixed in with a touch of envy. I wasn't proud of it, but it was the truth.

"I'd love to hear about how you met the love of your life," I said.

"I'm afraid to say it wasn't all hearts and flowers," said Dikembe.

Celestine
1929

When I looked at Marjorie, or even imagined being with her, I felt true unadulterated happiness on a level I hadn't experienced since sitting under a tree with Kabili.

And herein lay the problem—perhaps this was a happiness I did not deserve.

Was it not me who'd willingly left my entire family to suffer while boarding a ship to another country?

Skillfully, I soon managed to alienate Marjorie. Her presence at the registry was now strictly professional, with minimal words exchanged unless absolutely essential.

We no longer went out to tea.

I did everything I could to dismiss her from my thoughts because this meant ridding myself of any real feelings toward her—or so I thought. Yet at the registry it became more and more difficult not to be baffled by a belief she was the only woman in the world I could truly fall in love with—assuming I hadn't already . . .

I began reading books about romance, leafing through each page with a smugness I did not recognize, as they confirmed I was indeed experiencing something similar. This, coupled with the fact I could no longer erase her from my mind or my heart, told me I had indeed fallen in love with Miss Marjorie Cole.

The registry was thriving, and it wasn't unusual for a slew of men and women to walk through its doors each day. Marjorie often left for home before I had to close up and this was when I felt her absence the most, along with a longing to tell her how I really felt.

One day, less than two weeks into this new and cold interaction of ours, Marjorie turned to me. "As much as I enjoy working here, I can no longer do so."

"What do you mean?"

"You know what I mean. It is better I leave."

"I don't want you to go," I said, as if such words would be sufficient.

"This thing between us . . . it is strong, Celestine, and I am confused and—"

"Marry me, Marjorie!" The words were not planned and I had no idea where they come from. "Become my wife."

Marjorie's parents were thrilled, it seemed, because as soon as I walked into their beautiful home I became besieged by a multitude of relatives and an abundance of "congratulations!" A banquet including cassava leaves and yams, food which transported me back to my childhood, was presented in the finest of serving ware. Flavors exploded in my mouth, and for a moment I was transported back to my village, helping Mama cook in our little kitchen.

I wanted to ask where they'd purchased such items, but again, I couldn't expose myself in such a way.

After dinner, only the four of us remained, my own glass of wine untouched.

"I will try not to take to heart you not asking my permission first," said Marjorie's father.

"You have my sincere apologies, sir. It was never my intention to—"

"That is fine. We are meeting you now," said Marjorie's mother, a slightly older and just as beautiful version of her daughter. I would enjoy being a part of this family.

"Besides, Daddy is just happy to be rid of me!" said Marjorie.

"I've said nothing of the sort!" he said with a polite guffaw.

"My parents were very traditional," began Marjorie's mother. "This man here had to make sure a dowry was produced first."

I had no idea what she was talking about, and of course Marjorie sensed my confusion. Since our engagement she'd become even more in tune with me and this I found astounding, at times terrifying.

"Don't worry, Mama, my betrothed has a thriving business, as do we. He is more than able to keep me in the style I am accustomed to, if that's what you mean!" The two women laughed among themselves as Marjorie's father knotted his eyebrows, turning to me.

"Is the wine not to your liking?"

"Celestine is not a big drinker, let him be" said Marjorie, and I was grateful.

It was a joy to witness her happiness and it became easier for me to focus on that. Her father took me aside, admitting that to his relief his thirty-year-old daughter would finally be married.

"She's a rare jewel," I said, as he patted me on the back.

"That was sometimes the problem," he began. "Some men do not appear to know what to do with such a woman. She knows her own mind and is confident. That is not a way for a women to be, but alas, I am partly responsible."

I wasn't sure if he spoke with pride, disappointment or both.

After that night with Marjorie's relatives, we were both expected to decide and name a wedding date. Instead, I began to spend less time with my fiancée, citing work, the school—all the distractions which had always been there, yet were the only excuses I could think of.

When she wasn't with me, she would never leave my mind, yet

at times, to think of Marjorie was also to think of Agatha. The shame bubbled inside, heating up and burning through to my speech and almost every action I took. I felt transparent—as if everyone could see through me and to what had happened. There was a constant whispering in my ear that I was not good enough, that I was unlovable.

I hated myself for the way I was treating Marjorie; she deserved none of it and yet I felt almost powerless.

There were days I'd be absent from the registry and not inform her of why; times I promised to accompany her on a walk or to a show and just not arrive.

Once I traveled to the countryside for one whole week, after saying I would be gone for two days. I ignored her anger, dismissing her obvious pain.

I was never unfaithful to Marjorie, but I kept her away from my heart for as long as I could until she finally told me she was leaving me.

"I cannot and will not be party to this. I have never wanted to be a divorced woman so I will not be marrying you, Celestine."

I looked up. Her words had made their point. "I don't blame you. Why would you?"

"Do not try to turn this onto me. You did this, Celestine, *you*! What is wrong with you?"

Finally, she'd realized.

I wasn't good, but stained and used. She had finally seen me the way I saw myself.

I did not notice the tear in my eye, but she did.

"Celestine, I love you," she said, wiping my tear. "But I can't get through to you. Wherever you are . . . it's not with me. It never has been. I have no idea why you proposed. Perhaps you just believed it to be something you should do. Whatever. I love you, but I cannot and will not be subject to this anymore. I cannot sacrifice myself for you."

I shook my head, agreeing with her, silently begging her to stay.

When Marjorie gave in her resignation, I knew she still loved me, but the problem was I no longer loved myself and hadn't done so for a very, very long time.

Chapter Fifty-Five

Lowra
1993

"Tell me about your name," said Dikembe.

The money for the B&B had been well spent as it meant "popping round" to Dikembe's home daily for ten days, and truly getting to know not only him but his small extended family. It also meant being on hand for a chat with Sandra or just playing in the garden with the kids. I'd sometimes arrive in the afternoon or early evening, but I was a daily visitor and the strange thing about it was that nobody seemed to mind. Not least Dikembe, who kind of encouraged me to show up, even if it was all under the guise of recording his story.

Now and for the first time, Chris trusted me to spend the entire day alone with his beloved father.

"That's down to my mother, Vivienne . . ." I looked for any recognition in his eyes. There was nothing. Why would there be?

Now my family had been mentioned, I really wanted to tell him. To tell him he'd fathered a little girl called Caroline who then went on to have a daughter named Vivienne, and who then had me. I wanted to tell him we had a connection born from more than living in the same house, the attic and the artifacts; we were also connected by DNA and by blood.

"I've got something to tell you," Isaid.

It was now or never. Monty was at a meeting, and Chris and Sandra had taken the kids to see their maternal grandparents.

I stood up and started pacing the room. The sunlight shone so brightly though the glass windows and ceiling, a beautiful little oasis that Dikembe had carved out for himself—yet here I was about to change his life once again, with my words.

"Something's on your mind, isn't it?" he said. It was how he looked at me when he said this, as if an unspoken conversation had already started between us. And from the moment we'd first met just last week, surrounded by Monty, Chris and all the noise, there was always this conversation going on between Dikembe and me which nobody else knew about.

I took a deep intake of breath, ready to blow these secrets wide open and in doing so, risk alienating this man who had fast become my friend.

"I know," he said.

I sat back down.

"I have known all of the time."

I blinked rapidly. "How?"

"I think I've always known."

"But how—"

"Whenever I see you, it's there. The sadness in your eyes . . ."

"I . . . I never realized . . ."

"It wasn't obvious at first, but then I thought about the doll."

My eyebrows knotted.

"Tilly's doll, the necklace and the piece of paper. When you explained how you had found them as a child, you appeared so very matter-of-fact. There was no expression in your eyes and—please excuse me for saying this—a deadness. I know that deadness; I recognize it."

I felt a shot of confusion.

He turned to me. "You were there too, weren't you? Locked up?"

I couldn't answer at first, my mind switching to this new direction, and then finally and with no prompting from Dikembe: "Yes."

We sat in silence and it did not feel uncomfortable. There was no one I could sit with like this without wanting to say something, anything. Not even Dr. Raj, where the awkwardness had felt a bit too much. But with Dikembe it felt almost natural, I suppose because we'd been used to the silence . . . and the darkness.

Like Dikembe, I'd spent years of my life locked in that attic. Let out of it only for rare visits from social workers and education inspectors and my grandma before she got ill, the majority of my days and nights spent in there with just a flicker of sunlight when Nina would open the door, usually to inflict something on me I was sure I didn't deserve.

It had taken a long time to get to where I was now: functional. I'd even started to feel things again thanks to Dikembe, because for so long I'd made sure nothing could be felt except the drugs prescribed to me by Dr. Raj, which just numbed everything.

Now my feelings were awakened, and I couldn't be sure of what would happen if I went any further with this conversation.

So I didn't.

I'd not be telling Dikembe more than what he thought he knew. I'd simply acknowledge he was right: that yes, I too had been locked in the attic as a punishment. That I had willed away the moments thinking of my parents and writing poems on pieces of paper. Sometimes singing songs my father had enjoyed, like ABBA or David Bowie. Or recounting the alphabet. I wouldn't tell him anything more than that.

For my own sanity.

"Talk about being part of a club no one would want to join," I said. Attempting to throw light on such a huge chunk of darkness would never feel appropriate.

"Lowra, I see it as you and I being forever bonded by a shared experience. I for one welcome the thought because, well, it was a lonely time, and suddenly it feels like you were right there with me, albeit almost ninety years apart! Does that make sense or does it sound silly?"

"It doesn't sound silly at all." I sat back on the chair, suddenly feeling exhausted. My mind hadn't prepared itself for any part of this conversation. I was all set to tell him I was his great-granddaughter—not this.

"Just think, if the times were reversed, I would have seen those wonderful poems you said you wrote. They may have comforted me. Instead, you were lumbered with my useless doodling!"

"Which led me here."

"Indeed."

"Although it was the three photographs that did that."

"Only three?"

"There were three at the exhibition. Do you think there are more?"

"My dear, I do not think about them at all."

"I don't suppose you'd like to see the photographs again one day?"

"Everything to do with that day is planted in here." He pointed to his head. "There is no need for such pictures."

I understood. More than he could ever know.

"Do you still write?" he said.

"I've written a few lines, recently. I think you've inspired me."

"A poet's muse. Now that sounds like a worthy role."

"I wouldn't call myself that."

"Why should I be the only one to get all this catharsis?"

"I said a lot to Dr. Raj—my psychiatrist—because I needed some help a while back." I wished that hadn't come out, but it was too late to take it back.

"I'm from a bygone era where you had to be your own psychiatrist. I'm glad you had someone to talk to."

We were silent once again, as if we both needed space in which to wind up the running motor of our emotions.

That night, when Chris and Sandra returned home with the kids, they suggested we call it a night. The B&B was becoming too costly, and now I was confident Dikembe wasn't about to slip through my fingers, it was time to go back to my flat. He was here, alive and well, and we were already bonded by a history no one could ever take away from us.

The next day I met Monty for a coffee in Highgate Village, before heading up to Dikembe's home.

"I rather miss the Flamingo Club cafe," he said, raising the cup of tea to his lips. A jazz CD played in the background as we sipped on tea that was double the price of any I had ever tasted.

"You know we're coming to the end of the story now, Lowra."

"We are?"

"I have most if not all of the facts straight from Dikembe's mouth, which is wonderful. Probably would have been a lot more if you'd remembered to use the Dictaphone!"

"Well, it's not quite over. He's yet to finish telling me about the great love of his life; we always get sidetracked. All I know so far is that he was engaged and then he wasn't."

"I know you go over there and sometimes don't even discuss his story."

"I like spending time with the family. You know . . . doing normal things."

"I know."

"So, I will be patient and wait for the grand finale of how he found the love of his life, Chris's mother."

"That may be the grand finale to you, but the real end to this story is that he made it, despite all that happened—he made it to an age the average person does not. He made it, Lowra!" Sliding his hands across the table, he held on to mine.

"I want to know more," I said, sliding my hands away. Not because it felt odd—it felt OK actually—but because I wasn't about to go down the road of thinking we'd reached the end with Dikembe. I had only just begun.

"You've already decided not to tell him about Caroline—what else is there?"

"You're really asking that?"

He shrugged his shoulders. "I don't understand then."

"And that's it. Nobody can truly understand except Dikembe because we shared a very unique experience. I don't expect anybody to get that."

"I'm really not trying to upset you. What I'm saying is, if you're looking for him to change your life in some way, that isn't going to happen. He isn't some magical figure who's going to make everything all right. This isn't a Hollywood movie."

"How dare you!"

He looked toward the table.

"Monty, before you and I started this journey, I was just existing. After listening to Dikembe's life at almost a hundred years old, I see just how much he has achieved. Yet what have I done? If I live as long as him, I will have almost seventy more years to make a difference. That's how I think now . . . whereas before, I'd have just thought, *I have seventy more years before I can get out of this* . . . this fucking existence!"

Monty's eyes widened.

"This whole experience has changed my life and I'm not ready to walk away from it just yet. So I'm staying put."

His smile told me he understood. "If you need money to tide you over, let me know. You haven't worked in a while."

"I'm OK. The upside of having no social life is that I can save money each month and pop it into an account. It's not much but it's something I can live on."

"The offer's there if you ever need it."

"Thank you for understanding."

His hand reached across the table again, and this time, I didn't pull mine away.

The sun appeared just as Dikembe and I headed outside.

Chris insisted he take the walking stick, and I was happy to hold on to his arm if he needed me to.

"That boy treats me like a child," he said as we headed toward a bench. It felt lovely to get out of the house with just Dikembe by my side.

I had never seen him walk such a distance before and was struck at how stooped he was, his age much more apparent to me than usual.

He slowly maneuvered himself onto the bench and made a sigh.

"So much for making it to Highgate Wood."

"We can go back to the house and I'll call a cab. Chris gave me a number," I said, sitting beside him. A pigeon bobbed its head near my feet.

"Maybe next time. It's not as if I haven't been before. It's partly why I wanted to live in this area and bought this house."

"I can't believe you've lived here all these years!"

"After being cooped up in the big house for all that time, well . . . you'd think I'd prefer to be all over the place. But no. I like it here."

"It is beautiful."

"It is. I suspect you saw the trees on your way up. I developed a love for them just like my father, perhaps as a way of feeling closer to him. Whatever the reason, I feel a sense of calm whenever they surround me."

"You speak about them like they're people."

"Like humans, trees tell a story. In nine months they can go from nakedness to half dressed, to fully flourishing bloom. Then they repeat the process all over again. I think they communicate a metaphor for life quite clearly."

I nodded my head.

"Nothing stays the same. We're in constant transition even when we are stagnant. So either you go with that or you get left behind. I just went with it."

"We were kids, we had no choice," I said.

"We didn't then, but I suppose now we do."

A woman with a twin stroller walked past, followed by a man with a miniature dog jumping up and down on a red lead.

"I was always a workaholic as a young man and never really took the time to enjoy the sunshine, or the stars at that. After work, I'd teach in the evenings and arrive home really late to a meal my long-suffering housekeeper, Mrs. Markham, had prepared. That was my life and I felt content with it—until I met my wife, who showed me just how different my life could be."

"The love of your life, Chris's mum."

"That's the one."

To me, Dikembe was the most resilient human being I had ever met, and people needed to hear all his stories and not just the horrific parts. They also needed to hear about his joy. The fact this man had loved and been loved, after losing so much.

"Where's that machine thing?" he said.

I pulled out the Dictaphone. "You want me to use it?"

"I thought we were under strict instruction from Monty?"

"I didn't think . . . I mean, there are times I haven't used it, like when we talk about being locked away . . ."

His eyes followed another pigeon which flew across our gaze.

"You seem to speak more freely without it."

"You can tell?"

"Of course," I said.

His face suddenly relaxed. "She's been gone ten years now and yet I still miss her every single day of my life."

"If this is too hard . . . ?"

He gently took my hand. "No, I want to talk about her. That way it's like she's still alive, if that doesn't sound too silly."

"It doesn't."

"If you hear our story, perhaps you'll fall in love with your young man, Monty."

"He's not my young man!" I said, but I couldn't help smiling.

He raised one eyebrow. "Can't blame an old man for trying."

"How do you do that?"

"What?"

"Raise the one eyebrow."

"A trick I acquired in old age. The grandchildren love it!" He patted my hand and smiled. "Let me tell you about the girl who took my heart and never gave it back again. Her name was Marjorie."

"You met another Marjorie?"

"No, the same one. Marjorie Aminata Cole."

Chapter Fifty-Six

Celestine
1939

I thought my eyes must have been deceiving me, but they were not.

It was her.

Marjorie Cole.

"I can't believe it's you," I said, as I moved closer to where she stood outside a shop window, wearing a flowery dress and white hat tilted to the side, every bit as elegant as I remembered.

"It is me," she said with a wonderfully bright smile. I brought her slim hand to my lips, her skin also as soft as I remembered it.

Her eyes sparkled in a way that could only match how my heart was feeling in that very moment.

"Celestine," she said, and that was enough.

Perhaps for old times' sake Marjorie agreed to accompany me to a nearby teashop, where I found it rather difficult to take my eyes off her. As beautiful as ever, it was as if age had simply enhanced her flawless dark skin tone and added sparkle to those enchanting brown eyes. To me, she personified the beauty of the majestic ebony tree.

As we sat and drank tea, my mind whirled with words like "serendipity" and "chance." I hadn't seen Marjorie Cole in almost ten years and here she was, right in front of me. The past few months had seen the world begin to change again. Another war was imminent apparently, and while the nation believed everything to do with it would surely be sorted out soon—with England being the victors—I wasn't so sure. Having long since had such levels of optimism beaten out of me, sitting opposite Marjorie Cole, that cynicism I'd held on to for so long began to fizzle away.

As she spoke, as we conversed, it was as if ten years had faded away into twenty-four hours.

"It is so lovely to have run into you, Miss Cole."

"Oh, my name is now Mrs. Marjorie Denning."

The room, with all its patrons, tea brewing and activity, stood still. Of course she was married. I had been too much of a coward to offer her a life with me, and it was obvious another man would not be so shortsighted.

"I have been living in Somerset—a beautiful part of England. I would say it's nice to be back, but I do miss the tranquillity of the country."

"I can only imagine." My words now came out with great difficulty, weighed down by disappointment.

"I returned to London because my mother is unwell."

"I'm very sorry to hear that. Is there anything I can do to help?"

"Thank you, Celestine, but she is improving now. I think she just missed her only daughter. But I'm now here to stay."

"Will your husband be joining you?"

Her eyes rested upon the gold-lined teacup. "He passed away some time ago. Five years now."

I was not so callous as to see this as a victory. Marjorie had been hurt and that in turn was hurtful to me. I wanted only to carry what burdened her.

"My condolences to you."

"We had five wonderful years together. It was a good marriage." She gripped the handle of the cup. "Now it looks like I'm back in London for good. My parents are getting older, and it makes better sense for me to sell our house in Somerset and get on with it."

There was a pregnant pause which gave me time to unscramble my thoughts, from thinking she was married to discovering she'd been a widow for five years.

Marjorie Denning was now a single woman.

I smiled, and when she did the same it almost left me breathless, with what felt not unlike a swarm of butterflies flying around in my stomach. It was still there, this hold Marjorie had over me, and this time I would never let her go again.

Marjorie and I had spent endless days together since that afternoon three months ago in the teashop, my feelings for her reignited and never to be extinguished again.

Once again, as we sat in each other's arms, it was easy to fall into discussions on the political climate and possible war, as well as what could be done to enhance the lives of the ever-growing Black population in the city.

"I take it you are familiar with the League of Colored Peoples?" she said.

"Yes, of course, founded by Harold Moody."

"Let's not forget the other founding member, Stella Thomas. Who also just happens to be the first African woman to be called to the bar of England."

I smiled. Marjorie had lost none of her fire.

"I did not know about her."

"Of course you didn't. It's always about the contribution of the man, isn't it?"

"And it is you I have to thank for steering me in the direction of taking on women at the registry. When I sold the business it was thriving, with women making up twenty percent of my employees. So thank you." I took her hand and placed it against my lips.

"I shall take my commission incrementally," she joked, pulling her hand away. Marjorie, as ever, was not afraid to challenge me. She was a strong woman and one I desired with all of my heart. We'd hardly left each other's company in the last three months, slotting right back into the nook of each other's lives, as if the last ten years had never happened.

War was now imminent. Although Marjorie had injected a summer into my life that made everything appear constantly joyful, we also had to be realistic. Yes, we had been through war before, but nobody could foresee how any of us would emerge from this one.

I prepared dinner as I often did; just one of the ways I hoped to reassure her of my love, as my first attempts a decade ago had been weakened by my own obstacles. Of course, telling her I loved her no longer felt like the burden it may have in the past. I was now open, ready and willing to be all I could for this woman, perhaps keen at times to overcompensate for the pain I had once caused her. Marjorie often said my I love yous were voiced too frequently, but instead of the pull of rejection that could have followed, I felt happiness when she'd add, "But don't stop on my account."

We sat on my large Chesterfield sofa and I placed my hand over hers. "I truly love you, Marjorie."

"As I do you."

"I accept that sometimes you are still cautious about me after the way I treated you in the past."

"It was a long time ago. Plenty has happened since then. To both of us."

As she spoke, her head slotted into the crook of my neck, and I believed every word. However, I often sensed a hesitation with her, perhaps not only born from the past but the present too, as I was far from perfect. In those moments I still feared I wouldn't be enough for her. It was a small voice, yet one I perhaps had to accept would always be there, even if somewhat muted.

"I need to tell you something," I said.

She sat up, her face etched with concern.

In that moment, I could not have loved her more.

"I need you to accompany me to my study first."

That smile again. "If you are intending to have your way with me, Celestine, I am not that type of girl. You know this!"

Both smiling and hand in hand, we headed to the door of my study and I hesitated before opening the door. It felt as if we were standing on the threshold of something big and once we stepped over it, we could never return.

I opened the door and she immediately sat on one of the chairs. The room, as usual, was immaculate, with a desk facing the window, two cushioned chairs and a bureau in the corner.

"So, this is where you do your work. Why all the mystery?" Indeed, I had always kept my study out of bounds, even to Mrs. Markham. This was my room. My special room.

"Celestine?"

"My darling, this is my study but . . . but it is also where I sometimes sleep." My words were emerging with some difficulty but strengthened by my determination to tell Marjorie the truth.

"Why sleep in here when you have a perfectly good bedroom? Well, you have numerous bedrooms actually!"

As perceptive as ever, she clocked my expression.

"I don't understand, Celestine. There isn't even a bed in here. Where would you sleep?"

"There is something I need to tell you about me that I have never told anybody." I pulled up the remaining chair, close to her. "I should have told you the first time around but I just wasn't ready. I don't even know if I'm fully ready now, but if it is a choice between losing you and telling you, then there is no choice."

"You're scaring me now."

"You don't need to be scared, my love." I took both of her hands. "I just need to share this part of me, because to be closed off from you . . . Well, we know what happened the last time, and I can't take that chance again. I need to do this."

I hated how her expression had contorted into fear.

"Do not be scared, my darling. I need to do this, please let me do this."

So I told her about the attic.

During our time together a decade ago, I had reeled off a past that sounded palatable and reasonable, one that was steeped in unreality. Looking into her eyes now, I spoke the truth of what I had endured at the big house at the hands of Cyril and Agatha. In her expression was a reflection of the nightmare it had been.

Being taken from my family, my home; locked in an attic; treated like an animal; working for almost all the hours that existed and for no pay.

I also needed Marjorie to know this wasn't my full story, only part of it. That my actual story had been interrupted by Sir Richard and then the attic. Four long years I could never get back, but four years which would never define me. It was important she knew this.

Her eyes told me she did. After the pity, the horror and the sorrow, her eyes told me she did.

We said nothing for a few moments, which felt like an eternity. I was unable to feel the release I had expected; if I'm honest, those feelings of shame began to resurface, perhaps from what I *hadn't* shared.

We were still holding hands, until she pulled one of hers away and began to gently and softly brush her knuckles against my cheek. The room was dead quiet, not a sound.

"Celestine, thank you for telling me this," she whispered.

"Why would you thank me?"

"Because it means that you trust me, just as I trust you, and this means everything to me."

And then it happened. This avalanche of emotion I had not expected.

My shoulders heaved, and I was no longer conscious of her presence as I opened my mouth to a pained sound and a flood of tears: for the family left behind and never seen again; for the years spent in a cold, rat-infested attic; and for the years thrown away by letting Marjorie go the first time.

I slid onto the floor without realizing, my entire body turned to the side, Marjorie seated on the chair behind and over me.

I felt small.

Eleven years old again.

Then she did the most extraordinary thing. In her elegant royal blue dress, cut below the knee, she slid down and onto the floor beside me, resting her hand supportively on my leg as I lay with my back toward her, curved in the fetal position.

"What are you doing?" I said.

This was unbecoming of a lady and yet there she was, her entire body on the floor. I turned to her, my numbness thawing at the sight of her slightly disheveled hair, the hem of her dress rising untidily up her leg. She was uncomfortable on the floor, that I could tell by the way she shifted herself from side to side.

We were now shoulder to shoulder, which felt slightly odd until she grabbed my hand, and an immediate feeling of love and security ran from her to me.

Then it felt glorious.

"I used to believe you were coming in here to get away from me."

"No, never." I gently cupped her face, the lapels of my shirt wet from my tears. "You, you're perfect, my darling."

"You have a short memory, Celestine."

"I do?"

"Do you actually remember the way we met?"

I smiled, recalling the personal memory we often brought up in company. Of how she'd gone from telling me off to becoming the love of my life. Men like Royston were often horrified I would be attracted by a woman with such a spirit. Such a force of life. Yet it was a force I wanted to bathe in for the rest of my life.

"I love you," she said.

I felt the emotion begin to appear in my throat again.

"Don't fight it, my darling, " she said. "Just let it all flow from you. It will be all right. I'm here."

I'd never wanted Marjorie to see me as weak, but now that dam had truly burst and there would be no going back. The sailors and hardworking men I'd encountered over the years would balk at this level of emotion in front of a woman. Yet like me, I had seen them at the brink. An example: after a reading class, unable to leave because of the tears streaming down their faces; minutes later, dry faces and a silent promise never to speak of it again as they headed home to their wives and children. The baggage of a people far from home and too tired to cope in a country which had once welcomed them and just as quickly rejected them.

Marjorie held me in her arms once more, still on that floor, as I wept. I felt more naked, vulnerable, transparent and . . . embarrassed. Yet in that moment I had never felt closer to her.

As of that night, I felt a delicious shift.

While there were still times I would retreat to my study, she now understood. Sometimes she would join me and other times not.

Some days we'd play cards on the floor, sometimes we sang (badly) together. Marjorie was not only the most beautiful woman I had ever met, but I believed we had been placed on this earth for one another. That no matter who or what had previously come into our lives, we were always going to end up together.

Chapter Fifty-Seven

Celestine
1939

"What do you truly desire?" asked Marjorie.

We sat in the garden which, thanks to Marjorie, was now home to an array of wonderful flowers, half of which I did not know the name of. Among many things, Marjorie was also a keen gardener, and with the help of a landscaper had transformed what used to be a patch of land into a thriving bed of color.

Indeed, my house had become a home.

"Well, how about you lie in my arms forever?"

She smiled. "I mean, moving forward. I've seen a change in you since—"

"The talk?"

She smiled. "Yes, the talk. I can't help wondering what you could do now to keep that momentum." She leaned in. "Celestine, what would you like to take back from what happened to you?"

Perhaps Marjorie was too learned for me, because I simply couldn't understand what she meant.

"What I mean is, my darling, you are more powerful than you perhaps think. You have made a beautiful life for yourself despite what happened."

"It's just money," I said. "Of course it is nice to have, but it isn't everything. I would give it all up just to have you."

"Let's not get above ourselves!" she said, and we both gave a polite chuckle.

"Celestine, there is so much they did not take away from you. So much. You give to so many through teaching and your monetary contributions to all those societies, and no one can take that from you. But I wonder if there's anything that—"

"They took away my name." I swallowed. This had been on my mind from the day I had boarded that steamer aged eleven. "The one my parents gave me."

"Dikembe?"

"I only kept Celestine because, well . . ." I swallowed.

"What is it?" said Marjorie. She'd always sense when my mood suddenly changed. When a darkness would quickly flood over me.

I turned to her. "I kept the name Celestine Babbington because I assumed it would be easier for doors to be opened to me, especially with my business. When people see the name, they see a business owned by a quintessentially English gentleman . . . just like he wanted me to be. It was a name I loathed yet needed. Also . . . and I know this sounds ridiculous . . ."

"What is it?"

"I thought it would be easier for my family to find me . . . if . . ."

"Oh, my darling," she said, gripping my arm. It was still hard for me to accept her affection when it followed a moment of weakness, or in this case something which really made no sense, as I found it difficult to discern whether her reaction was pity or genuine comfort.

"My mama said I should answer to whatever name they gave me . . . or something like that . . . So she knew . . . she knew—or she feared—my name was going to be changed . . . Oh, I don't know, Marjorie." I could feel the emotion welling up inside me.

"I do understand what you mean about the name being more

palatable. However, my grandmother was given much more respect with her unpronounceable name because everyone assumed she was of high society back home, which of course she was. She never tired of telling me she was most disappointed when her daughter married a Cole!"

I squeezed her hand. "I am very tempted to change it, but it would mean a lot of paperwork."

"Not really. You wouldn't be the first or the last. So, Dikembe Ngoya . . . your birth name?"

"I'd want to honor my brother somewhere."

"Kabili?"

I had told her all the stories I could remember of Kabili and me under the tree; his cheekiness and our closeness, which had been so strong before he started working with my brothers and father.

"Kabili Dikembe?" she said.

"I don't know, what do you think?" Such a level of indecisiveness was not like me. But I knew that whatever combination of names I chose, I'd be dishonoring someone as I had four brothers and two parents, and all could not be included.

"To go by Dikembe Ngoya once more would feel as if I was still holding on to something unattainable."

"Celestine, this has to be your choice. It wouldn't be right for me to tell you what to do in this instance because . . . well . . . there's been enough people making choices for you."

How I loved this woman.

"This is something you have to decide for yourself."

I came to the decision I was to be known as Dikembe Kabili, in honor of my brother and the name my parents gave me.

Now, when I looked at Marjorie it was not as Celestine Babbington but as Dikembe Kabili; as a new man, and for the first time, one who truly felt worthy of her.

The day I decided to change my name was the day I asked Marjorie to change hers.

We married that summer in a very small ceremony, with just a few of her close friends and some of my ex-students from the school, including Dele and of course Royston.

Any life I'd imagined with Marjorie was so much more vivid and pleasurable in the reality we created together. At the age of forty-five I had experienced a rebirth which was joyful and full of unexpected surprises. This didn't mean my life was full of nothing but sunshine, but that on the dark days, I only wanted to spend them with Marjorie.

We expanded the school, and with Marjorie on board we were able to launch into more subjects. English and math were my specialty, the advancement of women Marjorie's.

With the help and advice of her father, I began to invest heavily in property with leftover money from the sale of the registry, which had just been sitting in a bank.

Some of the happiest experiences of my life were opening the door to a house which once felt large and empty, now bursting with contentment. The fireplace glowed with warmth, my arm around Marjorie's waist as we discussed our present *and* our future. Finally my house had been transformed, with a level of stylish yet homely decor only this woman, my wife, could have achieved: from the gilt-framed oil paintings hanging from the walls to the off-white lace table runners with scalloped edges. Marjorie was an amazing addition to my life and I could not imagine taking one more breath without her.

I accepted that my feelings of shame would never fully disappear, but I'd found a way of no longer allowing them to become a focal point in my life, by challenging myself to love Marjorie the way she deserved.

The way *I* deserved.

*

We had long since accepted that our marriage would be one without children. Marjorie's attempts to conceive with her previous husband had been met with heartbreak and a resolution that it would never happen—besides, this wasn't something we felt we needed to complete the bond we shared. So when, in 1943 in the middle of the war, Marjorie found she was pregnant at the age of forty-four and I at forty-nine, neither of us could believe it.

"Surely this is a miracle!" she kept repeating over and over again, as I stood in stunned silence. Her parents were ecstatic, of course, and Royston lifted me right up off the floor in congratulations. But none of it felt remotely real until the day the nurse said I could finally hold my baby son.

Dikembe Christopher Kabili.

Marjorie was exhausted yet beaming, and all I could do was stare at this tiny bundle which had been placed in my hands.

"Isn't this a dream?" she said, while I failed to tear my eyes away from him. Not because I marveled at how small and innocent he was, but simply because he would now be my responsibility. Having amassed enough money to ensure he would never experience poverty, I remained unsure of the other things expected of me. Like teaching him how to be a man, something I'd been on the brink of learning from my own father.

Also, what made me worthy of being this beautiful little boy's father, anyway?

When we brought him home, Marjorie sensed my hesitation, which was probably why she did one of the most unconventional things a wife could do.

She'd sometimes leave me to spend time with the baby alone, almost out of the door before announcing a visit to her parents or to the shops.

I fell into an utter panic the first time she did this. Well, the first three times, in fact. After which she'd return home to find us both snuggled up together on the chair.

When in 1944 another set of evacuations from the city was announced, I accompanied my wife, baby Christopher and a large group of children to Marjorie's former house in Somerset, which she'd never sold. During the previous evacuations, it had been difficult to place Black and mixed-heritage evacuees in homes, so Marjorie and I decided to do something to help. Once word got out, ten families were signed up within days.

That year in Somerset was one of the happiest of my life. Watching not only my son grow but ten others, while teaching and feeding them every day, was an experience that not only bonded Marjorie and I for life, but also reminded us we were happy with just the one child!

As always, I did most of the cooking because I was better at it than Marjorie.

Marjorie and I slept in the same bed and sometimes sneaked the baby in there too. Just the three of us: snug, free and in our own little world.

After the war, the children returned to their parents and we to London.

Our rather unconventional relationship, something not many understood, continued to work beautifully for us.

I truly felt part of a family again, only this one was of my own making. The thought was terrifying, humbling and exhilarating all at once.

Christopher and Marjorie were everything to me. In them I had finally found a reason to keep the fight going, or better still, not to feel I always *had* to fight.

When Marjorie died, it hit me in a way that was surprising.

If when I met her it had felt like I was in the presence of my mama again, it would only stand to reason that losing her would be the same type of grief. But I felt it so differently. With my mama, our journey had been cut short quicker than was natural, and I had felt the void ever since. With Marjorie, although so much time had been wasted beforehand, I still believed we had spent the most important years, the healing years, together, and that our time had come to a more natural end.

She was eighty-four and I was eighty-nine.

Lowra

1993

My face was wet as Dikembe finished the story of his life with Marjorie.

I wasn't sure if they were happy tears or sad, but again, I was just glad to be *feeling*, and had felt every single emotion throughout Dikembe's story.

"Thank you for sharing this with me." I switched off the Dictaphone, having recorded some of it: the least personal bits. Indeed, it had been a privilege to hear Dikembe and Marjorie's love story and there was nothing else I needed to add to it. Nothing.

"You'll make me start if you're not careful," said Dikembe, slowly wiping his left eye with a handkerchief.

"I can't believe you took in all those kids."

"I wish I remembered it all," said Chris, who had appeared at the bench halfway through the story.

"It was only for a short while."

"You've helped so many people," Isaid, astounded at how modest he was being.

"If you can't give back, then what is the point? Those are the only words of wisdom I can part with, I'm afraid!"

"Dad, you're getting tired now. Maybe we should get you back home," said Chris, and I had to agree with him. Talking about Marjorie had been intense for everyone.

"Don't fuss, son."

"Yeah, yeah, you've lived through two world wars, yadda yadda yadda."

"Do you see the way this boy continually mocks me?" he said, smiling.

I also smiled. These two people clearly loved one another deeply. They were a unit, while my idea of a happy family had been born out of TV shows, and mostly unreal and sanitized versions, which had felt safer to me. Yet watching Dikembe, Chris, Sandra, Aminata and Justin, and how they simply looked out for one another, had shown me what real family *could* be like. Did I desire something similar for myself? I wasn't sure. What I did know was that I still wanted to be within this one. These were real people, and I'd grown so very fond of each and every one of them.

Back at the house, Monty had arrived and was chatting with Sandra in the kitchen.

"It's not every day I get to speak about your mum and our romance," said Dikembe. "Let's take a look at the photo album, son. Young Lowra and Monty need to see pictures that depict me as more than just a little boy or a wizened old man!"

Now flipping through the second of four photo albums, Dikembe stopped at a black-and-white image of Marjorie, a stunningly beautiful woman standing proudly next to her husband, and another man holding baby Chris.

"That's my friend Royston, Chris's godfather. Took his duties very seriously."

"Uncle Royston's been gone five years now," said Chris.

Next there were shots of an older Marjorie holding Chris, who looked remarkably like Justin, and who, if I looked closely enough, reminded me of the first image I had seen of Dikembe in the museum. The one which had sparked this entire journey.

"That's Marjorie with Ammy when she was born."

By this particular photograph, it was clear that Marjorie's illness had caused considerable weight loss, but the delight in her face was matched only by that of her husband standing beside her.

"I'm so glad Mum got to meet her," said Chris.

"A wonderfully proud moment for us both."

By the fourth book, I sensed a frustration in Dikembe. "I wish there were pictures I could show you of my mama, father and brothers."

"The picture from your memory is so vivid."

"Not the same, though, is it? When I go, who will remember them?"

Chris looked toward me, perhaps wanting an answer, when all I could do was stare back hopelessly.

I spoke to take away the awkwardness. "Can you be sure it was your brother Pako you saw that day?"

"Do you mean, was it him or something I wanted so much I made it so?"

"Sometimes when we want something so badly . . ."

"I agree. And as time went on, as the hope faded, I began to think that it wasn't him after all. Then, twenty years later, I received an application at the registry from a man who needed work. Marjorie, who wasn't my wife then, took his details and I looked over them. Malcolm was his name. Malcom Sandersfield. The exact name he'd given me all those years ago. I had never forgotten it."

"That's amazing," I said.

"I waited for him to come back, but he never did. I visited the address, which turned out to be bogus—many men did that at the time. I just wished he hadn't." Dikembe's eyes lowered. "What a day."

"Dad, don't," said Chris.

"It's all right, my son." He turned to me. "When I looked at his application, I saw more than I had thought possible. You see, when my wife first joined the registry, she insisted on applicants writing down a bit about themselves, you know, to tell us why they wanted the job. A bit more than just *I need the work*. On his application, Malcom had gone into great detail about the pillaging and total destruction of his village. *The stench of death, the cries. There is nothing left. No one left. Men, women and children, perished and for what?* That's what he wrote—well, something like that."

Chris sat on the arm of Dikembe's chair.

"I believe he gained much catharsis the day he wrote the application, but it must have been too much for him, or he may just have known it was me because he never returned. I never saw him again."

"I'm so sorry, Dikembe," said Monty.

"Of course, I will never know if the man was my brother, Pako, or if indeed he was talking about the Congo. I'm no historian, but he could have been describing anywhere." He looked up at Monty and I could feel the electric connection that passed between them, one I could not penetrate even if I tried to. "Perhaps I'd so wanted to believe it because I needed to at that time. What was certain was that we were clearly from the same continent, and that in itself made him my brother."

I couldn't be sure, but I believed Monty swiped at his eye very quickly, before straightening his shoulders and clearing his throat.

When Aminata walked over to me and began circling strands of my hair in her palm, this was a welcome distraction. "I like your hair," she said.

"Thank you," I responded absently.

"Better than mine," she said, pulling at one of the large plaits resting on her head.

"Ammy, please leave Lowra's hair alone!" said Sandra.

"Your hair is lovely too," I said, before turning back to the conversation between Dikembe and Monty.

"I'm ashamed to say, Monty, that I do not remember much about my culture. Only the legend of the two kings, which I have meticulously kept stored in my memory over the years and then read about. I suppose I've tried to model myself on King Mbidi as much as I can."

"That you have, sir," said Monty. "That story again lends itself to the possibly that you are from the Luba tribe based in the Katanga or Kasai regions. But I can't say the Congo is my area of expertise. What I do know is, unlike a lot of the country, most of Katanga is an elevated plateau with poor soil and only a few places the rubber plant could have really flourished. So the main activity may not have happened there."

"When you say 'main activity,' are you referring to the atrocities?"

Monty cleared his throat and looked toward Sandra.

"Come on, you two, ice cream in the kitchen!" said Sandra. Not needing to say another word, Aminata and Justin were quickly behind their mother and out of the conservatory.

"As you may already know, it's estimated that over ten million people were killed throughout the country during the Leopold regime," said Monty.

I closed my eyes. Each of us sat in silence, knowing there was nothing we could say or do to change what had happened. Collectively, though, there had to be a way to let people know this had happened. That this terrible thing had happened in Dikembe's lifetime.

"What you are saying, Monty, is that if I was from part of the Katanga or Kasai regions, my small recollections would make sense?"

"Possibly. What we do know is that it would have been mostly in the 1910s to the 1920s, when mining and railway construction got underway in that region, that things would have become much worse, if that was even possible."

"So my mama saved me . . ." said Dikembe.

"It would appear so," said Monty.

"My grandmother was an amazing woman," said Chris.

"I am aware of articles on tribes such as the Luba people I could read as I am a lover of the written word, but just as I open the page, I am struck by a grief that clouds over me and does not leave until I close the book. As if learning about my culture now will just remind me of what I have lost. I have had to put my country to bed, so to speak. I needed to get on with my life without the distraction of memories . . . and a romanticized version of what could have been."

"I understand," said Monty.

"Do you? You are a Black man of history, and here you have a living relic from the past who tells you they know very little of where they came from, their own history. How much can you respect me?"

"Sir, I respect you more than you will ever know."

Aminata ran in, holding on to the remnants of an ice cream cone, perching herself on the edge of her grandfather's chair.

"Let me tell you something I do remember. Chris is an avid boxing fan and obsessed with Muhammad Ali. I'm more into cricket, as Sandra's dad, Kenroy, will testify!"

Sandra had walked in, smiling warmly toward her father-in-law.

"Anyway, this big fight—Muhammad Ali versus Joe Frazier, wasn't it?"

"George Foreman," said Chris.

"Ah, the Rumble in the Jungle!" said Monty.

"That's right. There was this wondrous spectacle before the fight. Men with yellow headbands and painted faces dressed in tribal clothing that I could not remember ever having been a part of my life and yet must have been, once. The women dancing in lines. They danced and danced and I couldn't take my eyes off the screen."

"That must have been very difficult for you," said Monty.

"The strangest, most ridiculous moments were when I looked into the crowds to see . . . to see if I could see . . . *them*. I mean, I told myself that wasn't the reason, but it must have been."

Dikembe slowly leaned back in his chair and the room fell silent. The heaviness of what had just been spoken weighed down the atmosphere. It took little Justin to walk in and lighten it. "Daddy, can I have a drink, pleeease!"

With Chris clearly hesitant to leave the room, Sandra took the little boy's hand instead and led him away into the kitchen.

Dikembe looked up at his son and then around as if acknowledging what he'd lost, while being joyful at what he had.

"Sometimes I'd moan to my wife about regrets. That I wished I hadn't let her go the first time. That if I'd married her then, we'd have had more years together."

When Chris's hand rested on his dad's shoulder and gently squeezed, perhaps this was letting him know he didn't have to continue. None of us really had any right to the thoughts of this wonderful man, anyway. Each word he allowed us to hear was a privilege.

"'You were not ready for me then, and if anything, we may have drifted apart in a year,' she'd say."

"Maybe she had a point!" said Chris.

"I don't want to be any type of show-off, but I will say this—if you find someone who makes you feel half the way Marjorie made me feel every single day of our married life, you are a very lucky person."

Collectively, we all just smiled.

"I went through losing my father, my mama, my brothers Kabili, Yogo, Djamba and Pako—everyone—yet I still consider myself a lucky man simply because I met Marjorie. Indeed, the major players I have encountered on my life's journey have never had such a pleasure, because if they had, they would not have turned out the way they did. So who's the true winner in the end?"

I smiled, because I knew the answer.

"If I hadn't gone through what I did, I wouldn't have Chris, Sandra, my grandchildren—and you wouldn't be here with us in the house today, Lowra."

I hadn't expected to be included in this way. Dikembe acknowledging me felt odd, strange and amazing all at once and I wanted to stay in that feeling, whatever it was.

"Are you going to tell him, then?" said Monty when we arrived again the next day.

"If you mean about being my great-grandfather, then no. You know what he's like when it comes to painful aspects of his past . . . he likes to keep them there. He even refused to be put in touch with Tilly when I suggested it."

"This is different."

"There's no need to tell him—he already sees me as family now because of the bond we share. Being blood-related doesn't seem to matter to him, and that goes for me too."

Dikembe and I had an intense and unexplainable connection, one which allowed me to be certain there were things he'd left out, even when the Dictaphone wasn't switched on. His eyes spoke to me before his mouth even moved. Dikembe at times embodied strength yet wasn't untouched by a lifetime of pain, some of which I knew he would never speak about.

What we now knew of Caroline and her conception—well, that wasn't my secret to tell and I respected his silence. But it was all there—through the expression in his eyes, and mixed in with the water resting in each corner of his eyelids.

"Lowra, you've said so many times how alone you felt in the

world. Now you have a chance to tell him what you know. Tell him about the daughter he never knew he had."

"The daughter who died before he could ever meet her? Why add to his pain?"

"We don't actually know she's dead; long life obviously runs in the family."

"My mother died young." My voice had risen above a whisper. "So you do believe he's my great-grandfather now?"

"There still isn't that much evidence for a historian . . . I just see that there's something between you two. Imagine if he knew there was a possibility you were related?"

"He has me, no matter what. We're bonded forever, and I don't need to break his heart to be that to him."

"I suppose if you put it like that . . . but what about Chris and Sandra?"

"What about them?"

"I know you probably don't want to hear this, but Dikembe's not going to be around forever, and when he does go, to Chris and Sandra you're just going to be a sort of acquaintance, a friend at best."

I hadn't really thought of that possibility.

"So, would you consider telling Chris after . . . ?"

"Maybe." But I didn't want to lose this family—one I never knew I had, or wanted.

Monty continued. "If it were me, I'd tell Dikembe now. He's been through a lot and I think he can handle it. Frankly, I believe he has a right to know."

"The shock could make him unwell . . ."

"Since that man was a child, people have lied just so they could control him."

"You mean, white people," I said.

"Yes, and here you are wanting to do the same. It isn't right and I think you know that deep down."

Monty hadn't finished speaking when I picked up my handbag and began walking toward the conservatory. Inside, as usual the light beamed through the glass ceiling and Dikembe was placing his mug of tea on the side table.

"There you are!" he said.

"His face never lights up like that when I walk into the room!" said Chris.

I managed a smile as I sat on the chair opposite Dikembe.

Every moment we spent together, all I ever pictured was the young boy in the black-and-white pictures that had started all of this. Now, in this moment, I was forced to look at him and see someone else: someone older—almost one hundred—and with the frailties that went with it. So while it had prevented me from telling him what I was about to, it would now be of help. Because it was only if I saw him as an adult that I could get the imagery of what had happened between him and Agatha Mayhew, almost ninety years ago, out of my mind.

Monty shrewdly called Chris away. I took a deep breath and exhaled slowly.

"What is it, Lowra? Are you upset about something?"

"Why do you *get* me so much?"

"I'm not even sure what you mean by that!"

"Dikembe, there is something . . . I need to tell you something."

"I am all ears."

"It's something I've known for a while now and not been able to tell you."

I turned my face away, closing my eyes. "I haven't been totally honest with you." I cleared my throat to buy time, my heart racing. "Agatha Mayhew had a daughter."

He stared blankly at me. "Go on."

"Her name was Caroline."

"So the Mayhews had a child after I left. I am unclear of what this has to do with me?"

"Caroline was of mixed race."

Dikembe's expression did not change.

"She was born in 1909—the year you told us you left the house. The birth certificate names the Mayhews as her parents but we have a photograph of her. Would you like to see it?"

"No, thank you," he said. The air had turned icy cold and it was already too late to stop the course of this conversation, even if I wanted to.

This was the moment I could lose Dikembe forever.

"We couldn't find any record of another Black person within the vicinity of Ranklin during that time. I mean, this doesn't mean there were none—there was Malcom for a start."

"Are you implying that one of us was Caroline's father?"

I had never lied to Dikembe before, but I had kept things back from him and maybe that meant just the same.

"Because . . . because you were only a boy, it did not occur to me at first, but . . ." I couldn't say the words. I shook my head instead, perhaps hoping they would come out anyway.

"In 1909 I would have been no more than fifteen years old."

There was a pause between us as I waited for some sort of permission to continue.

He gave me that. "Go on," he said.

"As I said—"

"I mean, go on and get out of here!"

My eyes widened. "What?"

"I would like you to leave."

I stood up quickly. My heart was breaking.

He had already turned his gaze away from me. Just like that.

I slowly walked to the door of the conservatory, willing him to call me back, but he didn't. I'd lost him just as I had feared.

I ran past Chris and Monty as tears began to fall down my face.

"Lowra," called out Monty, but I wanted to be as far away from him as possible. This was all his fault. He'd been the one who insisted I tell Dikembe everything, and now I'd actually lost him.

Monty caught up with me after a few hundred yards. The walk back to the tube station was a silent one, with nothing to add to my heartbreak but regret.

As we approached the entrance to the station, I felt a tap on my shoulder.

"Chris?"

"We need to stop doing this, don't we?" he said.

My thoughts were in a mess.

"Dad wants to see you."

I looked at Monty, hope in my eyes.

"Just you," said Chris.

Back in the conservatory, it was just me and Dikembe.

"I'm going to say it now—Lowra, I will not speak about anything regarding what you know or think you know. What I have already revealed is all I will say on the matter. So please do not ask me."

"I will respect that."

He suddenly looked every one of his years. "What became of her? The baby. Caroline."

I cleared my throat, not quite believing I was back here. "Caroline, as far as we know, couldn't speak. She was born with a condition—"

"She was mute?"

I nodded my head and then continued. "She became pregnant at twenty-six. She wasn't married and was sent away to have the baby. We don't know who the father was. Monty and I can't find anything, not that we've done a thorough search or anything. We wanted to stay focused on finding you. What we do know is that she didn't go back to the house after she had the baby; she was sent to an . . . to an asylum."

Dikembe slowly placed his hand to his chin. "What about the baby?"

"Agatha Mayhew took on Caroline's daughter as her own."

He placed his head in his hands, and once again I felt a wave of guilt for the pain my words were causing him. Yet, not telling him would have been a worse crime.

"The little girl . . . do we know what happened to her? Did she hurt her?"

It was in that moment and for the very first time that the real possibility my mother had been ill-treated was presented to me.

"Her name was Vivienne."

"Vivienne Mayhew?" he said.

I nodded my head. "She grew up in that house and lived there after Agatha died."

"What happened to Vivienne . . . after Agatha died?"

"Vivienne got married to a man named Patrick, and they had a little girl and that little girl . . ." I took a deep breath and my heart began to race again. "That . . . that little girl was me."

His forehead softened. "What did you say?"

Our eyes locked and in that precise moment, he knew, *we knew*.

It was difficult, but I tore myself away from his gaze and reached into my handbag on the floor, pulling out my purse.

I placed the only photograph I had of my mother into his hands.

"That's me, my dad and my mother."

"Extraordinary . . ." He swallowed. "She looks . . . happy. Your parents, forgive me, are they still with us?"

I shook my head sadly, and Dikembe stared at the photo with an expression I couldn't decipher.

"I did not know any of this when I started this journey to try and find you. I'd never been concerned with my ancestry or anything much, to be honest. Please believe me."

"I believe you." He carefully placed the photo to one side and slowly shifted forward in his seat, moving closer to me and grabbing hold of my hand firmly. With one touch, I felt everything he felt. When my tears came, so did his. This silent communication was louder and stronger than anything I had ever felt before in my entire life. I knew then, just as I had before, that Dikembe was my great-grandfather and now he was acknowledging me also. As I stemmed the tears with my lips, he stared at me so intently and I couldn't tell what he was thinking anymore. I hated that I looked more like Agatha Mayhew than any part of his family in the Congo. I hated that I must remind him of so much pain.

But then his mouth curved into a smile.

"What is it?" I said.

"I just knew there was something about you which reminded me of her."

I caught my breath, worried about precisely who I reminded Dikembe of.

"My mama."

"I remind you of your mama?"

"How gracefully she carried herself. How she would sometimes tilt her head to the side. These small things are the only things I remember of her and how she made me feel, and with you, I felt them all over again as soon as you walked through the door the first time."

"I tilt my head?"

"You do," he said.

I didn't want to risk breaking this bond which had accelerated in the space of minutes, but I had to say it. "I . . . I'm not sure if a DNA or blood test would confirm anything, but we could look into it . . ."

"I don't need any test. You already feel like you're part of this family, so why would I need one?"

I am eleven years old again. Reaching out for anyone to take away my hurt; to belong; to feel anything but pain.

"You're ours," said Dikembe.

My tears turned to sobs and then gasps, and then instant comfort when he placed both of his thin hands on my neck and moved me closer to him, his forehead touching mine. We remained there in a human triangle, both our tears falling and not quite believing that this was actually happening. That despite everything, we were family.

Chapter Fifty-Eight

Lowra
1994

The idea came to me when Dikembe showed me a piece he'd been reading about one of his favorite writers, Chinua Achebe: *Until the lions have their own historians, the history of the hunt will always glorify the hunter.*

The aim was always to record Dikembe's own story so that his place in history would be intact for centuries to come. Now Monty and I had come up with a way to make sure Dikembe would be the one to tell it.

Chris, Sandra and Dikembe were sitting at their dining table as we spoke.

"This is a remarkable idea," said Dikembe.

"This way your mama, father and brothers will live on," I said. It was a no-brainer really. "With the stuff recorded on the Dictaphone, there's enough to even use your voice as a backdrop to the narrative," said Monty, clearly in his element now.

"I don't know what to say," said Dikembe. "Although I do have one caveat."

"Name it," said Monty.

"I need you to make sure it is made clear that, although my story started a certain way, it ended with love . . . so much love.

Marjorie is as much of my life, if not more, than Sir Richard Babbington and the Mayhews."

"Of course," said Monty as he nodded his head vigorously. "Without a doubt. This isn't about Babbington. It's about you, Dikembe Kabili." He continued. "I've been talking to a few people already. We'll need funding, of course, but it will happen. It just won't be overnight, as applications to boards and charities take time. They may have conditions about what's included and we are clear that your wishes will be honored."

"I'm sure Chris will make sure everything is right."

"And you, of course!" I said.

"Lowra, I'm one hundred years old in less than three months, and chances are I won't be here by the time this happens. Everyone here knows that, except you, it seems."

I did not want to accept that and, looking over at Sandra, who'd been silent for most of the proceedings, she felt the same way.

"We'll contribute what we can, of course," said Chris. "It would be great for Ammy and Justin to see their ancestry up there like that."

"We're going to need a lot of money and I don't want that to be your responsibility," said Monty.

"I've done OK, and what Dad hasn't given away is mine apparently, so it's not a problem," said Chris.

"That's all for your children and future generations," added Monty. "Your generational wealth is a legacy to your family and an amazing feat considering what happened to Dikembe. It doesn't feel right taking from that. We'll find a way."

"Which is why I'm going to use the money from the sale of the house. All of it," I said.

A collective "What?" filled the room.

"I was never going to keep the money, and this seems like such a better way of spending it. The irony!"

*

I slipped into a thin jacket; even though it was a mild day, goose bumps had already begun to appear on my skin.

Although this was probably more to do with excitement.

The last couple of weeks had involved talks with English Heritage and finally being allowed to sell that house—with conditions. The estate agent had said something about decorating it first, to get a better price, but I wasn't interested. That tomb, that place of misery not only to Dikembe and me but clearly to Caroline too, needed to be sold and out of my life forever, with all proceeds going toward "An Exhibition of Forgotten Histories," Dikembe's audible voice being the centerpiece, along with photographs that would start with the one taken in 1907 which had launched my own journey.

Monty's excitement was infectious, seeing into a future involving a permanent fixture in a major museum: "The Centre for Forgotten Histories," he called it.

"Calm down" I said. "Let's see how this exhibition goes first."

"If I must!"

"Also, there's something else."

"What now?" He smiled.

"I'd like to try and find out what happened to my grandmother Caroline."

He shifted closer, clearly as intrigued as I was. "Do you know how hard that's going to be?"

"Harder than finding Dikembe?"

"Point taken."

"Not now, though, because I made a promise to Dikembe."

Lowra, I cannot stop you pursuing this—all I ask is that you wait until I am gone. I simply cannot take anymore expectations and disappointments, and I refuse to live my last days, weeks, months or years on earth in that perpetual state of limbo. Not again.

*

Babbington's house went for much higher than expected, and it felt great to know the exhibition and even a center for forgotten histories could one day be a possibility.

"Hopefully, one day that statue of Richard Babbington will be pulled down. I don't feel he should be celebrated," I said, standing in front of it after signing the last of the papers for the sale of 109 Ranklin Road. After today, I hoped never to set foot in Ranklin ever again.

"It should stay. A reminder of what he did," said Monty.

I'd never understand Monty.

I now worked with a new agency which found me part-time work. I attended the odd Friday night drink with Marnie, and even trusted her with news about the exhibition, giving her a sanitized version of my part in it. To which she responded: "Hark at you, all posh and intellectual! Who would have guessed it?"

The friendship was all surface at first, but then slowly and drip by drip, I began to show her a little bit more of me. I did draw the line at accompanying her, Rod and the kids to Butlins, though!

I made regular calls to Winter Pines, promising Tilly I would visit soon. According to my and Monty's calculations, she was my first cousin twice removed.

Another family member.

I visited Dikembe and the Kabilis constantly, at least once a week. The kids called me Auntie Lowra (which still felt weird) and loved nothing more than "hanging out" with me, apparently! Chris maintained he knew we were related due to the amount of gum I chewed (he'd been the same until Sandra had banned it in the house).

Dikembe and I often went for walks to the park, culminating with a discussion. I'd update him about the exhibition planning, recite some of the poems I now wrote regularly, and he'd update me on episodes of *Cheers*, which I felt was a fair trade.

One week, he looked slightly more stooped over than usual with the walking stick, but he was still quick on his feet as we walked past a bed of flowers heading toward "our" bench.

"Things are getting busy with the planning and my new job. I probably won't be able to come around as regularly. But we can still keep in touch by phone and stuff."

"And stuff? Is that good English? You young people! I despair for my grandchildren."

I rolled my eyes and smiled, patting his hand. "I'll come over maybe twice a month and we can go for more walks."

"That sounds nice, but shouldn't you be spending time with your young man?"

I blushed.

"This is the first time you have not corrected me!" he said with excitement in his voice. "Is there something I should know?"

"We're just taking it slowly. Very slowly!" I said, wanting to sink into the ground. I hadn't really got the hang of "us" yet or what that meant, or how to be in whatever it was we were even embarking on. Monty and I had been poring over some exhibition plans and it had just happened.

A kiss.

"I won't press," he smiled.

"You're probably sick of me by now, anyway!"

"You know almost everything there is to know about me, Lowra, and we've spent most of the spring and summer with one another, so you can't actually believe that?"

"I suppose being locked in an attic, there's always a reminder, this feeling . . ."

"That you're not good enough. Yes, that I can relate to."

We both chuckled, because we knew. We both knew where we'd been and, most important, how far we could go, despite the past.

Dikembe was living proof.

"Let me say it clearly: I would very much like it if you came around as much as you are able, without impacting too much on your time. Chris, Sandra and the children are lovely, but a bit of respite never hurt anybody."

"That's a deal!"

"Besides, who knows how long I have left, so better make the most of it."

I swallowed. "I hate to think of you not being around. I—"

"So don't. Let's just sit here in this moment and on this bench because that's all we—"

"Have. This moment. No control over tomorrow and the past is gone."

"Almost word for word," he said, squeezing my hand.

As Dikembe clutched my hand, patted the top with his other hand and then smiled, I knew here, and with him, was the only place I needed to be.

Epilogue

The four of us stood along the river, surrounded by lush and stunning greenery I hadn't expected before embarking on this trip. Sandra and Chris stood beside me holding hands, as well as their tears.

It had been many years since he'd gone and yet he'd stayed with each and every one of us. As his grandchildren grew taller, not a day went by without them hearing his name, whether it be from their parents, myself or even Aminata's college, who had made a field trip to the Centre for Forgotten Histories, in London.

It had been a long trip here to the Congo, in miles and in years, but finally we were able to fulfil Dikembe's final wishes.

Scatter me in my homeland so that I can once again be among the air, the water and the landscapes I left behind.

The man hired to accompany us offered experiences like "lessons with local fishermen" and venturing into a neighboring village, which, according to him, was still very much steeped in traditional ways. We'd never truly know if this was Dikembe's village or where that could actually be, but it was the closest we had and wouldn't stop us from honoring the final wishes of one of the most important people to grace our lives.

I, Dikembe Kabili, have seen it all, felt it all. At the end of it all, what really matters is that you allow yourself to love and be loved.

I turned to my side, my husband, Monty, wiping a tear from his eye, and I squeezed his hand. I wasn't going to cry today but smile and laugh, and remember the joy Dikembe had brought into all of our lives.

Chris, wearing his father's buffalo bone necklace, opened up the urn, and I looked away and up to that colossal waterfall, feeling sprays of water kiss the air, its mighty power reflected in the sounds around us. The wildlife, both hidden and obvious, the smell of nature and . . . life.

I turned back to Chris who was closing up the urn, and we just gazed at the water, watching as it gracefully carried Dikembe Kabili to where he wanted to be.

. . . *In the end, I just want to be back home.*

Acknowledgments

I'd like to thank God for the gift, for everything.

Thank you to Gillian Green for believing in this book and understanding what I wanted to do with this precious story. Thank you to Judith Murdoch for the unending belief—what a ride! A shout-out to all those who worked behind the scenes, including Rebecca Needes and the copy editors, proofreaders and more. It takes a village.

Thank you to all the professors and historians who graciously responded to my emails during their summer breaks: Guy Vanthemsche, Piet Clement, Koen Bostoen and Roger B. Alfani; special thanks to Maud Devos at the African Linguistics Culture and Society Research Unit in Belgium who located a 1909 version of the Kiluba dictionary.

To Ndugu M'Hali—your life matters. I hope I have done you proud.

Rest well, little one.

Author's Note

It has always felt like an honor to be in a position to tell stories. Chinua Achebe's quote, "Until the lions have their own historians, the history of the hunt will always glorify the hunter," resonates with me, particularly as a Black British Nigerian writer. Indeed, the history many of us learned growing up would have us believe the arrival of Black people in England started with twentieth-century immigration and the *Empire Windrush*, and their experiences limited to these. This can at times lead to the "single story" narrative, as explained by Chimamanda Ngozi Adichie.

I have always been fascinated with the lives of Black people in Britain before 1948, and was excited to hear of an exhibition at the National Portrait Gallery in London which promised a snapshot of this.

The "Black Chronicles Photographic Portraits 1862–1948" exhibition allowed me a moment in which to become mesmerized with the stunning images on display, some of which had remained hidden for over a hundred years.

One in particular, of a little boy in a clear black-and-white photograph, held my attention longer than the others. His sad expression spoke of an unspeakable experience, of trauma, displacement—the history of colonialism existing in all its guises. I couldn't tear myself away from this photograph, and that day in 2016 he not only captured my gaze, but also my heart. In that very moment, I announced to myself and to my friend beside me, "I'm going to write about him one day."

There wasn't much I could find out about this mysterious little boy in the photograph. I knew he had once lived in Britain during the 1800s, that his original name was Ndugu M'Hali, that he was born circa 1865, and that he died on 28 March 1877 at the age of twelve. It is unclear if Tabora in present-day Tanzania was his birthplace, but it was where his fateful journey with the explorer Henry Morton Stanley began.

Along with the sorrow of imagining what this little boy had been through—you only have to look at the photographs to read his trauma—I felt the need to tell his story, but in a different way and one which would not end so tragically at such a young age.

I was drawn to set the book partly in the Congo, for three reasons: firstly, Lualaba River in the Congo was where Ndugu M'Hali's life sadly ended; secondly, I drew parallels from my earlier readings about Ota Benga, a young Congolese man exhibited at the Bronx Zoo in 1906; and finally the fact that not enough people are aware of the atrocities that occurred in the Congo between 1885 and 1908—a period which saw the slaughter of an estimated ten to fifteen million African people.

Reading vivid descriptions of the brutality suffered by the Congolese people under King Leopold II of Belgium, and seeing the photographs that exist, meant that research for this book at times left me feeling exhausted with sadness, especially during that unique period in 2020 when the world seemed to be talking about race, and when statues of Victorian "explorers" and slave traders were being torn down around the world. I have purposely kept names and experiences of real-life "explorers" to a minimum in the book, determined this story be about a little boy and not those who captured and exploited him. So much has already been written about them, the hunters—something I came across time and time again during my research—with people like Ndugu M'Hali kept as mere footnotes, if they were mentioned at all.

Discovering the rich history of the Congo, the dialects, the countless tribes and amazing traditions dating back hundreds of years, felt joyful yet bittersweet, as such information would have been denied Ndugu and thus, my character of Dikembe. It's somewhat ironic, then, that I was unable to definitively trace Ndugu M'Hali's original tribe, as "born in Africa" conjures up so many possibilities.

Four years after first setting eyes on that photograph in the National Portrait Gallery and two published novels later, the need to tell Ndugu M'Hali's story never left me. It wasn't until the year 2020, when most of the world quietened as it experienced a global lockdown, that his "voice" became so loud I could no longer hear much else: *It's my turn.*

So, *The Attic Child* was born. It is the longest book I have ever written and the first inspired by a real person: the little boy in the photograph, alive again. While this isn't Ndugu M'Hali's actual story, it's his story reimagined.

My attempt to give a lion a voice.

Lola Jaye, 2022